WITHIN THE SHADOWS SERIES
BOOK ONE

# COFFEE AND FANGS

## AMY NEVILLS

ISBN 979-8-9909525-0-8

# CHAPTER ONE

*I'm being paid to sleep; it's a dream job.*

**W**ith eyes closed, savoring the last few precious moments of silence, she inhaled and exhaled slowly and deeply in a manner for which the elders who had taught her the technique would have been proud. Running her manicured hands down her silky gown doubled as a wardrobe check and a chance to smooth creases while making slight adjustments, ensuring no wardrobe malfunctions would appear in the late-night gossip shows or the morning papers.

As a habit that would appear to outsiders as a self-soothing technique to calm her nerves, she next slid her hands down her long, black hair; hair that had been blown, straightened, and lacquered to the point it wouldn't dare have a flyaway. A practiced, serene smile appeared as if by magic, a smile that bared no teeth but still made her seem approachable. Not that anyone would be allowed to approach. Security always made certain of that—and not the production company security that imagined itself having things well in hand, but private security that held her and her secrets to a much higher standard.

*Eyes strained to note and remember the finite details of the moments, details that often floated away with the rising sun: the smell of the leather seats, the crisp hint of whiskey lingering in the confines of the car, and the clink of ice cubes hitting glass.*

The white production company limo inched down the street before stopping in front of the Hollywood Theatre. She carefully adjusted the still-full glass of champagne on the small table. It was a prop—a prop just as much as her date, a former boy band member, who sat silently across from her, checking his phone. He did his job, just like the champagne.

A soft tap on the roof alerted them that the serenity would be broken within seconds, and the real acting would begin. When the door clicked open, without looking, she stretched out one pale, slender hand. It was immediately and gently grasped to guide her effortlessly out of the luxury car. One elegant stiletto led the way, hinting at what was to come.

For a split second, the crowd was quiet. Then, in less than a heartbeat, a roar filled Hollywood Boulevard as she seamlessly slid her small frame out of the car, her deep red gown brushing the red-carpet wrinkle-free.

A practiced smile in place and slow, steady steps took her toward the garish double doors held open by two men in dark tuxedos looking like matching bookends. Not quite matching, she noted as she drew closer, eyes focused on her goal. One looked like he had stepped out of a Norse legend with his resemblance to Thor, while the other appeared to blend more into the background as any good doorman should.

*When she looked at the doorman, whose blond locks were smoothed back into an impossibly high ponytail, her breath hitched, and she avoided looking his way again.*

Halfway down the carpet in rehearsed precision, she stopped to rotate toward the throngs of fans who had secured a place hours ago near the front with the paparazzi. Hand resting on hip, she appeared to peruse the crowd as her "date" slid a proprietary arm around her waist, careful not to wrinkle the dress but hinting at an intimacy that didn't and would never exist. The flashing of the cameras didn't bother her as it did some actresses; the young, pretty ones who complained that the lights hurt their eyes and washed out their complexion were utterly useless to her.

For a moment, she allowed the voices, the excitement, and the adoration to wash over her, filling her senses to the point that she tingled from head to toe.

"Ms. Sinclair, over here!"

"Is that an Amelia gown?"

"Who's the designer?"

"I love you!"

"Over here, I love you!"

"I'm your biggest fan!"

A slight sense of euphoria followed the tingle at the worship, and she mentally held it at bay, not allowing herself to bask in the temptation too much.

*The wave of energy floated over her. In her.*

*Through her. She drew deep breaths, savoring the moment, the near ecstasy enveloping her.*

Focusing on her hearing allowed her to pinpoint Meghan Malone's voice, announcing to her viewers that the star had arrived. She began her preplanned critique of the elegant red gown designed by her dear friend Amelia. Critics may argue the finer points, but ultimately, the dress was perfect. The red flattered her dark skin tone and black hair—so black one could imagine blue throughout it—perfectly, while also complementing the theme of her premier movie, *Vampire Nights*. Amelia had sewn her into the dress and would reverse the process at night's end. Amelia was the only one permitted to dress her petite five-foot-four-inch frame, and she found it endlessly amusing that at every significant event, the first question still asked was who had dressed her. However, asking kept Amelia's name on everyone's lips and minds, which was a bonus to her dear friend's design business.

As beautiful as her gown was, it didn't allow for quick movement, so with continued slow, short steps, she floated toward the double doors, allowing the crowd and photographers a glimpse of a curved calf from the slit on the gown. Once upon a time, a bit of leg would have driven men made with desire, but now it was expected and unsurprising; however, it was still sexy as hell.

*The gown swished against her calves, and the soft caress of her hair tickled her back, tantalizing her skin. The energy! The power!*

With one last glance over her shoulder, she looked directly into one lucky paparazzi's camera and added a hint of tooth to her smile as her lips fell slightly open. This would be the money shot for the photographer if he caught it. If he didn't, then at least she'd tried.

As quickly as the crowd's energy had rushed over and through her, it disappeared, and a sense of dark energy replaced it. The lights, power, and noise muted while the darkness pushed into her, down her throat, and throughout her body, an invasion that came on so quickly it choked the breath from her. The darkness slid across her bare skin, smoothing the still motionless hair, adding rough pressure as it caressed the naked skin of her shoulders and upper back. Coiling around her neck, a hot, fetid breath intimately assaulted the side of her neck, paralyzing her in front of the throngs of fans.

*Fear. Heat. Immobility.*

Ten seconds? Ten minutes? An eternity passed before it released her with a hiss and low laugh that curled around the back of her neck, intimately brushing her body, and then rushed away with a snap so loud her ears popped. She wrenched herself free from her startled date while simultaneously flipping her head back and forth, searching for an apparition over her shoulder, around her, anywhere!

Her escort looked at her with confusion as their carefully choreographed entrance fell apart just a few steps from the door.

Although she'd turned quickly, she couldn't quite catch the darkness that had pressed itself on her and just as promptly fled. No one stood on the carpet with her except her bewildered date, who indeed seemed to question if the paparazzi would still treat him kindly if America's Sweetheart looked afraid standing next to him.

No one could have approached her, and no one could have touched her. But the impossible had happened, and she could feel the mood change in the crowd as the roar dulled just a bit. The fans and paparazzi in the front were now frowning and shifting uneasily back and forth on their feet, trying to understand what had changed for her.

Plastering a larger-than-usual smile on her face, taking a deep breath, she waved slightly at the group while fighting the urge to spit out the arid taste of black magic that tainted her lips. Just a few steps, and she would be safe in the building. With two small steps toward the door, her ankle crumbled despite her customary finesse. With a surprised cry, she prepared to crash in front of a fickle world but before she did, hands reached out, grasping her forearms, steadying her, preventing her from face-planting into the red carpet.

One of the doormen had somehow managed to reach her and prevent the late-night gossip shows from having some tea to spill about a spill. Guiding her smoothly upright before a human eye could tell she'd stumbled was—the handsome one.

"Fenrir sends his regards. Come," the man who looked like Thor whispered in her ear, uttering the code words that marked him a member of her private security team. Words that should have given her some sense of relief from her newfound terror. And yes, after thousands of years, the feeling was nearly unrecognizable, but it was *fear*.

*Terror. The terror and fear pushed her over the edge into the abyss.*

# CHAPTER TWO

*No dream catcher here; I prefer to chase my dreams.*

*Beep! Beep! Beep!*

Jerked from the dream, trapped between waking and sleep, Eva thrashed about, caught up in what was surely a fiendish web set forth by some unspeakable horror. Groaning and still unable to open her eyes, she realized that they weren't, in fact, sewn together by a vengeful witch. Fighting with the vast sheet until both arms were freed, she followed up her battle by slapping wildly toward the blaring alarm clock until it was silenced.

Was it too late to return to dreamland? That was some good stuff. The excitement, noise, anticipation, and fear all felt so real, intriguing, and inviting. The arid taste of evil still filled her mouth from the strange dream encounter. Rubbing more sleep from her eyes, Eva managed to snuggle deeper into the sheets and blankets, pulling a pillow closer, hoping that the blissful sleep and the adventurous dreams would return.

A gentle *woof* interrupted those attempts. This was quickly followed by the butting of a cold dog nose against her bare skin, pulling her away from any attempts to reenter dreamland.

"Nooo," she mumbled, trying to hold tight to the energy the dream had left reverberating through her bones. Moving meant letting some of it go, and she wanted to bask in it and roll around in it until the energy rolled through her. Sadly, Apollo didn't seem to want the same thing she did.

Dog-sitting Apollo while the neighbors enjoyed a long weekend away had seemed like a good idea; sometimes, the quiet, comforting house got lonely. But the cost of such doggy entertainment came at a steep price. The Great Pyrenees-Labrador mix was determined to stick with his schedule and was absolutely unforgiving if his breakfast wasn't delivered on time, as well as his thrice daily walks and playtime on demand. Eva's work and sleep schedule were no deterrent to his schedule either. Hearing him shift back and forth while simultaneously tapping his feet reminded Eva that the impatient dog could follow through with eighty pounds of dog to the stomach if breakfast weren't immediately forthcoming. Sadly, that lesson had been learned the hard way during a previous visit.

Dragging bleary eyes open with blankets pulled tightly around her, hoping to avoid any more cold dog noses, Eva was met by Apollo's hopeful golden-brown eyes. Thumping his whip of a tail, knowing half the battle was already won, the overgrown dog barely suppressed the slight whine begging to escape. Reaching out with another groan, Eva questioned her ability to speak words. Hopeful of stalling getting out of bed for even a few more moments, she idly rubbed Apollo's soft ear. The fluffy beast moaned softly before letting out a putrid burp that enveloped Eva's face, immediately clearing up any confusion on her ability to speak as well as negating any chance of lingering in bed any longer.

"Apollo!" Waving a hand in front of her face to remove the foul odor while simultaneously groaning, Eva made a useless attempt not to inhale. "I love you, buddy, but save the ruck for someone else." Not that chastising him did any good. Making the same request for the last few mornings hadn't changed the outcome. She might think the dog didn't understand her requests if he kept this up.

With yet another moan and hopefully no more bad breath in her face, Eva began pushing the blankets and the clearly starving dog off her. "Apollo let's go. Let's feed you. Just quit hounding me."

With another more excited *woof*, Apollo took her movement as the perfect time to prance and jump toward her in response to the promised meal. Once he grew confident that Eva wasn't returning to her nest of blankets and pillows, his toenails clicked on the wooden floor as he ran toward the kitchen with another yip.

Eva took a deep breath to hold the manic dream energy inside her for as long as possible before committing to facing the day. With a quick flip of her wrist, she tossed the covers back into place, a half attempt to make the bed, before picking up two errant pillows that had fallen from the bed sometime during the night. Her king-sized bed with its wrought-iron frame took up most of the small master bedroom, completely dwarfing it. Although it was entirely out of place in the house that had probably last been updated in the 1980s, she loved the bed and had been thrilled at picking it out a few years ago, as it established that she was firmly entrenched in adulthood. Pulling her robe on as she made her way down the hallway, she made a quick detour into her office and pushed the button to turn her laptop on for the day.

Apollo impatiently pushed up against Eva, attempting to herd her toward the waiting food bowl in the kitchen, and she poured him a generous helping of dog food. She briefly offered a silent thanks for fancy upgraded coffee makers with timers and her ability to remember to set them, especially after a long evening working at the coffee shop, followed up with a few hours of writing. Her second shift of the week was tonight, but after that, she had freedom for the next five days, as long as Apollo's owners didn't delay their afternoon return. Working a few shifts a week at the shop kept her from becoming a hermit. As she poured the strong brew, the hearty smell enveloped her, and she paused for a moment to enjoy it, remembering the hint of whiskey that had hung in the air of her dream. Wondering if it would be too much to add a nip to her cup, she was also unable to wait for even another second, wincing as she sipped the still-too-hot beverage.

Wrapping it up with a quick trip outside for a still

impatient but now fed Apollo, she mentally began cataloging the dream while it still sat fresh and heavy on her mind.

Pulling her robe tighter around her, she took her coffee back to her booted-up laptop and pushed a few papers and books around to create a spot for the cup. In her immaculate house, her desk was an oddity. It overflowed with pens, pencils, scraps of paper, and odd bits of writing that seemed ready to fall off. A stack of old books perched precariously on the edge, and a simple nudge would have tumbled them to the floor.

Like her bed, the desk was oversized. It was one of the few purchases she'd made on her path to adulthood after inheriting her grandmother's two-bedroom house at the age of eighteen. For a few years, she couldn't afford to change the home furnishings, and when she could, she discovered that the oversized furniture she was drawn to didn't fit the place she called home. Much of the house still contained the smaller, older pieces that her gram had purchased years ago, while one bedroom housed her bed and the other her desk and books, with clothes overflowing the closets of both rooms.

Gram not only left Eva her home and all its possessions, but she'd also left tidbits of wisdom. Eva's favorite had been Gram's constant warning, "Watch your words flying around little ones. Words have power, so much power." So, Eva did, and she learned that words did, in fact, have power, and thankfully, such power earned her some serious money as well. Eva yoked and tamed the power of words through her writing. Although she sometimes imagined that the opposite might be true, she was a slave to the word.

Once again rubbing sleep out of her brown eyes before tucking an errant strand of chestnut hair behind her ear, Eva began to slide into her workday. Taking another swig of coffee, still wrapped in her robe, she settled deeper into her oversized office chair. Picking up a wayward pencil and scrap of paper that currently only held a few scribbles, she began jotting down the highlights of her dream, underlining a significant word here and there and adding a question mark at the end of others.

With practiced ease, Apollo slipped by Eva's feet to lie under the desk, sighing deeply as if he couldn't have planned a better day. Eva absently rubbed him with her foot. Another wayward lock fell in her face, and with a puff, she gathered up all her thick, shoulder-length hair, twisting and pulling it into a haphazard bun; with a grimace, she noted that it was way past time to wash the mass.

Pulling that morning's notes, as well as other scraps of paper, closer, she began earnestly tapping at her laptop. Book four in her series "Vamps in Hollywood" finally had the plot twist: the arc she'd been waiting for! Someone or something was stalking the mysterious and wildly successful exotic actress Fala Ishto! Would Fala's vampire origins remain a secret? Had someone discovered she wasn't a typical Hollywood starlet? Or was something even more nefarious after her? And why? What could frighten a two-thousand-year-old vampire who had no natural enemies?

The entire dream had been so clear this time, but often, after waking up, the memories proved fleeting. History had taught her to commit everything to paper before the tendrils of the dream blew away. Sometimes, they were just quick, short scenes, but this dream had been full and vivid, making it even more vital to put it to paper before it faded. This was the missing piece she'd been looking for. This book would continue to test Fala and her survival ability while she remained hidden in plain sight in present-day Hollywood.

Eva alternated between writing notes and typing into her laptop as she fleshed out the beautiful Fala's evening out and the visit from the mysterious cold entity. The minutes turned to hours, and the dregs of her coffee had long since grown cold when Apollo began impatiently nudging her to move her on to the next part of his day. Stretching herself up and pulling her neck side to side, she checked her phone for the time.

"Awe, buddy"—she ruffled the fur on his neck as he began to bounce side to side— "you're right, it's paws-itively time to get a move on."

He let out a happy yelp as Eva stood, stretching her limbs.

Prancing to the door, he waited eagerly for Eva to change into comfortable jogging pants, a tee shirt and pull on her walking shoes before she slid the leash on him. Then, leading the way out the door, he went out for his daily exploration of the neighborhood. Eva's house sat on the edge of town, saddled next to a large community park with acres of woodland and several miles of rolling trails. Often Apollo lunged ahead, followed by sudden stops to sniff a particularly interesting scent. As the entrance to the wooded trail came into view, he picked up the pace so they could quickly escape the heat of the late spring Ohio sun. The pea gravel crunching under their feet was the only sound as they walked, meeting no other pedestrians or bikers. Even the usual cacophony of birds was taking a break from their spring mating cries.

Eva held the leash loosely, knowing that although her neighbors had trained Apollo well enough, an errant squirrel or chipmunk might prove to be too much of a distraction for him to stay by her side. As Apollo happily sniffed his way down the trail, Eva allowed her mind to wander back to the words she'd been writing.

This fourth book about the vampiric Fala Ishto was proving more stressful than the first three combined. Of course, she'd written the first book for herself and put her overly active imagination to paper. Covertly, she'd joined online writing groups, then acquired beta readers, before finding herself with an agent, a contract, and what she'd thought was a stand-alone novel. Well before it went to print, book two begged to be told, and with book three, she was flying on success and excitement. In contrast, she told the story of a young priestess serving the ancient goddess Nephthys, who, as a young girl, had grown up splashing and mucking along the shores of the River Nile with her sisters before being called to serve the goddess. However, her innocent world was shattered when a zealot priest attempted to gain favor with Osiris and conquer death at the cost of the young priestess of the temple. The zealot's plan didn't take into account that as God of the Dead, Osiris wouldn't appreciate the interference. The young priestess, or Raven, proceeded to travel the world as one of the original vampires before entering the twenty-first century and the world of movie-making.

Now, nerves plagued Eva; she knew the success of the previous books and the readers' expectations. Although she knew how fickle fans could be, she also truly didn't want to disappoint them. Book four was the albatross. Although success had never been her goal, now that she'd tasted it, the fear of failure and disappointing others nearly crippled her. Last night's dream had reawakened her creativity and broken down the walls of fear that had sprung up over the previous few weeks.

Fala had a new, unknown enemy to battle. Although Eva Nance wasn't certain yet what enemy would frighten an infallible vampire, she knew her writing alter ego, A. Scriver, would create something truly remarkable for the heroine to overcome.

Caught up in thoughts of chapter outlines, plot holes, and character development, she nearly stumbled over Apollo when he stopped dead on the trail, staring directly into the dense foliage.

"Hey, buddy, easy there. Some of us only have two legs."

Late spring had brought a plethora of plants to central Ohio. Vines, Jack-in-the-pulpits, and leggy saplings cast shadows that made it impossible for her to determine what had caught the dog's attention. Tightening her grip on his leash and bracing herself in case this was one of the times he decided to forgo the leash rules and make a break for whatever was hidden in the shadows, Eva prepared for the large dog's next move. But Apollo didn't budge. He remained alert with fluffy ears pointed to the sky and woods while the hair slowly rose along his spine. He let out a long, low growl that ended in a sharp bark, prancing in place but not brave enough to break free and investigate on his own.

Raising her sunglasses, Eva squinted into the area that had captured his attention, but the shadows protected whatever might be hidden within the foliage. With a whine, Apollo looked at Eva and backed away. As Eva peered into the forest for a moment, the dark shadows seemed to move slowly around and, for a second, swelled and expanded out into the small trail, blocking even more of the sunlight that found its way through the trees.

A black squirrel slunk to the edge of the tree's shadows, stopping to sit on its back legs as its tiny eyes stared toward the pair with an intensity that suggested anger, if that were even possible. A nervous laugh escaped Eva at the momentary relief that it was just a squirrel. Of course, a squirrel. Crouching back to all fours, the squirrel moved a few steps forward and, as Eva blinked, the shadows seemed to ooze along with it, keeping the rodent just out of the sunshine.

As the shadows appeared to bob and weave before her eyes, Eva was transported back into last night's dream for a split second. A low, primitive scream shot out of her mouth as she joined Apollo in his backward walk. Somehow, she knew that if the shadows reached her, she would be frozen in place, powerless, just as Fala had been.

Powerless. Helpless. Drowning. Sorrow.

Apollo and Eva continued to slowly back away from the squirrel as it assessed them again with a strange, beady glint in its eyes before crouching down as if to boldly walk closer. The dark shadows drew around them, following the black creature closer and closer.

"Come on, boy, don't let those squirrels bug you; you're barking up the wrong tree," Eva muttered with false bravado toward the unusual creature whose black eyes suddenly flooded with a flash of red.

One slight misstep and the pea gravel rolled under Eva's feet. Before she knew it, she was on her butt on the ground, the backs of her arms and hands burning. She was up as quickly as she'd gone down, not wanting to take her eyes off the red-eyed squirrel and the strange, intense shadows. Shadows that were now gone. The squirrel had also disappeared from sight. The trail ahead and behind them was empty. Thankfully, no one had seen her embarrassing fall. Scanning the edge of the trail, she curled her hands up despite the burning from the scrapes and bits of gravel stuck to them.

Nothing. Everything was just as it should be. Apollo relaxed and gave an almost suspicious scan of the tree line, as if he hadn't been a quivering mess a moment ago.

They headed home; thankfully, the return trip was uneventful.

"Nice, nice." Pleased with what she saw, Eva reviewed her day's work on the laptop before ensuring it was saved. This time, she'd set her alarm to stop her progress in time to play ball with Apollo before she dropped him off at his owner's back yard and made her shift at A Latte of Coffee. They were due to arrive home within the hour, and he would happily soak in the spring sunshine until they returned.

Sliding the laptop, notes, and a few extra pens into her backpack, she mused that if things were slow she could always write to settle her mind, which was now bubbling, overflowing with ideas. Two chapters were done, and several more had a solid outline. She reluctantly admitted that this was precisely why she kept working a few shifts a week at the coffee shop. It was too easy to get wrapped up in the writing, too easy to go days without talking to anyone—Apollo didn't count—too easy to stay in pajamas all day drinking coffee, imagining another world.

The sunshine, which had continued all day, allowed her to ride her bike in comfort a few miles to the only coffee shop in town. Nice days made Eva forget her tendency to curse her commitment to riding in the rain and sometimes even snow. Entering through the back door allowed her to park quickly and jump into work. Grabbing an apron, she walked right into a surprising mid-week afternoon rush.

After a quick nod hello to her slightly frazzled co-worker Joanne, who looked relieved to see her a few minutes early, she jumped right into the fray of things. The beginning of the warm weather ensured that people were out, thirsty for iced coffees and boba teas. The women blended and scooped, falling into sync with the ease of two who had worked together for several years, quickly catching up on the waiting orders. From the corner of her eye, Eva could see Joanne bouncing along to the upbeat music of a small-town singer-songwriter as she blended a frozen drink, clearly enjoying the moment now that she wasn't overwhelmed with locals wanting their java.

When the machine paused, Eva asked loudly, "Joanne, what did the coffees say before their night out?"

With a grin, Joanne shrugged and poured the frozen concoction into a plastic cup. "Let's stir up some trouble." Good-natured but subdued laughter came from the impatient customers, who were beginning to thaw as the line moved more quickly now.

This time, it was Eva's turn to shrug and raise her brows. "Tough crowd today," she commented, knowing that many of them had used up their patience waiting for their orders. Passing a man his cold brew with a wink and a parroted request to "have a brew-tiful day," she wiped her hands on the towel, mentally working on the following order. The man nodded and dropped his change into the tip jar.

Once things settled down, Joanne swatted Eva with the tea towel she was using to dry the water along the workspace. "Good to see you. I have one for you today."

"Let's hear it." Eva pulled her high ponytail down to smooth it back in place before replacing the hair tie. Between the bike ride and the rush, her hair had taken a beating, and the heavy, silky hair took advantage, using the opportunity to escape from its confines.

*It really needs to be washed,* she reminded herself again.

"Why did Adele cross the road?" Not giving Eva a chance to respond, Joanne continued, rushing her words with a giggle, "To say hello from the other side."

"Perfect, that's what I like to hear." Eva nodded in appreciation with a chortle; who didn't like a good pun? "Might want to work on your timing a bit."

Joanne let out her own chuckle, shrugging as her curly, dark hair bobbed at her shoulders.

Knowing that Joanne could have handled the midday rush alone, Eva nudged the tip jar toward the single mom. "Don't worry about me; I have all night still." No one knew how Eva made her money. They either didn't care, or they assumed that she'd received at least a small inheritance from her gram and that her occasional shift subsidized her bills.

Eva knew that as a single mother of two preteens,

Joanne's budget was tight. Despite the initial protest, Joanne wouldn't argue about the fairness of splitting tips and happily went to work tallying the small bills and change, marking the end of her shift.

Eva busied herself with straightening, refilling, and wiping clean the self-serve bar. "Where's Cora? I thought she was here until I got here?" The owner and their boss didn't usually leave until late afternoon, preferring to be around to help during the busiest hours.

"It was slow earlier, and she had a contractor coming to her house today for that pool they're putting in, so she took off a little early." Joanne finished counting and tracking the tips on the tally sheet before sliding it back into the drawer and pocketing her cash. "I wish we worked together more often. You're such a hoot, and customers seem much happier when you're here." Leaning back on the counter, she examined the work area. "You caught on so quickly too. Were you a barista or a server before here?"

Sadness flashed through Eva, pushing it aside while flashing a too-bright smile. She truthfully responded to her friend, "You guessed it. I've always been a barista." To be completely truthful, she'd worked at A Latte of Coffee in various aspects since she turned sixteen just over thirteen years ago. Joanne had been slinging coffee alongside her for around eight of those years.

Eva liked to chalk her blanking on how long they'd worked together, or the fact that Eva had been there years longer than her, up to a frazzled single mom brain, but it happened too often not to still hurt. Joanne frequently mistakenly talked like they barely knew each other and was usually surprised when Eva repeated back something that Joanne had told her in the past. If she worked with her regularly, Joanne tended to remember more about her and the things they shared. However, the opposite was also true. Once, when Eva took three weeks off to meet a writing deadline on book three, Joanne determined she was a new hire and attempted to train her on the running of the coffee house when she returned for her two regular shifts a week. Face it, she was forgettable.

Not for the first time, Joanne told Eva, "If my brother were still single, I'd set you guys up. I think you'd be perfect for him. Not like that idiot wife of his," she added with an eye roll, still salty that he'd settled several hours away, closer to his wife's family.

Nodding, Eva didn't feel like explaining once again that she had, in fact, set Eva and Jonathan up. Yes, Joanne's parents had a theme when naming them; in fact, their father was Joseph. "Yup, too bad." There was no point in explaining that their chaotic relationship had consisted of a few dates, followed by a few fumbled nights, then ended with her avoiding Johnny until he dragged himself back to Cincy for college. Thankfully, he'd since met his wife, who was, in fact, a super sweet girl, and they had a toddler now. Eva did her best to avoid them whenever they visited, not wanting a repeat of the dramatic summer from a few years ago. Letting men close was a recipe for disaster. After several failed attempts at boundaries,

Eva kept sex to faceless strangers whom she could easily sneak out on after the deed.

"I hate to cut and run, but I'm out of here, if you think you can handle it. Got some big plans tonight." Joanne's attempt to leer was entirely out of place for the placid mom.

"Big plans with a book, I'm guessing."

"You got it, and a nice soak in the tub—if the kids let me. I'd call out tomorrow if the latest "Vamps in Hollywood" book came out. But alas, I must settle for a werewolf romance until she gets the next one out." A romance fan through and through, Joanne had a special place in her heart for paranormal romance and even a bigger space for vampires specifically. "I'll load up the washer in the back and start it before I head out."

"Yeah, yeah, get out of here." Eva tossed her wet cloth at Joanne, who caught it and tossed it back to Eva, who nearly missed it as it headed for her face. "Go," she ordered, red-faced, before returning to wipe the already clean counters.

Laughing as she walked out, Joanne tossed over her shoulder, "Fingers crossed for big tips tonight for you. Gotta build up that travel fund!"

Smiling, Eva began wiping again, shaking her head in disbelief. Of all the things for Joanne to remember, it was Eva's travel fund; a travel fund for a trip that never seemed to happen. Still, it was nice that she remembered.

# CHAPTER THREE

*What's the difference between a wizard who raises the un-dead and a sexy vampire? One is a necromancer, and the other is a neck romancer.*

**O**liver stepped out of the nondescript, mid-size gray rental car onto Main Street of what could be Any-Small-Town, USA. The GPS claimed it was Hubbard, Ohio. Despite the dipping spring sun, he continued wearing his sunglasses and fought the urge to reapply sunscreen. It was fine. He was fine. The sun had already dipped low in the sky, and despite the gnawing in the back of his mind, it was perfectly safe for him to be out in the sunlight and had been for hours now.

Clearly, the town rolled up the sidewalks at 6:00 p.m., if not earlier, and it was already nearer 8:00. He'd spent enough time in small towns over the years to know that they all consistently promised either nothing at all or drunken trouble after 10:00 at night. The only signs of life came from what he assumed was a family-owned restaurant or maybe a bar, which still had a red OPEN sign flashing. However, only an old truck was parked in front of the building, offering up what could be late-night drunken trouble in the future. Checking his phone, he saw that there was a coffee shop around the corner just off Main Street, but it would be closing soon.

He removed his black suit jacket and carefully hung it on the back of the driver's seat before rolling the sleeves up on his crisp white shirt. Despite his years on earth and his current financial security, the lessons of his youth prevailed: take care of your belongings.

Perusing the rustic downtown area, he realized his attempt to dress down for a town this size was coming a bit late, but perhaps this would help him blend in. Maybe the locals would believe he was a businessman traveling along the turnpike from Toledo to Cleveland, stopping for a bite to eat and a chance to stretch his legs. Even if he saw someone tonight, they probably wouldn't recognize the $500 shirt and assume it came from Macy's at best.

Strolling down the street in the general direction of the coffee shop, he kept his stride casual as he constantly scanned the streets. Stretching as if he'd gotten out of a long car drive allowed him to keep his eyes on all parts of the street, even if anyone was around to notice him. Adding in quick movements that human eyes wouldn't see, he followed up, scanning all buildings top to bottom, instinctively looking for places where someone could hide or an ambush could occur and noting the small boutiques and shops with their pretty window displays, but not missing the peeling paint or the equal number of empty storefronts. Nothing seemed threatening, but Oliver hadn't survived this long by being caught off guard.

Not for the first time that day, he half-cursed the loyalty that made him respond to Ravyn's plea for help. As owner of the security firm that protected the enigmatic Ravyn, he could snap his fingers and have any number of highly qualified paranormal employees eager to help their most important client. However, despite his desire to remain in his home, he couldn't ignore the bonds that tied him to her—and what he owed her.

If he was honest with himself, he might be stuck in a rut, working all day on lines of code and handing off the day-to-day business to Malthazar and Sebastian, only responding to their daily updates if needed. Oliver couldn't remember the last time he'd needed to do even that. It crossed his mind that it had been a few weeks since he'd heard from Malth. His previous call had been gruff, cryptic as usual.

*"Need time off and going off-grid."* That was Malth for you, though. He was a creature of few words and would show up when he showed up.

When Ravyn had Face Timed on his private number, the number only the few he called close friends had and even fewer dared to use, she'd looked wide-eyed and tense and sounded equally as frightened. Both exciting and disturbing. In the . . . was it 150 years now? He mused. Could it possibly be that long? Yes, around that. In the 150-odd years he'd known her, nothing—and he meant nothing—had frightened this fearless woman. As a human, she'd faced what nightmares are made of and, after she became a nightmare herself, nothing could. The relief on her face was palpable when he answered within a few rings.

"Ravyn Sinclair, it's been too long." Oliver spoke the words blandly. They texted most days, and it had only been a few days since their last video call.

"Darling, I'm so glad you picked up," she said, as if he had any other option. Indeed, his slow pulse had reverberated faster upon hearing the hesitation and uncertainty in his maker's voice. With her face clear of the makeup she usually wore these days and her hair hanging loose, she looked like the innocent, helpless human girl Oliver imagined she'd once been. She went on in an accented voice that spoke of the many combined lines she'd lived but was simultaneously indistinguishable. "I'm not safe."

Oliver immediately went on guard; his Ravyn couldn't feel that way. Keeping his tone even and gentle, he questioned, "Are the men I have on you not working out?"

Her studio hired human guards to watch her as needed, but as far as he was concerned, they were mere decoys. Two wolves stayed within her property during the daylight hours, and two vamps were always within striking distance during the nighttime hours, possibly more, depending on her needs and what Sebastian deemed necessary. Events meant more hidden security. Each guard was personally handpicked and vetted, knowing that if he couldn't watch her, at least those Oliver put in place might protect her with their lives.

As his creator, she would always hold a special place in his heart and life, more so because she never forced her will upon him using their bond. Even now, she wasn't demanding or summoning; she was requesting his help as a sister, not as a master. That was just who she was. He felt rage rush through his limbs at the thought that someone was making her feel unsafe

"No, they're fine and working out perfectly," she reassured him, unaware that she gnawed on her lower lip, "but there is just something more, something out there. I can feel it. I don't think they can handle what's coming."

Oliver bit his tongue to avoid standing up for the quality of sups he hired, waiting not so patiently for her to continue. In fact, his patience was gone within the half a minute they'd been on the phone, and he felt rage growing as a low growl of frustration escaped him.

Ravyn didn't appear to notice the precipice he balanced on. "It seems silly, but Ollie, something or someone is watching me. I could feel it at the premiere. And before you say it: yes, I know I'm an actress and someone is always watching me, but this was different. It was a separate feeling from the crowd and the regular watchers. I could literally physically feel it watching me. Whatever this entity is, it got close enough to touch me. It literally touched me, but no one could see a thing except me freaking out!"

Her voice sped up, hitting a higher pitch as the

words tumbled out in sudden near hysteria. "It was there, but it wasn't. And it's evil, and I don't mean like whooo hoooie evil. I mean that stuff that made me evil." Ravyn shuddered, wrapping her thin arms around herself as if to ward off a cold Oliver knew she couldn't feel. It was oddly . . . human-looking and he wasn't completely comfortable seeing his sire behaving this way. He'd seen her *act* human and helpless before, but this was no act.

She was utterly and completely terrified and trying to hide it.

A masculine hand with a scar across three knuckles appeared hesitantly behind her on the screen. It sat on her shoulder, and she reached up automatically, squeezing it for comfort.

"Who's there with you? A guard?" Oliver barked out sharply, guilt tight in his stomach that he wasn't there to offer her the same comfort.

Ravyn glanced over her shoulder as Oliver's head of security and lone wolf, Sebastian, leaned onto the screen. His blond hair fell in waves, surrounding his face as his deep voice vibrated over the phone. "It's Bash, sir. Due to the recent threats Ms. Sinclair has received, I came down myself to lead the premiere security detail." He didn't break eye contact with Oliver or even look down at Ravyn, who appeared shocked when she realized she was clutching his hand. She slowly released the hand and edged her own back into her lap.

Oliver noted with interest that she didn't push it away or shrug it off. However, Sebastian was lying;

he'd been there for weeks but apparently wanted Ravyn to think it was a one-off.

"I do believe there is a credible threat, sir."

"Oh my gosh, of course, there is!" Ravyn shrieked, pulling her shoulder away and shrugging his hand off. "What is wrong with you, Thor? I said there's a threat! I don't need you to say there's a threat." Another uncharacteristic reaction that Oliver filed away for later consideration; however, for now, he needed to know what the hell was going on.

She'd gotten comfortable bossing the regular shifter security team around, but an unfortunate side effect of her age was that the vamps on the team always deferred to her. Clearly, Sebastian didn't fall into either category, and Ravyn wasn't a fan.

Ravyn slowly explained, with Sebastian interjecting with additional details as needed, the feeling of being watched and stalked for the last few weeks. She'd been having vivid dreams lately, which went without saying aloud; neither of them had dreamed since, well . . . before. When sleep was upon them, there was nothingness, darkness, and meaninglessness. To him, it sounded as if she were being stalked and assaulted by witches, but few were powerful enough or stupid enough to try such a thing. Of course, it was against the agreements, but not everyone followed the accords set centuries ago to keep them hidden and prevent them from killing each other outright.

Then she told him about the books—books she'd known about for years and hadn't even hinted at their existence. His temper rose higher and higher at each word. They told each other almost everything mundane and absolutely everything of any importance, and she hadn't spoken a word to him about this. She'd tasked him to be her protector, then sent him away, making such a task much harder, but being dishonest and not telling him things was a betrayal of the worst kind. He was the worst protector.

Back to the books . . . When acquaintances had first talked about their hot summer read nearly ten years ago, Ravyn had only feigned interest, but then, hearing the hints and teasers about the heroine's origin story, she wondered if one of her sisters had, in fact, survived all these years and was making a profit off the pain. Without Ravyn saying the words, Oliver knew this was the hope she had—the hope that one of her sisters was out there—and in not saying anything, she could keep that secret spark, that bit of hopeful excitement, close to her heart.

Or was it simply the case of a creative mind stumbling upon an innovative idea that just so happened to be similar to what had happened to her thousands of years ago? Piquing her interest, Ravyn had begun reading the series that at the time consisted only of two books. Originally, of course, she'd felt the books were harmless, a crazy coincidence that could only happen in this wild world, but still, when not working, she enjoyed learning and devoured the written word. However, after a few chapters, she'd resigned herself to the fact that there were no coincidences in this deadly world. These books weren't written by a long-lost sister of Anat or a simple muse-inspired tale. No, the books were her biography. A biography that not even Ollie, or perhaps even herself after all these years, could have written so thoroughly.

These allegedly fictional books highlighted her very life, chronicling her present while revisiting her past lives. Long forgotten details caused her to chortle at times as the memories flooded back, and just as often hold back tears of sorrow at what was lost and the pain that she'd buried deep. Lovers she'd kept, lives she'd taken, lives she'd saved; so many fantastical secrets lay bare. So much was there, but at the same time, it was a highlighted edition. How could less than a handful of books tell her entire story?

Apparently, they were very popular, even best sellers. Thousand-page tomes that took a few years to write, but eager fans never let the stories fade between books. Three books so far over the span of ten years, with a fourth, and possibly final, on the horizon within the next two to three years. Not an exact retelling of her life—there were differences, for sure, creative licensing had been used—but enough correlation that it couldn't be random.

Oliver hadn't heard of the books, but fiction reading wasn't one of his vices. Give him a good article about new tech, though, and he was all in. On a separate screen, he rapidly scanned the info about the "Vamp of Hollywood" series while Ravyn explained the situation. How had he missed such a popular series? He knew why Ravyn had kept him in the dark:

such a secret had probably exhilarated her, and if she'd broken her silence on it, he would have been forced to intervene earlier. It was no secret that Ravyn had an ego. As an actress, she had to have one, as well as a thick skin. It had probably given her great satisfaction reading about herself, and she'd probably daydreamed about secretly playing herself if they made the books into movies.

Oliver said as much and knew he'd hit a truth when Ravyn drew herself up rigid and regal, pursing her lips and attempting to look down her nose haughtily at him.

Her guilty look.

From slightly off-screen, Sebastian admitted with mumbled tones that he'd read the books as well. They were highly entertaining, after all.

Oliver knew the bodyguards sometimes filled their hours at the house reading but had assumed the wolves were reading about how to gut and skin animals or maybe even war books, not paranormal romance. Since Bash didn't know Ravyn's history, he never suspected a problem within the pages, and Oliver couldn't blame him. The books alone should have been a red flag, one she shouldn't have ignored. The blame fell solely on his shoulders as well as Ravyn's. At her age, she'd seen enough that she knew . . . She knew there was no such thing as coincidence.

"Shut up, Thor," she muttered when the security guard whispered something so softly that even Oliver, with his enhanced hearing, couldn't pick it up over the phone. "Put that shit in your reports, don't tattle like

I'm a child."

Then the strange gifts of jewelry and flowers had begun to appear where nothing had been before, bypassing the best security system there was, a system he'd put in place. At the same time, she was guarded by the best paranormals he had. Another blaring, red flag that he'd once again not been notified about. Had he? Was it an email he'd scanned, a voice-mail deleted too soon? Maybe at this point, Sebastian's team had felt things were under control; he wanted to give them the benefit of the doubt. However, he would have their heads if the team had blown off these early warnings.

The gifts had escalated: small dead animals, heads of larger ones, and then even human body parts. By vampire standards, a few human ears and fingers weren't horrifying, but delivering them unrequested to a secure location while bypassing security was a final red flag, especially considering that Ravyn lived as a human in a very human world.

Due to her thorough security detail, Ravyn generally never knew the number of human threats she received. And calling those events threats was a disservice to real danger. These mundane human threats were delivered through the usual means, easily stopped, tracked, and deterred by paranormal means that Ravyn never needed to be bothered with. That was if they even made it past her human security team.

The gifts and messages making their way directly to Ravyn were true threats, and they should be treated as such, not swept under the rug and ignored.

Ending the call with a push of a finger wasn't

nearly as satisfying as slamming a receiver down into its cradle, but Oliver had to be satisfied with that. He ran a frustrated hand through his dark hair. He wanted someone to hit, someone to blame. But there was no one to blame. Security had done its due diligence and sent the reports up the chain of command to Sebastian. Bash, whom Oliver had hired to take over the entire physical security side of the business. Bash, who had followed every procedure in place and followed all physical leads. Bash, who had apparently been by Ravyn's side unseen and unheard, watching and protecting her even before this most recent escalation. Bash, who had insisted Ravyn call Oliver when he'd exhausted all means and knew that stronger methods needed to be utilized.

The books appeared to be the easiest of leads to track, and they were the reason he was in a town of 10,000 in the middle of rural America. Oliver supposed this hole of a town was probably fine enough if you were into this type of place, the kind where they were hanging onto 1950s nostalgia of mothers in aprons while fathers worked nine to five, forgetting that the female half of the population were second class, unable to bank, vote, or receive health care. Meanwhile, the current day idyllic small-town community had meth rampaging the back streets of the cutesy facade.

Frustrated, Oliver rubbed his chin; it really wasn't

a bad place. When had he become so jaded? Had it crept up on him over the years or had it just suddenly happened overnight as the years flashed by and civilization continued to repeat history, unable to truly learn from its mistakes while touting progress and values? At some point, he'd become his grandfather, a cynical, angry old man who could no longer find peace in the world around him. No wonder Ravyn had sent him off without her. If he could tire, he would be exhausted.

The town really wasn't that bad. No trash littered the streets. Apparently, the locals used the public trash cans standing on every block, or perhaps a Boy Scout troop picked up litter regularly. And the signs that adorned the neat but worn store fronts lacked the neon glow that was so common in Chicago. They reminded him a bit of the buildings in the small Illinois town where he'd grown up well before the first of the great wars. Maple trees grew on the lawns, surrounded with the starts of spring flower beds, and nearly all the stores—even the empty ones—boasted at least one planter bursting full with an array of freshly planted spring and summer flora. Tidy and welcoming, it was a place his parents might have chosen to live in if given a choice.

Ending up here was a twisted journey and not as easy as he'd thought it would be. Whomever he was looking for had hidden their tracks well. But he wasn't the best in the business for nothing. Sure, a human wouldn't have been able to track down this author, but there wasn't a chance she could hide from vampire persuasion.

After Ravyn's call ended, Oliver downloaded the books.

He breezed quickly through the tomes, marveling at the accuracy, while also dismayed that Ravyn had found them merely entertaining instead of downright frightening. Astonishingly enough, they did chronicle her life beginning in Egypt thousands of years ago, well before the birth of today's Christian God. A few things were embellished and fleshed out with apparent artistic license—Ravyn had told him that—but most things were factual. He couldn't be sure of everything because it was simply impossible to know all of Ravyn's stories. His heart broke for young Ravyn and for the centuries she'd chosen to slumber away, her soft heart too broken to deal with love and loss time and time again.

Nephthys was her new name after her death and rebirth. She'd taken the name of the ancient goddess of death and decay, winged protector of the dead. Her name before that had been wiped out, and even the book didn't reference it. It had truly been erased. However, the book's heroine went by Fala Ishto, which was yet another winged protector for an American tribe, a nickname cobbled together meaning "Big Crow," a nod to her resemblance to the bird. Ravyn had answered to the nickname Fala during the years when she'd lived with a Chickasaw tribe. She spoke little of those years, but enough that Oliver knew she'd felt happiness and love. Perhaps that was who she saw herself as still. Not simply Ravyn, but more.

As Oliver read, he realized that if even half the words on the pages were true and not artistic license, then this writer, this mysterious A. Scriver, knew more about Ravyn than anyone alive—even him. The digital book jacket contained a vague picture of the so-called writer shot from the side with her hair falling to hide the profile of her face. It was black and white, with the only color coming from a yellow ray of light fading off in the distance. Her biography was even more sparse. The space normally filled with accolades about inspiration and education, along with a summary of hobbies, kids, and pets was non-existent. Instead, riddles filled some of the empty space around and below her picture.

Book One asked, "What did the period say to the sentence? We'd better stop now."

Book Two stated, "Past, Present, and Future walked into a bar . . . It was tense."

Book Three was the shortest with just, "Broken pencils are pointless."

Was this supposed to be a clue about the writer's identity? Was she threatening Ravyn with the knowledge of past and present while threatening her future? Could broken pencils be a metaphor for the pointlessness of Ravyn's vampire existence or a tasteless joke about sharp objects and vampires?

Were dead animals and body parts a gift or a threat? Did any of it even mean anything or was he chasing the wind? Despite the lack of answers, Oliver couldn't suppress the slight thrill that swept through him as each unanswered question led to even more questions. Fingers flew over the keyboard as he typed out anything from his readings that might be a lead or a note to follow up on.

Sometimes the easiest answer was the most obvious; unless, of course, it wasn't. Internet searches turned up only the vaguest of details. Conveniently located in Chicago, the book publisher would be an early morning stop. Numerous fan pages dedicated to the books yielded few results. Apparently, A. Scriver avoided cameras, book tours, interviews, and basically anything remotely connected to promoting her work. He found no solid information, just speculations.

Oliver bookmarked a few promising sites in case his other ideas yielded the same results. He found teasers for a fourth book that was set to be released within the year, but again, nothing of substance. Despite the excitement the press releases generated from the fans, there wasn't a single clue on what was going to be in the next book. Even the author's name was a riddle, a generic German surname aptly meaning "writer." Literally "A Writer" or, if he was being fancy, maybe "A Scribe." However, this writer wasn't any simple teller of stories. She was a threat.

He rubbed a frustrated hand over his face and pondered. What could be in the next book? Book Three had covered Ravyn's life up until recently. Searching and scanning social media posts, he read through more fan pages and groups devoted to the writer and her works. Still assuming the writer was a woman, the picture could be a red herring designed to throw off searchers. But why? Why would someone go to such lengths to remain unknown? Even the most secret of persons must enjoy basking in the adulation of adoring fans. Surely she followed the pages under a different name, but going through each profile was definitely something he was assigning to an employee.

Finally, a page simply called Scriver, with a blue check mark and several thousand followers popped up in a search. Oliver scoffed. The writer must know that if she'd typed it like it was on the book, she would have more hits, or maybe she simply didn't care if fans followed her. Despite all the accolades posted about her, possibly she didn't need the affirmation. It was difficult to believe, but at this point anything was possible.

Oliver studied the sparse page, looking for clues. The posts were simple. The latest one from ten days ago included a closeup of the top of black coffee in a white mug. "So much happening . . ."

Cryptic and pointless, he scoffed, but the fans went wild guessing and begging for more interaction. A post from a month earlier was a stock photo of a salad captioned, "Lettuce get it on!" Absolutely no cohesive posts to give him even a hint on where to look next.

Oliver realized as he scrolled through posts that Scriver never responded to any comments or even came back to "like" a post or comment. Perhaps part of her appeal was her lack of accessibility? Clearly, she was a follower of the "less is more" ideology. Keep the audience wanting.

With a few clicks of the keyboard, he searched for the IP address that posted on the account. Another Chicago address. Could he find the writer without even leaving the Chicago area? He was already mentally patting himself on the back for successful tracking. No one could outrun tech.

A search of the address revealed it to be a live-in care facility. A few more clicks connected to and then opened the cameras at the facility, revealing a few early morning residents slowly strolling the halls using walkers. He flipped through camera view after camera view, scanning the early morning-shift workers and the residents alike. Oliver frowned. It seemed unlikely that a successful modern writer resided in an assisted living facility. The writing seemed younger; perhaps one of the workers? Without a flash of guilt, Oliver downloaded the employee files with the intent of viewing them after his visit to the publishing house or perhaps sending the mundane task to an underling. Sometimes the most obvious possibility was the answer: the writer had simply bounced around IP addresses until she landed randomly on this place, and there was no connection at all.

He sent the connecting files to an associate with instructions to continue scanning cameras while noting every visitor, employee, even delivery people. After a moment, he added an additional note to run background checks as well. Time consuming and quite possibly the most mundane task known to the company, he knew that direction coming straight from him would make it a priority without him needing to say it.

As he had maneuvered the early morning traffic, Oliver searched for information on the publishing house not available to the public. Voice command made simultaneous searches efficient as he drove. Contracts, author lists, email lists, and other secure information began to run through his customer sorter, searching for anything that mentioned the books by name, A. Scriver, and other key words such as "vampire" and "paranormal." The program estimated at least four hours to complete. Hopefully, he would have the information the old fashion way before it could even complete its cycle.

The publishing house was nearly a bust as well. Oliver confidently entered the modern offices on the outskirts of the city, thankfully not far from his own building, noticing the few cameras in place and even fewer that worked. He made a note to have his team erase him from the footage the minute he left, even though he easily slid around any clearly viewed areas.

Despite his vampire mind compulsion, Oliver's discreet inquiries were met with censure from most of his interviewees, who eagerly offered any assistance they could but were then unable to.

Frustration was mounting; admittedly, he was a bit out of practice with fieldwork, but humans shouldn't still feel the desire to hide information from him when he compelled them. Of course, despite their desire, they were unable to hide anything from him. It was just that they really didn't know anything. Despite her sales and apparent fame, no one he interrogated had even seen a picture of the writer, let alone met her in person. Apparently, she never came into the building. Despite claiming to have never met her, each person he spoke to announced verbatim that she was the loveliest of ladies and always so kind to everyone, a joy to work with. When pressed, they couldn't remember if she was young or old. Despite the fact that her book jacket showed long hair hiding her profile, no one could say if her hair was long or short. They could recall she had beautiful eyes, but not one person could say for certain what her eye color was. Blue? Brown? Hazel? Anything that appeared to be a memory of her was a canned response, and specifics were all uncertain and different.

Everything was done through her agent, who also apparently never came into the offices.

*What an asinine way to do business*, Oliver thought rather cynically.

Admittedly, if keeping hidden was the writer's goal, it was working. Business was conducted by email or courier through the unknown agent; one woman thought maybe the agent was Bess or Liz, but when pressed further, her mind became even more befuddled. The groundwork had been laid before he'd arrived to hide this writer from anyone who came looking. It smelled suspiciously supernatural, and where there was smoke there was fire. Combined with the mysterious gifts and visitors, all the paranormal activity tied together to spell out trouble.

However, after slipping in and out of several offices and chatting up receptionists with no luck,

Oliver found a chatty and bored assistant to the personal assistant of the editor-in-chief. Ironically enough, he didn't have to use any persuasion beyond a half grin and leaning close enough to speak in hushed confidence to gain the little information she did know. Setting aside her nail file, she seemed eager to speak to anyone who approached her hidden corner desk.

The editor-in-chief was the only person with whom the agent corresponded directly, and he was currently on another "vacay to a beach."

"The contracts with A. Scriver are, like, super confidential," the assistant babbled.

Oliver leaned on her desk, suppressing an eye roll while encouraging her with a nod and a flash of teeth with his smile.

"There are, in fact, no electronic copies." She leaned in closer to him as she ran a finger down her neck, dipping lower. "He keeps them off-site somewhere. His other assistant might know, but she's on vacay too." With a pout of her pink lips, she added with a huff and toss of blond hair, "My uncle said I had to still come to work this week, even with them gone. But sometimes I leave at lunchtime."

Now, with a whiff of persuasion and a hint of irritation, Oliver commanded the young woman to forget that she'd spoken to him, leave for an early lunch once again, and forget that she'd let him into the editor-in-chief's office. Then with a sigh, he added a healthy caution of stranger danger for her own protection to his compulsion.

# CHAPTER FOUR

*The sunlight wasn't so bad during the Dark Ages.*

The intense midday sun had forced Oliver to retreat and rest for a few hours. He was frustrated by this weakened state but accepted that it would worsen as the years passed. A few more centuries, and the sunlight would inhibit him even more than it currently did. The curse of the vampire meant that as his strength grew in power, so did his weakness. As the years ticked past, so did the amount of daylight his body could safely process. In the early days of his extended lifetime, the sunlight had only weakened him for a few minutes each day, but now he needed to slumber well hidden from the sunlight a good two hours of the day. Ravyn had reached an age years ago that had her hiding from the sunlight for eight hours a day and forced her to slumber for a good deal of those hours. It appeared to have leveled off for her, and he could only hope that if he survived as long as his maker, his limits might be similar.

Late afternoon brought him farther east of Chicago, entering a spotless, new live-in care center with a well-manicured lawn and bright spring flowers already blooming. It was, of course, the same care center to which he'd traced the Facebook IP address the night before. He cursed himself for not coming straight here and wasting time at the publisher's offices, but he also admitted that knowing a name and room number made it much easier than a room-by-room search for someone who might know the author. A hidden drawer in the editor's office had housed an address book with only a few names and places listed in code. He'd broken the code, easily determined which address he needed, and was long gone before the assistant returned from her early break—if she even came back that day.

Oliver knew he was in the right place as soon as he entered the room. The security cameras didn't invade the privacy of the home's occupants. A quick perusal revealed books overflowing from shelves, a few even stacked in tidy piles. Awards for various authors adorned the walls, and full-size posters promoting each of the "Vamps in Hollywood" book covers hung on the walls. A corner desk held a computer whose screen lit up half the darkened room, and just out of reach of the light in a wheelchair sat an elderly woman with long, silver hair and bright but unseeing eyes.

Just inside the door, Oliver froze for several breaths, his eyes darting around the room, measuring any chance of danger, before coldly examining the old woman before him. The years clearly showed on her expressionless, wrinkled face. Oliver observed her quietly, feeling she knew he was there despite the

50

glassy, unfocused eyes.

Finally, she spoke, breaking the room's silence, her voice sharp and clear. A futile attempt to feign fearlessness, but for her heartbeat speeding up and the slight catch of breath. "What will you be wanting . . .vampire?" Despite the straightness of her back and unshaken tone, her hands trembled ever so slightly as she hid them on her lap.

"How do you know I'm a vampire?" He carefully sniffed the air, relying on a third sense to ascertain possible danger. "Witch," he snarled out with a hiss. Moving closer to her desk with a careless ease he no longer felt, Oliver examined the notes on the computer's speech-to-text program without turning his back to her.

"I should be flattered you feel any fear of me," the old witch admitted, "and the same as you; I could smell you when you entered the building. Not all of us can rely on sight alone anymore. Plus, I still have a few charms and alarms around the place. We're not as helpless here as one of your kind might expect," she spit out bitterly. "Child, I'm not your enemy."

She softened her tone, which still trembled. "I'm just an old lady, and I've never had any problems with your kind."

Oliver said nothing; her assurance meant nothing. Still, he examined her closely while her pale eyes stared in a direction near him but not quite at him. More and more layers. A witch. Barely any magic left, and a good chance that what she held in reserve kept her alive and protected her home. Most likely centuries old, if he were a guessing vampire. It was doubtful that her magic was what held a danger to Ravyn, even if she had a reason to do so.

"If you're needing a witch, you're looking at the wrong one. I'm depleted. There isn't much left of me. I just want to enjoy my final years here with my friends." Gesturing throughout the room with withered fingers, she continued, "My only power is the word, nowadays."

"Interesting, because that's precisely the power I'm looking for: someone who knows the power of words." After the proverbial pregnant pause, he added, "A writer."

"I've represented a few of them over the years, but now very few keep in touch. They're all dead and gone, or they've grown old and forgotten me. Sometimes, a family member sends a Christmas card, but more often than not, it's a death announcement. It's doubtful that an old witch like me could help someone like you." Her blasé attitude again didn't match the heart beating so rapidly that it might explode.

"I think . . ." he admonished, squatting down, not caring that his previously crisp suit was creasing. He placed himself face to face with her, knowing that she could sense the danger inches away. "I think you still keep in touch with this particular writer and that you do, in fact, know where she is."

Oliver stared straight into her unseeing, pale blue eyes creased with the wrinkles that spoke of her longevity. He gently grasped both of her ringed hands in his, caressing the aged, wrinkled skin in awe of the age they belayed. As he pulled one hand to his mouth, turning it over to expose a paper-thin, pale wrist, he saw the tears well up. She let out a tiny gasp as he nipped at her wrist, careful to avoid tearing her fragile skin, and then she told him everything he needed to know.

Imogene hadn't lied completely to him; truthfully, she'd never harmed an innocent, presented no danger to anyone, and probably never had.

Oliver had a town—no address, just a PO box—but most importantly, he had a name.

Josephine. Josephine Nance. "Posy" to her friends.

# CHAPTER FIVE

*Being a fiction author is a novel profession, pun intended.*

Prep work for tomorrow's opening was nearly finished when the bell at the door chimed, letting Eva know someone had entered the shop. Wiping her hands on her black apron, she approached the counter with a quick glance at the clock: 8:40, nearly closing time. Steady business had ensured she hadn't had time to pull out her laptop and write, but the last stragglers, a chatty group of three young moms who were enjoying a reprieve from toddler duty, had just left for their respective homes and families.

"Hello! Welcome to A Latte of Coffee," she singsonged, expecting a local needing a decaf java before bed or a shift worker picking up a final jolt of caffeine. The remainder of her greeting got stuck in her throat when a stranger quietly closed the door behind himself.

Guppy-like, she opened her mouth and then closed it, foolishly rendered speechless by the man she quickly determined would forever be known as Mr. Tall-Dark-and-Handsome. Book Boyfriend flashed through her mind, and Eva felt her own face heat up at the scenes she could write with such a muse.

Strolling toward the counter, removing his sunglasses that couldn't possibly be needed as the sun had finished it descent earlier, but still looking as if he'd just stepped off the cover of GQ magazine, with his short, dark military haircut (how was his part so sharp?), pressed black pants with a few creases marring their elegance, and the sleeves of a herringbone white dress shirt rolled up as if he were trying to unsuccessfully play casual. All of this ended with, as her grandmother would say, "a jawline so sharp you could cut glass with it."

Eva's voice returned, and she managed to croak out, "Did you need directions back to the turnpike?" Damn, but Joanne was going to be sorry she'd missed this guy. Even if his being here was a mistake, who didn't appreciate a little eye candy? Obviously, though, this stranger couldn't mean to be here. Here was nowhere, and this gorgeous male specimen clearly belonged somewhere.

He let out a low rumble of a laugh, showing off, of course, perfect teeth. Eva tensed for a second; something was off. Although his laugh sounded genuine, she noticed it didn't actually reach his dark eyes, and it sounded practiced to her. A practiced laugh she could understand; after all, she worked customer service. "No, I'm looking to get a cup of coffee."

They stood silently for a moment, and he raised an eyebrow questioningly. "I can get coffee here, right?"

As if getting an actual coffee from an actual coffee shop might be an impossibility.

Dear Lord, she was acting like she'd never seen a man before.

"Oh, yeah, of course. Yes, absolutely," Eva repeated. *Shut up,* she demanded of herself. "Our specialty today is a 'You Mocha Me Crazy' light roast-mocha blend, and any size hot or cold for four dollars. Can I mix one up for you?"

This drew another raised eyebrow.

*He has blue eyes*, Eva noted. *Not pale blue or sky blue*. But holy moly, how were his eyes so dark? So deep, so dark blue they looked nearly black with barely a hint of difference in his irises. They were the eyes that writers dreamed up, eyes that a woman could get lost in. He would definitely appear in her next book! A mysterious man stopping by a small-town coffee shop? Thoughts flew even as she reminded herself that she was deep into a "Vamp of Hollywood" book, and there was no place for this man. Or was there? Scrunching up her fingers, she reined them in from searching out a pen to immediately take notes on the specimen before her. *Stop. Stop noticing his eyes!*

"How about a black coffee in the darkest roast you have?"

Eva nodded, letting out a genuine smile. "Perfect choice, our Déjà Brew. Regular or decaf?"

"Definitely regular."

Finally, muscle memory kicked in, and Eva managed to ring up his order and accept his cash before inviting him to have a seat while she brewed him up a fresh cup. After dropping a generous tip in the tip jar, he strolled around the shop, examining the locally made candles and jams for sale before pausing briefly at the bookshelves and lightly running a finger along the display of A. Scriver books. She immediately averted her eyes when he glanced in her direction before he settled down at a table for two, moving the chair sideways so that he settled firmly against the wall with her in sight, as well as the front door and the front windows.

*Military*, she decided. Her best friend Jackson had served two deployments in Afghanistan and now always took a position against a wall with eyes on everything. And he didn't always laugh fully or genuinely either, Eva reflected, her heart filling with sympathy for both men. It wasn't an easy life.

"You're brew-ti-ful," she whispered to the dark coffee filled within a fraction of an inch of the rim. Her eyes shot to the man as she thought she heard a snort, but his blank face was fixated on his phone. *He couldn't have heard me, could he?* How embarrassing if he had. But embarrassment didn't stop her from rounding the counter to deliver the tall, steaming mug to the tall, steaming . . .

Stepping carefully from habit over the wooden floorboard that creaked with age and then with just as much care not to block his view, knowing that even small things could trigger a former soldier's unwanted memory, Eva settled the coffee down in front of him. "Enjoy your Déjà Brew."

Before she could back off, he firmly grasped her

wrist to stop her from leaving, his fingers lingering briefly on her bluish veins. A sudden flare of static electricity flicked through her at the casual touch, causing her to start but not move away from the warmth.

Tilting his head toward the predominantly vampire book display, he casually asked, "Have you read the series?"

Eva felt more than just off-handed interest in the display even though he'd spent less time examining it than he had Lois Carter's strawberry-rhubarb jam display. Her grandmother had taught her much after her parents' death, and being too casual usually meant exactly the opposite. Another lesson had been to always trust your instincts. And those instincts were currently flashing some pretty crazy lights in her brain.

To anyone else, the dark-haired, blue-eyed stranger's question might have appeared to be a weak attempt at starting a conversation with a cute barista. Eva knew she was cute, maybe not gorgeous enough to remember for days, but cute enough for a casual night of fun. But his question, combined with his touch, had red alarms screaming and flashing in her brain. Folks just didn't stop halfway between Toledo and Cleveland in a small town to make idle chit-chat about novels—particularly her novels.

She pulled her hand back, stepping away to put space between them. "I've not read them," she said suspiciously, which wasn't really a lie. She was doubtful that he had either. He didn't quite fit her target demographic. If someone was out on a fact-finding mission, sending Mr. Tall-Dark-and-Sticks-Out-with-Nordstrom-Clothes to this small town wasn't very clever of them.

"That's too bad. They're quite good. A friend of mine is a huge fan." Picking up the coffee, he drew in a sip, still pretending to make idle conversation.

Seriously, did he think he was that good of an actor?

"I'll have to give them a go sometime," Eva lied. Her palms were growing damp, and she struggled to keep a casual, interested tone. "We close at nine, so if you've not finished up by then, let me know, and I'll get you a to-go cup."

She normally let customers linger as long as needed while she closed. The local clientele knew when closing time happened, and unless they were a group of moms on a rare night out, they didn't tend to lose track of time. But those alarms blaring in her head weren't shutting off, and it seemed best to get him on his way sooner rather than encourage him to linger.

Leaning back as if realizing his presence crowded her, he smoothly introduced himself and continued the conversation as if she weren't actively fleeing back to the safety of the counter.

"I'm Oliver Patrick. I'm looking for an old friend of my mom's. Mom passed away recently, and I wanted to get in touch with her friend, but all I have is this town's name, a PO box, and her name."

His voice flowed over her like silk, smoothly caressing her skin and gently beckoning her to sit down, relax, and help him find his late mother's friend.

Eva's lie detector continued ringing, but now curiosity also took hold. How far would he go in his lies?

"I'm sorry for your loss." Fighting the urge to move closer again, she murmured the platitudes from habit. "It's a small town, I'm sure I would know your mom's friend. Who are ya looking for?"

"Josephine Nance. Her friends call her Posy."

Eyes narrowing in shock, Eva jolted back farther, unable to hide her reaction.

Oliver leaned forward in his chair, clearly eager to hear what she had to say.

Pursuing her lips angrily, *pissed,* knowing that she couldn't hide that she did, in fact, know Josephine, she bit out, "When did your mama last talk to Ms. Posy? Or did they write?"

"Oh, they only wrote, as far as I can tell. I couldn't find any phone number in Mom's contact lists, just the PO box. Maybe Mom had the number memorized? Just a few days ago, a letter was forwarded from her to my mom. I wanted to come by myself and tell her the terrible news. It seemed wrong just to send a letter with such tragic news. Even though I didn't know her, they seemed quite close." The lies were rolling off him now.

"Right," Eva drawled out and attempted to casually dry her sweaty hands down her apron. "Well, sir—"

"Please call me Oliver," he interrupted smoothly. If Eva wasn't mistaken, he attempted to turn up his charm a whole other notch, smoothing down his shirt and sending a smoldering look up at her.

"Well, Oh-liver, I'm afraid you came all this way for nothing. Josephine Nance is my—was my—grandmother, and she's been dead for . . ." Now feeling annoyance and anger more than fear, Eva allowed an exaggerated thinking expression to cover her face, then slowly nodded, bouncing a few tendrils that had once again escaped her hair tie. "For yes, just over ten years now. So I'm going to assume and please don't tell me about assuming, I'm going to assume you've made some big mistake, and you're in the wrong town, the wrong state, the wrong . . . ."

In the blink of an eye or maybe even less than a blink, he appeared immediately in front of her despite the table and several feet that separated them. "Lock the door, and turn the Closed sign." His voice deepened.

Eva could hear a faint vibration in the command and, for a moment, she half turned toward the door. Yet her mind hesitated. *Did his eyes just flare red?*

Anger and annoyance raged through her, smiting any bit of fear that remained. She stopped abruptly, as if she hadn't been about to turn around and do just as he'd ordered. "Sir, it's time for you to leave. If you would like to be truthful about why you're looking for my gram—my gram, who has been dead for over ten years, I'll remind you—maybe then we can talk. But right now, you need to move on out of here. It's closing time."

The shock on his face surely reflected hers. Damn,

Gram had always told her that her temper would be the death of her. And this could be it.

But instead of murdering her like she feared, he let out a low laugh, this time genuine. Then he said in a low voice. "Little rabbit, you are a conundrum. Brave words, but I can hear your heart beating. And a woman's heart only beats that fast for two reasons." Without losing eye contact, he took a step closer. "I'll see you soon."

For some unexplained reason, Eva's mouth wouldn't stop spewing words. "Fur goodness sake, maybe you're just hopping mad, but you need to head back to your own bunny burrow." Crossing her arms, she gave a pointed look at the door, no longer in any mood to give him his coffee to go or to imagine what it would feel like to have those arms wrapped around her while his lips peppered hers. Seriously, what was wrong with her? She could easily admit that it had been a while, but seriously, this guy? Despite his good looks and Adonis-like body, he clearly lied for a living. What was up with moving that fast? Eva wasn't prepared to even dwell on that little oddity until much later and preferably after she'd made it safely home and locked all the doors.

Thankfully, but not without a small smile—assuredly a sexy, *genuine* small smile—Oliver continued moving forward right toward the door, flipped the Open sign to Closed, then before leaving, ordered, "Eva, lock up."

Letting out a deep breath, Eva sprinted to the door and clicked the lock as soon as it closed. Aware that the store lit up around her, making her visible to anyone outside looking in, she flipped the lights off before catching a breath to consider why on earth anyone would be looking for her grandmother. *And how the hell did he know her name?*

Gram Posy had brought Eva to live with her the year she turned twelve. The year a car accident had taken Eva's parents, the same accident that had caused Eva to spend her twelfth birthday in a hospital intensive care unit as well as the week before and ten days after said birthday with no reason or ability to celebrate.

All the doctors and nurses reminded Eva constantly of the miracle of her survival, the miracle that had brought her out of the coma. How lucky she was to be alive. But young Eva certainly didn't feel like a miracle or lucky. She felt like a little girl who had lost everyone and everything. And she had, and so had Gram, but they still had each other, and together, they would heal over the years.

Eva couldn't remember a time Gram hadn't been in her life. Of course, there was the year and a half when she was a baby before her mom met her dad, but she couldn't remember that time. For as long as she could remember, her adoptive father and his mother had been a part of her life. At least they had been, until the rainy night when the family car skidded out of control, hurling down an embankment and ending with only one member of their small family of three surviving. In an instant, Mom and Dad were gone, and life as Eva knew it up-heaved.

She had no memories of the accident and only vague memories of the day, flashes of riding in the back seat to the movie theater to see a movie she didn't remember. A splatter of fat, thick raindrops peppered the front windshield, not enough to even turn the wipers on, and the rays of the setting sun broke through the storm clouds that were rolling around.

"Turn this song up," were the last words she remembered uttering, but Eva couldn't remember if the words were before or after the movie.

She woke up in the hospital days later, bandaged head to toe, with an IV poking in one arm and a blaring monitor; she remembered nothing before that moment. Later, Gram told her they'd made it to the movies and were returning home after a torrential shower. Blackened skid marks on the road showed how the car had spun out of control at least twice before it careened off the road and down the embankment, crushing the edge of the guard rail as it hurtled through. Her parents were still strapped in their seat belts, lost at impact, Gram had quietly told Eva when she pressed for details. Eva herself was found just off the edge of the rural highway at the top of the embankment, a battered mess whose survival, let alone recovery, was deemed a miracle.

Gram was a witch, loud and proud, always saying the ditty with a giggle. Eva wasn't, and Eva's father wasn't. Gram had explained that men didn't inherit the power in her family line. And, of course, Eva couldn't inherit from what she hadn't been born to. She could learn a few things, but there would be no real power display because Eva didn't have a connection to the elements. Gram explained it all matter-of-factly, as if explaining why Eva had brown eyes and she had blue. They could both see, but that didn't change the color.

With a lower tone hinting at a secret, Gram told Eva that she had her own power to claim someday, when the time was right. Until that day, Eva was destined to follow Gram around the little house that had been in Gram's family for generations. Someday, it would be hers, Gram promised as they puttered through the garden, nurturing the plants and uttering incantations that Gram assured her would protect Eva as long as she remained within its boundaries. It crossed Eva's mind that such things hadn't protected her parents, but she never dared utter those thoughts aloud. Maybe her parents had been too far away from home for protection, or maybe there were no such protections. So she said the words, planted the herbs, and faithfully wore the black jade stone Gram pressed upon her, but it was all an act for her. As time passed, she believed less and less in Gram's supposed abilities and the possibility of magic and witchcraft around them.

The sad little girl eventually grew into a young woman whose broken heart and family appeared healed. But as Gram liked to remind her, once something was broken, no repair could ever make it as it was before. And that was okay. She could never be the girl she was before the accident, nor could Gram be the mother, grandmother, or witch she was before. But together, they tried; stronger in some spots, weaker in others, and even scarred in a few.

Just before her nineteenth birthday, Eva came home from her community college class late in the evening excited to share with Gram the discussion she'd shared after class with a few classmates. Since her best friend had joined the military, Gram had become her constant confidant. The darkened house immediately alerted Eva that something had happened; Gram always left a light or two on for Eva even if she'd gone to bed.

Eva ran through the house searching for Gram, and then started her search outside. A low sound brought her to the old woman's side as she lay half-hidden in the shadows under an overgrown mint bush, clutching a recently dug ginger root to her chest.

Wrapping her arms around her beloved grandmother, Eva begged her to stay as she shakily pushed the numbers in her cell phone for help.

Gram had held on long enough to see her beloved only grandchild one last time. "I've so much I should have told you, taught you," she rasped, drawing in each breath slowly, painfully. "I thought I had more time to tell you everything."

"No, Gram, you still have time to teach me." Eva pushed and willed her grandmother's strength to not fade as the shadows grew closer around them. The scents of lavender, sage, and mint enveloped them, caressing the two as they clung to each other.

"The house will protect you. I've made it so," Gram whispered. "Stay close to the house and you'll stay safe. I love you, dear child, and always remember you're good, no matter what anyone says or how they might try to convince you otherwise. You're good, you are goodness."

And that was it. As the emergency vehicle sirens grew closer and closer, Gram faded. And by the time help arrived, Gram was gone, and Eva was inconsolable. Again her everything was gone.

But Eva stayed at the little Firelands house Gram claimed was made safe just for her. And no matter how much she wanted to leave or planned to leave, those plans never seemed to come to fruition. Certainly, a therapist would have much to say about the matter, but Eva refused to return to therapy and continued onward. At some point, the black jade that Gram always claimed kept her safe and the bits and pieces Gram had strategically placed around the home—black tourmaline, labradorite, moonstones, and others—went into a small dish in the living room. Eva continued taking random classes that piqued her interest, working at the coffee shop, and eventually stumbled upon writing.

Tonight, after a breathless bike ride home and constantly whipping her head around to check the shadows for hidden dangers, she regretted for the first time the lack of streetlights on the dead-end street leading to her not-quite-secluded home. Built on the end of the lane, the street petered off into a curb just past her drive, and then grass and overgrown bushes followed, hiding from view the vacant land beyond. Her nearest neighbor was hidden by a tree line that seemed to not only block the view but also the sound.

An old, weather-worn sidewalk framed the front of her home, but time and nature had buried it between the neighbor's house and her own for several yards before it reemerged over the property line to lead the way across their front yard. They each assumed it lay buried beneath dirt and grass, but neither household was bothered enough to unearth it. The quiet dead-end road, just as easily used and mostly well-maintained by the township, meant that the buried sidewalk could remain unused and obsolete.

When Eva crossed the threshold of her home, the house welcomed her and wrapped her in a cocoon. She felt it settle down around her and, for a brief moment, she imagined she felt the wards her gram had always insisted were present after one of her strange rituals. Now that she stood safely in her home, she let out a soft, fearful giggle, cursing her out-of-control imagination. Today had been quite a day! But she couldn't deny how good it felt to be home,

"Home sweet home," Eva said to the silent house. Tossing her bag of things, as well as her keys, on the sofa, she basked in the comfort of home.

Safety. Security. Peace. Perhaps Gram hadn't been wrong about the early nineteenth-century home. Maybe her ancestors had imbued protective magic in its old bones. Or perhaps the series of events today were just a by-product of her own overly active imagination. Her mood was most likely due to her mind playing tricks on her. She'd been so wrapped up in her writing that maybe the fictional paranormal world was leaking into the real world when her mind didn't shut off. It definitely wouldn't be the first time her imagination had thrown her into chaos.

Of course, in the safety of the house, things started to seem silly. Apollo had found a sick-looking squirrel or some other creature on the walk today, and suddenly, her mind had replaced it with moving shadows.

And maybe this Oliver was, in fact, simply looking for a woman who had befriended his mother, but the passage of time had muddled things. Maybe he assumed an old letter was much newer or the mail hadn't been forwarded correctly for ten years. He'd never actually threatened her; he'd ordered a coffee and tipped well while asking his questions. Would someone who was planning something nefarious leave a cupful of DNA behind on a coffee table? Only a total idiot would do that; and his pricey shoes didn't give him the appearance of an idiot. Maybe she'd misheard his tone when he asked her to close up. Sometimes lights reflected weirdly in people's eyes; maybe it was worth bringing up at her next eye exam that she was seeing flashes of red.

Or maybe she was being a complete idiot by writing off someone who apparently knew her name, her gram's name, and who asked questions about the books she'd successfully kept the world from knowing for ten years that she'd written.

# CHAPTER SIX

*What do a stalker and a Pokemon nerd have in
common?
They both hide in the bushes trying to get a Pikachu.*

Leaving the discreet rental car on Main Street, Oliver
kept to the shadows as he followed Eva the few miles
to her home. Never once did his eyes lose her, even
though she frantically peddled as if the devil himself
chased her toward her destination. Technically, she
wasn't wrong, but sweet Eva didn't appear to truly
know anything about the devil. But like the devil,
perhaps she was the trickster, the beautiful face luring
in her unsuspecting victims with her innocent smile
and not-so-innocent curves that even a frumpy coffee
shop apron couldn't hide.

Eva. Like the first woman, full of life. Invigorating
life.

As his bunny fled, he felt his fangs burst forth in
excitement, reminding him of the early days long ago
when he'd fought so hard to control himself against
the blood lust. Different, but still the same loss of
control needed to be wrestled down. This leggy imp
provoked a side of him he refused to embrace. Just a
few inches shorter than his six-foot-two, she'd looked

only slightly up to stare at him defiantly in the eyes at the coffee shop.

Oliver forced his fangs to retract as he regained control of the strong desire to chase her down and pin her beneath him. Focusing on Ravyn, he reminded himself that Eva could be the enemy that tormented and threatened his maker. Although nothing about her struck him as such until he had proof either way, this investigation—this incredibly hot freaking mess of an investigation—would continue. Eva could easily be wearing a mask of innocence held in place by a beguiling face.

Settling down outside her cottage's boundaries under the branches of a buckeye tree older than him, Oliver reminded himself that too much time over the last few decades had been spent on the cyber-end of security, forgoing the thrill of fieldwork. He'd forgotten how fascinating and time-consuming it could be—and frankly, often tedious—but still enjoyable nonetheless. Leaning against the tree, he remained mindful of his white shirt, while also admitting it was probably going to be ruined by the unexpected stakeout and any future adventures the night might bring.

Hard to believe that just a few days ago, he'd set up a program to reset a certain genius billionaire's social media password every two minutes because that day's work hadn't interested him. Smirking, he thought of the extra add-on in which if the billionaire did make it past the password virus for thirty seconds the program would tweet random Disney emojis replacing all typed letters before it reset again. At the thought of the man's frustration, Oliver choked off a sharp bark of laughter. At the sound, a neighbor's dog let out a few low barks in the distance, and Oliver answered with a low growl of his own, carrying across the clear night to the distant yard, silencing the dog immediately.

Lights flipped on around the target's house, as if an attempt to fill it with light could keep anything out that really wanted inside. Why hadn't his compulsion stuck with Eva? For a second it had. After a flash of her name, she shook off the compulsion as easily as pulling off a jacket. That rarely happened. Yes, sometimes humans struggled against it, but to just remove it as if it didn't exist? Impossible. Impossible, unless maybe she was a demon or a witch, and a powerful one at that. But neither seemed likely. By all accounts, Eva was a normal, boring human, yet still a sense of otherness hung off her. In a few hours, his team would know everything there was to know about the intriguing Eva Nance, but until then, he was reliant on what he could see and hear alone.

Not even all the lights in the house could penetrate the shadows surrounding it. The house itself seemed determined to keep nosy neighbors from peering too closely into it.

Deciding to move closer to his quarry, he calculated that just a few steps would clear the yard and put him on the dimly lit porch. However, one aggressive step off the sidewalk edge had him jolted and shot back to the edge of the road on his backside.

"Shit," Oliver cursed at the unexpected jolt. Stunned, he sat momentarily in what he hoped was just dirt and gravel, knowing his overpriced pants were ruined. Embarrassment flooded through him; despite all of his training, he'd been knocked on his ass like a newbie.

Regaining his footing, this time Oliver eased forward much more cautiously. Reaching out gently with both hands, feeling the buzz that clearly warned of the impending danger, he detected the magic that flowed along the sidewalk edge marking the property but allowed anyone who ventured down the dead end sidewalk to remain unharmed. Maybe Eva wasn't a witch, but either someone who lived here was or she knew one who had cast this protective spell. Using the buzz of magic to guide his hands, he cautiously followed the protective shield around the shadowed boundaries of the half-acre yard.

As he rounded the back of the yard, his enhanced vision caught the plethora of vegetation overtaking it. It wasn't meticulously maintained and looked a bit overgrown, but it was oddly thriving and lush this early in spring. Sage, lavender, lemon balm, tansy, and yarrow could belong in any garden and were by themselves innocent enough. But among those plants, he spotted wolfsbane, belladonna, henbane, and monkshood—and those were just the ones he recognized. There was definitely something witchy going on here. Protection and poison weren't typical in most run-of-the-mill gardens. He suspected that the barrier keeping him off the land also kept the scents in.

If he hadn't seen the plants with his own eyes, none of his other senses could have alerted him to their presence.

Oliver continued his methodical journey around the borders of the yard, carefully moving his hands down to the ground and up higher than his head. The buzz threatened retaliation, but as long as he didn't press, he should remain unharmed. *Patience*, he reminded himself as he fought the urge to jump as high as he could to see if he could clear the barrier. So far it didn't appear that his previous attempt to enter had alerted Eva to his presence, but a stronger attempt might, and he had no desire to be knocked out by apotropaic magic as it protected its occupant. His staff witch would be impressed that he remembered her lesson on protective magic well enough to recognize it. Oliver made a mental note to mention it to her.

About forty-five minutes later and two-thirds around the perimeter, he found a silent spot just waist high. Probing the area cautiously and then more firmly proved that a dead space about two feet wide and maybe half as tall existed. More probing showed the area weakened several more inches outward. Even with this vulnerability, Oliver gave a mental nod, impressed with the creator of the rather large protective bubble. The witches in his employ hadn't created such a power barrier for him, so either they were weaker, or they were holding out on him. A powerful witch created and maintained this fortress, but nothing was impenetrable, as this spot showed. Time, patience, and power were all weapons against any sort of magic. This barrier required a combination of all three, but his goal was still to remain silent and unassuming, so he would have to add cleverness to the arsenal.

Of course, Oliver realized to actualize this plan, he had to get through this space. Unfortunately for him and his dress clothes, stepping through upright wasn't an option. Attempting to maneuver his tall frame through the fissure proved to be as awkward as he'd imagined, and also ended with him dirtying his knees and shins, as well as his hands. Due to its height and size, he considered a dive through, followed by a tuck and roll, but that would be irresponsible given that he didn't know if any traps on the other side would immediately rear up to attack him. Not for the first time, Oliver appreciated his tall, slight frame that permitted him to fit a bit more easily than a bulkier man would.

Half-way through the opening, he discovered that if he pushed up on the magic in its weakened state, it didn't react; it simply allowed itself to be pushed up or out, further enlarging the null spot. For a moment, regret about destroying part of the protective spell flitted through him. Clearly, it had been put in place for a reason, and he knew from his studies that it had been made of green hedge magic; whoever had cast it had done so with pure intentions. Delta, his staff witch, had been attempting to teach him to recognize various magical components beyond what his vampire senses told him; she would surely be impressed at his real-world practice. Grudgingly, Oliver admitted that her incessant chattering was paying off for him.

All of his employees would be shocked if they could see their normally impeccable boss in such disarray, and there was a good chance there was a hole or two in the seat of his pants. Certainly, dearest Ravyn would find it hysterical, reminiscent of their early days traipsing around various countrysides with muddy shoes, often filthy clothes, but with mostly high spirits.

Inside the yard, he realized how cut off the house and land were from the outside world. The garden scents were magically trapped inside the dome of magic. Not only did it smell different, but the air felt different; the crisp, clean magic permeated the very earth as well as all the plants. The air, nearly electric, flitted across his skin as if lightning were preparing to strike, and his body tingled in response, as if the hair on his arms could protect him if such a thing happened.

Of all the scents, naturally the most prevalent and irritating to him were the mustard seed and garlic. Of course, an earth witch with all these plants would have the most irritating, disgusting weeds among her plants. Contrary to popular belief, the plants didn't exactly protect a human from a vampire as much as irritate the hell out of their sinuses and enflame their eyes. Despite the lack of light, his eyes could clearly make out the glorious garden that had obviously been nurtured for years, if not generations.

Rubbing his burning eyes with a prayer that his nose wouldn't also begin running, Oliver made his way to the back ivy-covered porch, stepping lightly to avoid any errant boards that might let out a creak, alerting of his intrusion. Turning the doorknob, he gently tested it first, then with a crack, he popped the lock to the door leading into the kitchen, which thankfully opened with only a light sigh.

Walking in with all the confidence of an immortal vampire, he quickly ascertained that nothing stood in the way to threaten him. According to legend, vampires couldn't enter a home unless invited, but that simply wasn't true. It was a myth created to make peasants feel safer in their homes. And garlic didn't really offer any protection. It simply irritated eyes and sinuses; the same as mustard seed, but apparently draping oneself in yellow flowers never caught on quite the same way.

Surveying the kitchen, he began to wonder if he'd wandered on to the 1980s set of *Stranger Things*. Just as quickly, he came to the conclusion that he would never, ever tell Ravyn about these observations. Ravyn knew he watched a lot of Netflix, Hulu, and whatever other streaming services were offered, but he did try to keep the exact number of hours spent somewhat of a secret. Needing but a few hours of sleep left a lot of endless hours, and television easily filled them. Not everyone had parties and events most nights of the week, he ended the argument with Ravyn in his mind before it even started. Oliver knew she assumed he only watched science and tech documentaries, and truthfully, he did watch those, just not only those types of shows.

The cracked orange-and-yellow linoleum held a well-worn path between the refrigerator and the doorway with a lighter one toward the stove. Normally, he wouldn't notice a stove or refrigerator, but they were both yellow. Yellow! Yeah, the 1980s definitely called and wanted their appliances back. And of course, the countertops were orange. Why wouldn't they be? Bright flowered curtains that somehow both matched and clashed with the room hung from the small window over the sink. The counter next to the—yup—orange scratched up porcelain sink had been cut away, and a completely out-of-place stainless-steel dishwasher awkwardly jutted out from the space.

Was there still an eighty-one-year-old lurking around here somewhere? Eva had claimed her grandmother had passed years ago, but who didn't at least do some upgrades?

Oliver had assumed Eva lived here alone, but so far every single assumption he'd made about this investigation had been blown to bits. He really needed to do field work regularly, he reminded himself again. He couldn't possibly have always been this sloppy and incorrect. His senses continued rebelling against the scents of the garlic and mustard. Pinching his nose to hold off a sneeze, he hoped he hadn't brushed against the damn plants. The way the night was going, it wouldn't surprise him if his backside were covered in yellow pollen.

Silently heading through the door into what he correctly assumed to be the front room, he wasn't surprised by the green carpet. Not surprised one bit. Despite the drapes being tightly closed, he already knew the light leaked into the street outside. The plush baby blue sofas had blue-and-green matching knit afghans sitting across the back. No artwork adorned the walls or end tables; just family photographs, mainly on the walls and just a few on the tables.

Oliver picked up the picture of a young Eva with a man and woman wearing happy smiles, arms wrapped around each other. Eva had her mother's dark brown eyes, he noted, but hadn't inherited either's blond hair. On the wall, a graduate stood with her back to the photographer and arms spread out, flaring a robe while one hand clutched a diploma. The rich brown hair that flowed from the cap seemed like Eva was most likely the subject. Eva appeared to be the subject of most of the pictures, only none of them showed her entire face outside of the one with her parents. All the other pictures had her face angled away from the camera or hidden by hair or a book. A hint of cheekbone in one, an eye in another, but none showed her entire face.

Odd.

Opposite him, he could see a short hallway that, if he were guessing, contained the bungalow's single bathroom and two bedrooms. Sticking a head through the doorway, he saw that all the doors were closed, but also that lights shone from under all of them. Leaning on the door frame, pondering his next move while listening carefully to determine which room his prey occupied, he once again felt a distinct buzz of magic. Turning and placing his hands on the frame and the

80

wall simultaneously, he could feel the ebb and flow like waves on a beach as the magic buzzed through the house, moving down under the floor, testing him as it rolled along his feet, testing his balance and, if he were to guess, also his intentions.

He wasn't an expert but if he were to guess, this house sat imbued with powerful generational magic. Not just simple hedge witch magic worked here. Definitely not the magic of just a single witch, but several. Familiarity flowed with the magic, and it didn't battle with itself, but flowed as a unit feeling ancient, but at the same time new.

Fascinating.

*Achoo!* An unexpected sneeze rose up, bursting forth, followed by a shrill, sharp scream which broke his reverie of the magically infused home. Oliver found himself spraying mucus while standing face to face with a shocked, wet-haired, towel-clad Eva. Suddenly it became clear what door she'd been behind.

Her surprise immediately turned to fear at the realization that her sanctuary and her safety were under attack in her own home. Eyes wide, she opened her mouth, drawing in a deep breath to scream with more vigor, possibly hoping a neighbor would hear or it would frighten the intruder away.

Immediately acting on instinct as old as his existence, Oliver grasped her face with both hands, forcing her eyes to meet his, and ordered *"sleep"* with all the vampire coercion he could compel. She immediately dropped. Oliver easily caught her and her towel before either hit the floor. Thank the gods it had worked this time.

Resisting the urge to wipe his nose, he scooped her up, holding the towel tightly around her curves, acutely aware of her warmth and the feel of her in his arms as well as the sweet scent of spicy vanilla and a hint of lavender wafting from her, causing his fangs to once again pulsate. Holding his breath while pushing open the first door, he found a tiny room with a giant bed covered in an assortment of pillows. Squeezing around to the side of the bed, he lay her gently down and with a glance at her towel-clad body, briefly squeezed his eyes tight before covering her with the soft blanket strewn across the bottom of the bed.

*Well, crap.* Oliver ran a hand through his hair and then by habit smoothed it back into place as his stomach turned flip flops. The entire room smelled of her, and it placed him firmly on the outer edge of his control. Tonight wasn't going according to plan, any sort of plan at all. The hope was that once the compulsion wore off, he would have regained control of this bat-shit situation as well as himself. His control was an armor, and it was slipping tonight inch by inch. Grinding his teeth into submission, he held his jaw tight until pain emanated from the insistent canines.

The years had made him lackadaisical and inattentive, and in this world that was a death sentence. Falling victim to ego, consistency, and relying on his vampiric powers to override any threat would be his downfall. Even more sobering was the knowledge that it could also get Ravyn hurt—or worse. In any situation that required it, he could easily compel a person to do his bidding or tell him exactly what he needed to know without even getting up from a chair. But Eva had already demonstrated that she could shake off his power with ease. Even now, he had no idea how long she would rest. He needed to come up with an alternative and fast.

Ravyn's voice admonished him in his mind. "Brute strength," she'd scoffed long ago. "So many weapons in our arsenal, never rely on that. Seduction," the memory purred. "Innovation, flattery, cleverness, honesty. So many weapons at our disposal that brute strength would never be needed." The lessons had been learned and disposed of after years of relying on authoritarian relationships with his employees.

# CHAPTER SEVEN

*Two kittens had an argument; it was a cat-astrophe.*

**O**liver sensed her waking up before she opened her eyes. Her breathing lightened, and she no longer took the slow, deep breaths that had punctuated the last hour or so.

*Thank the gods,* he thought as she shifted slightly in her sleep. It hadn't taken long to search the tiny house which, speaking from experience, contained more books than any one person could read in several lifetimes, let alone a single mortal one. Amid the books, he found crystals and knickknacks imbued with warm, earthy vibes. Eva's home was what his friend Malthazar would call "boho witch style."

The thought produced a rabbit hole he wasn't prepared to go down tonight. He'd instinctively called Malthazar a friend. Were they friends? Neither of them really worked for the other; they weren't forced together, so any time they spent together was by choice, even if it wasn't too often. Similar interests had brought them together and, over the years, those interests had meant they could easily count on the other to have their back. It seemed like a friendship to him, even if it had started out more business-focused. He would have to ask Malth if they were friends, even if the man found such a question amusing, and surely Malth would. The answer might be interesting.

Oliver immediately removed himself from his seat on the only place to sit in the room, the bed; it didn't take a genius to know waking up with a strange man on your bed would *not* be a way to win friends and influence people without vampire coercion that might or might not actually work. He did so without spilling any of the red wine he'd liberated from her wine rack while searching the house. Good thing she was waking up; he was out of wine, a nice, apparently local vintage. Already an email had been sent to his assistant to have a case of the Buckeye Red sent to his home from the Ohio winery.

"Good doggie," Eva murmured before stretching her arms, one of which could only move a few inches. Oliver watched as she tested the range of movement again for her arms and then her legs before even opening her eyes. He could see when recognition for her current situation emerged.

"Eva," he began softly, friendly even, he hoped, while also once again attempting to push a bit of coercion into his request. "You can open your eyes. I know you won't believe this, but I'm not planning to hurt you. I just need you still, so you'll listen and answer a few questions."

Letting out a slow, deep breath, her reply was quiet but clear. "Exactly what someone would say who has someone tied to a bed in a, ugh, bath towel." As she assessed the situation, her heart rate remained fairly steady. Although it had sped up a bit as she awoke, it wasn't so fast that she was panicking. Her free hand pulled the blanket up tighter around her, as if that could protect her from the childhood bogeyman.

"What were you dreaming about?" He was genuinely curious; he didn't dream and dreaming about a dog seemed sort of interesting. Oliver had asked Delta the same before, and she'd always laughed and said her dreams weren't rated for his ears.

Eva's brown eyes did pop open at this, making his own breathing hitch for a beat as the pupils dilated in response to the lit-up room. They were just as pretty as he recalled; he'd nearly convinced himself that the speckles of gold in there were his imagination. Fire flamed from those gold-and-brown eyes, and he ordered his fangs to remain inert. However, this time his lower extremities throbbed, unaffected by his mental order. Keeping his face a mask of calmness, he didn't feel, Oliver tilted his head to hear her response.

"You stalked me, broke into my house, sneezed all over me, and tied me up to . . . what? Ask me about my dreams?" She shook her head in exasperation, making him grin a little as though they were friends joking about such a silly thing. "If you must know, I was dreaming about a talking dog in a tuxedo. His name was Thor, and he was annoying . . . a woman, because he kept talking so much."

Her face wrinkled in confusion as she contemplated this. "Although he may not have been a dog; maybe he was a coyote or wolf or maybe just a husky. I don't know." She waved her free hand as she spoke, letting loose another hint of vanilla and lavender. "Anyway, the woman was so annoyed about him talking. You'd think that a talking dog or animal would be interesting enough that you'd want to hear what he has to say, wouldn't you? I would want to hear it anyway. But she kept shutting him down." Cocking her head, considering, Eva added with an easy shrug, "Although she did call him 'asshole' enough times that that might be his name instead of Thor."

Eva's shrug released a thin shoulder that once again precariously crept free from the blanket, and her towel was sneaking dangerously low as well. Oliver decided not to tell her. Of course, if it continued on its journey, he would tell her or at the very least avert his eyes. No one could claim he wasn't a gentleman.

"Sooo, now that we've covered that I have weird dreams, you want to set me free and get out of here? Or heck, you can even leave me here and take off. Allergy meds are in the bathroom, if that's helpful. Whatever works for you."

He had, in fact, noted Benadryl early during his perusal of her home. Ignoring her proposed options and hoping his nose had stopped running on its own, Oliver gruffly moved forward with his traditional line of questioning.

"Are you a witch?" He still sensed no magic directly from her, but it oozed from her the same as it did from the house. If he tasted her, surely he would feel the sharp, acrid bite of magic in her blood, perhaps along with that sweet vanilla and lavender combo whose scent had slowly overtaken the acidic, blurry garlic and mustard deterrent from outside.

"Nope." Adamantly shaking her head, she simultaneously screwed her face up in confusion. Uncertain if his random line of questioning was serious or not, she still ascertained, "Absolutely no witches here, sir."

*Oh yes,* he recalled, *confusion and uncertainty.* Another weapon in the list Ravyn had rambled off years ago. Apparently, he'd inadvertently managed to utilize these weapons with muscle memory—or so he told himself.

"Does a witch live here?" he pressed. Despite her previous answer, deception and omission were a weapon common among women. No, not women. Witches.

"Nope, and FYI, if you plan to keep asking about them, witches really aren't real. So the answer is going to forever be no, although my gram liked to pretend with me when I was a kid. And before you ask, nope, I don't believe she was a witch either, and we covered the fact earlier that she doesn't live here and hasn't for a decade."

She shifted her free arm in an attempt to pull her towel tighter around her and ended up once again simply pulling the blanket higher up on her neck. Turning her head to look at him straight, another scowl crossed her face. "Are you high? Is this what this is about? Are you on a trip? We can get you help. I have a bit of cash I can get you."

The relaxed look on Oliver's face was replaced with a scowl of his own. Affronted, he snapped, "No, I am not high nor intoxicated. I can't even . . . Why would you even ask such a thing?" For a moment, he felt a flash of guilt over her now empty bottle of wine, but that hadn't even allowed him to relax.

Waving a hand over her face, she responded, "Because you're kind of a mess. Like, red eyes, and a little teary, runny nose, and all that stuff. I know sometimes some drugs cause bloodshot eyes. Not that I'm an expert or anything, but you sound crazy, and your face is all kinds of messed up." Eyes wide, she amended, "Not that it's a bad thing, you're not really that bad. I'm just . . . concerned for you. And when I say drugs, I mean medicine."

By the gods, this was awkward. Oliver admitted, "I'm having a reaction to some of the herbs growing here. Namely the garlic and mustard." He watched her for a reaction, seeing if the revelation meant anything to her.

"I have those allergy meds in my bathroom," she reminded him with a wave toward the doorway. "Help yourself and then take off." Noticing the empty wine bottle next to her bed, her sympathy then turned to indignation. "Please don't tell me you drank my last bottle. I thought you said you weren't intoxicated."

"It's quite good," he admitted and then grumbled, "I can replace it. But we are way, way, off course. Medicine won't help. It'll be fine later." Oliver hadn't realized the herbs had such an effect on his face, but obviously in the past, he'd simply avoided the

90

annoying little plants. His hand twitched, begging to touch his tight face and see if it were as "messed up" as she claimed.

"First, yes, witches are very real. And you live in enough magic that it should be obvious, and I'm not sure why it's not. Second, I want to know what you know about Ravyn Sinclair."

Eva's face wrinkled in confusion again. "Who? Ravyn Sinclair the actress? I don't know her, know her. I mean, I know she's an actress. I guess she lives in Hollywood, if I were to guess, and she acts in movies and maybe . . . TV shows? If you're trying to stalk her, you're way, way off base. I mean, you're, like, two-thirds of the country away from her."

Oliver sighed. "This is ridiculous."

Eva nodded eagerly in agreement. Maybe they were coming to an understanding of minds. Slowly, he watched her face deflate in her belief that they were on the same page. "I'm not stalking anyone. I already know Ravyn. I work for—with—her," he amended before barreling forward. "Someone or something is stalking Ravyn. Could that someone be you? I'm simply here to determine if it's you or perhaps someone powerful you may know."

Sitting completely still, he watched her carefully for any signs a magical attack might be forthcoming. A single zip tie would be no match for a powerful witch and, in fact, some might attack just for the insult, but he liked to think he was giving her the option to not feel he was a real threat. Yet. Even his explanation for being there could be considered insulting and childlike to a paranormal the strength of whom lived in this house, like explaining basic addition to a mathematician. But on the other hand, he felt no magic signature directly from her at all, and that in itself kept him from laying all of his cards on the table. His stomach twisted in knots, reminding him yet again that he sat on the edge of his control, and that he needed to remain calm and in control.

Eva responded just as slowly to Oliver, "O-kay. But I'm guessing first, that tons of famous people have stalkers or whatever, but they don't normally go searching for them thousands of miles away in the Midwest cornfields. Disclaimer: I'm no stalker or again not classified as an expert, but I would assume they have some sort of proximity they try to stay in to actually stalk people. And I'm not the one with zip ties at the ready." A constrained hand wiggled at him, admittedly giving her argument more merit.

Growling lowly, Oliver ran a hand through his hair again, and then began smoothing it back down. At this rate, he would be bald by the end of the week. When Eva's eyes went wide, it hit him that his display mimicked every insane stalker shown on every television show. A part of him wanted to shout that *he* wasn't a crazed stalker, but without his coercion, how could he convince her of this? And more importantly, why did he want to?

"Argh"—he ripped through his hair again—"how are humans so frustrating?"

"You know, um, sir, humans . . . like to be dressed when they're talking, especially to people they don't know. It makes *humans* more comfortable and more likely to listen."

Oliver wasn't certain he appreciated her tone, and even he recognized a placating tone. God knew Ravyn had used the same one often enough on him over the years.

*Maybe that tone is the reason we don't travel together anymore*, he mused. But Eva did make sense. Allowing her to get dressed might open her mind up to listening, understanding, and more importantly, answering some questions about her connection to Ravyn.

Opening a few random drawers while ignoring Eva's sighs of indignation, he pulled out a bra and panty set from the top drawer. He tossed it at her without looking, trying to ignore the feeling of the satin and lace between his fingers. The next drawer contained some tees and leggings and with no concern for color tossed another set at her, followed by a pair of well-worn tennis shoes found near the doorway. Proof he could be as reasonable as anyone.

Gesturing toward the pile of A. Scriver books he'd brought into the room, he noted, "Thought you said you hadn't read them. Seems like someone who has all the series in every cover made, as well as a few international translations, might just be a big fan." He didn't expect an answer. Clearly, she was obsessed with the books and most likely shared an obsession of Ravyn with the author. All signs were pointing straight toward this cozy little witch house in this quiet little town. Now he just had to figure out who Eva was protecting.

"I'm going to release you, so you can dress and we can talk things out like reasonable people," Oliver monotoned, ignoring her snort and releasing the zip tie with a twist and snap. "It goes without saying, don't try to run, escape, or whatever. It's a waste of time. Blah, blah, blah. I'm much faster." The art of interrogation; give a little freedom or comfort, and they'll return it tenfold as they grow complacent. Here was a chance to show he was reasonable, as well as prove to himself that he had more skills than just compulsion in his arsenal.

"Yet, you still said it," Eva grunted as she contorted herself under the blanket, quickly maneuvering each article of clothing into place while not taking her eyes off him. Sliding out from under the protection of the blanket and towel, she slipped her shoes on quickly, fearing he might change his mind and leave her barefoot.

Remaining quiet for a blessed moment, she sat up, letting her now clothed legs hang over the side of the bed. Mesmerized by the pumping artery running up the length of her pale neck, he remained close enough that if she stood up, they would be crammed together in the small space between her bed and the dresser. Casually, he continued where she'd left off. Regardless of what she said or thought, Eva wasn't completely lacking in information. "You said your grandmother was a witch?"

"No. I said she claimed to be one," Eva corrected, craning her neck to look up at him and causing more of her delicious scent to float up toward him.

*Semantics, however delusional.* Either she truly had no idea, or she was a consummate liar.

Either way, Oliver needed to gain her trust by either pretending to believe her or telling her the truth about the world she lived in. He hated trying to explain the real world to those with blinders on. The same arguments, the same shock of disbelief, and finally, at some point, acceptance. He knew it so well he could recite both parts, and it was such a waste of time and energy. Tilting his head while looking down at her, he realized he could see straight down the soft tee he'd tossed her. Suddenly, standing over her wasn't the intimidation factor he'd planned. *Ignore, ignore!* The rational part of his brain took over, and he dragged his eyes up from the soft, inviting curve and swell of her breasts and looked into her eyes.

"What I hear you saying is that you lived with a witch and had no idea she was one. Wait! No, you didn't believe her, which is, in fact, worse. She was actually completely honest with who she was to you, and you didn't believe her." Oliver stated this in a bit of shock himself as he watched Eva open and close her mouth, trying to make sense of his words.

Her heart fluttered and sputtered a bit as confusion strummed across her face. She truly hadn't known or believed her grandmother was a witch.

How to convince someone that the entire world they believed in wasn't the real world?

Of course, being brought back from the dead as a vampire made it difficult to hide from that. Not that he would turn her just to prove that supernatural creatures existed. "We really don't have time to go through this entire futile exercise." He intoned flatly, "The world you think exists is just a small part of the entire world. A blanket, so to speak, and under that blanket hides all the things that go bump in the night. Some are good, some are bad, but all fall under the category of 'paranormal.' You know witches, werewolves, fae, vampires, spirits even. Demons of various types, but of course, if you believe in God you know about angels and demons, so you're already halfway there. Just a little hop, skip, and jump to accepting the rest."

Nodding firmly, he hoped that perhaps this proclamation could simply lay things to rest, but he also knew that telling someone that the world they lived in was a lie . . . Well, not so easy to reset the brain to reality. Sort of like *The Matrix* . . . Hmm, maybe he could use *The Matrix*'s Real-World analogy to start explaining the paranormal world to others. Not that he planned on ever having this conversation again. It was going about as well as the last three times he'd explained it; thankfully, without the typical screaming and tears that had accompanied past conversations.

Eva stared blankly at him, turning even paler, if that were possible. Sighing, Oliver sat down on the bed, half turning to face her, bumping her knees as his lanky body struggled to fit in the tight room.

"I'm messing this all up, trying to hurry, but I don't have all night. Well, I do, I just don't want to be here all night doing this." The thought rose unbidden that he could, in fact, think of several things he would rather be doing in that room all night. *Think of Ravyn! Focus. Grandmother! Surely, talking about her grandmother will kill any elicit thoughts!*

"Did your grandmother ever lie to you about anything? And not the little stuff like Santa Claus or that Tooth Fairy thing. But the important stuff?"

"No," she whispered. "Words have power, and she wasn't one to misspeak."

"Then why would you think she would lie about the essence of who she truly was?"

With a bit more firmness to her tone, she replied, "Because literally, witches don't—can't—exist. Besides, I think I would've noticed if I had a broom-mate." She shut her mouth firmly in a tight line, as if trying to keep any more stray thoughts from escaping or in an attempt to end the conversation.

"But you didn't. And says who? You're living in a house seeping with magic. Hell, it may have been created with magic. You've never wondered why your stove and refrigerator still work? Why your roof never leaks, and why you've never had to paint, or update the windows?" Oliver worked with a few assumptions, but the look on Eva's face showed he'd hit the mark. Maybe he wasn't so out of practice with field work and conjectures after all.

Again she opened her mouth to interject, but he pushed forward. "Don't say its craftsmanship or things used to be built to last." See, he could use sarcasm too. "No matter how well made, it's impossible for appliances to last fifty years—or more, by the looks of some of that stuff—with no maintenance or repair.

And I'm guessing you don't weed or even water that jungle of a garden out there either, yet it thrives. And again, that's not how gardening works. Even I know that." Oliver knew that very well, his childhood having been spent weeding his mother's garden; backbreaking work at times and never by chance or without intervention.

Oliver paused, looking at her to see some sign of acceptance or argument, but Eva stared blankly at the dresser, hopefully beginning to process. "She was a witch and by the laws of genetics, you should be too." Oliver stopped, quite pleased with this argument; maybe he should have been a lawyer. Maybe he still would be. He had years ahead of him and studying for the bar might pass some time.

"Except she's not my biological gram," Eva whispered so softly that he wouldn't have heard her if he wasn't a vampire. "Her son adopted me after he met my mom."

Oliver gave this some thought. "Does her son visit here or stay here often?" He had no sense of another person on the property, male or otherwise. All of his senses convinced him she lived here alone with an apparent untapped arsenal of magic at her fingertips. Depending on the lineage, males rarely inherited this level of power. Not likely, but also not impossible. And to be honest, it seemed likely that Ravyn's stalker was a man. The gifts and messages were almost like a man courting her for attention.

Eva gave a sardonic laugh that nearly broke into a cry. "He and my mother died years ago, even before

Gram, so yeah, not a lot of hanging out has been happening unless it's the case of those spirits you were talking about earlier."

"No, there are definitely no spirits hanging around," he solemnly promised her in case she needed reassurance. "Did she have any other children? Did your . . . father?"

Eva shook her head no.

Oliver gave this new information some thought, typed out a quick text on the cell phone he pulled from his pocket, and hit Send. They sat silently watching his phone until the soft *ding* announced a response after several minutes.

"My source says that she must have been from a powerful lineage and imbued the house with her magic and possibly her ancestral magic as well." Letting out a soft sigh, he went on, "I'm sorry to ask this, but where did she pass?"

"Here." Eva nodded, her voice growing misty at the memory. "Here."

Oliver could understand loss; after living for so long, it was inevitable. In the past, at times he'd pulled away from mankind and others to prevent himself from having to deal with the loss year in and year out. It only protected his heart a bit; even vampires weren't meant to be solitary creatures. It was a lesson Ravyn had shared with him long ago, but she'd also admitted that he needed to experience most of life's lessons to truly learn from them. He supposed that was why this decade she surrounded herself with work, parties, admirers, and fans instead of his morose ass. Being alone took a different toll on the soul; loss could fade, but it never left.

"Thus she is here." He gruffly tapped the wall behind him. "I know this is tough to understand, but I really am trying to track Ravyn's stalker. This stalker doesn't follow typical rules, because he or she"—he glanced at her, not really believing anymore that she was the stalker—"he or she is a paranormal, and all the regular rules don't apply."

"So you didn't say witch; you said paranormal. What paranormals? Werewolves? Vampires or fae, whatever fae are? And who exactly are you? Some paranormal police officer? A witch? Something else?"

Acceptance had moved in quickly, or she simply planned to placate him into complacency and mount an escape. Either idea was acceptable, and one option was definitely more exciting than the other.

"Yes. I don't know yet. A friend and private security. No, no, and yes." Oliver watched Eva match his responses to the questions that had poured out of her. A new twist; now she was asking the questions and he was answering, but maybe unconventional would track down whatever crazed creature was stalking Ravyn.

"What private security company? How do I know you're who you say you are? Not that I even know who you are. And most investigators would have simply asked a few questions, not broken into someone's home and tied them up. You make it a little hard to trust you."

Oliver considered this. "I don't have a card.

Anyone in the business knows who I am and what I do. If they don't, then I'm not the one they need. My name is Oliver Patrick, and I run a personal security business with an emphasis on cyber security." A full introduction this time and a reminder of his name.

"Oliver." Eva nodded in greeting, as if they were still sitting in the coffee shop, before all the awkwardness. "I'm Eva Nance, but I guess you knew that."

He nodded. "You told me." He didn't mention that it had been under a brief moment of coercion that she'd managed to push off anyway. Seeing that she appeared more receptive to the idea of life being different than she'd known, he continued to question her. "Do you know anyone else who might have been a witch or a part of your grandmother's coven?"

"No. She had friends around town she would see. I never heard her use the word 'coven.' It seemed like just normal friend things they did. She did have a friend near Chicago whom she always called sister. This just doesn't seem possible. Gram was just normal, so normal."

"The literary agent?" he asked, connecting some dots, thinking of the elderly witch he'd visited in the human care facility, surrounded by the books she loved.

"Yes," Eva agreed, then realization and fear flashed through her eyes. Wrinkling her forehead, she quietly asked, "Is Imogene okay? You didn't . . . Well, you didn't do anything to her?"

"Imogene is fine"—he waved off her concern for

the older woman—"sleeping things off after telling me to come here to find Josephine Nance. A long-passed Posy, who would, in fact, have known about my world, but gone too long to be writing and publishing the stories now."

"Good. She doesn't deserve bad, anything bad," Eva amended. "She has been a good friend to me." Hesitating a beat, she asked, "What other paranormals are we talking about?" She examined him as if she could decipher his DNA despite the fact that she'd ignored all proof that she'd been surrounded by magic her entire life.

Warmth flowed through him. Oliver knew his blue eyes flecked red at interest, and she jumped in surprise. "Are you sure you're ready for this? Once you know, you may never un-know. It's much easier to give knowledge than to take it away." Regardless of her answer, she needed to know the obvious, but by asking her, he gave her a sense of power. At the same time, she gave up the chance to later blame him for her blinders being removed and to knowing the world around her.

Eva nodded shortly and quickly, as if not completely sure that she was ready to accept this new knowledge, but not wanting to give herself a chance to reject it.

Oliver took the moment to lean in closer to her and inhale her sweet vanilla and lavender scent, while focusing on the now frantic beat of her heart as it attempted to escape her chest. His fangs quickly dropped at her scent, and his vision blurred as the red in his eyes deepened. Instinctively, his tongue ran along the tips of his teeth, enjoying the sharpness and freedom.

A gasp flew from Eva as she leaned back from him, nearly as fast as the bunny he called her. After the initial shock, she peered closer at him, and he curled up his lips, baring his fangs to allow a closer look for a few quiet moments.

His vision returned to normal as he retracted his fangs, the thirst reined back in where it belonged. "Vampire, in case you're lacking that basic knowledge," he drawled, fighting to control his own urge to catch the prey he saw in her.

"So have you caught up?" he demanded, then checked off, "Grandma was a witch. Vampires exist—as well as a plethora of other supernaturals. You live in a house of magic, and something in this town is stalking my friend, another vamp, and all signs point toward . . . you, little bunny."

"Are there vampire squirrels too? Or a creature that moves with the shadows and feels like it wants to rip your soul from your body?" Eva rattled out immediately considering that the early threat might not just be in her mind.

"Vampire squirrels?" Confused, Oliver shook his head contemplating her words, before immediately going on guard, "Was this creature controlling the shadows and moving toward you?"

Before Eva could formulate a coherent thought, let alone an answer, a massive thump rattled and heaved through the house from top to bottom, strumming through the both of them, as if a giant was attempting to punch a hole through the roof.

Oliver steadied himself by reaching out to the dresser, while Eva knocked into him. Instinctively he reached out to keep her from falling to the floor.

Guilt, unfamiliar but unmistakable guilt flashed. "By the gods," he cursed, "I may have cracked open your barrier just a tad, leaving things a bit vulnerable." He hated to confess his sloppy actions as the house trembled again. "I mean, the magic had faded in a spot, and I just helped it along." Clearly, he should have known the barrier protected the home and its occupants, and that by expanding the weakness, he left it open to be exploited by others.

"Dude, Oliver, I don't even know what that means, but I really don't like the sound of whatever that is. Did that squirrel find me again"

The house trembled again as it took yet another hit. Pictures on the wall fell from the impact, crashing and shattering the glass. The few knickknacks on the dresser jumped and scooted, threatening to also dive to the ground. The foundation below the house seemed to creak and heave against the onslaught.

"No, whatever it is, it is much bigger than a shadow creature. That creature was being used to locate you, a scout of sorts. This creature is being sent to hunt you. It can't fit through the protection spells; yet. Sounds like it's trying to jackhammer its way through."

"What protection spells?" Eva shrieked at him as he pulled her to her feet. "A protection against rough

104

and rumble?"

"The protection spells your grandmother and quite possibly your ancestors put on this place. Imagine a literal dome placed over the top of the house, sealing everything in, protecting it as it stands unchanged but also out of sight. It's a powerful spell and if she hadn't passed, I don't think it would have lasted as long as it has," Oliver quickly explained as he attempted to look through the well-worn lace that framed the small bedroom window, hoping to catch a glimpse of the attacker.

Another crash, harder this time, pulsated through the walls and rattled the windows. More pictures crashed from the walls in the front room and realizing she was clinging to him, Eva used the iron headboard to pull herself to a standing position.

Oliver turned away from the window. "Eva, you have no reason to trust me, and every reason to run. But I need you to trust me so we can make it out of here. The barrier isn't going to hold much longer, and if we stick together, I'll do everything in my power to protect you until we can both get all of our questions answered." Looking into her eyes, he willed her to trust him. He didn't care if she did it under faith or compulsion, but if she ran all bets were off. While he didn't know what manner of creature was out there, he did know it was enormous as well as powerful. Alone, Eva wouldn't have a chance, and Oliver really did want to learn more about her.

# CHAPTER EIGHT

*Fight of the Living Dead*

*E*va instinctively rubbed the spot where the zip tie had loosely trapped her to the bed frame earlier. Body tingling, every single fiber in her being demanded that she run and never stop. But she held herself in place as she met Oliver's deep blue eyes with a false bravado.

*Fake it till you make it*, she chanted over and over, willing herself to remain calm. *Vampires, werewolves, and witches, oh my!* Seriously, was this crap real, or had she crossed into a dream so real that she could literally feel it? If it was a dream, at least it included a hunky vampire and not some old, decrepit one like Nosferatu.

"So, we have to just hang out here until whatever that is out there breaks in and then what?" Eva attempted to look through the closed blinds but couldn't see past the darkness before Oliver pulled her away from the window. Flinching away, she pushed both hands against his hard chest. "And personal space, please."

"Do you have a death wish? Don't show yourself to something that's hunting you, Eva, unless you plan to be bait," he chided, hints of red once again trickling throughout his vision. He inhaled deeply. "We won't sit here and be prey either."

So, she hadn't imagined red eyes before. Clearly, the color was dependent on his mood, but she hadn't decided yet what that mood was.

"Again, not an expert on being hunted either, Oh-liver," she mocked, ready to reconsider his nickname from Mr. Tall-Dark-and-Handsome to Mr. Everything-Will-Kill-You. Or EWKY for short. She smirked at calling him EWKY to his obnoxious, chiseled face. "Can't you do some vampire whammy or mind trick on whatever it is?" Eyeing him suspiciously, she continued, "Or are the flashy eyes and pointy teeth your one trick?" Was she seriously considering that all of this stuff was true?

The small but mighty house once again rumbled in protest as it powered through another hit, shifting the floorboards beneath them like waves on an ocean. This time, the flickering lights ended in blackness, while only a bit of light from the nearly full moon shone in through the lace over the window.

Oliver didn't move, but it threw Eva off balance, and she steadied herself on the first available surface, which once again was his solid—very solid—chest. Hanging on a few extra moments just in case the house was torn from its foundation, she then pulled herself back, grinding her teeth in frustration as if he personally had knocked her off balance.

"And who says it's hunting me? It's probably after you, and you just led it here." Realization dawned on her that this completely serious and possibly deadly threat had been brought right to her doorstep. Popping an accusing finger in his shadowed face, Eva continued in a harsh whisper, enraged that he might have a hand in destroying her home.

"You! You did this! I've lived here almost my whole life without any of this! Maybe I can just leave and this whatever it is can stay and duke it out with you. Wait! On second thought, maybe you can leave. It will just chase after you, away from my house before it's destroyed completely!" Considering the damage already inflicted on her beloved home, Gram would roll over in her grave thinking of the mess.

"That's a negative all around. First . . ." Whispering back, he ticked off a list. "I don't have any natural predators or current enemies, especially ones that would follow me to the middle of Ohio. Second, I think you've always had a threat and just not realized it because of all the protections wrapped around this house. Third, I'll admit with prejudice that I did add some damage to your protections, but in my defense, they were already beginning to fade, so this attack was inevitable. At least the way it's worked out, I'm here to help you. Add in the shadow scout that spied on you early today leads to the conclusion it is definitely you they're after." Finality touched his voice, and he raised an eyebrow, as if his points made any sense at all to her, and she should be thankful for his mighty protection.

Looking at him in a mixture of awe and shock, fighting to keep her voice low from whatever was outside, Eva questioned incredulously, "Are you wanting me to thank you for all this? Are you trying to be the hero of *my* story?"

Shaking her head, she continued, "Assuming I believe anything you've told me, it doesn't add up that anything out there would be interested in me. Any chance you have a super fast car parked outside?"

Despite the momentary silence outside, the house quivered as if gearing up to brace itself against another assault. Again the lights flickered, this time ending up bathing the room in a soft light from the lamp that lay on the floor. If Oliver was telling her the truth, and the house protected itself or her, then that was quite possibly what was happening.

"Actually, I have a rental that I left downtown. I followed you on foot." This time, it was his jaw that clenched as they both ran through any possible scenario that might aid an escape.

"Super vamp speed and kung foo fighting skills then, by chance?"

Another hit sent a stronger rumble moving through the house, as bits of ceiling fell around them, and the bed jumped closer to the opposite wall. This time, a roar of triumph followed by other excited yips and howls bit through the air, hitting Eva straight in the chest while the house continued vibrating around her. Whatever was out there wasn't a singular creature. It sounded more like a pack of wild animals; wild animals that were apparently huffing and puffing and blowing her house down. Were these possibly the werewolves Oliver claimed existed?

"Yes, super speed, but while also carrying you and fighting off what unfortunately sounds like an entire pack of hellhounds . . . Not entirely a feasible plan if we want to assure we aren't ripped to pieces." His serious tone cut through Eva's snark, but at the same time, she noted how he bounced on his feet as if in barely contained excitement. How the red bled entirely through his eyes, hiding any hint of blue.

Was he happy with this development? Was he insane?

So hellhounds, not werewolves. Was there a difference? Her books didn't have werewolves in them, and the books she'd read didn't cover hellhounds—assuming they had any of the other stuff right. It wasn't like smut books were a guidebook to paranormal creatures.

"Hellhounds do not sound good." Ignoring her amped up companion, Eva realized she lacked any real weapons as she glanced around her small room. Dropping to her knees, with a wiggle she shimmied partly under the bed and pulled out the never-used aluminum bat that she'd purchased after Gram passed, leaving her alone in the house. Quickly back on her feet, she hoisted it like a character from *The Walking Dead*, wishing the small room allowed for a few practice swings. "Not good at all, are they?" she repeated, really hoping he would suggest they were the size of kittens and easily defeated.

"They are not." In a tone that didn't allow for arguments or hope, he added, "When I said I have no natural enemies, I hadn't considered hellhounds being set loose. Barely controllable and completely unpredictable, they hunt in packs and rip their prey to shreds. Only a fool would call up that many; they could turn on their summoner as easily as follow directions."

Standing to the side of the window, he peered over quickly before asking her, "Any chance that old Suburban under the carport still works?"

Shocked, Eva nearly looked out the window herself again. How had he seen it in the dark and through the overgrowth of the garden? How long had he crept around outside getting a lay of the land, before sneaking into her house? Had he watched her from the yard while she undressed and showered?

The 1982 blue two-toned, diesel Suburban sat under the carport rain or shine. It had most definitely seen better days with its faded paint job and a few touched up rust spots. The carport was covered in vines, protecting it from the elements, and the hedges and vines on three sides hid it from casual view. There was just enough room to park it under the small but sturdy structure. A few times a year, the beast got pulled out by her or her friend Jackson when he was home on leave. She would take it for a tune up or oil change, drive a few miles in it, and then park it again. Jackson would use it as long as his leave allowed, always making sure the diesel was topped off, oil changed, and the tire pressure still good. It had run two, maybe three weeks ago. Within a few yards of the house, it might as well have been a mile away if the beating that drummed through the house was an indicator of the creatures' desire to get to them.

Head bobbing and fingers crossed, Eva confirmed it ran. "Keys are under the tire." Despite the possibility of teenagers taking it for a joy ride—that had happened to a few neighbors—no one bothered her old heap, probably forgetting that it did on occasion run. Or maybe it was safe in part due to the protective magical dome Oliver kept on about?

"We need to make it there before they break through, and I think that's going to be soon. Very soon," Oliver admitted, listing their options. "If we could wait until morning light, they would have to go back to hell, but I don't think we have that much time, and unfortunately, I don't have backup anywhere close. We have to move fast and just try to stay ahead of them until morning light."

The pounding grew stronger while they whispered, causing nonstop, fevered tremors on the house. The creatures' shrieks and howls blasted through the windows, rattling the pictures that had already crashed to the floor and causing a flurry of ceiling popcorn to fill the air around them.

Eva wasn't mistaken. Claws seemed to grow slightly from his long fingers, and the red eyes quickened with excitement as he ran through their options. Despite his ruffled appearance—was that mud on the knees of his pants?—Oliver was clearly looking forward to the battle to come. Keeping a firm two-hand grasp of the bat while wishing she shared a bit of his excited optimism, she let him pull her by the elbow in the direction of the hallway.

"Won't you go *poof* yourself in the morning light?" she whispered, wondering if that would be a bad thing, but also realizing that all her newfound questions would go *poof* as well.

Face furrowed and nose wrinkled, his red eyes shot back at her. Tight lipped, he shook his head in the negative, leaned close to her ear, then out of the side of his mouth, said in seeming disgust, "Stupid superstition."

A single lamp remained lit and on its side in a corner of the now mostly dark living room. Normally a comfortable, tidy room, it currently lay in shadowy shambles. As they crept through the room, the ground crunched under a plethora of shattered memories and keepsakes. Not even the sturdy settee remained unscathed; tipped on its side, pillows eschewed, it was missing the soft afghan that normally rested on its back. Near the upset furniture, Eva could see the outline of her work backpack she'd tossed onto the settee just a few short hours ago.

Pulling free from Oliver's guidance, she shifted the bat to one hand while squatting to retrieve her bag splayed out upon the floor. No matter the circumstance, she wasn't prepared to leave her laptop behind and was thankful she'd been too amped up to unpack it earlier. Maybe her phone was still inside the bag as well? Definitely not as important as saving her currently unbacked up files. Twisting the bag around over her shoulders, she settled it comfortably into place, once again freeing her hands to grip the bat with firm resolution. She nodded toward Oliver, indicating that she would follow and that holding her hand wasn't necessary to ensure compliance.

Oliver immediately stepped in the direction of the front door. She hesitated, then whispered lowly, assuming that if vamp hearing was a thing, he would hear her above the house's moans of protest, "The back door is closer to the carport."

Shaking his head no, he jabbed a finger toward the front door, clearly indicating for her to follow his instruction.

*Like I'm a dog*, she thought in disgust, following anyway although her mind insisted that the back door sat much closer and in a direct line to the suburban. *He'd better not get me killed,* but nonetheless, Eva stuck closely to his backside. *Is that dirt on his pants?*

Oliver exited first, then with one arm extended, added protective cover while holding the door for her to silently walk through.

Even in the dark, Eva could see the flash of his eyes constantly scanning the tree line as well as watching both blind corners of the house. As soon as they exited the house, she realized the pounding and annihilation came from the back of the house. Leaving through the back door would have put them directly in the beasts' line of sight. A miscalculation like that could have been detrimental. Inside the house, the pandemonium had been too much to pinpoint where it was coming from—or at least for her. The backyard must hold the weakened spot that Oliver claimed existed.

Noiselessly, the pair turned in tandem, hoping to

go around to the side unheard and unseen. One last thud reverberated through the dark house, its foundation, and through the very core of the ground beneath their feet. This time, the powerful shock waves knocked both of them off their feet into a dazed pile on the ground. After a slight pregnant pause, the sound of the animals reached a new frenzy of growls and howls. Eva's heart pounded out of her chest as she tried to catch her breath, refusing to lose grip on her only weapon even as she lay shaking on the damp ground.

"They're in," Oliver whispered, reaching around to wrap an arm around her in one swift movement, half pulling, half carrying her toward the corner of the house, reaching it in a flash. Pausing before peering around to ascertain the direction the hellhounds would go, Eva felt certain whatever the creatures were, they would surely hear her loud, ragged breath and pounding heart.

A tiny cry mewed forth when she heard the sound of the back door smashing and perhaps part of the outer wall itself crashing in, followed by the beating of heavy paws rushing through the house. The squeals, howls, and yips of excitement turned to sharp barks of frustration as they tore through, destroying her sanctuary, unable to immediately find their quarry.

Oliver never gave her a chance to mourn the devastation that had been unleashed in her home. They continued their journey in a blur down the partially graveled, mostly dirt drive that led under the darkened carport. Stopping just short of the bumper, Eva caught her breath and tried to get her eyes to adjust quickly.

"Keys?" hissed Oliver.

"Under the passenger side tire. I'll grab them, you drive?" she whispered back, assuming that being in the security business he might have a bit of experience evading whatever it was they were trying to evade. Later, she would mourn the loss of Gram's cottage, her safe place. Her home.

In a zip, Oliver silently opened the driver's door and slid in, as Eva cautiously crept down the other side of the Suburban. She'd parked too close to this side of the carport, and the vines and bushes that had grown up here had also begun to encroach on the side of the vehicle. Squeezing down with relief that she fit, she ran her hands around the wheelhouse. Triumphantly, she felt the magnetic key that Jackson had put there years ago. Relief flooded through her when it popped out easily into her hand and bouncing up, she could nearly taste her freedom, at least from the hellhounds at her door. Opening her door with a resounding creak, she stopped short as it banged sharply against the side of the carport. The frantic, fevered crashing in the house paused briefly before another resounding crash. This time, it came straight through the front door.

"Get in!" Oliver shouted as she reached her arm through the small space, blindly tossing the key at him, not knowing if he caught it or not.

The door couldn't open all the way; surely not far enough for her to fit inside quickly.

Eva cursed herself and her own bad luck. Last time she'd driven the car, she'd parked it closely to the right side, knowing she seldom had passengers get in. Now that might get her killed. Squeezing in with her backpack on wasn't working at all, so she took it off and tossed it on her seat, watching as Oliver threw it in the back seat, reaching a hand across the console to finish pulling her through the tight space.

She was going to make it, surely she was. Eva could hear the creatures pounding across the yard as their shrieks and snarls ripped through the air. How could something cause the entire ground to quake as it moved? How many were there? Turning sideways, hoping to slide into the Suburban, she cursed herself for not leaving more room. Gram had told her to always be prepared for anything, and at the first test, she'd failed. She'd failed, and she was going to die for it.

Facing the seat, she looked through the car, reaching with her right hand toward Oliver's hand, knowing his brute force could get her through the too small opening if they could just reach.

For a second their eyes met. His were surely just as wide as hers, but not filled with the panic she felt. They boiled red and angry, anger that she knew wasn't directed at her. However, the next second, just as she was about to grasp his hand, just as she felt the brush of his fingertips, the Suburban shuddered and heaved sideways.

At the same time, a searing pain shot through her right calf. Time slowed down as she tumbled and thrashed, fearing that the vehicle had been body slammed on top of her. Her head hit the door with a resounding crack as she was yanked fully away from the Suburban. Blackness and silence, then pain as a creature jerked her backward along the driveway where the other two waited. The gravel tore into her stomach and arms as she was ripped backward. A breath later, she screamed in agony from the fiery pain shooting through her leg up into her ribcage, while her head pulsating from the pain.

The hellhound shook her leg violently, rolling her half over, then released her with a deep growl. Lifting her heavy, throbbing head, she felt the blood dripping down along her face raw from the gravel. So much pain. She pleaded with her body to move but instead came face to face with two other predators. If she were standing, the creatures' backs would reach her shoulders. Black as sin, with eyes red as blood, the hellhounds moved closer, snapping and snarling with smoky breath, reeking of sulfur and what she imagined was brimstone from the fires of hell. Closing her eyes tightly, Eva painfully braced herself for their next movement. There was no doubt they were here for her and not Oliver.

A sharp yelp cut off a growl, followed by yet another crash. Opening her eyes, Eva realized that only one would open now, but still she saw the savior standing above her. Oliver had thrown one hellhound, launching it into the other, sending them reeling across the lawn to land in a heap. They lay stunned for a moment before thrashing about, untangling themselves from each other. Like a warrior god of old, in a fluid movement so quick that if she'd blinked she would have missed it, he snatched up the bat that lay by her side. Rolling over, struggling to regain her footing enough to stand, Eva watched Oliver beat the remaining hellhound away from her while he roared an unholy sound. Winding up, his last swing sent the stunned hound back into the street, where it lay motionless.

Eva could already hear the other two recovering their breath as they huffed and snarled, attempting to regain their feet and clearly preparing to launch a vengeful counterattack.

Swooping her up, Oliver placed her gently in the Suburban's passenger seat, plenty of room now since the determined brute's body had slammed the vehicle sideways, nearly yanking the door off its hinges.

The fire in her leg refusing to relent, Eva cried out in agony. She grasped her leg in both hands, unable to control the tears flowing down her cheeks. She was barely aware of Oliver manhandling the broken door and pounding it closed.

Squealing tires, the Suburban reversed into the street, thumping against the hound that lay there, then with a hard shift, screeched forward down the street.

Eva tried breathing deeply through the worst pain she'd experienced. Looking at Oliver through her one good eye, she gasped, "My leg feels like it's on fire." Her entire body was a combination of dampness, fire, and pain. She couldn't decipher where one injury ended and another began or even if she bled or if the dampness she lay in was due to perspiration from the fire she was in.

Compassion and concern filled Oliver's now blue eyes as he looked at her, hands gripping the steering wheel. "It's the hellfire from the bite. We need to get you to my healer." Glancing in the rearview mirror, then shifting his gaze back to her, he let out a slow breath. "When the sun comes up, the hounds won't be able to follow us, but for now we have to keep moving." He hesitated before adding, "I can give you a bit of my blood to help ease the pain until we reach the healer, but if we stop right now, we're dead. I know this is all new and unbelievable to you, but it's the best chance you have right now."

So great was the pain, Oliver could have offered to punch her in the face, and if such a hit diminished a fraction of the pain, she would happily accept it. She nodded in agreement and leaned in, unsure what to do, but willing to try anything just to relieve the pain.

Fixing his eyes on her, Oliver bit his own wrist as they barreled down the road before placing the dark offering to her. "Just a sip and then rest," he instructed with a strong push behind the words.

Not even needing to lean forward, Eva set her mouth uncertainly on the wrist that had two thick, dark streaks of blood oozing up to stare at her. "You don't need to be gentle," he told her as he turned his eyes back to the highway.

Her hair fell forward, surrounding her face, hiding from view what she did, and she placed her mouth more firmly over the wounds. Sucking, she moaned with a jolt as the sweet and salty fluid touched her mouth. It wasn't what she would have imagined as the nectar slid down her throat. Running her tongue along her savior's wrist, she became determined to savor each succulent drop even if it caused the death of her. Greedily gulping now, she felt the essence move down her throat, then through her body, leaving her energized and heady at the same time. The pain in her body faded, and she took another swallow, this time hearing Oliver moan next to her. Raising her head, she looked at him apologetically as what appeared to be agony filled his tense face.

"I'm so sorry. Was that too much?"

"No, it's fine," came his terse answer. His lower jaw tightened and he again brought his wrist to his mouth, licking the wounds as he watched her, removing any trace of the injury. "On hellhound bites, it will unfortunately wear off, so we'll need to continue doing it. But the pain may worsen each time."

Eva nodded in understanding, then let out a giggle as her head continued to bob up and down. "Haha, my head is floating." She bobbed it back and forth and laughed again. "I feel like one of those bobble heads."

Oliver side-eyed her as she began examining her hands, doing jazz hands in slow motion. "Wow, look at my hands. They're so perfect and they move so fast." Placing her hands on her lap where they continued to bounce, she lay her head back against the seat. "I feel sooo good right now. I can feel my blood pumping through every part of my body, even my head. Oh wow, yeah, you're, like, a real, live vampire. Can you feel my blood pumping through my body?"

"I can hear it," he corrected her. "It whooshes through, echoing through my ears. I can only feel it if I'm touching you."

"Oh, feel this!" she squealed as she removed his hand from the steering wheel and cupped it next to her chest with both hands. "Can you feel it? It's moving so fast."

Oliver shifted uncomfortably and admitted that yes, her blood was moving super fast through her. "Eva, I think you may be high or drunk. You need to rest now."

"I don't do drugs, and I only drink coffee," she replied indignantly, tossing his hand away from her.

"I think you've reacted to my blood, but you need to relax and rest. We've got a long drive ahead, and this is only a temporary fix," he cautioned.

"Ugh, don't be such a prick," she retorted, followed by another bout of giggling. "Get it? Prick? Prick yourself for blood? Not my best work, I admit, but my head won't stop floating."

"I know. Just lie back and rest. How's the leg?"

"Better, a bit. Low burn instead of hellfire burn," she mumbled. "Why am I here?"

"Because a hellhound bit you, and we're on our way to get you fixed up."

*But why?* she wondered, but her mouth wouldn't move to form the words. Continuing to float, she listened to his voice.

"On our way near Chicago. That's where I live, and I have people there. I'll have someone meet us, and we'll get you fixed up. Then we'll figure out our next move."

*Our next move* . . . Eva liked the sound of that. *Oh, yeah, I was in Chicago once or maybe twice.* She couldn't remember right now, but later, when she remembered, she would be sure to tell him. Nestling down, she mused, *You taste nice.*

Silence, sweet silence, then she heard Oliver whisper, "Thanks."

*Oh, Lord, now her mouth worked.*

# CHAPTER NINE

*All this driving is tire-ing!*

Taking no chances, Oliver continued driving as if the hounds from hell were giving chase. In fact, they probably were. Unfortunately, the old Suburban didn't recognize the danger they were in and refused to go over eighty-five miles per hour. And even at that speed, the engine groaned and thumped and, on occasion, a belt let out a frantic screech. After a few miles, he dropped the speed, hoping that the hellhounds couldn't keep a pace like that for this many miles, especially with at least temporary injuries.

Going slower seemed a better option than breaking down along the road. Not for the first time that night, he cursed the fates that put his plane on the west coast. Transporting Ravyn had been a priority and, despite the wealth accumulated over the years, he'd never seen the necessity to budget two modes of air travel for the two of them. Rarely did he fly, so he shouldered the cost and allowed the pilot to focus mainly on Ravyn's transport.

So many regrets, and the night was still young. Oliver deeply regretted not ripping the three hounds apart with his bare hands, but during those frantic moments his only concern had been getting Eva away to safety. He kept glancing across the console at her as she slept. He could hear her soft breathing and the slow thump of her heartbeat, but he needed the extra reassurance. Oliver rarely shared his blood, but in the few times he had, never had he seen such a reaction. After just a few sips of his blood, she'd glowed! If she hadn't been held down by her injuries, she might have floated around the SUV.

Opening his phone, he sent an all hands on deck message to his assistants, instructing them to prepare for his and Eva's arrival and what to expect. Sending a similar one to Ravyn, he informed her that their schedule had been moved up due to the circumstances. She needed to adjust her schedule to fly in immediately to meet them outside of Chicago.

A thick silence filled the vehicle and made him anxious. Sadly, he'd found over the years that silence was no longer the blessing it had once been. The quietness disconcerted him, leaving him feeling like he had too much time on his hands or, when he really cared to admit it, silence made him feel empty. Over the years, Oliver had filled his ears with music, television, noise, and business. Anything to keep his mind going and hold the emptiness at bay.

Not wanting to waste his precariously low phone battery, he tried the old radio. Clicking it on, he spun the dial only to find dead air and occasionally bits of static. Thumping on the dashboard a few times did nothing except leave him frustrated. Clicking the radio back off, he listened to the music of the thumping engine, followed by the whine of the stressed belt when he pushed the accelerator too hard. Under all of that, he followed the soft thumping of Eva's heart, accentuated by the mostly steady inhale and exhale of her breath.

Settling into the cacophony that filled the small space, Oliver continued driving as fast as the vehicle could manage, quietly watching the early morning sun in the rearview mirror chase them west. Thankfully, his specially made sunglasses had survived the night's adventures, and he pulled them on to protect his eyes. He'd been truthful when he told Eva vampires could survive the sun. It did, however, like certain plants and herbs, cause irritation and even temporary blindness without protection. He stopped just once to fill the vehicle's voracious gas tank at a quiet dual pump gas station in the middle of nowhere with no cameras and a sleepy attendant who forgot them before they pulled away.

Continuing to monitor Eva, he knew before she woke up that she was waking, and the pain was returning quickly. The changes in her heart rate and breathing clashed with the sounds he'd become accustomed to as they harshly sputtered and grew ragged. Before she could even attempt to blink her eyes open, he had a wrist in front of her mouth, and she greedily suckled down what he offered. Prepared this time, he managed to suppress his moan, but not the pleasure it brought him.

"Thanks," she muttered as the pain again eased.

She began to glow again as the calm settled back over her, covering her like a blanket.

Groggily, still without opening her eyes, she requested he talk to her until she fell back asleep.

"I will," he promised as she wiggled her glowing fingers, which despite the early morning sun still lit up the passenger side like a luminous beacon. After driving for hours, they were close, so very close to making it to his home. To help.

"I grew up in a small town much like yours, except mine was surrounded by even more corn and soybean fields in central Illinois. I lived and died over a hundred years before you were even born. When I was a boy, I did the normal things: Ran around town with my friends from sunup until sundown or sometimes even later. Did chores for a few pennies, played in the crick outside of town, and had a pretty secure childhood, which for those times was pretty special. I suppose that's why I like to stay in Illinois. I'm close to the city, but I still feel the wind that rolls off the dusty fields on a hot summer night, still smell the freshly cut hay in the spring when I take the time."

Sighing, he went on, "Sometimes I forget to take the time." The memories of his idyllic childhood gave him a pang of homesickness, then with a chuckle, he continued, "One summer, probably the hottest on record. One of those scorchers where nowadays people cook eggs on sidewalks or bake cookies in cars to really show how hot it is. Three of us decided we'd had enough of lying around in our own sweat, and our mothers were simply sick of us coming into the house filled with complaints and reeking like only little boys do, plus more due to the heat."

The words flowed softly from him as he spoke of that hot summer and the fun they'd made—for themselves, anyway. Surely their mothers would have argued differently. Oliver continued to glance at Eva as he spoke, reassuring himself that her breathing remained steady as her body with the help of his blood fought to keep the hellfire at bay. Turning the old vehicle's air conditioning on high, grateful that it seemed to work fairly well, Oliver turned all the vents toward Eva to try to keep her body cool. Despite the outpouring of cool air, she continued sweating.

"Howda you stay coool?" slurred from her barely moving, dry lips.

Oliver could hear the slowing of her heartbeat, and he pressed the gas pedal deeper to the floorboard as he continued telling her about the hottest summer on record. Apparently, she was listening.

"And it wasn't mud that surrounded the cattle pond at all." Oliver stopped his story as Eva let out a low moan. The effects hadn't lasted as long as the first time and with several hours of driving still ahead of him, Oliver knew he had to give Eva more of his potentially life-saving blood. Yet he hesitated. Although not wanting to consider the possibility, if she couldn't stave off the hellfire and, gods forbid, she died while under the influence of his blood, would it turn her? The hellfire burned off the vampire blood, but who could say how much of what she'd ingested stayed within her? Hellfire burned unpredictably, and all he was working with currently was secondhand knowledge. When Oliver transitioned to a vampire, he'd been given a choice; although admittedly, he didn't have all the facts and with death beating your door down, you tended to make hasty decisions.

Eva should have a choice as well.

*Act in haste, repent in leisure.* With those words in his mind, he pulled into an abandoned gas station with cracked concrete that had weeds and even small saplings growing from them. He parked the Suburban near the back side of the boarded up, faded building, out of sight of anyone who might pass by on the rural road. This time, Oliver released her seat belt before scooting over to cradle Eva in his arms, opening his wrist and forcing her to drink a few more drops when she would have stopped sooner. Her glow had dimmed, and this time, despite him having forced more blood into her, she hadn't the energy to even mumble at him.

# CHAPTER TEN

*The doctor is in; time to tickle your funny bone.*

*A*rriving at Oliver's home and despite being held up by Oliver, Eva swayed heavily, her head feeling like it was stuffed full of cotton. One part was due to the lack of sleep over the day and another part was due to Oliver swooping her out of the Suburban and moving with breathless speed. No longer feeling like her body burned from the inside out due to the hellhound's bite, she now felt a cool numbness spreading throughout her.

Without sitting her down, Oliver barked out, "Where's my witch?" His breath panted out as he scanned the room, apparently not seeing whomever he was looking for among the group sitting casually around the room.

Cradled in the comfort of his arms, Eva pressed a light hand to his tense chest, not sure if it was to comfort him or herself.

*It's all good,* she tried to tell him, but despite the fact that her lips moved, no words came out. *It doesn't hurt anymore; maybe I'm better.* He felt so good, both warm and cool at the same time, that Eva just wanted to stay curled up against his cool body and close her eyes for a minute. As they drifted closed, she remembered his voice had been begging her to keep her eyes open. With a guilty flash, she forced her heavy lids back open to focus on the room.

Reclining in a chaise lounge with a glass of red wine—well, maybe—was an elegant, black-haired woman. Eva's addled mind realized that most likely the long-stemmed wine glass held Ravyn's dinner.

*Wait, dude, that's Ravyn Sinclair.* Despite hearing the truth of Oliver's words during the night several times, in no way did she imagine that the famous actress would casually be sitting in this stranger's home. Ravyn. His friend. A vampire. What a strange, strange dream.

*Yup, it's dinner,* Eva concluded when Ravyn lowered the glass from her full lips, and the thick substance slowly slid down the side back into the bottom of the glass. *Wait, does that mean Ravyn is a vampire too? Didn't he tell me his friend was a vampire? Maybe? Wait! Whoa, I just thought all this . . . It makes sense if Oliver is, and they're best friends, probably lovers . . .* Eva scowled. *Yeah, lovers making beautiful vampire babies together. Not that it matters to me, not one bit.*

Bleary eyes fluttering from the force required to keep them open, Eva noted the menagerie meeting inside the living room with windows tightly closed, but still brightly lit from within. One man stood guard near the door where they entered, drawing himself up taller although Eva was still coherent enough to see his disappointment with Oliver failing to address or acknowledge him.

"Hey, State Farm Jake," she slurred toward the disappointed and then confused khaki-clad guard.

"I'm not Jake," he began, but already Oliver had blurred past him and any possible introductions the man in khaki could have stumbled through.

After Oliver's abrupt movements, attempting to focus on the other man proved to be a bit more difficult. He was farther across the room, behind the chaise but within touching distance of Ravyn, and he may have been moving, but at this point, Eva couldn't swear to anything. Once the figure settled into place, a gurgle of laughter escaped her, and a sluggish finger managed to point in the general direction of the tall-large man, her eyes going wide with recognition. The hand on Oliver's chest lightly tugged at his no-longer-white shirt.

"Heyyyy, I know him! Look, it's Thor the talking, tuxedo-wearing dog." Slowly, the tongue twister managed to work its way free from her cotton-filled mouth.

A loud, unlady-like laugh escaped Ravyn's mouth. She didn't even attempt to hide her glee. "She does know you, Thor, you dog."

*Ha!* She'd made the beautiful woman laugh. If they were laughing, then she couldn't be dying, right?

The man growled lightly under his breath, and Oliver returned it with a half-feral growl of his own that echoed off the room, causing the man to nod and drop his eyes.

"Where is that witch?" Oliver demanded as the group bobbed and weaved around them, turning fuzzy as the light grew too bright for Eva's eyes. "I pay her to—"

Eva weakly slapped a hand toward Oliver's tense jaw. "Calm down, cash more bees with shugar, or you cash more honey wif flies." She slurred out her words, feeling her eyes roll up. Then she hastily jolted her eyes open again as the remnant of memory demanded in a harsh tone that she remain awake.

A flurry of erratic red hair blocked the rest of the room from her fading line of vision and a gentle voice chided, "Boss Man, I'm here. I've gotten everything ready. Calm yourself." Scents of cinnamon and earth enveloped Eva as the colors moved around her and tendrils of the hair tickled her face. Closing her eyes, she told herself, now she could rest. Surely, now she could rest.

Cool hands pressed the spot on Eva's calf that had grown inflamed again despite numbness throughout most of her body. Eva couldn't stop the moan of pleasure that escaped her at her soothing touch. "Ah, girl, that hellhound got you good, but I'll get you taken care of. I'm Danika." The same cool hands brushed her sweat-laden hair away from her face, smoothing it gently behind her ears. The same cool, soft hands, so much like Gram's, gently pried open her eyes, while Danika's green darted around, examining them, before releasing them to slowly close in relief from the bright, hot air.

"She's Delta." Oliver's arms tightened around

Eva, offering both comfort and protection, as he corrected the witch.

*Witch?!* Belatedly, his demand for a witch fired alarms off in Eva's head. *I'm dead or dying. There is no, no, no . . . no what?* Already, the heat had driven the thought from her mind. *Vampires, witches, and werewolves, oh my!*

"Today, I want to be Danika. Come on, Boss Man. I'm set up in the first room down the hall. Just bring her in there." Delta/Danika snapped her fingers at Oliver, and he swiftly followed the red pixie down a hallway.

*I wish I could get him to do that,* crossed Eva's mind, but she couldn't get her mouth to form words.

Eva felt herself being placed onto another bed. "Got to stop meeting like this." When no response came, she doubted that she'd spoken the words aloud. Maybe she'd just thought them. So damn hot. Was it possible for a person's blood to boil from the inside? Could someone survive if that happened?

A cool, wet cloth pressed to her lips, and she instinctively drew the coolness into her mouth, feeling a rush as the taste of chamomile and mint seeped past her lips. *Gram? Gram?*

"Keep having her sip or suck on that until she can't drink any more." The red-headed witch's no-nonsense voice left no room for its listener to disobey.

A rush of air stirred up beside Eva as one gentle hand switched to another, pressing the infused water cloth to her mouth as she feebly tried to suckle on it.

Delta began examining Eva's swollen calf. Eva winced as she mouthed the cloth, wanting to scream against the returning pain. Her leg felt so tight, she wondered if it were possible it could split open, and her stomach lurched despite the cool chamomile. Squeezing her eyes closed against the pain, then once again remembering the persistent demand that they stay open, Eva forced them back open but was unable to focus on the flurry of activity around her.

*Can I rest yet?* She couldn't remember now if he'd told her to open her eyes or close them.

"Ah, sweetie, it got you good." Clicking her tongue sympathetically as she swiftly pulled back the shredded leggings from Eva's legs, Delta added, "I think you're going to want to sleep through this."

*Oh, precious, that means I can close my eyes.* It just felt like too much work to close them now though.

Eva heard Oliver grudgingly admit, "My compulsion won't work with her. She's either enchanted or immune. There's been no time to determine the cause." His smooth voice, so low and comforting, nearly made her weep as its dulcet tones caressed her.

"I've given her blood four times, and it's burning off quicker each time."

Eva struggled to tell him that it was okay if he needed her to sleep again now. She would; however, each time she opened her mouth wide enough to speak, more minty water filled it.

"I can take care of that." Reaching down, the flurry of red hair pulled out a small jar, tipping it around in the light before placing a pinch in her hand. Tossing her hair over her shoulder, she leaned in close to Eva's face, so close that despite her fading eyesight, Eva could see the gold speckles dancing and moving in the woman's green eyes, the same gold that streaked through her red hair.

*So pretty,* Eva thought.

Then Delta blew the dust and whispered, "*Somnum.*" The dust expanded, then expanded again, sweeping toward Eva's face and filling her nose, eyes, and ears with the impossible, expanding powder. Then darkness came; sweet, sweet darkness.

# CHAPTER ELEVEN

*You can hear the blood in your veins, if you listen
varicosely.*

**W**aking was a slow and arduous process. Eva felt like she was swimming through cotton, but at the same time she couldn't determine if she needed to go up or down, over or out. Thick and heavy, her eyelids fought both opening and staying closed.

"Water," she whispered through cracked lips, not even recognizing her own raspy, torn voice, hoping whoever was in the room would recognize the word. Thankfully, a straw was instantly placed between her lips, and the cool, refreshing, minty water soothed her lips and throat. A gentle hand wiped away the liquid that dripped down the side of her face, and she sighed with the contentment and coolness of it. Perhaps she didn't need to open her eyes after all, and could just remain here in this bliss halfway between sleeping and awake. Floating, cool, and pain free.

"Eva," a voice prodded, insistent, annoying. "Eva? Eva, it's time to wake up."

She wanted to hurl a pillow at the offending voice, but her arms were too heavy to move. Eva felt the straw being placed between her lips, and again she drank, this time more deeply than before, and again the offending drips were wiped away. "Thanks," she muttered a bit begrudgingly, because surely the same person who gave her water was demanding she open her eyes.

Then she remembered: she wasn't dead! Pushing the cotton out of her way, she struggled to find her way to the surface toward the demanding, ridiculous voice. Opening her eyes, she was unable to see at first; it was too bright.

"Let me dim that," said the voice, sounding farther away than before. The lights went dimmer in the room.

Eva's eyes no longer had to struggle to focus but still felt too heavy to keep open for more than a few seconds.

"Is that better?" asked the voice, closer again.

Eva nodded in affirmation, struggling to lift her head to see who spoke to her.

"Hold on." Arms reached around her and sat her up, clearing her head more and bringing the room into focus. "Easy. You've been out for a while."

"Oliver?" She looked blindly toward the voice that had brought her from her slumber. Memories rushed in. *Is he real? Is this all real?*

"I'm right here, next to you." Eva felt his cool hands gently untangle and brush the hair off her face. "Do you need more water?"

Shaking her head no, she tried once again to open her eyes and keep them open. It was easier this time, and she could now see the fuzzy outline of Oliver's head and dark hair. After a few more seconds, his features came more clearly into view as he moved closer, a solemn, serious look on his unsmiling face and worry lines surrounding his eyes, moving up his forehead.

"Keep frowning like that, and you'll get wrinkles," she told the immortal, who gave a small, almost angry chortle. "We cut it close, didn't we?"

"We did," he quietly replied, nodding slowly and repeatedly. "We really did."

"So, this is your bedroom? Some guys will do anything to get a girl in bed." The electric shades were drawn tight, and Eva couldn't tell if it was day or night. Black floor-to-ceiling drapes with gold lattice framed the darkened windows, contrasting greatly with the 1950s floral and lace in her own bedroom. Even in the dim light, she could see the piles of black and white wax that were all that remained of something like twenty candles originally on every flat surface of the emerald-green room. Cinnamon, if she were to guess, due to the circumstances, if she remembered a bit of Gram's rambling instructions correctly.

Eva grimaced, realizing the candles were definitely not a part of Oliver's regular decor. A pile of blankets covered a chair in the corner. Mixed with the cinnamon, she caught a hint of sage and other unidentifiable, burned herbs, which seemed to permeate the air as well as the pillow her head lay on. "No offense, but your room smells like my grandma.

Like, so much so."

The pile of blankets in the corner began moving, and Eva slowly turned her head a few degrees, giving her eyes a chance to refocus on the movement. First one long, thin arm appeared, and then a full head of wavy red hair.

"Big stretch," the woman's voice said.

*Is that Delta/Danika? What was her name?*

"Why does a stretch feel so much better when you say 'big stretch' with it, Boss Man?"

Eva felt rather than heard Oliver's low rumble in reaction, hitting her low in the stomach and causing an unexpected, but not unpleasant, lurch deep within her. "Quit calling me Boss Man. And no, this isn't my room; it's a guest room on my property. It was closer," he admitted from next to her ear.

The red-haired woman finished tossing the blankets on the floor and stood up, stretching again with both arms above her head. "Argh, rough night or two or three, wasn't it?" Her black tank top edged up over her hips, and Eva glimpsed a tattoo on the flash of white skin just above her black leggings that were riding low on her hips. When she finished stretching like a cat, she pulled her leggings up and her tank top down, before making her way to Eva's bedside, solidly hip checking Oliver until he pushed his chair away from Eva's bed and stood up with another grumble.

"Hey, sweetie, remember me? Probably not. I'm Daphne." Leaning in closer, she pried each of Eva's eyes open one at a time, taking her time examining each closely, her eyes flitting around as if the windows to her soul would release their secrets.

"It's Delta," Oliver corrected with an air of impatience. "Seriously, why do you do this, witch?"

Delta rolled her eyes as she continued her thorough but gentle exam of Eva. "Ugh, what was my mom thinking? I'm literally named after a wetland. She might as well have called me Swamp." Tossing a look at Oliver, she drawled, "Tell me, Boss Man. Why can't I try out a few names for myself, especially when I'm called on my one day off?" She raised her hand, cutting off any attempt of a rebuttal. "My one day off for an emergency of epic proportions, the one day I can stay up all night playing D and D with the peeps—and in the middle of an epic battle fighting a demogorgon. They were probably all wiped out without me there."

She ended with a huff of disgust, continuing her exam downward, pressing on Eva's stomach and ending with the bitten calf, which thankfully no longer burned like hellfire. In fact, it was only Delta's gentle prodding that reminded Eva that she was wounded there. "Besides, maybe I love hearing you say my name, Boss?" she added brashly with a cocky grin.

"Looks good; looks great, in fact. First, it smells like your granny in here because I'm using earth magic like her, so thank you and you're welcome for the whole healing and saving your life thing on my day off." She waved her hand over Eva. "So anyway, what are you? I can't quite put my finger on it." Finally taking a breath, she cocked her head as she studied Eva, waiting for an answer.

Eva took a wary glance at Oliver. She knew this woman had helped her, but who in the heck was this crazy, weird girl Oliver had delivered her to? "Um, I'm a barista? A human? A human barista. Sometimes I take college classes, and I do a bit of writing," she amended, because omission wasn't really lying. She did dabble in writing as well.

A dubious expression crossed the petite redhead's pale face, frowning as she looked back and forth between the two of them, popping a hand on her hip. "Yeah, no. That's what you do, not what you are." Delta was younger than Eva had first thought, at least a decade younger than her own twenty-eight years. Not a single wrinkle or crinkle marred her smooth face, not even a laugh line, despite what appeared to be an extensive healing repertoire that included possible concussions, road rash, and big ole flaming demon bites.

Now the young red-head glanced at Oliver, who refused to meet either of their eyes as he studied an apparently interesting spot on the opposite wall. "What do you know, Boss Man? You're looking mighty suspect. And you, Miss Eva, are definitely not human—or not completely human. That hellhound bite would have killed you dead if you were just human. Nothing I could've done would have saved you. And this wound"—she tapped the side of the bed near Eva's calf, causing her to flinch despite the fact that it didn't hurt her—"is healing much faster than it would on a shifter, and even most fae. I gave you a boost to get you started, but much of this is you. So,

I'm asking you again, what are you? This whole debacle messed up my day off, I'll remind you, and do you have any idea how hard it is to coordinate days off for a decent game of *Dungeons and Dragons*?"

Eva swallowed. Was she supposed to answer the irate redhead who barely looked out of her teens? "I've never played *Dungeons and Dragons*, so I guess I don't know. I've always been human." Anytime now would be a good time for Oliver to jump in with his brooding voice, agree that she was human, and quiet down this prodigal teenage witch doctor. But he still remained silent for someone who, in the short time since she'd met him, appeared to have an opinion on everything.

Gram had always said she was special, but what parent or grandparent didn't think their little rug-rat was special? And what else could she possibly be? Just learning that vampires and witches were real was pretty mind blowing—if it were, in fact, true—but what had Delta said about shifters and fae? Maybe she was still in a coma, a dream, a coma-induced dreamland. Clearly, she had a fairly active imagination.

After all, her dreams had inspired books that had made her quite comfortable financially. Could she be dreaming and not realize it? Maybe she was still dying from an accident, and this was an elaborate hallucination created by her mind to protect herself. What if a car had hit her on her ride home from work, and everything after that moment had occurred in dreamland to hide from her the fact that in reality she was dying? Wrinkling her forehead, she recalled that she'd read about that. Or maybe it was a movie? People living entire lives within a few minutes as they died, completely blissful and unaware.

"It's all real," Mr. Tall-and-Broody finally broke his silence in a dry flat tone. "You're not hallucinating or dying. Not anymore."

Eva turned an incredulous look toward him, squinting at him, and focused her thoughts to mentally scream, *"In case you can read my mind, don't. Just don't!"*

Aloud, she said, "Maybe you could tell me what I am? Because to be honest, this is all one big, crazy mess to me. Until last night or whatever night, my life has been normal." This wasn't feeling like a dream. The aches in her body said otherwise, and her vision had cleared out any dream-like qualities, but still she couldn't help the sardonic tone in her unbelieving voice.

"Oh, girl, I was hoping you would ask me." Dropping the firm tone, Delta moved to the bottom of the bed, bouncing down on it, yet careful not to hit Eva.

Oliver opened his mouth to intercede, but Delta again waved him away.

He continued, "If I'm Boss . . . Man . . . why don't I feel too much like I'm in charge of all of this? And I've explained everything to her. A lot of things. Some of the things," he amended before shrugging and lifting a sardonic lip to encourage Delta to continue. "As you were."

Certain that the sparky witch had a reply, Eva's head volleyed back and forth as the two bickered. Could they be siblings? Could a witch and a vampire be siblings? A witch and a vampire walk into a bar . . . No, no, two siblings suffering from a mass delusion. Wait! If she wasn't in a coma, there were other people in the house.

"Because, Mr. Oliver Patrick, you pay me—all of us—damn good money to find out things. And this is something I can definitely find out."

Oliver stuck his hands in his pockets and again slowly nodded at the witch. He still wore the clothes they'd traveled in, and the once crisp, button-up white shirt was now wrinkled, missing a few buttons, and covered in spots of mud and blood. Her blood. She'd almost died last night. Was it last night? Delta had made it sound like there had been several sleepless nights. She still wasn't sure how long she'd been here, but really, did it matter?

"You're both giving me a headache." Pointing a finger at Eva, Oliver injected, "You're not dead or dying. This is real." Gesturing between himself and Delta, he added in a slow, firm, nearly angry tone, "We. Are. Not. Siblings. No relation at all, no respect apparently, either. That one is not a child, not a teenager. I don't employ children. And I can assure you she is neither and is, in fact, older than—"

"Hush," Delta's voice cut through the room with a crack. "You of all people should be old enough not to discuss a lady's age."

Mouth opening and closing like a flounder out of

water, uncertain what part of that to even start on, Eva decided to ignore him and his tone, as well as Delta's response. Who needed all that attitude anyway? Bestowing what she hoped was a gracious smile toward the not-a-teenager, she said, "Yes, help me. I want to know who I am. Writing with a dull pencil is pointless. I need to know everything." Who was she to judge someone for not looking their age? She herself still got carded regularly and could probably shave a couple of years off if pressed.

"First of all, I want to get rid of all this." Delta gestured over Eva's entire body, causing Eva to pull the soft blanket tighter around her, covering herself under its protective layers.

"All of what?" Step one already confused the hell out of Eva's brain. She really, really hoped Delta didn't want her to get naked. Glancing at Oliver, she felt her cheeks heat up.

"Don't overwhelm her, witch," Oliver demanded. "She's still looking a bit flushed."

Eva closed her eyes, thinking, *Sure, now he speaks*. Couldn't she just die now? It would be simpler and much less . . . everything.

"Oooh, someone still feeling like the hero? You've saved her, Ollie. That's the easy part." Delta clasped her hands together in mock awe, fluttering her lashes toward the glowering vampire. "This spell or charm that's hiding you: I can feel it all over you, and it was done with good intent, but I didn't examine it since it had nothing to do with your injuries. I would never, ever examine someone or remove something without

148

consent," Delta solemnly promised Eva.

"Thank you?" Overwhelmed, Eva didn't even understand the words coming from Delta's mouth. "Are you speaking Latin again? Wait . . . you spoke Latin to me before? How did I—"

"You're right. You're so good at this." Delta giggled, as if this were the most normal conversation in the world. "We're going to have so much fun. But first: is it okay if I check out your aura and this spell? I did check out your aura just a tiny bit before when I was healing you, but those were extenuating circumstances with you being unconscious and almost dead."

Delta animated her words with hand waves so violent that Eva couldn't even attempt to track the movement and fought the urge to hold them in place or duck so she wouldn't get hit by the flaying girl.

"Witch, calm yourself and focus." Force punctuated Oliver's words and took away any doubt who really stood in charge here, at least for the moment.

Inhaling and exhaling slowly for several beats, Eva watched as Delta found her center before telling her, "Do what you need to do to figure this out, because in the last twenty-four hours, my life has gotten crazy."

Incredulously, Delta sat speechless. "Oh, honey . . ." She squeezed Eva's leg as she stretched out beside her face to face. "It's been more than twenty-four hours. You were out for almost three days. Only the one day was my day off; I've been firmly on the clock since then." She paused a beat before adding, "And whatever is going on with you has been happening a lot longer than that; you've just not known." Closing her eyes, she moved uncomfortably closer to Eva, and then appeared to just listen.

"Your grandmother was an earth witch. This I know."

"In the spirit of honesty, adoptive grandmother."

Delta's eyes flew open, nodding speculatively. "That does change things a bit, but it also makes more sense. I can feel magic on you, in you, a part of you. But at the same time, it's foreign. And your aura is muddy, like, muddy, muddy. I've only seen this when someone charmed themselves hidden, and it was never this murky. May I lay my hands on you?"

Consenting again, Eva nodded, and Delta immediately placed her hands on the closest arm and leg while closing her eyes. Eva waited, looking away from the silent witch, while holding herself completely still so as not to disrupt whatever it was that Delta did.

Oliver remained seated a few feet from the bed, back stiff, but leaning slightly forward as if prepared to launch from the chair at a second's notice. Eva realized that his disheveled, bloody appearance didn't mean he'd spent the night by her side, but in fact had spent at least two full days next to her without taking even a moment to change. His eyes moved away from Delta's work and held hers captive in stony silence as they waited for Delta's analysis.

"I've got something." Delta's soft announcement broke off their contact as they both turned toward her.

150

"You've definitely had a concealment spell done on you. And it's still earth magic, mostly green with a touch or so of gray. How long ago did you say your grandmother passed through the veil?"

"It's been about ten years now."

"Did she give you a talisman to carry?" At Eva's confused look, Delta explained with an air of impatience, "A crystal, a necklace, a ring"—back to waving her hands—"any sort of jewelry, even a button?"

Understanding dawned on Eva. "Something that would have held the spell?"

Delta clapped her hands in excitement for her best pupil. "Held the spell or really a focal point to enhance or direct it, but potato, potahto. Anything you can think of?"

"When I went to live with her, I had a lot of nightmares. Bad nightmares. Gram gave me a few things: A stone—black jade—to wear, a dream catcher for my room, and a pen; one I could write with." Eva made handwriting motions with her right hand and uncomfortably cleared her throat. "She told me to never take the jade off, but after . . . after I lost her, I did. I tossed it in my purse for a while." She'd carried it around with her for a few years, not bearing to look at it, to remember the love and warmth her gram had poured into it.

"And then one day, I added it to a pile of other stones. Any of the interesting ones I found, I put in a little bowl and kept on my dresser. Whenever I found a pretty stone, I liked to imagine it was Gram saying hi."

At the memory of her home, sudden panic overtook Eva; she should be at home. Why had she let Oliver take her away? It wasn't safe here!

Chest tightening in panic, Eva's eyes took in the room, searching for an escape route. She needed to get home. Now. The overwhelming desire to jump from the window and run home nearly overtook her despite the fact that she had no idea where she was or how far or where home was. Lifting herself from the bed brought Oliver closer to her side in the blink of an eye. He held onto her firmly. His touch brought a flood of calmness through her, but the desire to get home didn't fade entirely.

"Oh, wow! That thread just came alive!" Delta had been listening intently, but as panic took deeper hold of Eva, she reached out to a spot that as far as Eva could tell was just empty space. Pinching her forefinger and thumb together, she twisted while uttering, "*Dimittus. Confractus. Libartus.*"

The tightening panic in Eva's chest began to dissolve as Delta spoke the words.

"What just happened?" Oliver demanded, for the moment not content to be on the sideline, and not quite loosening the hold he had on her.

Ignoring him, Delta gently spoke to Eva. "Honey, have you ever left your house or the area around your house?"

"Well, yes, of course. I go all over the place in town, and for a few years, I went to community college about ten miles away." Triumphantly, she added, "and I've been to Chicago a few times."

"Were you ever able to stay the night away, or did you need to get back home immediately?" Delta continued speaking gently, sympathetically, as if to a child.

"I could have stayed the night, but I didn't need to." Indignation flashed through Eva. She wasn't a child! Like a punch to the gut, realization strummed through her. No, she hadn't been able to stay long each visit to Chicago. Any visit had been punctuated with the work she needed to do, and then she'd gone straight home. She didn't always plan it, but she would worry that maybe she'd forgotten to lock up the house, no reason not to drive the few hours, or perhaps they would need her to fill in for someone at work the next morning. Silly reasons, in hindsight, but at the moment they'd given her pressing needs to get home. "I just like to sleep in my own bed." It was a feeble excuse in a long line of excuses to go home after squeezing in an afternoon coffee shop visit or maybe finishing up a day at a museum.

"Eva, that strand connected you to your home. Think of it like a tether tying you to your home. You might be able to stretch it out, but the farther you get, the tighter it tries to pull you back. However, I don't think you'd have been able to travel far enough, fast enough to have it snap and set you free. More likely it would have snapped you back home if you'd fought it."

Delta gently gave Eva permission to forgive herself for not being able to fight an unknown spell. Or was it a curse?

"However, that's not what is muddling your aura, but it is one of several threads that have been placed on you. Several, as in hundreds, perhaps."

With horror, Eva thought of all the trips she'd hoped to take and some she'd even planned, from camping trips ruined by broken water heaters, to road trips thwarted by flat tires. Flat tires on every vehicle of every person planning to road trip with her. One year, after the success of her first book and she had extra funds, she'd even created an itinerary for a trip to visit London.

Her computer crashed and destroyed the plans and then, when she bought a new one, she'd just forgotten about it. Forgotten she'd wanted to see the castles, go up in the Eye, see the yeomen! Forgotten she'd wanted to have tea and biscuits with clotted cream and stand among the stones at Stonehenge. "Did my gram do this? Did she do this to me?"

Delta sadly and slowly nodded. "I think she did, and I think she did more than that. There are more threads to trace and destroy, but all of this has taken everything out of me. The healing, and the single thread. Your grandmother was very powerful," she admitted, "gone ten years and that thread still stood active and strong as if it had been formed yesterday. Clearly, it's tied to something in the house or maybe even the house itself, but that's some mega power."

Looking intently at the young woman, Eva now realized she stood on the brink of exhaustion. Dark circles encompassed her eyes, showing strongly against her pale skin. Clearly, her energy waned, and she hadn't gotten enough sleep in the pile of blankets in the corner. For days, the woman had sent all of her healing energy into a complete stranger, and even now at the seeming snap of her fingers, she still used the last of her energy attempting to heal and help her.

Eva sat her own unusually pale, nearly translucent hand on Delta. "Go rest. And thank you for everything. I'm alive. Everything else can wait. I've had all this going on for many years, so we can wait a few more hours or days, or whatever you need. Then you—we—can figure all this out together. I don't need to leave now. I can stay."

"Let's get you to your room, witch." Oliver spoke gruffly, but Eva recognized that he cared about the young witch in his employment.

Delta pulled herself into a sitting position on the side of the bed. Her last act in releasing the thread had drained both of them, and Eva doubted the girl could stand herself up. Oliver hoisted her to her feet, then half carried, her half led her from the room for much needed rejuvenation.

Oliver's low tones whispered to her as he left the room, although Eva couldn't hear what he was saying and didn't hear if Delta responded. Hopefully, someone would treat Delta to a cup of rejuvenating tea and tuck her into bed. The girl—no, the woman—she mentally amended, deserved it.

Although he wasn't gone long, exhausted, Eva found herself drifting off to sleep again, waking back up as he reentered the room. Oliver stood across the room in his grubby, battle-worn clothing, watching her. Eva felt like the obvious needed to be stated. "You're filthy and you probably stink. Don't you have a shower around this dump? And maybe some clean clothes?"

His sexy laugh undid her. Sticking his hands in his pockets, he nodded slowly. "I'm sure I could scrounge up some clean clothes and a shower. I'd hate to offend your sensibilities and all that." His laugh was nice and hit Eva low, deep in her stomach. She'd done that, brought out a genuine laugh that had caused his deep blue eyes to sparkle.

Standing in place looking down, he sighed and closed those blue eyes briefly before meeting her own eyes intently. "I'm so sorry this happened to you. If I'd ever thought that you or anyone would have been in so much danger, I would have done things differently, taken more precautions, and brought more people. Anything. I deeply regret that you got hurt so badly on my watch."

Incredulously, Eva opened her month and then closed it before opening it again. Ugh, this was becoming a common reaction from her. "My God, if I wasn't so sure I'd fall over right now, I'd stand up and smack you in the head. Sounds like those creatures would've found me regardless of you showing up. In fact, if you and your particular brand of crazy hadn't shown up, I'd probably be dead now. Dead. They were coming for me anyway. You saved me. I don't even know what else to say, except thank you and please, for the love of God, go shower!"

Closing her eyes and laying her head back deeper

into his pillow, she wondered if he would respond. *Damn, these pillows are amazing. Maybe when this was all done, I'll ask him where he got them from.*

Silence followed. Then the click of a door that she assumed led to the on-suite bathroom. As the water turned on, never opening her eyes, she smiled and indulged herself a bit as she imagined him undressing for the shower. Just before sleep overtook her, Eva wondered why he hadn't gone to his own room to shower.

# CHAPTER TWELVE

*What do you call witches who live together?*
*Broom-mates.*

Eva gently broke through the dreamless sleep. Unlike the last time she'd woken up, this time she felt refreshed and less like a Mack truck had run over her. Letting out a low sigh, she stretched deeply, relieved that the painful injury to her calf had now subsided to what amounted to a pulled muscle. However, she stiffened and her eyes grew wide as the bed shifted behind her, realizing she wasn't alone in the bed this time. It wasn't a pillow she'd snuggled against, but a very comfortable, comforting body. The room was entrenched in darkness so thick she couldn't determine who lay silent and unmoving next to her, although she had a suspicion.

Waking up next to someone—anyone—never tended to end well for her, and Eva didn't anticipate this time would be any different. To her surprise and embarrassment, her stomach let out a long low rumble reminding her that it had been too long since she had eaten.

"Hey, it's me." Confirming her guess, Oliver's

husky whisper broke through the silence and darkness of the room. "I'll open the shades a bit so you can see." He moved again, presumably to find the remote, since of course wealthy people didn't just walk over and open blinds.

The soft whirring of the motor near the window confirmed that he did, in fact, use a remote. Not only did the shades open, but the darkened windows behind them began to lighten up, filtering in bits of sunlight, gently easing her out of the dark.

Blinking as the soft light infiltrated the room, Eva attempted to ascertain how much time had passed. With no internal sense of direction and complete lack of familiarity of the house's layout, Eva couldn't tell if it was sunrise or sunset; only that it was one or the other.

Not for the first time, as if reading her mind, he said, "Sunset of day three." Oliver's voice remained soft, but Eva could feel his gaze pinned on her, perhaps waiting for the shock of this revelation to hit.

And it did. Panicked at the passage of days, Eva flipped her head around to look at him, no longer embarrassed at waking up in a bed with a man she barely knew. "What? I've been gone that long? I've got people who'll worry. My work will be freaking out. My friends won't know what to think."

"Eva," Oliver gently began, and Eva hated the pity he'd heard in her voice. "You had a text from Jackson asking what's up? We said you were writing. And that's it. No other missed calls or texts."

Of course. Closing her eyes, sadness filled Eva.

Really no one cared since Gram had gone. Jackson probably wasn't even in the country and had taken a chance that she could talk.

*He believed that?* Bullishly, she considered how well Jackson knew her. *I would've stopped writing immediately to FaceTime with my best friend.* Her friend group wasn't large at all. The few others she had were married with children and didn't always reach out. Running into her while she served them at the coffee shop with promises to keep in touch better wasn't a great way to preserve a relationship. Admittedly, she'd given up calling and texting after repeatedly reminding her friends who she was when she did see them. It sucked being a wallflower, but sometimes more wasn't worth the effort. Apparently, shutting people out was becoming her profession. Ohhh, wait . . . Her profession?

Eyes open now, lying face to face with Oliver, she tentatively asked, "Why would I be writing?" She pulled the blanket up to her chin, tucking her hands under it, and then suddenly a strange feeling flowed through her. Regret? Trepidation? Unable to recognize this unfamiliar but hopeful feeling, she waited.

"There are a few things we need to talk about." Oliver closed his mouth tightly before continuing, "I had to give you my blood for you to survive the journey here. If I hadn't, you would've died. We never would've made it in time."

This time it was definitely regret that flooded Eva, along with a healthy jolt of fear, "Wait, what? Am I going to turn into a vampire? And why are my emotions all over the place? If I was going to be a vampire I wouldn't have emotions, right? Aren't they, like, stone cold or whatever? Or am I going to die? I'm going to die, aren't I?"

Sardonically, Oliver chuckled, "No, I promise you aren't going to die or turn. If you were, it would've happened already. And you would've had to die to turn. It was close," he admitted, sincerity marking his words. "I wouldn't have done it differently, but it was way too close, and everyone deserves a choice when it comes to that.

"The matter of your emotions is actually a little bit more complicated. First, vampires are, in fact, very emotional. Easy to anger, easy to laugh, and all that. In fact, emotion is sometimes what makes *some* vampires so unpredictable. We have to learn to control our emotions, like Spock." Holding up a flat hand to pause her from a barrage of questions, he separated two fingers from the other two as a way of explanation. "But the emotions you're feeling aren't because you're becoming a vampire."

Oliver's steady voice, flat and nearly devoid of emotion and inflection droned on, pushing through quickly, as Eva fought to not interrupt. "Sounds like you're feeling my emotions. Since I fed you"—Eva raised an eyebrow at this—"I've been feeling like I'm inside your head, and now that you're awake it appears you're feeling my emotions through some sort of psychic connection. I thought it would fade, but here we are three days later, and I'm still getting a lot from you. I'll try to work harder to hold mine in check, but I admit it has been difficult."

*Kill me now. Wait! Is that him? He's embarrassed by this? Does that make the entire situation even more embarrassing? Is that possible? Yes.*

"Did you just make a *Star Trek* reference? Are you a Trekkie? Can vampires be Trekkies?" Raising her own hand up in the air, she struggled to separate the right two fingers from the left, mimicking his Vulcan greeting. Blinking owlishly several times and again not waiting for an answer, Eva continued straining to keep her voice a casual reflection of his. "Sooo, why would you tell Jackson I was writing? Coffee shop, middle of nowhere town, a very human barista. Remember? One who still isn't sure all of this is real."

Lying flat on his back, Oliver ran a frustrated hand through his rumpled dark hair, next to her on the very edge of the large bed, clearly exhausted.

Eva couldn't remember much of the last few days, but she did remember he seemed to do that quite often. No one had ever appeared quite so frustrated by her before. Of course, outside of Gram and possibly Jackson, no one had spent this much uninterrupted time with her before either. Wearing clean clothes now, Oliver lay on top of the bed, smelling of a sharp, clean soap. Gray sweats. OMG. She swung her eyes back to his face before her thoughts or feelings took an embarrassing turn or, dear God . . . Was it already too late? Keeping a blank expression, Eva focused intently on his face. *Don't think about the sweatpants, don't think about the sweatpants*, was the frantic mantra running through her head on repeat.

"I like watching television," Oliver confessed.

For a moment, Eva wondered why he was telling her that, then she remembered the *Star Trek* reference. "I get that. I mean, I don't watch a lot of TV, but *Star Trek* is a classic that everyone should watch. Personally, I like to read. Most of my days are booked, for sure."

"I like watching it a lot," he continued, staring up at the ceiling. "I binge anytime I get a chance. I don't neglect my work or anything like that. But the last couple decades, I've been bored, so shows and movies keep the boredom and quietness away. And well, yeah, I like *Star Trek*. They're doing more than exploring the earth; they've visited galaxies and planets."

Even if Eva hadn't been connected to Oliver, she would have recognized his embarrassment and what it took for him to open up about such a thing. Apparently, binge watching Netflix wasn't on the list of approved things for big, bad, self-proclaimed vampires to partake in.

"And the writing . . ." He sighed. "You're A. Scriver. You're not German but still, calling yourself a writer or a storyteller is simple enough." It wasn't a question, but a statement, so Eva remained silent, unwilling to lie but refusing to admit the truth. "You pop out puns similar to the biography in the books." He listed, "You're definitely smart enough to be a writer and, well, I sort of cranked up your laptop and looked through it while you slept." With the last sentence, his voice lowered and he mumbled a bit, while he stared up at the ceiling.

Shocked, Eva sat up, letting the blanket fall from her to the waist. "Woah! I did *not* give you permission to go through my things." Spinning her head from side to side, she searched for the backpack that carried her latest work.

Finally he looked at her again, turning his head to meet her eyes and giving her a shrug that said going through someone's highly personal laptop and highly personal work wasn't even in the same category as touching a metaphorical aura.

"It's in the other room." Oliver waved a lazy hand toward the door. Dropping his eyes for a moment away from her shocked look, he seemed captured by a spot just below her chin. Mesmerized, in fact, by Eva's collarbone where the strap of the thin tank top was supposed to sit. "And it's not like I touched your aura or anything like that."

He *was* reading her mind. He had to be. Then, as if it had a mind of its own, the strap at the edge of her shoulder slid a hint farther. Eva's breath hitched as a lusty feeling moved through her body and ended between her legs. Was that Oliver's emotion or hers?

*Don't look down at the gray sweatpants*, she reminded the slutty, lusty goddess inside her.

When Oliver's brown eyes moved up toward hers, she knew that the lust she felt belonged to both of them. A surge of power shifted through her, causing tingles that ran down her arms and legs. Her breath caught in the back of her throat. "Is it?" she verified in a low, husky voice that wasn't her own.

He did fill out that white tee shirt nicely. See? She

could avoid looking at his gray sweats. Running a finger down his bare arm, Eva gasped as a bolt of energy shot between them, buzzing them both.

"Oops!" She giggled. "Static electricity." Jerking her hand away, confused, she slapped it over her own mouth. *What is wrong with me?!*

Oliver continued watching her, silently examining her every movement, while rubbing the spot where she'd touched him as if it burned. His phone buzzed next to him, jarring him from his slow perusal. A few quick clicks on the phone later, he said, "Everyone is here, and they want to meet you. Do you want a shower and change before this meeting?" Waiting for her response, he added his own official nod. "I'll have things brought in for you to wear. Then you can eat while we talk."

Eva's stomach grumbled at the thought of food. If it had been days, then no wonder she was feeling out of sorts. Food suddenly became a priority.

# CHAPTER THIRTEEN

*Now you're a real pizza work!*

It wasn't the quickest of showers, but definitely one of the best of her life. Eva made the decision that if her house had survived, she would definitely upgrade her bathroom. Finding a new bottle of vanilla lavender body wash made her not feel quite so far from home. She lingered long after she'd washed the remaining grime and blood away from her body and out of her hair enjoying the comforting scent. She didn't only spend the time basking in the seemingly unending stream of hot water. She carefully examined where she knew wounds had been just days before, while prodding the puckered, scarred bite marks on her calf that looked weeks old and not just days. Thoughts of the promised food kept her from remaining in the shower indefinitely.

After her shower, she found a few simple items folded neatly and waiting for her on the bed. Fresh sheets and blankets had also replaced the ones she'd lain on for the last several days and nights. The soft leggings and tee were clearly not new, but they fit well enough and felt heavenly to pull on after her shower.

No shoes but socks, so she wouldn't be forced to parade barefoot before strangers in an unfamiliar place. Dressed in someone else's clean clothes, Eva left the room to follow the soft murmur of voices down a long hallway with closed doors, before entering a lounge filled with seating and an almost familiar yet still strange grouping.

Slipping quietly into the room, Eva wasn't sure who or what to expect when Oliver said everyone had arrived. She recognized Delta, who was attempting to fit an entire slice of pizza into her mouth while lying half-reclined and barefoot on a sofa. Eva was fairly certain that the two women in coordinating jewel pantsuits near her were related; they looked just similar enough they could all be sisters.

However, they were cutting their pizza into smaller bits, eating it with a fork while perched on the edge of upholstered armchairs with shoes that matched handbags sitting upright next to them. And while Delta's hair fell down in wild, unruly curls, their equally red hair had been pulled into submission to form sleek, matching chignons. They topped off the look with expertly applied makeup. Similar and clearly related, but not quite the same aura floated from them, and definitely not Delta's earthy, free spirit style.

A sense of déjà vu smacked Eva in the face when she spied a dark-haired woman alone on another sofa, bare feet tucked next to her side and a glass of red wine in hand.

*Wait! Is that the actress Ravyn Sinclair?*

Oliver had said he was doing security for her, but

why was she here barefoot and casually dressed? Had she been here before or was that a stress- and injury-induced hallucination? Eva couldn't trust her own memory at this point. Had she spoken to this group of people when Oliver brought her into his home or was that a false memory created to fill in the blanks of this new world she was discovering?

Tipping her wine glass in a small gesture of greeting, Ravyn gave her a faint smile that spoke of knowing exactly what Eva was thinking. Clearly, shoes were optional in Oliver's house, and the women were comfortable enough to slide out of them.

Three men—huge, oversized men in crisp, black suits—stood at various points within the room, their straight backs near the walls but not quite touching them as they also surveyed the room, eyes in motion like animals stalking prey or wary of unseen predators. One of the giants, blond with curly hair, who had tried to pull half of his frazzled mane into man-bun, stood closer to Ravyn and his darting, wary eyes tended to land on her much more often than the others' eyes did.

Eva allowed a lip to curl up, wondering about this relationship. Somehow, even when recovering from being torn apart and impending death, she'd managed to start "shipping" paranormals. Perhaps she'd lost her grasp on reality and now life had begun imitating her art in a crazy twist of events. A bark of a laugh that immediately cut off into a slight cough drew her eyes directly to Oliver. Despite knowing exactly where he was when she'd entered the room, Eva had avoided looking at him.

Sitting in yet another upholstered chair, Oliver owned the space, leaning forward with elbows on spread knees, sucking all the air from the room when she looked at him.

Delicious.

He'd apparently been in the middle of a conversation with the possible Delta relatives and sat frozen with his eyes upon her and a quizzical look across his face. He'd changed from those delicious gray sweatpants into fitted khaki pants, with what in Eva's mind was becoming his signature look, a white button-up with rolled sleeves. Despite the fact that room separated them, Eva began to fear that perhaps she was the prey as Oliver's eyes flared darker and deeper at her, losing the look of amusement. It was his eyes that drew her farther into the room in spite of the fact that she could have happily stood in the doorway and silently observed the group until she could slip away again.

A startled feminine voice broke her trance as Eva watched the room.

"Oh dear, whaaat are youuu?" an unfamiliar woman questioned in long, drawn-out vowels.

"Hungry?" Eva quipped sardonically, wondering how often she could be asked this in a day. Almost before the sarcasm had completely escaped her mouth, Oliver stood next to her with a plate of pizza while simultaneously managing to lead her deeper into the full room. Delta snorted around the pizza in her mouth, giving Eva a thumbs up while somehow still managing to hold onto a second slice.

The elegant woman who had questioned her so abruptly managed to pull her face into a look of embarrassment that Eva doubted was sincere. "I beg your pardon! My own mother would be appalled by my manners. It's just that you're . . . so interesting . . . just as mysterious as my daughter said. She also said you're amusing."

These last words were said in a flat tone and definitely not a compliment—perhaps even an insult—but that wasn't what Eva found most interesting. "Delta's your daughter? I thought you were sisters."

Delta rolled her eyes as the older witch tittered, perhaps finding her more amusing now than with her first impression. "Ugh, don't encourage her. Eva, this is my mother High Priestess Hecate of the Midwest and Greater Northern Coven Regions, Supreme Leader of all within her domain. Mother, this is Eva . . . Well, Eva Nance, adopted granddaughter of another Nance."

A wave of her hand followed the introduction that Eva wasn't quite sure was reverent, but at the same time she couldn't put her finger on how much was the truth and how much wasn't. Funny coming from someone who made a living writing fiction or evil devil lies, as some of the more colorful reviews liked to point out.

"Her mini-me is Athena, next in line for the great High Priestess of the Midwest and Greater Northern Regions, Maiden of the Midwest and Greater Northern Regions. Of course, the greatest title bestowed upon her is elder sister of me, the unexpected and unexplained." Sarcasm and even a hint of disdain followed the latter's introduction, and Eva didn't need a degree or even a course in psychology to see that there was a bit of sibling something going on there. "And 'maiden' doesn't mean she's a virgin; it's been a lotta years since that was a problem and not relevant to the maiden title."

With a sigh that showed she couldn't quite ignore her daughter's confusing and possibly irreverent introduction, Hecate nodded regally toward Eva as Eva stumbled out, "Nice to meet you, High Priestesses or, eh, both of you."

"Please, just call me Hecate. Those titles are nothing to you. The pleasure is all mine, and I greet you on behalf of our coven."

"And Athena," the other announced in a shrill, cartoonish voice that didn't quite match the elegant lady before her.

Delta groaned at her, continuing to shove pizza in her mouth even after her sibling gave her a dirty look.

Oliver pressed the plate at Eva. "Sit and eat. They voted on pizza." He lowered his voice, leaning in close to her ear. "And by voted, I mean honestly, Delta threw a tantrum until it was ordered. Don't hesitate to let me know if you want something else. You need to regain your strength."

Smiling at the image and acutely aware of Oliver's soothing coolness against her, Eva took the fine china plate she suspected usually served a much fancier fare. "Pizza is perfect, and I'm starving." Sitting crossed-legged on the only empty space in the loosely gathered furniture grouping, a sofa across from Ravyn, she nodded hello to her, feeling a bit self-conscious eating in front of the glamorous woman who had sat silently, watching the greetings play out around her.

Smiling a toothy grin framed with rosy lips, Ravyn waved her wine glass toward Eva. "Eva, it's really so lovely to see you up and about. When Oliver brought you in a few days ago, we weren't sure how things would end up." Her soft, lilting voice had an accent or combination of accents that Eva couldn't quite pinpoint. "But I really am glad you're doing well." Leaning in toward Eva, hinting at a camaraderie with her, she lowered her tone, although with Oliver's vampire hearing, who was she kidding? "Oliver has been quite beside himself. I don't think I've ever seen him so frazzled, and I've known him a long time." Raising an eyebrow, she once again raised her red wine to her lips, sipping. Waiting?

Eva's mind hadn't played tricks on her; Ravyn had been here when they arrived. Slowly, she chewed her pizza without tasting it. *So, Ravyn is surely supernatural too? A vampire?* Oliver had said he worked for her, that they were friends, birds of a feather and all that. Swallowing the food in her mouth gave her time to formulate a response, but still all she could come up with was, "It's nice to meet you?" This came out more a question than a statement, because Eva still had no idea why she was here or really where she even was. A few days ago, simply writing, existing, and working a few shifts at the coffee shop had summed up her life. Now it looked very different.

"Ah, yes, it really is. I'm delighted as well. Since Oliver is being so rude, I suppose I should introduce myself. I'm Ravyn, dear, beloved friend of Oliver's, and hopefully you and I will be great friends as well. We sort of met earlier when Ollie brought you in. And just to face one of the elephants in the room, I am a vampire as well. Ollie says you're new to our world, and it's understandable that this is all very overwhelming and confusing, but it's important to just begin with honesty. Don't you agree?"

The pizza turned to sawdust in her mouth. Her world had always been small, but Eva was learning that it could be squished even smaller than she could imagine if all of this were true. And unless this was a huge practical joke or mass hysteria, it was, in fact, very true, and the sooner she accepted it as such, the sooner she could move on and go . . . home?

"I agree, fangk you very much." Hell, what was wrong with her? Couldn't for once her mouth just say what it should say and drop unnecessary puns that instead of drawing laughter might cause someone to literally kill her? She hadn't seen much of this world yet, but half of it had tried to kill her, and she definitely needed to be wary if she made it through the next few minutes unscathed.

Thankfully, laughter boomed from Ravyn at the slip of her tongue. "You're a riot and so refreshing. I can see why he's enamored with you."

*Who, Oliver?* Eva felt her face flood with the heat of embarrassment while her breath hitched, releasing the momentary panic she'd felt at her faux pas.

Continuing to eat the tasteless pizza, she casually scanned the room to see who or what surrounded her. She remembered seeing a few members of the unlikely group earlier through her fevered haze. The three huge men still stood on the perimeter despite the numerous seats available in the large sitting area. The blond giant nearest to Ravyn had moved a few steps closer when Eva had sat down, but the others remained bookends to the room.

With a wave of her hand, Ravyn mostly dismissed the men around her. "These are my current bodyguards, hired thugs, protectors, whatever they choose to be called this century. Maybe you remember Thor the Dog, leader of my protection?" She gestured toward the tall, glowering man who rolled his eyes so quickly that if Eva had blinked, she would have missed it.

"I'm so sorry, I don't completely," admitted Eva. "When we arrived, I truly was out of it. I definitely don't recommend getting bitten by a . . . wild animal . . ." She trailed off uncertainly. Oliver had called them dogs or hounds. That was it: hellhounds, some sort of beasts from hell by the sounds of it, and they'd definitely looked the part. Craning her neck upward toward the huge bodyguard, whose bad side she didn't want to be on, she added, "Apologies if I said something, um, weird. I wish I could say it was due to my injuries, but my mouth gets ahead of me sometimes."

"Pfft, I haven't laughed so hard in ages! Ollie told me about your dream. You're nearly prophetic with those things. In all seriousness, though, hellhounds are nasty, nasty creatures. Really, they should all be put down. The only purpose they serve is being assassins for cowards who can't get their own hands dirty."

"They were quite hideous and scary-looking, and that was before all the biting and venom and near dying went down," Eva admitted, thankful that no one in the room would think she was crazy. "I've never seen anything even remotely as terrifying in my entire life."

All the quiet conversation occurring around the room drew to a halt as her words hung in the air. Delta sat with another piece of pizza hanging from her mouth, while her sister posed with a fork midway to her own mouth. Even Oliver looked shocked, and he'd been with her during the entire horrible ordeal.

"What?" Eva asked with confidence draining from her faster than her old tablet's dying battery. "Don't you all find them ugly, or is it different with you? All black and angry snarls with gray smoke seeping off them? Bits of red here and there?" Maybe they were the unicorns of the paranormal world, and their state of attractiveness was relevant to who was looking at them. Dear Lord, had she insulted them all? Ravyn had said they should all be put down, but maybe there was some other unknown rule she'd broken.

Ravyn leaned back onto the sofa after sitting her wine down on the small side table, peering intently at Eva with her dark eyes, tilting her head slightly as her messy, dark bun bobbed. "You . . . you could see the hellhounds?"

"Well, yes. I mean they chased us, bit me. Oliver fought them off. It wasn't for very long, and it happened so fast." Eva flushed at the memory of Oliver roaring as he went into battle with the large, black creatures, flinging them as if they were the size of puppies. Shivering, she hoped to never see their red, glowing eyes, bloody fangs, and sooty, wiry black coats ever again.

Ravyn slowly clapped her hands, smiling in admiration. "This is going to get interesting, my dear, because you shouldn't be able to see hellhounds at all. Humans can't see them. They can see the destruction they cause, they can feel the pain they inflict, but they're blind to the physical manifestation of demons." Gesturing toward the three witches, she continued, "Witches can't see demons." Pausing, she looked at the man she called Thor and questioned, "Can shifters see hellhounds?"

He nodded shortly in affirmation but offered no additional information.

"And dearest Eva, demons see demons." Picking up her glass of wine, Ravyn announced, "I feel I've done my part in determining she's not human and not a witch. We're narrowing this down, people. Now, it's time for some of you to start earning your paycheck."

With a flash of panic, Eva repeated to herself the question that had seemed so odd each time it was asked.

*What are you?*

Admittedly, the answer might not be as straightforward as she'd once thought. "I'm human though, aren't I? I've never looked like or felt like any sort of demon, or vampire, or shifter. Okay, I don't know much about shifters except from fiction books, but I don't turn into anything else at the full moon or any other time."

Looking around the room, all Eva found were puzzled faces reflecting her own. "I mean, I've always assumed I was human, because that was all there was. My mom, as far as I can remember, was human, and I assuredly was born from her. And Gram claimed to be a witch, but she wasn't blood related to me."

Setting her now empty wine glass down, Ravyn leaned forward, her voice low and almost threatening. "Eva dear, that is only one question in many, many we need answers to." She continued staring gravely at Eva until she set her plate of food down, no longer hungry as the gnaw in her belly turned into something else. "Do you resemble your mother or your father?" This was said casually enough, but Eva wondered if this was truly one of the many questions that apparently needed answering.

"My mother," she answered hesitantly. Honestly, why could that even matter at this point? "But to be honest, I've never even seen a picture of my father—my biological one, that is. So, I really only know part of the story." Shrugging, she tried to let the group know that the story of her origins was unimportant. "I was young when Mom died, and she hadn't said much about him; just that he didn't know about me. Later, way after she died, Gram told me it was a one-night stand and that he didn't . . . couldn't," she amended, "know about me." After losing the only parents she'd ever known, a young Eva had often woken from nightmares in which a mysterious man claimed he was her father and ripped her away from her gram. Gram always assured Eva that nothing would take her away, a fact that held true until death did.

"Could she be like Malthazar?" Oliver asked the group, as if they all knew this Malthazar.

"It's rare, but not impossible, and would explain her being drenched in magic," Delta volunteered from her reclined position, restarting her eating frenzy.

Hecate interjected, "If her mother was truly human, then it perhaps could be her father. But it's still possible that her mother wasn't human. You need to have someone look into that. But it's doubtful that two females would be born from demon lineage. One would be rare, but two with enough undiluted blood to trigger this sort of magic would be statistically impossible."

Ravyn ignored the interruptions and conjectures around them and leaned closer to Eva. Examining Eva's features closely as if seeing her for the first time, she whispered, "When and how did your mother die?"

Oliver started at the brusque line of questioning, but Ravyn waved him off, adding firmly, "This is important and besides, you're being paid for this, lest you forget." Gesturing for Eva to answer, she ignored Oliver's growl of frustration.

Eva looked hesitantly between the two and explained her mother and adoptive father's deaths—as much as she knew, anyhow, and as much as her gram had filled in for her: the rainy night, the car careening down an embankment, being found outside of the car, her coma, her memory loss, and the miracle that was her survival.

Despite Ravyn's intensity, Eva found her easy to open up to and soon forgot about the others in the room.

Ravyn listened intently, never interrupting. She "tsk"ed over certain moments and smiled sadly at Eva's loss, setting a gentle hand on Eva's knee. When Eva finished, she felt heart wrenched, but also strangely invigorated at the same time. Outside of the therapist, she hadn't shared her story with anyone. She always just assumed Jackson knew and, aside from him, she had no friends close enough to ever ask about her past.

"Ohio, you say." Again, this wasn't so much a question as a statement. Ravyn perched on the edge of the sofa, her body quivering in excitement. "By the end of the night, perhaps I will solve all of this mystery, and during my next lifetime I could be an investigator too." Eyes flashing, she zipped next to Eva in the blink of an eye, eliciting a gasp from her as she grasped Eva's hand loosely in her own, flooding her with warmth at the touch. "It looks like my foray into the Midwest didn't go as unnoticed as I'd planned."

"I'm fairly sure you couldn't go anywhere unnoticed," Eva admitted. Why wasn't she pulling her hand away from the vamp? If even a fraction of vampire legends were true, Ravyn was a creature who craved blood and could snap her in half on a whim. Instead, she felt comfort and peace.

*Oh, shit, am I being mesmerized or compelled or whatever Oliver called it? I have absolutely zero survival instincts,* Eva lamented in her head even as she happily returned Ravyn's gentle smile, as if the two shared a secret.

Delta, who had finally ceased eating, interjected, "Um, why is Eva glowing?"

Eva turned toward her quizzically, realizing that she wasn't compelled if she could do that. This pronouncement had Delta putting her pizza aside and sitting up.

Hecate looked thoughtful as she examined the glowing Eva from across the room. "Interesting. Not a usual half-demon trait, although I'll admit I've not studied the subject, since typically those beasts don't last long on either plane." Her eyes widened guiltily as she uncomfortably fanned herself, seeming to remember that Eva might be such an abomination.

"She glowed when I fed her," Oliver admitted casually, and Eva turned a startled glance at him before looking down at her hands that were, in fact, gently glowing. "Brighter, but the same sort of thing. Malth didn't when I gave him blood."

Who was Malth? Another half-demon? Why was she even entertaining these thoughts? She was nothing special. It had been proved time and time again that she was forgettable, ordinary. Life happened around her, not *to* her.

"How do you feel, Eva?" Hecate questioned. "Is it pleasant, warm, cool? Anything you can tell me would be helpful."

Without looking at Hecate, Eva explained, "I feel energized, like I could go for a jog. I'm a little tingly, sort of like when your leg goes to sleep, but in a better way."

Hecate nodded. "I think you fed from Ravyn's energy, perhaps her excitement or her emotions. Unusual, but empaths and other creatures can do that." Plucking the air, she grasped things that the others couldn't see and, turning these invisible items in her hands, examined them thoughtfully. Moving closer to Eva, she asked, "May I?" and held out her hands.

Eva slowly nodded yes, assuming wrongly that the elder witch wanted to examine her hands, but instead, Hecate plucked more invisible items from the air, examining them and muttering in an undistinguished language.

Ravyn continued as if the entire interruption hadn't occurred. "As I was saying, I can fill in a few more parts." Noting her empty glass, she held it backward to her bodyguard, who sighed and muttered under his breath before taking it for a refill. "I was there the night of your parents' deaths. Sometimes I go on walk-abouts or hitchhike across the states to break up life. And I remember that night. An unholy storm rose up quickly, and although I can get wet, I just don't like it. It's uncomfortable and unnecessary. So, I walked down a culvert and decided to wait things out perched on a ledge inside."

At her bodyguard's snort, she took the glass from him. "I've waited in much more uncomfortable places than this, mind you," she retorted haughtily. Sipping daintily, she continued, "I saw the car go off the ledge. It hurled down the side of the embankment like a freight train, or like something had plucked it up and tossed it. I immediately slipped down the hillside, not sure if anyone could even survive. Perhaps I was getting wet for no reason. But despite what I am, I'm no monster."

When she paused, the room remained quiet, waiting. Ravyn's throat pulsated at her memories. She smiled softly and sadly to a shocked Eva. "Your parents were already dead. There was no saving them. The trees, the stones, they were gone. But you, I remember clearly. You were in the back seat, so badly injured. One of the branches bypassed both your parents and went clean through your chest. Here." She pointed to the spot between her own breasts. "You were pinned to the car. Life barely clung to you, but I could see it in you. I thought maybe I could help you. Not turn you. No, that would have been wrong, but you had more life left in you. I was sure of it. So, I fed you my blood. Removed the branch."

Shuddering as she remembered, she went on, "Oh, your screams, poor child, your screams. I fed you more. Then I made you forget it all. No one should remember that. I placed you up by the road and flagged down the first car that passed. I gave them instructions and then made them forget me."

Shuddering as Ravyn's words stirred unformed

memories, Eva gaped in shock at Ravyn, then at Oliver, and back to Ravyn. "Is this true?" The words felt familiar, yet the actual memories of the moment still lay unformed, out of reach in her mind.

Ravyn nodded sadly. "I left quickly to search for the cause of the crash. It was no accident. And interesting enough, it was another hellhound that had thrown the car off the road."

For a moment, a memory of darkness flashing as it pounded into the moving car crossed Eva's mind. Was it real or imagined by the scene Ravyn painted as she filled in the gaps of Eva's memory? "Is the hellhound that attacked me"—she pulled a breath that choked off a cry of pain—"is it the same one that killed my parents?"

A blood-thirsty yet satisfied look crossed Ravyn's face. "Child, I assure you, that hellhound is not alive to attack you again. I made sure of that, that very night."

Eva hadn't been mistaken. Ravyn was strong, very strong, if she'd managed to fight off and destroy one of those creatures. "You?" formed on her lips, although she wasn't sure if she planned to cry out or thank her.

Again Hecate interrupted. Had this witch never been taught manners? "Well, that would explain the thread between the two of you. It's one of the oldest and strongest in the bunch. Delta told me you had a mess of them, but I didn't believe it until I saw all of this." She nodded approvingly to her younger daughter, who beamed under her mother's praise.

"And absolutely more proof that Eva is something . . ." As if being human was nothing, Eva thought sardonically. "No human could simply have a thread of this sort tied to a vampire, especially one of Ravyn's age and strength."

*Mama Hecate is sucking up now,* Eva thought, not just a little bitterly. "So, how are we connected then? What does this connection do?"

Ravyn shrugged, but Oliver interjected softly, "Eva, the Ancient Egyptian goddess Ma'at was depicted as a winged creature. Ravyn is a representation of Ma'at. Throughout her history any winged creature, a bird, a crow, or a raven have been a part of her name.

Ravyn smiled gently at a shocked Eva. "The name given to me when I was taken, but you knew that; you know all of it. You just didn't know it was me. To some, during that lifetime, ravens symbolized death, but also rebirth and starting anew. I am the raven; the raven is me. Over the years, I've needed different names, but I prefer the truth or at least a version of the truth in whatever language that might be in. It always comes back to the raven. Fala was one such name, only my people during that time didn't have a name for 'raven' and during that time I was the crow. And Ishto means 'big.' I was simply called a big crow. Translated, it doesn't quite have the same ring to it."

Like the pieces of a puzzle fitting together, things were snapping into place. "But that was my dreams, just my dreams."

Delta's mouth gaped yet again as she looked

between the two of them. "Oh, wow! I did not see that! That's you? And that's you?"

Her sister sat by her side, perplexed, her shrill voice asking, "Who? That's who? Who is?"

Eva knew exactly how she felt!

"So, you're some sort of a dream hijacker? Interesting. Although you know not everything is completely right, I will assume artistic license." Ravyn pondered, "Or is it just my dreams? Is it a different connection than a true dream demon would have?"

Demon? Dream hijacker? Was that what she was doing? Infiltrating Ravyn's dreams and stealing her life to share with others for money? And a demon? Surely, she would know if she were a demon!

Ravyn looked at Oliver. "So this is our little writer, but she's not my threat. There is nothing coming from her at all that even remotely feels threatening. In fact, I feel sort of peaceful and relaxed in her presence." Giving Eva a side eye, Ravyn continued, "Unless of course she's a black widow, and it's all a ploy to make me feel comfortable before she strikes."

Gasping at the insinuation, Eva opened her mouth to offer reassurances that no ploys were involved, and it was all just chance or circumstance.

Exasperated, Oliver shook his head. "Eva, there are no black widows. She's joking; poorly, but joking."

Hecate, who hadn't spoken to anyone in several moments, just moved around to examine the air around Eva, gestured to Delta to come closer. She pointed to several spots for Delta to examine.

Face furrowed in concentration, Delta examined

the areas that were apparently only visible to her mother and her. Communication passed between the two with no words.

"May I?" Hecate reverently asked Ravyn.

"Of course, High Priestess." Despite the invitation to call her Hecate, it didn't seem right. Eva noticed that everyone else in the room, barring Delta, spoke reverently to the woman. The witch began an exam as thorough on Ravyn as they'd conducted on Eva. Eva noticed that tension had formed around Ravyn's eyes. Despite her languished expression and the sipping of her wine, there was concern about what might be discovered.

"I would've died if you hadn't stopped for us," Eva ascertained. "Was the coma because I still had so much healing to do or was it something you did?"

Ravyn smiled sadly. "Yes, you would have died. And I took a huge chance with you so close to death." She plucked at an invisible piece of lint on her silky lounge pants. "But I felt so compelled to help you. I couldn't just leave a child. And for your parents, it was truly too late. I knew at the time that you would face so much sorrow and heartbreak, but still, it was better to live."

"Oh, Mother," Delta cried out in happy surprise, interrupting the reminiscing. "That's amazing!"

Looking pleased with herself, Hecate nodded and half-smiled serenely at her daughter. "My fledgling, you would have found it yourself, I'm certain. Though I'm honored you called for my assistance. She's learning much in your organization, Mr. Patrick."

Deflecting the praise, she snapped her fingers at her elder daughter, who smoothly stood. The two of them strolled out with one of the bodyguards following close behind, as if nothing astonishing had occurred or as if no one was waiting for answers.

# CHAPTER FOURTEEN

*When white blood cells fail to fight off any infection,
their effort goes in vein.*

Even though three people had just left, Oliver felt the crowd of people in his home pressing down upon him. Unbuttoning the top two buttons of his shirt did nothing to alleviate the unfamiliar anxiety coursing through him. Glancing around the room at the remaining occupants, he realized two things: aside from one, these people were his inner circle, not a random horde pushing him out of his space; and second, these were Eva's emotions.

He casually set a cool palm on her shoulder, giving a gentle squeeze and mentally conveying support and comfort, hoping Eva could feel something from this strange connection they shared.

Ravyn gave a slow, barely discernible but knowing wink to him as she looked over her wine glass, and Oliver pointedly looked over her shoulder to the shifter guard, both his business partner and one of the few beings he called friend, who stood within arm's reach of her. Ravyn responded with a casual shrug before returning her attention to Delta.

The wolf ignored his glance and stood at attention with his eyes fixed at some point beyond them all.

"Sooo, Oliver's young, enlightened witch, what have you and your high priestess discovered?"

Oliver snorted quietly. Eva had most likely bestowed a title on Delta after all the confusion surrounding the fledgling's name. Delta did like her titles and nicknames, and the young woman beamed at the question, completely unbothered by the disrespectful nomenclature.

Rushing through her words, Delta began explaining what she'd discovered while plucking and pulling unseen areas from the air again. "The magic strands that surround Eva are more complex than anything I've seen before. Some are old, and some are newer." Her cheeks reddened as she looked at Oliver with the last bit, but he returned the look with his own passive expression.

Delta continued with her explanation in an excited voice. "Most are tangled and have been set to confuse and muddle. This one here . . ." Picking an invisible thread from the air with a thumb and forefinger with her other hand, she gave it a pluck as if it were a guitar string. "This one here is the oldest of them all. It's magnificent."

The group waited on edge for her to continue, but for several minutes, Delta was caught up in the beauty of a mysterious magical thread that no one else could see. Finally, Oliver demanded, "Delta? What's so special about that one?"

"Oh, yes! I forget sometimes you can't see them."

Delta sighed as if the loss were too great to imagine, and then confessed to Eva, "Probably similar to how most people can't see hellhounds, but you can. Nothing interesting to outsiders, but to our eyes, it's like, wow!" The red-haired witch released the thread to make explosions with her hands. "But yes, this thread, the oldest and the most wrapped up in all the others, leads to"—she circled her body around to Ravyn—"*you*! It's directly linked to you. And in case anyone was wondering, the newest leads to Boss Man." Gesturing toward him with her head, Delta raised her eyebrows expectantly.

Sighing, Oliver tried to move Delta along. "Is it because of the blood gift? I've gifted others my blood and never had this reaction. And Ravyn, I'm assuming the same."

Ravyn shook her head. "No, never. To be honest, I've never heard of this. And what sort of magic would do this? We're certain Eva isn't a witch"—she waved her hand toward Eva—"though clearly, she's steeped in witches' magic. I have no magic, per say. So, what is the connection? And why?"

Delta nodded. "It's definitely the blood gift. It has given her a link to your emotions, thoughts, and, I'm guessing, memories as well, if the award-winning 'Vampires in Hollywood' novels are anything to go by."

She strummed the title out and Oliver mentally groaned, knowing without a doubt the young witch was also a fan. Had everyone read the books but him? What was it Delta often said? Better late to the party than to not show up at all? Or something like that. He'd read them now. They were a good read, and even he could admit he understood why they were so popular. They would make a great television series.

"The only similarity is that you both gave blood to Eva, so whatever has created this thread, it's due to whatever she is." Delta added thoughtfully, "But also don't underestimate magic; the magic that made you. Just because we don't understand how you've been made doesn't make it less magical. It's just a magic that I can't recognize or see or control."

Oliver felt Eva's panic rising even higher, as Ravyn shrieked while raising her hand to her chest. "I can even feel that. I don't miss being human and feeling all the fear and uncertainty." Eyes wide, she looked at Oliver, giddily asking, "Can you feel that? It's . . . it's amazing, even exhilarating!" she gasped out, eyes wide as she clasped her chest, looking at the group, open-mouthed, as Eva's fear ebbed throughout her.

Oliver understood how she felt as a score of Eva's panicked emotions flowed through him as well, but Ravyn seemed to be forgetting these were Eva's own overwhelmed, nearly out of control feelings. To suggest otherwise belittled the overwrought woman before them.

When the initial emotions surged through him, Oliver nearly found himself bowled over. Biting down to suppress the overwhelming emotions surging through him, he forced himself to stay upright as other sensations flooded him. The desire to protect her enveloped him, the desire to hold her in his arms until the pain and confusion fled from her body; emotions as unfamiliar as her panic and fear.

Oliver seated himself next to Eva, pressing his leg gently against hers, again trying to convey reassurance. "I know this is overwhelming," he began.

Eva snorted, the color beginning to return to her face. "That's an understatement. My entire world—my entire existence—is apparently not what I even remotely thought. I feel like the old frog in a blender game on phones. I've been shook up, shaken so hard that I'm just liquid now. I'm not even close to what I was just last week."

Despite Eva's rather grotesque explanation, Oliver felt her lean into him as she absorbed some of the calming he was offering. "Can you remove these threads?" She assumed her mother had left because this was in Delta's realm of capability and not because even the high priestess couldn't untangle this magic. Surely if Delta needed a boost or help, her mother wouldn't have left so abruptly.

"Actually, I think I can. Of course I can," Delta confidently confided in them. "But it's going to take time. And I'm going to have to search and shift through the mass to unravel the threads. Most of them, however, were made at the same time and just raveled around intentionally as a mess. I think your grandmother did this to hide you, Eva. Most of these muddle, confuse, and cause people to forget you. You're as deeply hidden as any person can be magically."

"Is this why she doesn't have any pictures of herself?" Oliver began connecting a few dots. Eva's surprised look showed he wasn't wrong in his assumption.

"Yes," Delta excitedly replied. "Do you not get your picture taken? Like, is it an aversion?"

"No," Eva admitted, "not even that. It's more like I'm un-photogenic. Every picture after I turned fourteen has, like, a blur filter on it, or it's out of focus, or something. I can manage some profile shots if I'm mostly turned away. And my driver's license picture is a mess, but they tried so many times. They managed to add some sort of filter to give me features, but they're not my own."

"Ah," Delta acknowledged knowingly, "based around puberty too."

"I suppose." Eva nodded thoughtfully in agreement, still leaning on Oliver. "Yes."

Oliver noticed her heart rate had steadied, and she unknowingly leaned deeper into him, with her dark brown eyes intently on Delta.

"Is it my gram's magic? I mean, it seems like you're able to tell this stuff."

Delta nodded. "Not all witches can, and I come from a powerful line. The Witch Who Wasn't Supposed to Be." Her voice dropped theatrically, but Oliver knew it was underscored with a tinge of hurt that she refused to acknowledge, and he followed suit. He had no desire to get caught up in the affairs and inner workings of the witches, even if he did like Delta.

Oliver knew Delta's story well. Despite her accidental and highly unlikely conception and birth, her power parentage could make her more powerful than the high priestess when she matured. Unfortunately, despite being born from Hecate, she wasn't a contender for the role. Her sister Athena, as first and supposed to be only child, would take Hecate's leadership position in the coven if Hecate ever deemed it time to step aside to the position of Crone and give the Maiden her time as High Priestess. Whatever her reasoning, Oliver didn't even pretend to understand the workings of coven politics. And despite Delta's power and parentage, she didn't have a defined place in her world, which made her a perfect candidate and employee for him. *Witches and their traditions; their loss is my gain.*

"Yes, it's your gram's magic. You still reek of it after her death, what, ten or so years ago? And it probably actually began earlier than that. Puberty is my guess; so much revolved around those changes. This is important, Eva. Your grandmother obviously thought she needed to hide you from something. Something that we have no idea of. You need to really consider if it's worth dropping these charms and leaving you to be found. Right now, you're hidden . . . or mostly hidden."

Ignoring Oliver's look of indignation, she continued seriously, "Eva, no matter what Boss Man says, I won't do this without your consent. And even then, I'm not sure we should do it without having full knowledge of what you're hiding from. If you decide to do it, I will, and if you decide to stay hidden, I'll strengthen the wards on you and on your house. They'll last your lifetime and beyond." Glancing at Oliver, she added, "Unless some buffoon decides to rip them apart by hand and lead hellhounds right to your door."

Oliver sat quietly next to Eva, waiting for some sign of her decision. Even through their new bond, he couldn't get rid of these emotions and thoughts. "How does this affect Ravyn?" Asking that question got a spike of some unidentified emotion running through him, as well as increasing the rate of Eva's beating heart.

Delta held her hands out in a gesture of acceptance. "Unfortunately, Ravyn's thread is buried under all the other layers. I cannot remove Ravyn's without removing the others. If they stay, all the threads stay in place."

This time, Sebastian interjected. "Witch," he hissed, "if you're all about consent, what about Ravyn's consent to that? She'd be subject to this chain until that one dies." He tossed a hand toward Eva.

Oliver hissed at the threatening motion the shifter made at his . . . at his what? His Eva?

Delta smirked at the wolf and opened her mouth to most likely tell him to go take a flying leap and that his opinion mattered less than the doormat's, but it never came to that.

Ravyn held up a beautifully manicured hand to stop the exchange before it became volatile. "Ah, Thor, so touching you're worried about me, but I consented to a connection years ago when I gave the child my blood. True, I didn't fully understand, but regardless, I gave it freely. Consent has been given and will not be revoked no matter how you howl."

"I have to think about all this. I-I don't know," Eva stuttered. "Imagine going to the same school and every year being asked if you're the new kid. Imagine everyone you meet never remembering the first time or the last time you met," she mused. "This explains so much. I'm not really just an unforgettable wallflower; this was put on me. Imagine people seeing me, really seeing me. And people remembering my name."

"Does no one remember you at all?" Oliver asked, finding it impossible that anyone could forget the delicious beauty before him. Stupid, blind humans.

"If I've met them enough times, like my neighbors, they remember me. Sometimes they forget specific things we've done or talked about. My co-workers remember me as long as I work regularly, although not all the customers do." She laughed dryly. "God, the times I've been asked if I just started working there. My editor remembers me."

"The witch who knew your grandmother? She sent me to your town with only your grandmother's name. She might have been a safety net and even under compulsion, the spell held."

"And my friend Jackson. We don't even see each other that often anymore, but he has always remembered me and everything we've done or talked about, maybe even better than I remember."

Through the bond, Oliver could feel the

excitement from Eva, the excitement of others remembering her and connecting with her, like Jackson. He wondered if she could feel his desire to kill Jackson for being the cause of her happiness but quickly squashed the thought in case Eva could feel his anger and hatred. He couldn't bear the thought of the disgust and fear she might feel if she knew his true thoughts on this matter. Besides this Jackson was Eva's *friend*, no one deserved a life of loneliness.

Still examining the air around the room, tracing unseen lines with no beginning or ending, Delta casually tossed out, "He's probably a member of your gram's coven. There is a hint of other magic around you, but none seems masculine aside from Mr. Tall-Dark-and-I-Drink-Blood. He's most likely closely related to either your gram or other coven members, so the magic recognizes him or was made to omit him from it."

"When we find the answer to one question, five more appear in its place," Oliver mused, feeling inordinately pleased that his was the only masculine energy currently on Eva. Then he ticked off, "We still don't know what the threat is to Ravyn and if it's even connected to Eva. We don't know what Eva is. We don't know why the connection has formed between Ravyn and Eva, as well as Eva and me. We know the blood is the catalyst, but how has it happened? And why the need for such protection on Eva? What does she need protecting from? I suspect her grandmother sacrificed herself to create a bond between her magic and the house Eva lives in to maintain these spells."

Delta opened her mouth, then closed it, then opened it again. "Boss Man Dude. Can we have the win for just a second before you go all Debbie Downer and Negative Nellie on us? Despite the fact that I need Eva's consent to remove the threads, I do want to add that the magic is fading. The threads are weakened. I don't know how long they'll last; they could drop next week or in ten more years. They could go one at a time or they could drop at once. You could be anywhere when it happens, and then whatever you're hidden from will immediately know you exist. But if you do consent to their removal, I promise I'll protect you when they drop."

The seriousness of the young witch's tone and her brave promise brought tears to Eva's eyes. Her voice low and with a hitch, she said, "But you don't even know me. No one knows me."

"Yet you're worth knowing." Delta twisted her red locks into a bun and secured it on her head. "I would hate to have saved you from a hellhound and then let something else happen to you. I mean, if we can kick a hellhound's ass, we can beat back whatever else is out there."

Not wanting to remind Delta that she, in fact, hadn't directly defeated a fire-breathing beast from hell, Oliver gently and earnestly promised Eva, "You'll have my support too. I vow to protect you with all I have if you choose to drop the magic that binds you. I apologize if my actions, although unintentional, led any evil to your door or further weakened the spells placed on you."

Delta continued, her tone gentler, "It won't be an easy task. Even working non-stop could take days, and that is even if it were possible to work non-stop. Imagine, if you will, that you're connected by literally a magical tether from here"—she pointed to Ravyn's heart and drew a line across to Eva's chest—"to here. Simple enough, surely. However, on top of that, you have an absolute mass of other tethers overlapping, twisting, and winding together, intertwined and imbued by both old and relatively speaking, of course, new magic."

Looking pointedly at Oliver with that statement, she continued, "We can't just snap the tether."

"Why not?" Oliver questioned. "If Eva has a mess of magic, why not cut the tether you see extended from Ravyn? That seems simpler than sorting through this mess you're laying before us."

"Excellent question. However, if we cut it from Mistress Ravyn, the magical snap will be unpredictable. The remaining tether won't necessarily dissipate. More than likely, it will snap back into this mess, as you've so aptly described it, and cause . . . well, even more of a mess. A magical backlash mess that we can't predict, because mixing magic like that, especially magic we didn't create or control, and allowing it to recoil is bad, bad news. Very bad," Delta slowly enunciated.

Nodding, Eva mused, "It sounds like a rubber band ball. At work, we'd take any rubber bands that come on packages, letters, products, whatever, and use them to create sort of a bouncy ball. You have to wad up the first few bands and then start wrapping other rubber bands around them. No rhyme or reason to it, just an organic growth of rubber bands, and if one starts to slip, you twist it around differently to stay in place. Then, unlike what's happening to me, we could bounce this pretty amazing ball around, but when a band inevitably broke, it never really came free. It would just tangle up and hang onto the rest of the chaotic ball. And then to actually unravel the ball became impossible without destroying it entirely."

"You've summed it up perfectly. Add in a pretty serious magical slap to the head when a band breaks, and it's nearly a perfect analogy. This mass needs to be magically unraveled with surgical precision. And I'm offering myself as your humble surgeon, if you would allow me." Delta held her hands out in offering at the end of her announcement.

"There is no way the hellhound attack was random. She had a shadow scout stalking her early that day." There was no way both the hellhound and the demonic squirrel had just happened upon her. Something or someone was looking for her. Ravyn was not the one being stalked.

Laying her head back on the sofa, Eva closed her eyes, clearly overcome by the past days, the attack, the healing, and this new news. Oliver wished everyone was gone, so he could wrap her up in his arms without their judgmental eyes upon them. Why was he overcome with the desire to take care of her, to comfort her, to promise her the world and at the same time protect her from it? Even if a magical tether compelled him to protect Eva, Oliver could at least pretend at this moment in time that the feelings were real. Thankfully, he could make at least one of those items happen immediately. "Everyone, out. Head back to your area for a few hours. Let's give Eva time to decompress and determine her next step."

"Ollie, this is quite gallant of you; we so rarely get to see this side of you." Ravyn's tone held a light, mocking note, but she was already rising, and both of the remaining guards moved with her. "Are my rooms stocked with this delicious vintage?"

Oliver sighed, mentally questioning why Ravyn didn't seem to be affected by the magical attachment to Eva in the same way he was. "Just take the rest of the bottle, Ravyn, and have one of the men ring down for another to be brought up."

Blowing Oliver a kiss, Ravyn swooped up the bottle and headed toward the apartments he always had prepared for her rare visits. Apparently, he needed to have an assistant order a case of the Buckeye Red for Ravyn and another one for himself. Who knew she would like the Ohio wine as much as he did? It seemed Ohio hid all sorts of delicious secrets within its farmland.

Snatching up a pizza box, Delta also headed for the door, crumbs flying off her as she walked. "Have fun, kids. I'm gonna head to Mama Hecate's research library to pick up a few things I've requested. Time to research, prepare, just in case, and all that. I'll grab a few things and then be back before you know it," she warned with a teasing lilt to her voice.

*Peace and quiet finally.* "Do you need more to eat or drink?" Oliver asked Eva. "The pizza is probably cold, but I can get something else." Again that pull to see to Eva's comfort.

The quiet of the room settled over them, giving a much needed reprise from the revelations of the last few hours.

Shaking her head no, Eva pulled her feet up on the sofa, curling up toward Oliver. He liked how that felt. Reaching over with his free arm, he pulled a soft throw off the side of the couch and wrapped it around her.

"Thanks, Oliver," she whispered.

"It's nothing."

"I wasn't talking about the blanket."

"I know." The comfortable silence stretched out between them. Oliver listened as Eva softly breathed in and out, relaxing as the truths that had been revealed were slowly set aside, and they sat in the moment.

"What do you do normally when you're home like this?" Eva asked him, raising her head to look into his eyes.

He felt his heart skip a beat. "If I'm not working, I like to watch a movie or TV." He admitted with slight chagrin, "I told you I like watching shows."

"Where's your TV? Not here."

"I have a separate entertainment room. I suppose some would call it a 'man cave.' In fact, Delta often refers to it that way. This room is mostly used for informal meetings and get-togethers that need fewer distractions. It's also closer to the kitchen, so during such gatherings people can grab what they need quickly."

"Let's go watch something." Eva smoothly stood up from the sofa, grabbing Oliver's hand to pull him as well.

"Does your injury hurt?"

Stretching her leg and foot, Eva smiled. "Actually, it doesn't hurt at all anymore. I've always been a fast healer, but Delta really added a boost." Now that Oliver stood, Eva pulled on the hand she still grasped. "But I'll follow you. I have no idea where I'm going in the big place." Frowning, she added, "In fact, I have no idea where this big place even is."

"Southeast of Chicago, outside of the city for privacy for myself and anyone who works for me, but close enough we can be there in under an hour." Oliver found himself not wanting to release the hand she'd casually grabbed. Tightening his grip just slightly, he continued, "This way. Any ideas on what you want to watch?"

Several hours later, and just as many laughs, the second romcom ended. Eva hadn't cared what they watched, and Oliver discovered she truly didn't watch much TV. He'd realized her situation might require some laughter to escape from the heavier thoughts of the previous hours and days, as well as to celebrate being alive.

Perfect choice.

Oliver knew from experience that stepping back and letting the mind relax was sometimes the best way to find an answer to a problem. Of course, relaxing in a plush, theater-style recliner while watching a high definition, wall-size TV and having every snack available at the push of a button clearly helped set the mood. Keeping distractions to a minimum, his housekeeper silently brought in refreshments, even his own special drink which Eva probably assumed was red wine similar to Ravyn's drink, not realizing that the wine only made up a small portion of the nourishing beverage. His phone silently alerted him when Ravyn and her staff reached her quarters, and then alerted him again when Delta returned from her mother's library. No one had disturbed them, so he knew at least emergencies had been kept to a minimum.

Despite the problems they faced and the fact that they now had more questions than they'd started with, he felt content sitting with Eva and laughing together at the ups and downs of romantic movie life. Oliver caught himself several times not even watching the screen and just observing the woman in the next seat over laughing as she enjoyed the moment. It might have been easy to forget the danger she and Ravyn faced. Too soon, decisions needed to be made, and answers needed to be found. Oliver's promise to Ravyn continually proved to be much more difficult to keep.

At the end of the second movie, Eva stood up,

stretching with her arms above her head, showing a small expanse of skin between the black tank top and leggings that Delta had picked out. The witch was a walking contradiction of all black, but at the same time bubbles and unicorns.

Despite the spiked wine he'd sipped over the last hours, Oliver's fangs threatened to burst free again as Eva unassumingly stretched back, tossing her curls back over her shoulder, exposing the blue vein running down the pale skin of her neck. Shifting uncomfortably in his seat and unable to take his eyes off her, he gripped the armrest with his free hand to remind himself to stay seated.

Unaware of Oliver's inner turmoil, Eva asked, "Another one? You want to pick?"

At the same time, his phone buzzed next to him. Without removing his eyes from her, he answered the phone.

Listening to the chaos on the other end of the line, he knew the reprieve had only been momentary. "Call Delta and get her there immediately . . . good . . . we're on our way now." Hanging up, he fought the urge to crush the phone in his hand. He could sense Eva's tension returning despite the fact that her face remained impassive.

"Break time is over. We're heading to Ravyn's rooms. Something has happened." Was it just last week he'd been overwhelmed with boredom and the monotony of ordinary days?

# CHAPTER FIFTEEN

*I got into a fight with 1, 3, 5, 7, and 9. The odds were against me.*

The urgency of the moment kept Eva on Oliver's heels as he zipped down various hallways, and just as she would have lost him, he stopped in front of a set of double doors that he nearly ripped off the hinges when he tore it open. Eyes wide, afraid to blink in case he flashed away, she hurried after him, covering the last few yards just as he entered the room. Hesitation never crossed her mind. What threat could there be in here, a fortress, a maze, a maze fortress?

Of the areas Eva had visited, the entertainment room was the most comfortable and lived in. The kitchen and living rooms felt formal and unused. Clean and sterile came to mind. Even Oliver's guest bedroom, where she'd spent time healing, had a minimalist feeling, although Eva would be the first to admit the bed and bedding were out of this world comfortable. Maybe after all of this was over, she would upgrade her own bedding again, then with dismay she realized that after the hellhounds' attack, everything might need to be replaced and not simply upgraded. Did she even have a home anymore or had the hounds destroyed everything? Images of the large, soot-covered beasts shaking her mattress to pieces and playing tug of war with Gram's old sofa brought tears to her eyes.

Following Oliver closely into Ravyn's rooms, she instantly encountered complete pandemonium. Wind rushed at them as if trying to force them back from the room. On the floor the stoic bodyguard who had spoken so sharply about leaving Ravyn tethered to her, held a foaming-mouthed Ravyn, who thrashed wildly, as if something were attacking her from the inside while the wind rushed around them, teasing them and whipping her hair into tiny knots.

The other protector stood on guard with claws extended from his hands, scanning the room, preparing to shield the duo from whatever the mysterious windstorm blew into the room. So far, whatever led this attack seemed to be invisible. Eva couldn't help trembling at the thought of hellhounds springing forth from darkened corners of the room. Had the creatures found them here and managed to infiltrate the fortress?

Red hair waved, rising in the air as Delta stood like a Valkyrie in the middle of the maelstrom, ignoring the chaos, chanting as she circled, gesturing in the air with what to Eva looked like weeds in hand. It crossed Eva's mind that as much in awe as the witch had seemed over Eva's ability to see the invisible hellhounds, she spent a lot of time poking around empty air space.

Pushing through the violent storm to Ravyn's side,

Oliver knelt beside the two. "What the hell has happened?" he asked furiously. His hands clearly itched to fall upon the helpless woman, but he held them in check, perhaps fearing that whatever held her in its thrall might transfer to him, or his touch might make things worse for her.

Claws out and moving in closer to keep a tight guard on the incapacitated vampire, the shifter shouted, "We have no idea yet, sir. We were sitting in the lounge area here. She was, uh . . . asking Sebastian about his sexual conquest, then mid-sentence she fell over and started screaming. Delta heard and ran in and said something about an attack."

As Eva clutched the door frame, fighting the wind that threatened to push her off her feet, she felt an inexplicable, urgent tug in her chest, drawing her to Ravyn. Uncertain and still clutching the door with outstretched arms, she took a few steps closer as the invisible tightening chain urged her on. Without hesitation, she quickly covered the last few steps and knelt beside the woman, grasping her hands in both of hers, acting on instinct.

Pulling Eva closer to her, Ravyn opened her eyes, blood red as they silently screamed in pain and panic. "Help me, please," she begged Eva as red tears began to flow and her body continued convulsing violently.

Feeling Ravyn's pain and fear as if they were her own, Eva let them flow through her hands and into her, nearly stopping her own heart as they hit her. Not sure what she could do, but continuing to follow whatever was driving her, she worked to stifle the panic, fear, and pain that were overtaking her through Ravyn. Peace and calming, she attempted to focus back on the vampire, mentally urging Ravyn to calm down. Working on instincts to protect Ravyn, she continued to draw in the panic and feed back the calmness. She imagined a protective bubble settling in over the two of them, cradling them in safety and security.

The tug on her chest drew her closer to Ravyn until she was pushing the bodyguard half away in her own attempt for nearness. Leaning in close to Ravyn's ear, Eva whispered, "Drink," and pushed a wrist to Ravyn's mouth.

Still half-crazed in panic, Ravyn pulled her other hand free from Eva's and grasped the offering with both hands before extracting her fangs and biting deeply.

Grimacing, expecting pain, but surprised to find none, Eva shuddered as Ravyn drank deeply from her wrist. Hearing a roar of pain from Oliver, she broke eye contact with Ravyn and tore her eyes to Oliver as his own eyes darkened. In a segue state, Eva's eyes went back to Ravyn's as a wave of guilt flashed through her. Wide, clear eyes filled with guilt stared back at her, and Ravyn removed her mouth from Eva's wrist, pushing herself away as Sebastian also pulled and rolled away with Ravyn tucked protectively in his grasp. But was he protecting Ravyn from Eva or protecting Eva from her?

Like a flash, Oliver appeared at Eva's side, cradling her wrist where a few drops of blood still lingered. Snarling, he glared at a panting Ravyn, hidden half behind the shifter guard, who crouched on all fours as if the wolf had already pushed forward to protect his charge.

Still feeling as if in a dream, Eva found herself floating around the room, noting that unlike the rest of the house, this apartment had touches of homeyness around it. Despite the mess, a few plump pillows littered the floor, the sofa turned on its back now looked plush and comfortable. Paintings adorned the walls, and the unmade bed wasn't utilitarian gray, but filled with colors and textures. Eva's attention floated back to Oliver and the wrath emanating from him like the heat from a fireplace and hot enough to burn. Grasping his face, she forced him to look at her, knowing that his misplaced anger wasn't with her.

"Hey, hey, it's okay," she whispered to him.

Oliver's eyes regained focus on her, and a horrified look spread across his face as he regained control of the hot anger coursing through him.

"Oh, God, I'm so sorry." Looking from Ravyn to Eva, he begged forgiveness from both.

"I hate to interrupt all this going on," Delta began with an all-encompassing wave of her hand, "but in case you guys didn't notice, we have some serious shit going on." Ignoring the exasperated looks everyone in the room sent her way, the witch continued. "That was clearly another attack on Ravyn. A thread similar to what connects her to Eva is the culprit, only this one isn't connected. It's trying really hard to connect, though. Whatever is on the other end really wants Ravyn, and it's attempting to mimic the magic between the two." Glancing at Eva, she added, "Clearly unsuccessful due to previous claims."

"Thank you, Delta, for fighting it off," said a breathless Ravyn, pushing the wolf away as she stood wobbly on her own feet.

Oliver lent a hand to raise Eva off the ground as well but neglected to release his grip on her. Finding she didn't mind, Eva allowed herself to lean into Oliver, basking in his strength, but also finding the terror that had engulfed him.

"That wasn't me," Delta admitted. "All I was able to do was find it and see what it was doing. It was testing the thread between the two of you, basically prodding at you to find a weakness and attach to you. Eva was the one who basically fought it off, strengthening the bond between you both even more. It was like watching a protective shield going up. Whatever or whoever controls that thread knows that you two are attached, and I think it's trying to break the attachment and replace it with its own link to you.

"I'm just guessing here. I've not seen anything like this before. I mean realistically, it could also be after Eva and indirectly attacking Ravyn to get to Eva, but my gut is telling me it's after Ravyn. Eva could be considered collateral damage." Delta no longer spoke to the group but appeared to be talking aloud as she figured things out.

"Was it witch magic or some other kind?" questioned Oliver.

Eva agreed that was a good question. Was a witch searching and attacking or was it something else?

*Something like her?* she considered with unease.

"Definitely a witch," Delta answered with confidence, before amending, "Definitely magic; however, it doesn't necessarily mean that someone isn't paying a witch for the work. And it could have been a witch who called up the hellhounds; at this point, anything is possible." Her head flipped in a double take to Eva. "Uh, Eva, you're glowing again, even brighter than before."

Twisting and turning her hands and forearms, Eva looked from them to Oliver in disbelief. Upon seeing her white limbs glowing brightly from her fingers and hands up through her wrists and above her elbows, fading under her tank top, she whispered, "Enlightening."

"Actually, it is." Delta scrutinized the glow and looked from Oliver to Ravyn. "I think Eva boosted Ravyn during the attack, and I think she's drawing from Oliver now. How are you feeling now and before the attack?" She directed her questions to Eva.

"Super energized before I put my hands on Ravyn. That's why I did it and why I, uh . . . gave her my wrist. I felt a surge, and it just felt right. Like it was something I was supposed to do."

"Hmm. Driven by instinct maybe? Protection or self-preservation?"

"Afterward, I felt tired for a few seconds, but when Oliver touched me, I surged again. To be honest, I want to run around the room as fast as I can or jump on the bed and touch the ceiling." Eva gestured toward the bed, wondering if it was as comfortable as the one she'd been sleeping in or Oliver's? As the master of the house, surely his was more comfortable. Would he let her lie in it and test out the theory? Maybe she could lie in all the beds in his home and test out their comfort level? Did a vampire need a comfortable bed? Did they sleep in beds or coffins?

Her mind raced, peppered by question upon question. "I feel like I could climb a mountain or hell, even jump a mountain. And my mind can't slow down; it just keeps spinning and spinning." Waving her hands to articulate her point, she stopped mid-wave to study them, as if the appendages were somehow new to her. And they were; sort of, anyway.

What she couldn't say was that she didn't want Oliver to let go of her or to let go of the energy pulsating from him. It was all she could do just to stand there and not lean into him until his arms caught her up and held her tightly, filling her from head to toe in his delicious energy. She admitted, "I'm not really feeling like myself right now."

"You sound like a rechargeable battery. Taking energy in and letting it out, only you're not using electricity." Tapping her finger on her mouth Delta, considered it all. "Interesting,"

Horrified, Eva asked, "Am I some sort of parasite?" The glowing dimmed as she stared at her hands in horror.

"No, no." Delta seemed to consider it, apparently not noticing Eva's horror. "Neither Boss Man nor Ravyn seemed harmed by this exchange . . . well, possible exchange. In fact, it clearly helped Ravyn in

214

this instance."

Oliver shook his head and shrugged, as if the exchange hadn't affected him at all. Eva continued to resist the urge to pull the man holding her even closer, wrapping herself in him like a blanket of comforting, sexed-up, snapping, sparkling energy. He would be horrified. Ugh, it was horrifying; her thoughts were starting to alliterate! *Focus.*

"We're still working with hypothetical situations. I think if what I'm seeing is correct, it's more of a symbiotic exchange, perhaps mutualism, but we don't understand much about what's occurring. Reminder, people: it's all conjecture until . . . well, until it's not. Exchanges of power potentially are positive to all the parties involved, and I'm not certain if you keep any of the power for yourself, or just enough for survival."

"These threads, these bonds need to be broken now," Oliver demanded, not noticing the hurt that surged though Eva. How could he act like she was a parasite, after Delta just said she wasn't? Was the idea of having a single thread to her so repulsive that he would endanger them all by having it destroyed? Did he even consider it would leave Ravyn vulnerable to whatever had attacked her? And maybe she'd misread the room, but she sort of thought Oliver had some interest or attraction to her, or at least thought enough of her to not recoil in disgust.

"Oliver," Ravyn said gently, "destroying it will just leave us all vulnerable. Right now, the only protection we may have are these bonds. If I have a soul still, that parasite was trying to attach itself to it. I feel that deeply."

"Yes, Eva can protect you. But who is protecting *her*? In this whole scenario, she's the only one apparently vulnerable! She's the only one who's nearly died from a hellhound attack. She's the only one whose home has been destroyed." Oliver's anger simmered in his voice as well as the air around him, so thick and heavy it nearly slapped Eva in the face. Unexpected relief flowed through her when she realized it was concern he felt about her, not disgust, but it also made her question why his opinion of her mattered so much to her.

Sebastian interjected with more than a tinge of anger and a hint of fear that he tried unsuccessfully to keep hidden. "Yes, but your *friend* Ravyn paid for your—for our—protection, and quite the sum, if I'm not mistaken. It has been promised to her. An oath was sworn." Looking toward Eva with a sneer that nearly crumbled her, he added, "We don't even know what kind of creature she is. Clearly, she's been in Ravyn's head. She could be lying about everything and is part of whatever plan there is to get to Ravyn. You're acting like some love-struck, smitten boy who can't see past the tits in front of his face."

Oliver's eyes instantly went black, so quickly that Eva couldn't even react. With a roar, he leaped the few feet separating them, grasping a snarling, now choking Sebastian by the throat. "You dare threaten her? You dare question my loyalty?" Lifting him from the ground, Oliver snarled with fangs extended and enraged black eyes filled with blood as he held the man's life in his hand. Kicking and thrashing, Sebastian's hands formed claws, fighting to rip Oliver's hands away from his throat.

With a shriek, Eva froze as Oliver tackled the larger, broader shifter with his lithe form. This couldn't end well, but for whom she wasn't sure. Shaking off the initial shock, she looked from Ravyn to Delta, speechless in her hope that one of the two would end this standoff before it turned deadly. Delta used the time to examine the split ends of her long hair and Ravyn simply rolled her eyes at the men.

"Sometimes they like to posture and pull this crap," Ravyn explained casually to Eva. Then, changing her tone to a near roar unlike Eva could have imagined from the woman, she screamed, *"Boys! Stop! Now!* You are frightening our guest and new friend Eva. Sebastian, quit spouting nonsense and quit provoking the man who quite literally signs your paycheck. I don't need you to speak for me. And Ollie, stop acting like a child ready to tear anyone apart who touches his toys."

Smiling apologetically at Eva, Ravyn shrugged, her tone once again calm. "Not that you're a toy, dear. I just like comparisons; it makes a monologue punchier, if I do say so." The actress gave a nod to her chosen profession.

Snapping her fingers at the other bodyguard and baring her teeth, Ravyn ordered, "Jake, take Thor for a walk around the perimeter to check things out and cool off. Put a leash on him if necessary." She lifted a chair with ease despite her small frame, sitting it back upright for her to sink down into as she raised a weary hand to her own head. When Sebastian moved to take a step toward her, she waved him off and snapped her fingers. "Now. I can't be around you when you're like this, and I'm fine. Jake, get him out of here. I dislike repeating myself."

"Yes, ma'am, and I'm not Jake," he grumbled under his breath, moving closer to the now still men, but not quite within striking distance, smoothing his hands uneasily down his khaki pants, uncomfortable with the idea of getting between the two.

"Oliver, come sit with me," Eva suggested, still feeling his anger. Although nothing like the initial blast that had caught her off-guard, it still simmered and snapped through her veins, waiting to once again boil over. Glancing down at the oversized sofa, which still lay on its back with cushions strewn about, she amended, "Maybe you can help me set up the sofa first, then we'll sit here and hear Delta out."

With another snarl, Oliver shoulder-checked Sebastian aside as he stomped toward the sofa. A low growl escaped the frustrated shifter as he left the room with Not-Jake after a long stare at Ravyn, who gestured again toward the door with her head and tense jaw that warned of a reckoning if he didn't listen.

Oliver picked the sofa up with ease, sitting it upright as well as another armless chair.

Eva dropped the cushions back in place, settled onto the edge of the sofa, and gestured for Oliver to join her, again keeping as much contact between them as possible while enjoying the feelings of comfort and protectiveness. She could feel Oliver relax against her, and the brush of him against her bare skin left her craving for more contact, more emotion. Biting the side of her cheek to ground herself, she allowed her hand to rest on his bare arm for a moment before it began moving almost of its own accord the length of his arm, enjoying the feel of his skin.

"I'm sorry," he whispered sincerely as black and red bled away from his dark blue eyes. "I don't . . . I normally don't lose control like that. My deepest apologies." Even if Eva hadn't been able to feel his shame and embarrassment through the link, the sincerity of his words was easily heard as he lowered his head. A part of her wondered if he'd apologized more tonight than he usually did. It struck her that he normally didn't do things he later regretted.

Delta let out a disgruntled noise and closed her eyes, rubbing her head as if warding off a headache. "By the goddess, if you would all just listen to me, we might actually get through what I've learned. I keep trying to sugar coat things, and it gets out of control. You three have a weird connection that is magnifying everyone's crap and causing all this craziness."

Another wave of the hand. Eyes still closed, she gestured toward Eva. "You're some sort of part-demon, part-human hybrid. Still working on the exact type, but it explains the fact that you can see hellhounds, and that you were born of a very human mother. Don't ask," she ordered. "I checked: her mother was human. Don't ask for more details. The details apparently bog us down, and I've had a very,

very long seventy-two hours. I've spent more time with my mother than I have since I was seven. I've looked through old books until my eyes bled. I've listened to my sister twitter on and once my day off went *kapuff*, my D and D group went on a raid without me—idiots—and all of them died. So, I really can't handle any more of anything from you all. Capiche?" Opening her eyes, the young witch examined them all, waiting for a sign of agreement.

Eva's mouth gaped open, then closed, then opened again.

Ravyn appeared to examine her in an appraising way and found her acceptable since she nodded.

"The d-devil really is in the details," Eva stammered, not sure what else to say, then deciding maybe, just maybe she'd misheard Delta or this was all some witchy slang she wasn't understanding, she asked, "A demon? So, you really think I'm a demon?"

They existed? Demons were a thing? Truly? Despite the earlier speculation, it hadn't truly sunk in that she might not be human.

"Oh, no, just half or less maybe. Probably your missing daddy was full or half. Probably full, to be honest. Halflings don't last down here, and nod to your gram that you stayed hidden for as long as you did. But I would most definitely say you've got some demon blood running through you. Just your healing ability alone puts you in the supernatural category, but the fact that you were bit by a hellhound and survived the hellfire so long with minimal treatment puts you firmly in the demon camp. And unless you're lying about seeing the hellhounds up close and personal," Delta reminded her, "like sees like." Turning over a fallen chair, the young witch moved it closer to the three before picking up a large, leather-bound book from a pile near the door.

Settling down in the chair with the ancient book on her lap, she wiggled her fingers before opening it to a book-marked page. "I'd narrowed it down to three, maybe four choices, but this little interaction just knocked a couple off the list. I'm down to one, I think. Yes, I'm fairly sure it's this one. Drum roll . . ." Delta ordered. When no one complied, she sighed and continued, without giving up the fanfare, "I think you're part succubus."

# CHAPTER SIXTEEN

*Hellman's is the demon's favorite mayo.*

Looking expectantly around, Delta appeared a little disappointed at the small group's lack of reaction. "Look, I still actually think it may have come straight from your father. We've just never been offered an opportunity to study half-demons. So, maybe it could be from your mother's side and it never activated, or perhaps unknown daddy's mother or father had some demon blood, but to be honest, it doesn't matter where it came from. I think when Ravyn gave you her blood . . ."

"My demonic blood," Ravyn spat out the words flatly, harshly, as if the idea that she'd infected a child with demon powers could destroy her. "My demonic blood awoke the genes that might have simply lain dormant and been passed down and slowly diluted out of existence. My existence and my blood have put her in danger."

"Well, yes. That's not quite how I would have phrased it, but yes, essentially that's what happened. But it's also what saved Eva's life." Clearly, Delta was uncomfortable attempting to comfort people.

"Ray, Ray," Oliver said the intimate sounding nickname softly, causing Eva's stomach to twist in pain at the tone.

"Ravyn, no matter what it did, you did it with the purest of intentions. You saved my life." Eva squeezed away from Oliver to lean forward and grasp Ravyn's hand. "I owe you my life."

"Assuming that your succubus powers didn't start to come in until you entered puberty, your grandmother would have made more attempts to hide what you were and possibly suppress your more succubus-like qualities."

Thoughtfully, Eva considered, "Gram did have a nasty concoction that I had to drink weekly after I started my period. I began having nightmares, and Gram acted as if it were a part of puberty. She always told me that it helped with cramps, hormones, Mother Nature, you know, but honestly, I just drank it. I didn't care, and I wouldn't win an argument with her, and we just do what our adults ask of us. The nightmares went away, and life went on. But after she passed, there was no one to make it, and my period wasn't really that bad, so I never really thought about figuring out what she'd made me. But," she pondered, "it would actually make sense, because it was after Gram's death that I started dreaming about Fala Ishto and her life."

"As well as her death," Ravyn added, still holding herself rigid with what felt like guilt as they unraveled the past.

"Right!" Delta's voice rose in excitement. "If you were suppressed, so was the thread. It was there all along, but just unable to be explored and traveled. In your dreams, you were more open and susceptible to exploring the realm. But were you feeding from her? A succubus needs to feed, and Ravyn should have noticed some energy loss, unless her being a vampire somehow counteracts it all." She paused to consider the possibilities. "What we're seeing is unprecedented. I wouldn't even know what to reference to see if this is the norm or an entirely new event. Demons aren't exactly forthcoming on this plane."

"Even when I fed Eva on the trip here, I never noticed any diminishing strength, and she was definitely being powered by me," Oliver interjected.

"Interesting." Delta ran her finger down the page, scanning the handwritten words in the old tome. "*Sex*! I mean, assuming you've had sex and all that . . ." She blushed as Eva nodded slowly. "That's like prime feeding or energy gathering for a succubus demon."

"Dear Lord, this could explain so many awkward encounters . . ." Eva trailed off, not wanting to offer up too much in the way of explanation. She chose her words carefully, popping a gust of air out of her mouth, completely aware that Oliver had gone tense. "Yeah, awkward would definitely be the word I would use." Mentally, she added, *and unsatisfying.*

For Eva, sex often ended unsatisfactorily when the man she was with claimed exhaustion and fell asleep immediately after the deed. No cuddles or little kisses, no lingering caresses. Nope, they acted as if they'd run a marathon: rolled over, held her if she were lucky, and were snoring within minutes.

Meanwhile, Eva lay there irritated, lacking, and wondering why there couldn't be more, but powered up enough to run her own marathon. Definitely orgasms were possible—she'd practiced that one enough on her own—but the partners she picked seemed to skip that part for her. Sneaking out past sleeping men had become her standard operating procedure, despite the fact they never woke up after the deed. And when they did awaken hours and hours later, they would call begging for more, for another chance, giving excuses. They never understood what happened: too much to drink, too tired, overworked. Please, please.

*Ugh.*

"And unsatisfying for me," Eva ended the carefully worded explanation of her dolefully inadequate sex life. "Still, I kept trying, and I'm not going to lie; one-night stands are much less headache than dating." Covering her face with her hands, she let out an embarrassed laugh. "Gosh, I'm pathetic, and now you all officially know more about me than anyone else alive."

"Tit for tat, little one." Ravyn reminded her that all of her own life and vulnerabilities had been laid open for Eva as well as anyone who read her novels.

"Oh, my!" Eva's eyes widened. "I'm so sorry. I guess I didn't really say that. Everything is just out there. If I'd known you were a real person, I would have never—"

"Honestly, not everything." Waving her hand, Ravyn reminded her, "I waited three novels to even consider who you might be."

"Did you ever enter anyone's dreams or memories?" Delta asked curiously. "Like the men you were with? Or . . . laying it all out there, did the men survive the encounter with you unharmed?"

"My God, I didn't kill anyone!" Not that some of them didn't deserve it for the mediocre encounters and days of harassment for a repeat. "And their dreams? I doubt it, but I'm not sure how I would even know."

"Maybe being only part succubus means that entering dreams isn't necessary," Oliver offered. "Or perhaps she does, in fact, feed from Ravyn through their link and doesn't need nourishment that way. But honestly, I don't know that any of that matters. Eva clearly isn't harming anyone. Any demonic qualities that might call for her to be put down don't apply here."

"Whoa, put down? Was that a possibility?" Gram really had been wise to put all the protections on her and the house if that was the conclusion others would jump to. Not a single part of Eva felt demonic or dangerous; it was crazy to think that others might want her dead just for existing. Sliding into one person's dreams and years of overly obsessed sex partners hardly seemed a crime worthy of death.

"Well, yes and no. Typically, the paranormal community looks down on demons running amok and causing problems. A little mischief is okay, but most don't stop at that. And to be honest, like Delta said, we don't have a lot of knowledge about half-demons. As much as they come to Earth, they don't often leave a lot of evidence. Dammit! I wish Malth were here. If anyone could be considered a half-demon expert, it would be him. And I have no idea where he's currently holed up."

"Well, what about you and Ravyn? Aren't vampires 'demonic'?" She added air quotes in case her sarcastic tone wasn't obvious to the others.

"The paranormal community has elected representatives and leaders that we call the Faction. The Faction is fairly young, but attempts are being made to give us rules to live by and standards to follow, an accord if you will. Since the faction signed the accord, we—all of us, including vampires—have rules of conduct to follow. Do no harm isn't necessarily a rule; it's more like, if you do harm, stay under the radar. Demons aren't a part of the accord and so we, as a community, police them as necessary."

"Oh, wow, Oliver, I'm thinking you missed your calling with that answer. Are you sure you're not in politics instead of security?" When Oliver remained silent, Eva thumped her own head. "You're involved in the politics and policing, aren't you? Of course you are."

"People, focus," Delta ordered. "Eva, I think your grandmother put the spells and protections on you to hide you from our kind, the supernatural. But you're safe with us. She may have been worried about demons searching you out, but honestly, I don't think they would be concerned enough with you.

"I don't have Malthazar's apparent expertise," she added sarcastically, "but I can research and read a book. You're part human and part lower demon. And that lower demon part might have only been noticeable due to Ravyn's blood activating it. You're not a threat to them, and you're not of use to them. And in a pinch, due to Ravyn's blood, she could lay a claim on you that they couldn't supersede. So, what I'm saying, is I think you're safe. Safe at least from us, and whatever your granny feared." Hesitating, she continued, "I think whoever sent the hellhounds after you did so because of your connection to Ravyn and for no other reason.

"In my professional opinion, we should remove all the layers of magic at least down to Ravyn's thread, and we can examine it closer." Delta closed the book firmly and met the eyes of each of the three sitting across from her. "It's obviously your choice, but that's my suggestion."

Eva felt the confidence rolling off the witch; she felt Ravyn's calmness and Oliver's concern. The mixed-up conglomeration of emotions empowered her as she recognized them for what they were. Perhaps this was what she was missing. Gram had meant well, but until now, Eva had never stayed the night away from her home due to the protective spells in place. Surely, Gram had never planned for Eva to live her entire life in chains. Perhaps she'd planned to remove them as Eva matured and they determined the next course of action. Had Gram known what Eva was? Or did she just have a sense of the danger she might face? Eva would never know, and she would never know what Gram's long-term solution would have been, but she knew what hers had to be. From this day forward, the choices would be hers and hers alone.

Nodding with firm resolution while her skin danced in anticipation, she said, "Let's do this. Let's break these chains."

# CHAPTER SEVENTEEN

*Oh no! I'm under a tack!*

*H*elplessness engulfed Oliver, followed closely by frustration that he had nothing to offer, no way to help either of the women before him. Never had he felt as useless as he had when they entered that room. Instead of remaining rational, he'd reverted to anger to cover his inability to help. Eva, however, had been magnificent and fearless, immediately dropping to Ravyn's side to help her. Not even knowing what to do, she'd trusted her instincts to guide her. Despite being thrown into an unknown world, she was seemingly taking it all in stride. Of course, coming that close to death might have something to do with her openness and willingness to accept their world and its inhabitants.

The best he could do was focus on the things he could handle. His own security had been shredded, obliterated by this attack. The facts were clear and didn't need to be stated, but of course he said it anyway.

The wards had failed, and failed badly.

Delta needed to contact her coven and find out

what had gone wrong with the wards and protections on his home; in his mood, he couldn't trust himself to speak to them. Once he'd caught his breath and ensured that everyone was safe, it struck him that owning a paranormal security firm meant that his home was the most protected place to be. It was humbling to realize it wasn't, and that some sort of dark magic had been able to penetrate the extensive and rather expensive spells put in place to attack an unwanted guest. Spells that had been purchased for an exorbitant price from members of Delta's rather powerful coven. In a short and clipped tone, he informed Delta that he expected her coven to immediately determine what had happened and to fix it.

Delta admitted the failure but argued that this was the result of a combined attack by unknown entities. Witch magic clearly laced the attack, but there was also unrecognizable magic intertwined with the former. Dark, black, blood magic, and it had dissipated before Delta could even begin to trace its origins. The sacrifice had been huge for such a strong spell, she whispered to Oliver, who knew without her saying that the wards hadn't been brought down by an animal sacrifice. This had cost someone—or perhaps even several someones—their life. And for what? Just to prove that Ravyn wasn't safe? That nothing could keep them out? It was a futile waste of life just to prove a point.

After Eva's adamant agreement that spells and protections needed to be removed from her person, the process was anything but quick. The intricate magic that had been woven around her acted like a living, sentient being. Again working on assumptions, Delta admitted that the magic had layers upon it, probably placed and reinforced, and shored up and patched repeatedly by Eva's grandmother during the years she'd lived. Her death may have added another layer, and then Eva's own part succubus magic that had been suppressed for years most likely had merged its way in as it fought to gain its own freedom. Within it all, the original thread of magic connecting Eva and Ravyn was raveled among the oldest of the disarray.

Even without understanding the exact mess of magic, Oliver did grasp that undoing it safely would take time. He understood time. Always too much, too little, or not enough, but regardless, it always passed.

As Oliver vetted one of his most trusted employees, Delta worked alone on the task of unraveling the magical chaos. Additionally, her ability to literally see magic was an anomaly that few, if any, other living witches currently possessed. Working alone, and occasionally consulting with Hecate for guidance, meant that the task took longer due to limits on Delta's energy and own magic. Acceptable, since outside of his company, Oliver found few he could trust explicitly, and Delta without conjecture had told them there was no one capable of helping her even if she wanted to waste precious time explaining what she saw. Time. Always time.

Ravyn and her entourage left within hours to go back to California. "Too much to do, to sit and wait," she'd announced. "After all, this thread has been attached for eighteen years. What's a few more days? Call me when you're ready for me."

Once they left, Oliver felt he could breathe easier. Never before had he felt relief when Ravyn left. Lonely, yes, but not relieved. The big house just felt so damn crowded with those extra bodies in it. And despite the cooling off period, his temper flared every time his supposed good friend and partner Sebastian came into the room. Even the thought of Bash made Oliver's temper raise.

Oliver also suspected Ravyn absolutely hated the waiting game, and more than likely she knew the tension between the head of her security detail and him needed both time and distance. At least in LA, she could be back on set, working and keeping her time and mind occupied.

A few days after Ravyn had left, and countless layers and threads of magic had been removed, Delta announced that she needed an entire twenty-four hours off to regroup, recharge, and refresh away from them. She'd spent all of her days and nights at Oliver's compound, taking up residence in another guest suite she'd long ago claimed as her own. Alternating between studying, tracing and removing magical threads, and resting, following up with eating copious amounts of food, she needed a true break.

Oliver suspected that meant playing that

*Dungeons and Dragons* game she always talked about, but he didn't ask because he simply didn't care to hear the answer. He pretended to abruptly consider her "request," but his heart sped up at the news.

Twenty-four uninterrupted hours alone with Eva.

As Delta walked out the door to be driven to her apartments in her coven's home, Oliver began composing an email to send out, letting his people know that outside of an emergency such as maiming or death, he would be unavailable for the day. A quick amendment added the exception that if anyone heard even a whisper from or about Malthazar to let him know immediately. Going forward, he needed to be able to find the half-demon no matter where he was in the world or how deep in a mission he went. When he caught back up with Malth, he needed to re-explain the importance of being able to contact each other when needed, especially as partners in Malth's endeavors. Neither Delta nor Bash went so far off the grid that he couldn't send out an SOS signal or vice versa.

Another text was sent to the standby security detail to prepare in case the rest of his plan came to fruition, a mix of work and pleasure.

Oliver then went in search of Eva, finding her in the entertainment room, lounging sideways across a theater seat, reading a novel while music played softly over the speakers.

She took his breath away. For a moment, all he could do was watch her quietly after he'd slipped into the room with her. Her face was pale, but slightly glowing as it was most days now. Oliver suspected she drew from him without realizing it and surprisingly, the idea that he kept her sustained pleased him.

Eva's hair was still damp from washing, and the waves just barely skimmed the tops of her shoulders, peeking out from another one of Delta's borrowed tank tops.

Rubbing his chest, he wondered if Delta had removed the thread binding them. She never explicitly said which ones had been removed and his was so new that it seemed likely that it had been one of the first to go. With or without the magic tether, he'd been drawn to Eva since he first laid eyes on her in the coffee shop just a week ago. Sometimes, Oliver thought she felt the same way, but Eva apparently walled up her emotions better than a master vampire.

Sitting in the theater seat at her feet, Oliver plucked the novel from her hands and studied the paranormal title and cover while she smiled at him. Raising an eyebrow he questioned, "Not enough magic and supernatural mystery in your life currently?"

Shrugging one of her tantalizing shoulders while giving him a crooked grin, Eva replied, "I mean, I guess I do have a type, and I have to stay on top of the competition. Keep up with the writing trends—solely for research purposes, of course."

"Of course," Oliver smoothly agreed, loving the sound of her teasing tone. Despite the fact that her other books weren't inspired by Ravyn's life story, she still created popular works that her fan base loved when they weren't demanding a sequel to their favorite series. The fact that the mundane world ate up anything paranormal didn't surprise him. After all, he did enjoy the movies and shows himself; even if they weren't always entirely accurate, they were enjoyable. Her new insight into his world would grow her writing by leaps and bounds, and he suspected after she finished her latest novel, a demon hero or heroine might make an appearance. If nothing else, Eva had the ability to bounce back and embrace the changes in the world around her.

Breaking eye contact first, Eva looked past him toward the door, shifting positions as if preparing to get up. "Is Delta ready to get started again?"

"No, Delta is going AWOL today. With permission, of course," Oliver added, wondering what it would take for her to not break eye contact every time it was made, or not go running from a room when it was just the two of them. Holding onto her feet seemed desperate, but despite knowing that, he still casually laid a hand on them, hoping to still her before she left the room.

"Not much of a rule breaker, are you, Mr. Patrick?" she teased with a laugh. "Well, good for her. Although that doesn't leave me much to do except read and, to be honest, I'm sort of getting tired of that. I may even have to break down and write some more." She said this as if she wasn't spending most of her downtime typing away on her laptop in corners of various rooms.

Oliver's blood began pumping faster at the teasing tone. *How could everything she says sound so sexy?* A plan began to formulate, as he realized that today had just become the perfect day to both spend some time with Eva as well as see if their enemies were still lurking about. The wards had been quiet, not even a sizzle from an unassuming animal, but perhaps that was just a ploy to lull them into complacency. "Want to get out of here?"

"Do I ever!" To prove her point, she swung her feet free from his hand, aiming for the ground but instead nearly hitting him in the face. He caught the offending appendages before they could bump him.

"Okay, I get it. The whole gilded prison bit." Holding onto her ankles longer than necessary to stop their momentum, he noticed the happy expression on her face turn to a slightly guiltier look.

"I'm sorry"—she put her feet carefully and firmly on the floor—"I can't imagine that my barging in here and staying is all that great for your vampire bachelor life. And I'm not ungrateful. You've given me a pretty great place to stay, but yeah, it would be nice to get outside anywhere and see anything at all. These walls are great and all, but they're still the same four walls."

"Walls worth a few million," he teased back, "and you hardly barged in here. I brought you here after you were nearly killed under my watch. And before you grab onto that with both hands, you're not here out of any sense of guilt. It hasn't been so bad having you around."

"You just like having someone to play board games with."

Groaning, he retorted, "I'm sure I'll beat you at Scrabble one of these rounds."

"Not if I can help it. What kind of wordsmith would I be if I lost at Scrabble?"

Hesitating, she asked, "I don't know all the facts about what you and Ravyn are. But are you okay to go out in the daylight? I mean, you must be if you asked me to get out of the house today. And I don't know; I always thought vampires must sleep during the day or something, but you, you're like a machine. I don't even know if you ever sleep."

Nodding, Oliver explained, "Yes, it all depends on a vampire's age and who made them, and how old that creator was. But popular belief has garbled some things—or maybe it was intentional. A younger vampire can actually handle more daylight than an older vamp. That's often why an older vampire makes a companion and then discards them every few hundred years. I can still function quite well during most of the daylight hours, but every decade takes minutes from us, centuries take hours. While I'm weakest during a few hours of each day, Ravyn is old enough that any amount of sunlight can be detrimental to her. That's why she picks and chooses her work so carefully. Thankfully, people this era are more accepting of a sunlight allergy than they were in the past.

"The early years were rough," he admitted. "Even when traveling, you always needed a plan for those hours and a backup plan for the plan to keep your creator safe. Not that Ravyn really needed it. After surviving a millennium, she really didn't need my help, but helping her gave me a sense of purpose, a purpose I needed in those days. Nowadays, sometimes if I choose to, I could nap or recharge during the hours I can't be out, but mostly I'm just weaker than normal, but a little sunscreen and sunglasses still allow me out at most hours."

He'd left a lot out; some secrets just weren't his to tell despite how honest he wanted to be with Eva. Hesitatingly, he added, "A lot of the myth and lore are put out just so people feel safer. No one wants a creature of darkness who can enter a home uninvited at any time of day.

"But it's not just a simple chance to go out and get some fresh air. I mean, that's a bonus for you, but maybe we can get a team together and do a little recon and see if there's anything outside these walls." It was only sort of a lie. Teams had kept the area secure in approximately a ten-mile radius outside the perimeter established around his home. Layers upon layers. All traffic and any camera connected to the Wi-Fi within even a wider radius was fed into his offices in the city, where they were manned day and night by yet another team. If anyone was in the area, they would know long before they could physically get close to his home or Eva. This was a chance to get out and spend time with Eva away from the house.

Wrinkling her forehead, Eva considered his words before questioning, "Would I be . . . are you wanting me to be bait? Bait to draw them in or out?"

Tapping down the need to tell her it would be perfectly safe, but uncertain if she would simply want to spend uninterrupted time with him, Oliver worked carefully to choose his words.

What he wanted was to spend time with her. What he wanted was to keep her safe inside the walls to his compound. But what he wanted wasn't for the best if they ever wished to move forward.

"I dislike the word 'bait,' but yes, I think if anything is waiting out there, you may draw it out, just test the waters, so to speak. Everything is quiet, very quiet in LA with Ravyn and her team." This bothered him as well as Sebastian. First the constant bombardment of gifts, as well as the physical manifestation of magic, then complete silence. Whatever was out there, it was waiting. Waiting for what, they didn't know, but the waiting was draining. And when you were drained, edgy, and tired you made mistakes. This enemy could be waiting for them to make a mistake, but still it seemed to be better to go on the offense and try to draw it out early on their own ground.

"I can have a team ready to go within an hour." Oliver bit back the guilt over already notifying his security to prep despite not knowing if she would agree. They were probably ready to roll out in fifteen, but she didn't need to know that. "We can go out, get some coffee, shop a bit. Whatever you want. If all goes well, you won't even realize the team is about and if it goes really well, we can get our hands on the witch who's attacking us."

Oliver watched Eva consider his words. Despite all the security in place, he still half-hoped she would deny his suggestion and stay safely within the fortified walls. Layers upon layers of security, he reminded himself. Teams scattered throughout the enlarged perimeter, prepared to leap into action if anything appeared out of the norm.

Nodding with a half-smile still etched with concern, she said, "Let me change, and we can go do whatever. I'm game for anything. Better to be on the offense than constant defense. Who knows? Maybe if we're lucky, we can end this today."

Optimism. Oliver swore her trust in him wouldn't be misplaced. If she was willing to face her fear, he was willing to stand beside her and protect her.

He noticed she was still wearing pajama bottoms. Pajamas covered in tiny flying dragons that clung tightly to her thighs, clearly belonging to Delta, he thought with more than a little guilt. He hadn't been a very good host; he simply wasn't very good at thinking of such things. He owed Delta a huge Christmas bonus this year; actually, it might be a summer solstice bonus if he really wanted to stay on her good side.

"Coffee and shopping then? We could even scrounge up some late lunch or an early dinner. We'll stay away from the city and stick with a few smaller areas just to feel things out," he proposed, acting as if he hadn't already mentally planned a route that kept them circling about well inside an extended perimeter.

# CHAPTER EIGHTEEN

*There are no such things as vampires, unless you count Dracula.*

Within the hour, Eva and Oliver met back up in the kitchen. Eva's wavy hair was now dry, secured back on one side with a clip. She had the backpack she seemed to carry everywhere and wore another borrowed black (of course) hooded sweatshirt and jeans that Oliver suspected Delta had swiped from her sister's closet, as the two sisters were the same size. Delta's complaints about clothes and their textures had included a tirade cataloging the uncomfortable stiffness of denim, a product apparently created by Satan himself.

Eva immediately zoned in on the one misfit of the garage filled with shiny black vehicles. The lone stand-out had been brought in the same day they'd arrived and, in fact, had been towed then pushed by two shifters into the spot it currently sat.

"Gram's Suburban made it here? Is this how we got here? I never even thought to ask."

Oliver noted tons of shock and awe in Eva's voice; after driving the vehicle, he felt the same.

"I just assumed it was destroyed. I remember so little about the trip . . ." Eva's voice trailed off as she grinned at the old SUV.

"It made it a few miles from here and then died. By that time, my men had convoyed up with us, so we rode the rest of the way in a different vehicle. Later, they towed it back and replaced quite a few parts, and got you a new battery, as well as tires." The trip had been rough on the old SUV and if it had been his own, it would have been retired to the junkyard, but something told him even then that it meant something to Eva. Oliver's heart swelled as Eva looked at him with shiny, bright eyes. It had been the right choice to fix it up.

Shrugging in a way that he hoped conveyed no problem, he placed an arm on her waist and led her toward the modern-day tank they were going to take out for the day.

"And new parts. I can pay you back. I have plenty of money." She seemed embarrassed. Oliver was getting better at reading her, he thought, strangely smug in the knowledge. "It just wasn't a priority since I barely drive it, and usually Jackson takes care of things when he's back visiting."

His ego took a hit with those words. "Well, Jackson won't have to now," he clipped out, tightening his grip on her waist, feeling the flush of jealousy wash through him. "And the money is nothing." Despite the extensive background check that had been done on her best friend, who apparently had been born of a witch and was off serving his country on classified missions, Oliver couldn't stop the sting that came when Eva referred to him with such fondness.

Opening the passenger door of the monstrous, armor-plated SUV, he once again assisted her into her seat. Sunglasses in place, he opened the garage doors with a remote control, then rolled down the long driveway. Oliver knew that as they entered the roadway, two other vehicles with three men each would fall into place as a part of today's orchestrated event. One in front and one behind and if all went as planned, Eva wouldn't know they were there. And if she did, either something was going terribly wrong or his men needed additional training.

"I don't mean to sound ungrateful; I just do miss my own things," Eva admitted as they drove. "I've gone from never, ever spending the night away from home, to now not even being sure if I have a home to go back to." She'd immediately opened the tinted window to let in the fresh late spring air and sunshine. Oliver removed another pair of sunglasses from his console and offered them to her.

"Is this okay? Not too much light? And thanks!" Lifting the sunglasses, she slid them on her face and let the sunlight dance across her face.

"The sunlight is fine. We've passed the hours I need to remain inside." Taking a breath, he added quietly, "Your home is being set to rights." Oliver had hesitated to tell her, despite knowing how much she cherished her childhood home. Somehow, Eva seemed reluctant to accept any help, although in reality none of this could be done alone. Things like her vehicle and house were easy; nothing money wouldn't solve.

"A crew repaired what they could, removed what they couldn't. Your belongings were set as right as they could be." He shuddered, remembering the size of the holes in and out of the house. The hellhounds must have run shoulder to shoulder trying to fit through the doorways in their eagerness to reach her. "I've had witches set protective spells and alarms around the perimeter again, not as specific as your grandmother's but acceptable until you decide what to do next." Cringing in memory, he continued, "Unfortunately, your clothes were all destroyed. Apparently, hellhound piss burns holes in whatever it touches." This also verified that the hellhounds had been after her; it didn't clear up, though, whether or not they were in league with whomever was after Ravyn.

Eva sat so silently that Oliver feared he'd made a terrible mistake in telling her. Finally, after several long moments, she turned to him with tear-filled eyes. His heart dropped. Had he messed up? Why did it seem like he never knew what to do around Eva?

"Thank you so much, Oliver. I know I'm not good at saying it, because I've been alone for so long. But thank you for fixing all of this. No one has ever done so much for me."

Thankfully, she wasn't angry and had seen it as the gift that it was.

"It's not all fixed yet, but you're welcome. And I do feel a bit of responsibility in showing them the doorway in."

A laugh escaped her as she lay her head in her

hands. "And hellhound piss! Really? That's just ridiculously disrespectful. Of all the things to do, of course they do that. As if just destroying my home wasn't enough."

Eva fiddled with the radio, syncing it to her phone, and the playlist filled the background. Leaning back into her seat, she caressed the supple leather armrest, admitting, "I may have to spring for one of these. As much as I love the old Suburban, this is a much better ride. And maybe after . . . after Delta is finished, I'll be able to travel and take road trips like I always imagined."

"You think?" Oliver asked, raising a questioning eyebrow. Even though her books sold well enough, he wasn't certain if her budget would allow for the customized vehicle. He hadn't scrutinized her bank accounts during his investigation, and at this point, it was no longer necessary or appropriate. Maybe she could afford it if she skipped the bullet proofing and specialized satellite link up. "It's a nice ride," he agreed, "and one of my favorites."

"Sure beats a horse-drawn carriage, I bet." This was quite seriously spoken, nearly a question, but Oliver could hear the hint of amusement hiding behind the tone.

"Okay, now, I'm not that old."

"If you say so," Eva continued in her teasing tone. Oliver liked seeing this side of her. At his home, people were always around, magic spells needing broken, security issues and questions for his job. "So, why security? What made you go into that?"

"It makes a lot of money," Oliver replied flatly. Then flashing a smile, he continued, "And it's something I'm good at. Years ago, before, I attended engineering school. I like to build and create things, so I always kept my hands in the thick of things. Then at some point, I heard whispers of the military creating circuits, and a crazy new idea called a computer. I managed to persuade a few key players to teach me about them. Then I continued to keep up with them. If they learned it, they taught me. If they built it, I knew how and why.

Before that time, I'd also done some moonlighting as muscle and run with a few crowds of questionable character. I could often talk people out of causing trouble, and that was without compulsion, and I didn't have to rely on the old muscle part of it as much. I hired a few others, mostly shifters and vampires, then hired a few more. Eventually, I focused more on the logistics, setup, and cyber features, combining the two into a few viable businesses. And hey, like I said, it makes a lot of money."

"I thought the truly rich found it crass to talk about money?"

"I was born working class; of course I'm crass." This was nice; it had been too long since he'd had conversations regarding things other than work. "And writing? Why did you decide to start putting everything down on paper?" he asked, curious to learn what motivated her.

"Sometime after Gram passed, and most likely after that herbal mixture got out of my system, I began having the most vivid dreams about a little girl growing up in ancient times along the Nile, and progressively intense dreams that followed her throughout her life. My therapist at the time, and yes, several therapists over my lifetime . . . Childhood loss, losing parents; it's supposed to be helpful, and it was."

Pausing, she went on, "I'm getting all off track. She suggested I start writing the dreams down, sort of an additional journaling assignment, I suppose. They like having their assignments and love journaling all around. Perhaps she thought it would offer insight for me, or it was a secret reflection about how I was dealing and feeling. So I did, then I started adding in details. Remembered to fill out the who, what, when, where, and how we learned in elementary school. Took a creative writing course at the community college, then another, then dropped out of school all together. Took a break. Found on-line writing communities, then by luck my gram's old friend reached out to see how I was doing. Serendipity, kismet, fate, chance; whatever it was, she happened to be a literary agent—retired, but still willing to see what she could do for me. And here we are." Spreading her arms, she explained, "Writer extraordinary, magically linked to a vampire or two, with a few hellhounds thrown in the mix. All a part of my ten-year plan."

"Sounds like the makings of another bestselling novel."

"Maybe, if I survive it all. I mean, I'm having to borrow clothes from a witch ten years younger than me and a lot snarkier. I really don't have the snark to pull off Delta's wardrobe."

"Not many do, that's for sure," Oliver admitted. "And I can also assure you Delta isn't ten years younger than you."

Quizzically, Eva looked at him, doubting his words.

He mimed locking his lips with a key, not willing to share any woman's age.

"It's none of my business, but why does Delta work for you? Unless that's a secret too. It seems like her family and her coven have plenty of money and status. I can understand freelancing a bit as needed, but she puts in a lot of hours."

"Yeah, normally her hours aren't so . . . aggressive." Knowing Eva, she would feel a fair amount of guilt, but Delta was well compensated for her time, and he refused to apologize for that. "But she does have set hours. The High Priestess thinks the structure is good for her, or at least that's the story she tells. Delta is the witch who shouldn't be. Hecate had one daughter about seventy years ago. Athena, you met her." Glancing down at Eva, he added, "And whose jeans you're probably wearing."

"First, don't mention these jeans! Those sisters are tiny. I can barely breathe! And what, Athena's seventy? Hecate doesn't even look that age, and Athena looks younger than me."

Oliver glanced at Eva. "Well, you look younger than twenty-nine as well, a byproduct of the succubus blood, I assume." It hadn't taken much research to find out her age; a simple flip through her wallet and her license had freely given that information. Despite the fact that in a few weeks she was turning thirty, Eva also looked to be in her early twenties and would remain that way for at least several decades or more, if he were to guess. Demons were immortal and depending on how the human side fared, a hybrid could theoretically live much longer than normal humans. Malth had been alive for decades longer than Oliver, but had said on occasion that most hybrids had a shorter lifespan due to circumstances out of their control.

"Finally, a good side to all this! So, you're telling me I've been wasting time and money moisturizing daily for a decade, and this is all natural?" Eva fist pumped with feigned joy. "So, I'm guessing witches also don't age like humans?"

"No, and I don't dare ask the High Priestess her age. Typically, witches of her power have a single daughter during their lifetime. A protege, not just a daughter, but a novice who is trained, groomed, and will inherit the High Priestess position when the time comes. Only Hecate got pregnant again, years ago after fooling around with a visiting mage during some witchy moon ceremony, I'm sure. Thus Delta. To be honest, I don't think half the time Hecate knows what to do with her. Delta is powerful, definitely more powerful than her sister, and quite possibly will someday rival her mother and at a much younger age. But tradition says Athena inherits all that Hecate has: the title, the position, the wealth.

"Athena doesn't see Delta as a rival, but that doesn't mean it can't change in the future. If Delta didn't exist, there would be no question or threat to the future of the coven or Athena's future. But Delta does exist, and no one is quite sure what to do with her or what her existence means for the future. Sooo, she works for me. She's disrespectful, dresses inappropriately for the job, but hands down is the best witch I've worked with. Power levels aside, if she doesn't know something, she researches until she does. I've helped her make additional contacts around the world, and that has opened her up to learn even more, which also makes her even more of a threat to the standards that her coven lives and follows."

Oliver could almost hear the wheels turning in Eva's brain as she digested the story that wasn't truly his to tell, but what she said next surprised him. "You're a really nice man, Oliver Patrick." Holding up a hand and shaking her head, she added, "And no, don't try to tell me otherwise."

"I'm really not." Oliver suddenly became very interested in the straight road that lay out before them. He could feel Eva's eyes on him, and she laughed. Her laughter rolled through him, giving him the same feeling of contentment that her compliment had. He was no longer the man she imagined him to be, but perhaps he could become that man once again.

"Whatever you say, 'Boss Man,'" she mocked. "Anyway, where are we getting lunch? I could eat a bit now. Your housekeeper, chef, whatever makes out of this world meals, but I would kill for a big ole greasy burger and fries. Not a chain, but someplace that uses real beef and if it has sticky floors, that's a huge bonus! And did I say huge? I hope I mentioned that as well."

"I think we can manage that. I have to admit, though, I expected you to go for a big *ole* cup of coffee first thing." Mimicking her tone, he considered the nearby options for her request.

"You jest! The day is young! However, I literally had a pot before you found me. And you have a setup that rivals most coffee shops. I need some food to soak up some coffee before the cycle starts again. And I swear if we get attacked before I get some junk food, I'm going to fight off the hellhounds with my bare hands myself!"

"Perfect," Eva moaned around the medium rare burger as she bit into it. Oliver suppressed a groan himself; if she kept this up, he would remain in a permanent state of hardness. Eva had moaned identically when she took the first drink of her beer from a glass he suspected wasn't quite clean. Oliver had polished his silverware with a paper napkin before digging into his own rare burger, hold the bun. Pushing the toppings to the side, he cut into the barely warm meat, savoring the taste as he rolled it around in his mouth.

"Good?" Eva asked through a mouthful of food as the neon bar sign flickered, alternating lighting her up in red and then darkness. She'd alternated between the thick burger and the extra crispy French fries. He needed to make a note to his chef to include a few less healthy options in the daily menu for Eva.

Smiling, he nodded. It was, in fact, quite good. However, as much as he enjoyed spending time with her, Oliver continually scanned the bar. They slowly enjoyed their meal and when Eva had a second beer, Oliver added one for himself. He could drink all day, and it wouldn't impair him or prevent him from noticing anyone who approached.

Perhaps emboldened by her second beer, Eva waved a fork toward him. "What do you normally eat, or how, I guess. I know you can have coffee, wine, beer and rare beef. Is it enjoyable?"

Carefully, Oliver wiped his face with a paper napkin before responding with a slow nod, "yes, I do enjoy those items, but they don't satisfy me. Of course, I drink blood." His voice dropped lower. "Ravyn taught me to survive on animal blood and the blood of the dying. War brings that in droves. But these days I get my meals discreetly packaged and delivered from a few local blood banks." After a breath he admitted, "I wouldn't down a meal directly from a willing source, if the opportunity allowed."

Giving a small smile, Eva considered his response. "But doesn't that lifestyle put you at the mercy of others. If the blood bank doesn't deliver or no willing donor is on hand then what? You starve?"

"Possibly, but not probable. A certain amount of hunger can be uncomfortable, but not detrimental. And

254

Ravyn and I aren't the only ones who live like this. A European conglomerate has been working on creating a laboratory blood that can keep my kind sustained. I hear they are very close."

The jukebox played just loudly enough that the conversations around them were slightly muted—or would be to anyone who wasn't a vamp. Oliver heard nothing that worried him. He noted the six guards rotated through the bar as well, ordering a single beer or soda to sip as they sat casually, but on alert to any dangers. A few of them ordered food to go, and Oliver could imagine the werewolves' order of half a dozen rare burgers causing bemusement in the kitchen. Oliver could almost relax. Almost.

"Why do you use a pseudonym for your writing?" It was one of the things he couldn't understand. Her work was good. Successful. "Why remain hidden?"

Eva carefully wiped her mouth and hands with several of the paper napkins before tilting her head, considering his question. "In the beginning, it was sort of about not being seen. Would it be embarrassing for people I know to know or read my writing? Regardless of what is written, it's still a baring of your soul, personal. Then it evolved into realizing it didn't really matter if people knew who I was as a writer, because I've never really been seen. It was just an extension of that."

With a sardonic laugh, she continued, "And eventually, as my work actually became well-read, dare I say popular even, it became about ego. I could be sort of smug in the knowledge that they, the readers, didn't know who I was, but I did. They could guess, and wonder, but I could revel in the knowledge that I knew this secret that they didn't."

After they finished their food and only drops of warm beer remained in their glasses, Eva sighed in contentment. "I'm so full. And thanks; this floor is the exact right amount of sticky." Gesturing toward his partially finished plate, she asked, "Do you enjoy any other regular food? And drink?"

"I do, depending on what it is," Oliver admitted. "Any strong alcohol, although it doesn't affect me. And a bit of meat—the bloodier the better—although I have to be careful not to overdo it.

"Shopping next? Or just drive? Lady's choice today." *And every day*, he mentally added. Oliver cringed at his own thoughts. When had he become so needy and obtuse? He did feel a tad guilty at his selfish behavior. He craved spending time with Eva, and she'd appeared happy to stay in his home, content to watch movies and play board games, but clearly she was making the best out of the situation.

"Ugh, maybe I should have shopped before we ate!" She lay her head back against the green vinyl booth and groaned. "Maybe just a Walmart or Target if there's one nearby. I'm not picky. Just need a few things that fit me a little better."

"I think we can do a bit better than that. Besides, it's my treat." An assistant had already sent Oliver a list of various boutiques in the area that might appeal to her. While he might know a dive bar or two off the top of his head, boutique shopping was definitely out of his area of expertise.

"You really don't have to pay. I have money, and I barely spend what I have." She reached for her backpack, where he knew her ID and credit cards were kept.

He held up a hand to stop her, shaking his head.

"Yes, but I would like to buy you clothes. It's the least I can do. Perhaps those hellhounds wouldn't have gotten in so quickly if they hadn't followed me."

Looking him in the eyes, Eva questioned, "How about bras and panties? Because Oliver, that's what I really need. Delta and I aren't close enough to share panties, and that poor girl has no time to run around buying me stuff. And bras? Don't even get me started." Pointing to her chest, she reiterated, "We certainly aren't the same size, even if she was willing to share."

*Don't look at her chest*, Oliver ordered himself as his eyes were immediately drawn toward her full breasts despite the fact that a bulky sweatshirt mostly hid them from view. Where both Delta and her sister were thinner and several inches shorter, Eva was all curves and softness. It was no wonder their castoff clothes didn't fit her properly.

"Eyes up here, sir"—she pointed at her eyes—"and no, I'm not wearing any underthings at all. They were still wet from being washed last night." Hesitating and then emphasizing "wet" could have been his hopeful imagination, but her heartbeat speeding up definitely wasn't his imagination, nor was the wide-eyed look she gave him. "They have to hang dry, or they would already be in shreds."

Torn between apologizing for not thinking of his guest's needs after he'd dragged her away from her home in the middle of the night with barely the clothes on her back, or focusing on the fact that she wasn't wearing anything under her ill-fitting clothes, he remained temporarily speechless. His mouth went dry as he thought about the snug, borrowed jeans with nothing underneath them.

His fangs begged to drop, and his tongue ran along them, ordering them to remain in control.

"Yes or no to buying me the personal items I need?" Eva refused to look away, meeting his gaze with a steady, challenging look as her heart continued to beat rapidly, waiting for his response.

"Of course, whatever you need." Thankfully, he had enough experience in the art of interrogation to keep his voice as steady as hers, but Oliver still somehow felt as if he'd lost a round to the enticing woman in front of him. "I'll buy you whatever you need, Eva."

# Chapter Nineteen

*That was almost as good as an orgasm.*

Sitting once again beside Oliver as they sped down the road, Eva nearly cried. Had she really told Oliver that she wasn't wearing panties? What was she even thinking? Well, she knew what she was thinking. Here she was, sitting beside a rich, sexy man who had saved her life and offered to buy her anything she needed after listening to her and asking her questions about herself. That romance novel wrote itself, and she was the unlikely bumbling heroine, only Oliver had only been kind and interesting to her, not *interested, interested.*

If she'd been wearing panties, they would be dripping from the way his eyes watched her intently as she spoke, or the way his shirt pulled tight across his chest when he leaned toward her to slide her drink closer. And why couldn't she stop thinking about the word "panties"!?

They sat for several long moments inside the car while they both digested what she'd said.

*Idiot*, she cursed herself. What if this interest she was feeling was a byproduct of his blood or her apparent demon blood? She'd been a waitress long enough to appreciate that sometimes men, as well as an occasional woman, misunderstood kindness or service at the coffee shop as interest. What if he was just doing his job, keeping her safe, until the perpetrator was caught? How embarrassing to be on that end of the equation.

Wordlessly, Oliver drove to a small outlet mall that offered an array of shopping options for the average shopper as well as a chain bookstore. Silently, he quickly rounded the SUV, opening her door before she was able to lay a hand on the handle. Despite the fact that she could easily step out of the vehicle on her own, Eva took his offered hand as she slid out into the parking lot. He smoothly pulled her toward him until she was nearly touching him.

She held her breath as he leaned toward her ear and lowly announced, "Be careful, my little bunny. Your every move has me wanting to chase you, and when I do, I won't be able to stop."

Eva's breath hitched in her throat as she stared up into his dilating eyes, knowing hers also reflected desire. But he was correct: this was neither the time nor the place. Still, she couldn't stop her hand from lingering on his arm before slowly pulling away, dragging her fingertips down his arm and hand and stopping briefly before releasing her grasp.

"Tease," he whispered softly with a smile before bopping her nose. *Bopping her nose?!* She smiled back up at him before turning to scan the options, immediately zoning in on the intimates store. Thank

God! Underclothes that fit and didn't need to be washed daily.

Oliver did, in fact, buy her several bras and panties, although she hadn't shown them to him. As she picked them out, however, she couldn't help but imagine his reaction to them. He'd remained a perfect gentleman, sitting in a chair outside of the fitting room, scrolling on his phone as the sales staff found her the items she needed. Several days' worth, plus a set she left the store in, although Eva groaned as she squeezed back into Athena's jeans. If it were up to her, they would have been set on fire, but she supposed she needed to return them.

At another store, she carefully selected two pairs of jeans a size larger and a curvier fit than the ones Delta had swiped from her sister's closet. Wearing those as well as a V-cut, gauzy white shirt leaving the store, Eva told herself it was because she'd dripped ketchup on the hooded sweatshirt, but she couldn't deny the pleasure she felt when Oliver's eyes ran up and down her body, dilating slightly.

Armored up, wearing all new, well-fitting clothes empowered her and added a sway to her step leaving the store. No more hand-me-downs making her feel too tall or too big. Despite the fact that Oliver had given her *carte blanche* in the shop, she kept her spending to the necessities as much as she could. Undergarments, socks, jeans, three tops, and a pair of soft pajamas that she could call her own as she continued to lounge around at Oliver's home.

Apparently remembering her drawers from home

before they fled into the night, Oliver added a few pairs of black leggings with matching tanks and tees, raising an eyebrow with a challenging look as if daring her to complain. Apparently on a whim he added a Lavender scented body wash and shampoo set to the pile as well, as if the pricy soap in his guest bathroom wasn't good enough for her.

Leaving the store ladened with packages, Eva spotted a display of graphic tees in the bookstore window. Her eyes barely flickered on them, and she overcame the impulse to look at them. Her mood plummeted, as she thought of her collection of graphic book-themed tees she'd collected over the years. All destroyed within a few moments by hellhounds who had decided marking and burning through her clothes with their acidic urine was a grand finale to destroying her home.

While wearing his dark shades, Oliver had continually scanned the parking lot as well as the sidewalk in front of them and behind. He hadn't appeared to look at the window, till he told her, "Grab a few if you want. We still have some time before we need to get back."

Eva had forgotten that their true mission had been to draw out whatever was after Ravyn and her. Caught up in talking, shopping, and eating, she'd briefly forgotten the trouble she was in and how, at least for now, she was a job for Oliver despite how things might otherwise feel or appear. The plan had been to be out and about, but to arrive back in the security of Oliver's home well before the sun set. Ideally, they would have drawn out whatever was hunting them after they were safely back inside Oliver's fortress with supernaturals on guard and prepared for an assault.

"I'm good," Eva protested as he pulled her inside. Finally, to silence him, she pretended to examine all the tees carefully before choosing a medium gray graphic tee that said "I Like Big Books and I Cannot Lie" and a soft pink "I Closed my Book to be Here." Despite his protests to pick more, Eva found that she couldn't. Each of her previous tees had a story behind them. Not only had they been cute or sarcastic tees, but they held a memory from the moments she'd chosen them. The story of these two would be a good one: the first of a new series after a hellhound attack and marking the day she went shopping with a handsome vampire intent on treating her like a princess. They would mark a good—no, a great—memory, she mentally amended.

At the counter, Oliver slid over five hard-cover books he'd picked up from the paranormal new release table. At Eva's quizzical look, he shrugged innocently. "I figured I could expand my library a bit."

Laughing, she agreed, "Yup, exactly what I figured you'd pick."

"What?" he asked mockingly. "Can't a man enjoy romance? Besides, I've just read some lately that have me wanting to read more."

Settled again in their vehicle, they determined their next stop as they began circling back. Oliver's suggestion of coffee was shot down by Eva. Apparently, not only did his chef cook delicious healthy meals, he had an amazing coffee setup. Eva hadn't been suffering without her coffee while visiting. She'd enjoyed strong espresso as well as a plethora of mixed drinks. This was when Oliver learned that she'd been mixing up drinks for the rest of his staff with the setup.

"You don't have to wait on those ingrates," he said, laughing, before a horrified expression spread across his features. "Has Delta been getting caffeine?"

"Haha no, I'm not that crazy! She gets decaf with all the extra sugary syrups you can imagine. And I don't mind making drinks for everyone." Honestly, it made her feel at least a little bit useful, and it pleased her how much everyone liked and appreciated the drinks.

"You'll spoil them all, and then they'll be useless when they don't get it." Oliver chuckled, but it starkly reminded Eva that her presence in the household was temporary. Even if they didn't know the end date, leaving still loomed ahead of her. And she would miss all of them, from the security guards who began and ended each shift with a cup of either hot or cold java, Delta, who probably didn't need all the extra sugar she consumed, the housekeeper/chef, who made sure the coffee bar stayed stocked with her favorites, and especially Oliver.

They ended the road trip at the edge of Lake Michigan with only a few minutes for Eva to dip her feet in the cold water. In the distance, she could catch glimpses of the Windy City through a haze of light fog. Someday, she promised herself, she would visit and even stay the night there. Although this day hadn't been too bad; an entire day spending uninterrupted time with Oliver. Sure, occasionally he would tap a few things out on his cell phone, but he never waited for a reply before replacing the phone in his pocket. No discussion of magic, demons, or threats marred the day. Despite the fact that the reality of it loomed overhead, they managed to do a pretty good job of ignoring it.

They had plenty of discussions about books, shows, movies, and, to Eva's delight, she learned that Oliver was a fan of the theater. Or as he put it, "A perfect mix between a book and a show." For a brief moment, Eva allowed herself to imagine they would get to attend shows together, but sadly nearly immediately recognized that such a thing probably wouldn't happen when things settled down.

Eva's chest tightened at one point in their discussion as she wondered if, when the tether connecting them was removed, she would feel the loss of Oliver or if her untethered heart would just simply no longer feel him or anything for him. Perhaps that would be the easiest of the two options. The idea of an emptiness or nothingness broke her heart, but it wasn't fair for Oliver to be magically tied to her against his will.

Sitting together on a bench on the empty beach, while Eva slowly enjoyed a scoop of dark chocolate mocha ice cream, they watched the sun cut lower into the sky, a vivid reminder that the day was coming to an end. It had been a perfect day of freedom, and although Eva never saw any security detail, she suspected they weren't as alone as they appeared to be.

Reluctantly, Oliver apologized that they couldn't stay longer, but it was important that they were back home before nightfall. Despite the fact that nightfall made him the strongest, if the hellhounds managed to track them down, it would put Eva in unnecessary danger.

Eva agreed, shuddering as she remembered the slobbering beasts that seemed determined to hunt her down. The reminder of the dangers around them put a damper on Eva's mood, and she sat in her seat a little quieter as they listened to music on the return trip. Despite the miles traveled that day, they'd simply driven in a large circle, not going too far from home as they tested the waters for any possible threats that they could draw out.

Eva recognized a few of the landmarks as they neared the gate of what she now realized was a mini-fortress fenced in with elegant, yet foreboding reminders that it could easily serve as a prison as well as keeping others out. A glance in the side mirror showed the two black vehicles pulling into place closer behind them.

"Ah, there they are," she whispered mostly to herself.

Jolting out of his own silent thoughts, Oliver glanced in the rear view mirror to confirm what she saw. "Without knowing what we face, I didn't dare skimp on protection. Even if they were hidden all day, they were still there. I'm glad we didn't need them.

Needing them might have ruined an otherwise perfect day out."

Eva's heart swelled with warmth; despite the fact that their intention had been to draw out the stalker, it had been a perfect day. There was always tomorrow to try again or, of course, whenever Delta needed another break or finished the magical unbinding—whichever happened first. Pursing her lips, she struggled to find the words to agree with his assessment, and perhaps even her hope that they might have other perfect days together. But nothing seemed to want to come out.

Oliver hit her with a small smile that nearly blinded her, opening his mouth to form words that had no sound. Panic tightened in her chest, expanding outward through her limbs, and Eva struggled to raise a hand to her chest as Oliver's expression slowly turned from happiness to concern and confusion. Blinking slowly, she struggled to focus as his face turned fuzzy.

As if in slow motion, that light in his eyes left, and panic filled them as something slammed into the side of the SUV, rolling it over twice. Flashes of trees, ground, sky, and light filled Eva's vision as the seat belt pulled tight against the violent rolls. She immediately flashed back to a similar time years ago; a time she couldn't remember until this moment. She'd been here before.

It felt like long moments in time, when in fact it was surely just seconds before the vehicle settled on its side with Eva panicking, gasping for air in horror, hanging from the taunt seat belt as her body strained toward Oliver.

She flinched as an explosion behind them again shook the vehicle. Roars filled the air as Eva hung frozen, now recognizing the sounds of the hellhounds just as she felt the door above her being ripped from its hinges. A shadow immediately blocked the sun. Helplessly, she stared at Oliver, pleading for his help; it was all happening again. Oliver's own eyes raged, turning from panic to black with anger as he strained, unable to move against whatever black magic held them in place.

Floating above him and unable to move even her eyes, Eva watched the bags of newly purchased items slowly float, suspended around them as they attempted to once again settle into place. In slow motion, her own blood dripped through the air toward Oliver, so slowly she could see the molecules as they twisted and turned. Coming from some injury she hadn't yet felt, drops of blood plopped onto his white shirt, slowly spreading to once again mar the beautiful white fabric.

Still unable to move, she felt a familiar hot, putrid breath on her face. The fear and confusion she'd been feeling was replaced with unadulterated panic as the air was sucked out of her lungs. By her neck she felt what must be a claw cut the seat belt, releasing the tension. Before she could even fall a fraction of an inch toward Oliver, her body was flung from the vehicle. Mentally bracing herself to hit the ground, and sure of the agony that would follow, she stopped falling with a jolt midair. A gasp of surprise puffed out as she felt herself being zipped away, leaving a path of cut air in her wake.

Light came—and then blessed darkness.

# Chapter Twenty

*It's as dark as a hellhound in here.*

Eva awoke slowly, swimming once again through the darkness and the alternating dull throbbing and excruciating sharp pains that shot through her skull.

Alive. Pain meant she still lived. She prayed that the same could be said of Oliver as well as the men who had been guarding her.

Before she even opened her eyes, she gingerly touched the spot on her forehead that the pain seemed centered around. Blood no longer flowed freely from it, but if all the dried blood indicated anything, it had flowed profusely and freely. Her quicker than normal healing ability meant she could have been out for twenty minutes or two hours.

A low moaning had her opening her eyes and slowly moving her head back and forth to determine who or what made the noise next to her. Big mistake; her head rattled even with careful movements, making her lose what little remained in her stomach. Retching caused the shaking to worsen and for several moments, she was caught in a cycle of dry heaving as her vision wavered fuzzily back and forth.

Too late, Eva determined that the noises were coming from her. She probably had a concussion. She'd never had one before, but it seemed likely. Closing her eyes again, she remained lying on the cool, damp floor until the dampness began to permeate her clothes and the stench of vomit filled her nose as it slowly dried on and around her.

*Oh, my new clothes!* She mentally moaned again, doubtful that the once flirty white peasant top had survived a car accident, all the blood and most likely, her own vomit. Fitting. She chastised herself for even concerning herself with clothes after clearly having been attacked and kidnapped. With a shiver, Eva pulled her now bare feet closer to her body in an attempt to ward off some of the chill. Her captors had removed both her shoes and her socks, most likely to discourage her from running.

Worrisome; it didn't bode well for her future if her kidnappers hadn't tended to her wounds. Despite her concerns for her own safety, she hoped Oliver wasn't trapped with her. The last thing she remembered was the fear and anger in his eyes as he lay trapped in the overturned car, apparently paralyzed by what seemed to be a magical attack of sorts. If he'd been left behind, surely he would mount an attack to rescue her. Despite the fact that they'd only known each other for days, Eva knew that Oliver's character wouldn't allow him to leave her behind with an enemy.

Or would it? Doubt crept into her mind, and loneliness settled through her. She was alone, more alone then perhaps ever before. Surely someone would

272

come for her.

Slower than before, she gently raised her head, feeling her way along the damp dirt floor until she felt a wall only a foot behind her. Pulling herself up enough to lean on the wall, she spent the next several minutes with eyes closed, allowing her stomach to settle again. Despite its emptiness, it still battled against her every movement. Finally, Eva opened her eyes again, this time just tiny slits to peer out into the dark room, scanning ever so slowly for any light source, any clue as to where she might be and hopefully a way out of what appeared to be a basement—or maybe, if she were lucky, a barn.

The pitch black corners of the room loomed outward, covered in shadows and darkness, leaving her unsure how far it spanned. A few tiny spots of light shone through at the top of the room only a few feet above her head. Eva opened her eyes bit by bit, stopping when the pain rose. Finally, she could focus on the room around her. It must be a basement, she ascertained.

The tiny streams of light were allowed in through quarter-sized, oval-shaped windows with a few bars across them near the top of the room. The light just caught the beams that she assumed ran clear across the room. Squinting at the window, she doubted even without the bars that she would be able to squeeze her hips through the frame. Scanning the walls the best she could from her spot on the floor, she didn't even see a door or any stairs. Surely they were in one of the darkened corners? Every room had a way in and out.

She refused to believe otherwise even as the panic settled in, blood whooshed through her body up into her head, and for the second time that day, everything went blissfully dark.

The next time Eva fought her way out of the darkness, a bit more light streamed through the small windows. This time, she managed to keep her head upright without the throbbing headache and nausea. Still leaning against the wall, she determined that either not much time had passed or her captors really didn't care about her health enough to check on her wellbeing. This still didn't bode well for her future, and since rescue wasn't assured either, she had to take care of herself and get moving.

Taking a deep breath and bracing herself for any possible pain, she nearly vomited again, this time from the heavy, rotten smell hanging thick in the air. Almost like baked dog crap, but from the bowels of ten dogs. Taking shorter breaths from behind her crusty-sleeved arm, Eva gingerly pulled herself to her feet, keeping the wall to her back in case she couldn't support herself.

Despite a brief wobble, she made it to her feet and stayed upright. The ceiling wasn't as low as she'd feared. She could stand upright with a few inches of clearance. The light filtering in showed the beams of the room stretching out and dust particles floating about. On the end farther from the windows, she could make out a frame that appeared to be the structure of the enclosed staircase. The extra lighting didn't raise her hopes of escaping; it only showed truly how bare the room was.

And that stench. What was it? Pulling the inside of her blouse up to cover her nose, she slowed her breathing to short, shallow breaths in an attempt to get past the odor that permeated the air.

In the hopes that maybe her captors hadn't searched for a phone, she patted the back pockets of her once new jeans. Although she'd expected that her phone was gone, Eva still felt the flicker of disappointment. One could hope; surely the universe owed her some good news for a change. However, if she were trying to find a bright side, admittedly it would have been worse to be captured in too tight jeans.

Her heart rate once again shot up, as tiny scratching and shuffling noises came from a corner across the basement from her, just for a brief second. Rats? Had they crawled on her while she slept? Holding very still in the following silence nearly had her believing she'd imagined the soft shuffles and that she was truly alone down here. Holding her breath, she once again heard a scratching noise followed by a low whine and a huff that cut through the darkness. Eyes whipping back to the area, she caught a glimpse of red pierce the darkness from the same far corner. Were cameras set up down here watching her every move, seeing the fear and panic in her?

"Hey!" Eva attempted to shout, but only a low, garbled mumble came out. Clearing her aching throat and watching the area just past the darkened staircase frame, she tried again, still without any force. "Hey, let me out."

Not original, but what else did her captors expect to hear? Above her head, it sounded like a chair being dragged across the table and then boots stomping across the floor as dust gently rained down on her from the ceiling. Blinking, she attempted to look up to see any signs of light or life. Angry tones came through the ceiling, too low for her to make out any words but loud enough to understand the intent.

A door opened at the top of the stairs, shining more light down into the basement. One of the angry voices replied, "Shut up," making Eva step back a beat farther from the stairs. She heard more dragging sounds, then a silhouette stepped down the stairs, hauling what looked like a hose behind it.

"Shut up," the man's voice repeated in anger, "or I'll give you some of this too."

Eva's eyes strained against the darkness and new light, but she was unable to make out any features. The man was big enough to block much of the light from the door as he thumped a few steps down the stairs, giving her no indication who—or what—he might be.

Grumbling, he clopped halfway down the stairs, turning sideways, and aimed the hose toward the corner, sending a powerful spray of water back and forth for several minutes. It beat the floors and walls, followed by a gurgling sound as it drained away.

"It's your turn next time," he shouted up the stairs. "This crap stinks. We'll all be better off when this thing's gone!" Thumping back up the stairs, dragging the hose, he slammed the door shut once again, leaving the basement in mostly darkness but a bit less stench.

Taking several moments to still her pounding heart and allow her eyes to readjust to the darkness, Eva gingerly walked toward the corner the man had just angrily sprayed. A part of her was thankful that for the moment she appeared to be forgotten by whomever was upstairs. A small, sad huff and feeble hiss escaped the corner, followed by what sounded like the clank of a heavy chain, then silence. As she inched closer, the camera light she'd seen earlier turned on again. Wait! No, make that two red dots just a few inches apart.

Not cameras. An animal, then? Was a dog trapped down here with her? Moving to the side, to allow just a little more light to filter toward the end, she realized with dismay that this wasn't any regular dog. Yes, it was the size of a regular dog, a bit smaller than Apollo, so maybe forty or fifty pounds. The poor thing was soaked through where the man had sprayed it and the area around it down. It lay limply in the mud-soaked corner near a drainage grate at the bottom of the wall and floor. Black fur dripping, it lifted its head just a few inches from the ground, letting out a soft growl before dropping its head back down to its mucky paws. No longer shining red, its dark eyes followed Eva as she moved closer to examine the situation.

The large link chain was wrapped tightly around its neck and fastened somewhere behind it.

"Oh, no, no," whispered Eva, recognizing the small hellhound for what it was: just a puppy, a baby.

Why had it been trapped here with her? How long had it been down here lying in the mud and muck, being sprayed down regularly, leaving it weak and without a parent?

"Hey, baby." Eva attempted to keep her tone level as the listless puppy eyes perked a bit at her voice and actively scanned her every move. Despite having been attacked and bitten by hellhounds at least four times its size, she couldn't help her heart breaking for the poor trapped puppy. Reaching her hand out in front of her, she wondered if approaching it like a regular dog was the correct thing to do. It let out a halfhearted growl, its eyes flaring briefly red before it whimpered again, shifting uncomfortably as the too tight, heavy chain links clanked against each other.

Taking a chance, Eva gently reached out farther, putting her hand near the pup's nose, but not too close. It puffed out a fizzle of hot air as it attempted to smell her without touching her. Encouraged, she slowly moved closer, tentatively touching the side of the puppy's head. Letting out a heart wrenching mew, it pressed its head farther into her palm, obviously enjoying the warm touch.

"Oh, baby, you're freezing," Eva muttered, at least knowing from Delta's constant barrage of knowledge that hellhounds were meant to enjoy the molten hot pits of hell. Being cold made for a pretty miserable pup, especially one that might not be old enough to regulate its body temperature and was regularly being power washed with frigid water.

Eva continued to rub the puppy, which wiggled a

little bit in what she hoped was happiness and not anticipation of an attack. Running her hands down its side, she was dismayed to feel ribs instead of a well-rounded puppy belly. Once she stroked the dog, feeling confident enough that it looked at her with hope, instead of fear, she felt the chain tight on its neck. An ice-cold carabiner clip digging into its neck held the links together. Using her soothing voice to keep the puppy calm, Eva simultaneously worked the clip free while caressing the hellhound.

"Hey there, let's get this nasty thing off you. It will feel sooo much better when it comes off. You're a cute little fellow—fellow or girl. Not that it matters too much to you. Oh, yeah, right there, I think I have it. Just hold still, little one, while I take this off. Such a good little hellhound," she crooned.

The chain fell to the floor and the pup froze briefly for a moment, eyes flaring up, then it shot forward with unexpected energy. Eva suppressed a scream and jumped back; afraid she'd made a horrible mistake. But no, the pup gave a putrid lick to her face before heading toward a bowl set just beyond its reach and gulped down in about three bites whatever had been inside.

"Those dickwads . . ." Eva scowled despite her own circumstances. What kind of people would tie a puppy up and then leave food just outside of its reach? Even if they weren't murderous kidnappers, they were jerks.

Eva backed slowly down the basement again toward the light of the small windows, in case she did need some distance from the pup, but after it carefully examined the now empty bowl, it bounded toward her, shaking its body from head to toe in an attempt to remove some of the water from its wiry fur, as well as shake and stretch its poor neck.

Slowly reaching down to again rub the dog's head, she whispered, "How long have you been here, little buddy? Do you have someone looking for you?" *I hope I do,* she mentally added.

Squatting down, she used both hands to deeply massage the puppy's neck where the fuzzy fur had been flatten and partially worn off. Anger flared as the puppy moaned and flopped on its side. This allowed her to identify that it was, in fact, a male.

"You like that, don't you? And oh, I guess I can call you Baby Boy now." Continuing to rub his stomach and sides, she moved from a squat to fully sitting on the floor, again pressing her back against the wall closest to one of the small windows. The pup moved from the floor up onto Eva's lap, pressing his relatively small body as tightly against her legs and warmth as he could while she held him. When he opened his mouth in a yawn large enough that Eva could almost count his teeth, she noted that they were much smaller than those of the hound that had bit her. Did he still have puppy teeth? Should he be nursing? Did hellhounds nurse?

Despite learning that a small part of her was demon, she still didn't know that much about demons. Some laid eggs. Were hellhounds born or hatched? Not that it mattered; she had a feeling whatever had been in the bowl hadn't been enough food or the right food, if the puppy's ribs were any indication.

Stroking the puppy, who within a few minutes began to snore lightly as he relaxed under her ministry, Eva channeled good energy, health, and healing for him. At least one of them felt safe enough for a few minutes. Pulling him a little closer, Eva noticed he didn't quite feel as cold to the touch, and his fur was beginning to dry. Continuing to run her fingers along the dog's coat, she noticed some of it was still soft, fuzzy puppy fur; only bits had started to turn wiry like the adult versions. Poor, poor baby.

After several minutes, her legs began cramping under his weight, so Eva maneuvered him to lie alongside her, keeping him pulled in close to continue the warmup. Resting her hands on him, she continued to envision energy flowing to him. Despite not knowing or understanding if her power worked that way, the positive feelings were all she currently could offer. She forced herself to stay awake since she was concerned that if she fell asleep she might accidentally draw energy from the puppy in order to heal her own body. During her days with Delta, they'd speculated about how her energy worked, but it was only guesses on the give and take on the human-demon power.

Silently, the light and shadows continued moving up and down the walls and floors of the basement, proving that time was passing, but how slowly or fast Eva wasn't sure. Finally, she heard a door slam again somewhere above her and heavy footsteps across the floor. Was someone staying at the house at all times or were they coming and going? She knew from before at least two people had been present, but there could be more. She tensed as they stomped toward the doorway above the staircase, and the door creaked open again. This time, Eva didn't bother shouting anything, deciding it was better to be ignored than receive the same attention as the malnourished pup.

"Grub time," the voice announced at the same time the man threw something down the stairs, bouncing it off the walls and onto the floor. Baby Boy sat up stiffly and growled softly as he approached the stairs, then looked eagerly up at Eva, awaiting her approval.

"Good boy," she muttered, patting his head before firmly requesting an ignored "stay" command. Both of them walked in the dim light toward the edge of the stairs where the items had hit the wall, searching for whatever "grub time" offered.

Eva easily found a water bottle, since she nearly tripped over it after it had rolled free. She'd gulped down half of it before reminding herself it might be a while before they considered her needs again. Getting down on her hands and knees, she swept the dirty floor, searching for whatever else the man had tossed down to her. Thankfully, all the other items appeared to have stayed safe and clean in the bag. She scurried back to the slightly more lit side; Baby Boy followed closely, not wanting to be left alone any longer.

Opening the plain brown bag, Eva unhappily examined the contents. "Not very well rounded," she told the young hellhound, who watched her hopefully

282

with those puppy eyes yet again. Two lukewarm fast-food burgers, a bag of generic chips, and an apple. Opening the first burger, Eva broke it into pieces and hand fed it to the puppy, who eagerly gulped down each piece whole. Then she ate the chips, sharing a few of those with him as well.

"Your mama trained you well. What a good little beastie," she complimented him when he patiently waited for his share. After taking a bite of the second burger for herself, she broke off another piece for Baby Boy, who left behind a string of drool as he gently took it from her hand. Another bite, and she gave him the rest as he looked at her with big hopeful eyes, knowing he needed it more than her at this point. This left her the apple, which she gave a crunchy bite, enjoying the tart flavor. Biting off another piece for the now uninterested pup, she ate the rest herself. One last short swig of water, then she followed up by cupping a bit in her hand and offering it to the hellhound. He was equally uninterested in that. Maybe they didn't drink water.

Turning in circles, he again lay down next to Eva, this time keeping his eyes open to scan the room.

Tightening the cap to prevent unintentional leaks, Eva lay the bottle near her. Who knew when her captors would deign to give her more? The over-sized puppy left out a soft belch, and Eva groaned and fanned away the putrid scent of hellfire. Ugh, but maybe it was a sign of good hellhound health. Snuggling down and kissing his still fluffy, sleepy head, she whispered to him, "I'm glad I'm not alone."

# CHAPTER TWENTY-ONE

*Icy what you did there.*

*R*age.

Hate.

Loathing.

Blood red, hot anger flooded Oliver's body as he lay helpless in the damaged SUV. Everything that could go wrong had just gone wrong. Despite his promises, they'd taken Eva, and it was entirely his fault. She'd trusted him to keep her safe and he hadn't.

Mind screaming, begging to break free and rip into anything, he was unable to move.

Frozen.

Helpless.

Unable to do anything but watch with blood-filled eyes seething with fear and rage, he saw a single claw as the beast severed Eva's seatbelt where she hung for an eternal single second in time, before being scooped up and disappearing in a flurry of blackness and wiry fur. Never would he forget the horrified look frozen on her face, the pleading in her eyes as she was snatched and hurtled away, blood dripping from her injuries. That wouldn't be the last look he saw on her face,

Oliver swore fiercely despite the fact that the stasis that hit him left him unable to even blink.

One instant he'd turned toward her, smiling at her beautiful face, opening his mouth to say something he hoped she might find interesting as they reentered the safety of his home. The next moment, they were hit simultaneously by what he assumed was an exceptionally powerful frozen time spell and slammed by a hellhound. And if he were a guessing man or one who could foresee every possibility, he realized that each of the SUVs had likely faced the exact same concurrent attacks in military precision. If he could see every possibility, he would have considered that a witch powerful enough to wiggle through his wards would also be able to spell hellhounds to search out their prey during the day. Just because it had never been done before didn't mean it wasn't a possibility.

Eva had fallen victim to his hubris, but in the end, her enemies would pay. Oliver didn't make the same mistakes twice. He'd underestimated both their strength and determination, but he swore it wouldn't happen again.

Within seconds of the attack, he was surrounded by his men pulling his immobile, helpless body from the wreck, while another of his staff witches fought to counteract the spell he'd been hit with. It was too late. She was gone. He'd failed her.

The armed guards, guards who had mostly been hidden from sight during Eva's stay, circled around, claws and weapons at the ready, while others carried him and the stunned men inside the safety of the gates.

His body grew hotter as his blood and rage attempted unsuccessfully to burn the spell from his system.

With trained precision, the guards locked down the gates, windows, and doors as they brought him deeper into his home. Helpless, Oliver knew the soldiers would follow the protocol that he'd laid out on the rare chance that something like this would occur. Once the lockdown began, only three people would be able to come and go from the compound or end the lockdown. Of the three, he was incapacitated, and Malthazar was still unreachable on a hunt. This left Delta, who hopefully hadn't ventured far during her twenty-four-hour reprieve.

Inwardly, he fought for his men to deny their training and to immediately go after Eva. Go after her before she was gone. His eyes raged at them as they carried him inside, mentally ordering them to go after her, but also knowing the directive had previously been clear. He felt his phone buzzing in his pocket, startling one young soldier who with a stumble dropped Oliver's right side.

Grunting, Oliver mentally demanded the young wolf answer the phone if he planned to keep his head once Oliver was free. Gulping, the youth felt around in this pocket while the other kept a firm grip on Oliver, holding him upright.

"Helllllo?" his voice squeaked as he clicked the phone on.

"Is this a test?" Delta's voice screamed over the line for all to hear. "Who is this?"

*Thank the old gods*, Oliver thought. At least the

system had alerted Delta of its activation. Hopefully, it would do the same for Malth. He needed the half-demon here; he needed him here days ago. Even if they couldn't find him, the magic should. This particular system had never been used, and theoretically they should get a notification of some sort, according to those who had set it up.

A scar-faced guard pulled the phone from the recruit's shaking hand. "Delta, system activated, not a drill. Code one, eight, eight, seven. I repeat: this is not a test. One, eight, eight, seven. Active and safe."

"I'm on my way." Despite Oliver's immobile state, his hearing still picked up everything around him, and he knew Delta's arrival meant that if he or the current witch on duty couldn't break this spell, without a doubt, Delta would smash it.

Instantly the phone rang again. Gruffly, the guard began, "Code one—"

"I come," said the deep voice on the other end, followed by a click.

Momentary relief flooded Oliver, as the men continued half walking, half dragging his dangling body between them to the house, while others circled around, on alert for a secondary attack. His legs were beginning to tingle as feeling slowly returned; already the spell was either dissipating or the witch's counter attempts had helped. Oliver fought to move his mouth, but it still refused to cooperate even as his fangs itched to burst forth.

*Work faster*, his mind screamed at the calm-faced older witch as she jogged sideways along with the

288

men, attempting to weave magic over him with her hands as they bustled him down the drive to a hidden door that led underground back into the basement of the house.

As they entered the doors, the popping of his ears confirmed that the security spell was settling into place. All security guards would be moving to their assigned spaces around the compound, if they weren't there already. Alert and waiting for whatever happened next.

Oliver was settled into the well-finished basement where the bulk of his security staff worked and typically moved in and out of the property without being noticed by the occupants on the higher floors. Gritting his teeth, determined to will the breaking of the spell, he glared around the room while the security teams checked in with the leads. With care, the witch grasped his face with both hands, turning it toward her own.

"Hold now, sir." She maintained eye contact as she firmly issued the order. Despite her apparent calm demeanor, she obviously feared that when she dropped the spell, he would rage.

He hoped his eyes conveyed that despite the rage he was sure she could feel boiling from him, he didn't lack control.

Clenching her jaw, the woman nodded before laying her hands on him and uttering, "*Praevaricator glaciem*." Her hands pounded on his chest as she demanded, "*Praevaricator glaciem*."

Ice breaker.

Beginning slowly and then building as the moments passed, louder and louder she beat her hands upon him, ordering the spell to break the frozen state of his body. Faster and faster, she repeated as her hands followed the tempo. The sounds vibrated as they filled the air, echoing in his head as she unrelentingly fought the spell, refusing to surrender as the long minutes passed.

Oliver watched as the world seemed to slow down around him, noticing the details of the moments. The sweat slowly gathered along the witch's forehead and temples from the exertion until it pooled down the sides of her face, catching her hair as it went. The shifters moved anxiously around her, their animals uneasy as the sharp magic filled the air, hanging thick and threatening. Their voices slowed as they continued to monitor the situation, ascertaining the next threat. His vision blurred as he watched the guards' slow, methodical movements, checking doors and monitoring the cameras outside.

One final time her hands rose, hitting his body as he felt the spell weaken, then crack and break away as he regained control of his speech and limbs.

As soon as he felt the spell finally quiver and shatter around him, Oliver attempted to leap to his feet, ignoring the full, heavy feeling in his limbs. Instead of finding himself immediately upright, he in fact rolled over and off the settee, barely keeping to his feet and not face planting only due to the fact that one of his men reacted quickly enough to settle an arm around him, pulling him upward. The hired witch had collapsed to the floor in exhaustion, and he would have found himself on top of her if not for the shifter's quick reflexes.

Slowing down, he held onto the man's arm as his equilibrium regained its sense of up and down, while scanning the room. Scattered across the floor were the other guards from the accompanying vehicles, recovering on their own from the effects of the powerful spell. Despite the blood on them, they appeared to have only suffered the effects of the spell and only minor injuries from the hellhounds tossing their vehicles aside like toys.

Delta had arrived. Already she had a map strewn across a large table, with a well-worn, deeply stained wooden bowl on one side. A pendant swung from a chain in one hand, and she held a bone-bladed athame in her other as she barked orders at his men. While a few looked uneasily at each other, three shifters moved without hesitation to stand near the table, holding out their right hand to her. She quickly sliced deeply into their palms. Blood welling up, they promptly turned their blood-filled palms to the darkened bowl that had clearly held blood sacrifices on more than one occasion. Oliver noted those who had offered their blood freely, intending to acknowledge the sacrifice once Eva was returned to them. Already the blood slowed and their bodies began to heal the wounds.

Magic lay sharp and pungent in the air. Its thickness verified that this wasn't Delta's first attempt to locate Eva. For a moment, fear snapped around Oliver's heart before he immediately squashed it. Fear was the enemy, making a mockery of hope and intent; there was no place for it in a search for Eva.

Nodding at the wolf who had led the group during the attack and subsequent incapacitation, Oliver acknowledged that despite his own misgivings, everything had been done according to plan. Gaining his footing, he was able to shrug off the helpful hold and stand by himself.

"Move all of them to the infirmary down the hall," he instructed, gesturing toward the exhausted witch and still incapacitated guards who littered the ground.

Several men immediately stepped to it, working together to move them down the narrow basement hallway.

"Any ETA on Malthazar?"

"Not yet, sir. He went back to dark mode."

Malth was always in dark mode. He lived in the shadows, drawing them deeper and deeper around him as each journey out seemed to take a bit more of his soul despite the good he was doing. But if he said he was coming, Malthazar would come.

Still moving more slowly than he liked, Oliver made his way to Delta's side. A frustrated sigh escaped her. Placing his hand gently but firmly on her arm, he commanded, "We've got this. Let's find her, so when Malth gets here we're ready. Then we'll go get her and bring her home."

Delta gritted her teeth and hissed out, "And then they'll pay. They will all pay."

Grimly, Oliver nodded in agreement. By the gods, they would pay.

# CHAPTER TWENTY-TWO

*Keep your spell book under war-lock and key.*

*E*va woke up with a start, not sure exactly when she'd fallen asleep. Somehow, she'd used the fluffy young hellhound as both a pillow and a blanket as he'd wrapped himself around her, likely seeking comfort as well as much needed warmth. The shadows had grown long, and once again only moonbeams sparkled through the small windows. A cursory glance at the pup showed her that he too was now on alert. Hackles rose on the back of his neck, and his eyes glowed as he glowered toward the staircase where surely the threat would emerge.

"It's okay, Baby Boy," she whispered to the pup in an attempt to calm and reassure both of them. She patted his head, allowing her hand to soak in the now warm body.

Doors slammed above them and this time, several sets of feet stomped across the floor overhead. No angry shouting; instead, hushed murmurs whose tones couldn't be deciphered. By the time the upstairs door pushed open, Eva and Baby Boy were on their feet. Standing protectively in front of the puppy, Eva took a wide stance, sure that whatever was coming next didn't bode well for either one or both of them. But they weren't going to get to him without going through her first. Baby Boy, despite his initial aggression, hovered behind her as memories of previous bouts with cold water and beatings apparently filled him.

Despite her will to fight, the standoff ended quickly as three men walked single file down the stairs and spread out evenly across the room.

Gruffly, one of them suggested, "Make it easy on yourself."

Still, as they approached, Eva swung wildly with both arms, trying to keep Baby Boy behind her. The hellhound growled and snarled, just as intent on trying to serve justice to his captors despite his fear.

Two of the men easily restrained Eva, half lifting, half dragging her toward the stairs while the other brought up the back. He served a solid kick to the frantic pup, who hit the wall a few feet away and slid unmoving to the ground.

"Stop!" Eva screamed, fighting tears and pulling harder against the unmovable men. One gave her arm a sharp twist, while the other open handedly struck her in the face. Tears fell for the first time since her capture as they forced her up the narrow wooden stairs, the silence behind her deafening. Her face throbbing and barely able to keep her feet under her, she was dragged up the stairs as if she weighed nothing.

If looks could kill, they would all be dead. Unfortunately, wishing someone to death wasn't a power Eva possessed. Despite being knocked around by the three men, whom she started to suspect were shifters, she refused to go easily. She'd read somewhere that allowing a captor to take you to a second location could be a possible death sentence, so surely another location wouldn't lead to good things, although at this point, Eva wasn't even certain how many different locations they'd taken her to. Surely death was imminent?

Their iron grip gave no room to wiggle free, and kicking them only resulted in hurting her own foot. A solid knee to the groin hadn't worked out either; one had caught her knee so tightly with his hand that she thought he would break it.

The kitchen sat at the top of the basement stairs. A table with four chairs along with a trash can overflowing with fast-food wrappers and pizza boxes piled alongside it were in the otherwise bare room. What must have been a front room with no furniture or rugs was followed by a trip down a narrow, darkened hallway with several closed doors and another stairway at the end.

Despite her pain and fear, Eva continued noting everything she could about her surroundings, but what she was seeing didn't look hopeful. The old place was clean, not spotless, but outside of the trash area, nothing marred the simple, empty rooms. Windows were haphazardly boarded up, enough space between the boards that during the day the occupants probably didn't need to turn on the overhead lights. The dampness didn't cling to the air quite like it did in the basement, but a hint of it still hung in the air along with a sense of foreboding—

or perhaps that was Eva's own terror.

The men pulled her up another set of stairs, not caring if her feet or even her legs hit each step as they dragged her along. In exasperation at the top, one of them wrapped large, bare arms around her from behind, pinning her arms to her sides. He grunted at another to grab her legs and despite her frantic, shoeless kicking, she was picked up unceremoniously for the remainder of the journey.

As she wiggled and writhed in a pointless attempt at freedom, they carried her effortlessly through one last door into a room that unlike the others, wasn't at all empty.

While the emptiness and decay might have been disturbing, the items in this room terrified Eva to her core. Nothing good would happen here. The very air sat thick with warning and promises of pain. Wrestling helplessly against the arms that immobilized her while pleading wordlessly not to be taken inside, she was all but ignored. She might have been a piece of furniture as they impassively carried her into the room of horrors.

The smell of rotten eggs filled the air. Newly lit black candles illuminated the room, the thick, dark wax just starting to drip down the sides. Unidentifiable words and symbols covered every inch of the once white or gray walls in black and red smudged writing. Layers upon layers overlapped the symbols at times or retraced old ones. Horrified, Eva prayed that the older, rust-colored symbols hadn't been made in the blood of previous victims and were just faded paint.

Thick, heavy drapes covered the windows from floor to ceiling, and black pentagrams decorated a large portion of the ceiling as well as the floor. The air dripped with magic, and even if Eva hadn't known anything about magic or its existence at all, this room would have terrified her. The primal need to save oneself would have kept anyone and everyone from venturing past the threshold by choice. The room reeked of physical pain, suffering, and death.

In the center of the room sat a block of wood and even before the men pulled her toward it, Eva had the horrible sense that it was for her. It was stained deeply with what was without a doubt blood, the dark stains following the path of the marred grooves cut crudely into and around it before angling toward the floor at the corners. Shiny new shackles attached to the four corners with O rings drilled deeply into the thick wooden platform promised horrors she couldn't even begin to imagine.

As if they could read her panicked mind, and before she could launch another assault, one of the brutes simply picked her up by the throat with one hand and laid her on the table. Meanwhile, the other two made quick work of the shackles and chains, while she simply choked, gasping for breath with feeble struggles against them.

Eyes wide in horror, she lay pinned to the table, forced to stare at the ceiling painted with a thick, black seeping pentagram. Her neck and head were trapped between two boards that the men cranked and tightened into place before placing a strap between the boards and under her chin, making certain her head remained immobilized. Her eyes darted from side to side, barely catching her captors moving back, out of her peripheral vision, to different areas of the room until they were out of her line of sight completely. They stood still, no shuffling. The only sound in the room was Eva's ragged breath that she tried to slow down. Breathing in and out, pause, silence, in and out, straining slightly against the straps and board, causing her to choke again.

Then another set of steps, firm and crisp, echoed through the house. Striking heel, toe, *click*, *click*, closer and closer, moving with purpose, not speeding up nor slowing down. The men inside the room shifted slightly, making the floorboards of the old house creak as they bore their weight.

"Here he comes," one whispered, then another and another.

*Who comes?* Eva wanted to whisper her question but knew it would remain unanswered at best; at worst, someone might strike her again. Her heart rate sped up again as she strained to move her head even a fraction of an inch toward the door, her eyes blurring painfully as she strained to see to her side. The footsteps didn't even pause at the door; heel, toe, heel, toe, crisply into the room but still unhurried.

"Awwweee, here she isssss," a raspy voice stretched out, as if some damage had been inflicted on vocal cords and tongue.

Eva struggled to see who was just out of her eyesight. One more step and she could see the outline. Two more after that and *he* stood above her, peering down in examination.

Wrinkled and scarred, the gray, sunken man looked down at her, his pale blue eyes strangely devoid of actual color, tongue moving in and out as he perused her face.

Eva nearly screamed when she realized that his tongue was, in fact, split, as he caressed his dry lips with the short, severed pieces. Several scars ran vertically across his throat, leaving three long slashes that suggested someone had perhaps tried to behead him. Well, this explained the raspy vocal cords as well as the hissing sound that created his speech. Tufts of white hair floated wildly around his head, peppered with bare areas covered in dark spots.

"You're hisssss troublemaker," the withered man stated. "Notthhhhing," he spat, and Eva flinched as the flicks of spittle hit her cheek.

The man raised his hand toward her face, and her eyes grew wide as just three fingers and a thumb hovered above her. Wiping the spit around her face with rough, dry hands, he then held up the appendage for her examination. "Sssssacraficcccce for the Masssssster," he wheezed out, explaining the missing ring finger. "You will know." A coughing fit cut him off from saying more, or perhaps he'd finished for a moment.

He walked back away from her line of sight, and Eva struggled again to see where he was going or what he was doing. Finally she begged, hating the pleading hitch in her words, "What do you want from me?"

A sharp smack shook her head, banging it deeper into the wood surrounding it, bringing tears to her eyes. The headache that followed reminded her that not too many hours ago she'd suffered a concussion.

"S-s-sorry" she whispered. Would they even give her a chance to give them what they wanted? Why didn't they tell her what they wanted or ask her questions? Surely they would realize quickly that she wasn't who they wanted.

"Silence," the guard who had struck her muttered, as he and the others moved around the table close enough that Eva could catch occasional glimpses of them. A bang near her head caused her to flinch again. A large book had dropped onto the table next to her head, letting off a cloud of dust and an odd leather smell that floated across her face, gagging her as she struggled to catch her breath.

The wizened creature stood over her, alternating licking a finger with his forked tongue, then turning the pages of the book. The smell of old pages and sulfur floated up as each page flipped. Grunting and wheezing, he examined the pages before stopping, then continued his intense, uncomfortable examination of Eva, without touching her.

*Thank God for small favors,* Eva thought as she shrank away from his beady gaze.

Without a word, he began grasping points of the air above her, twisting and turning invisible strands as he examined them, similar to what Delta had done, although she'd had permission.

"Dissssgussssssting," he hissed and nodded at one of the men near her head, who then grabbed her throat again, prying her mouth open with his other hand.

The old witch bent closer and stuck a finger deep into her throat, prodding around while she choked and gasped for air. Just when Eva started seeing stars, he removed his fingers, casually wiping them on her face, while she sucked air into her screaming lungs.

Eva gave up any pretense of bravery and began crying, softly gasping as she fought to breathe.

"Shhhheeee isssss wrapped in magic," the old man said, revulsion filling his voice. "Thisssss isssss what blocks him." More shuffling and banging outside of Eva's vision. "We mussssst rip it out, for him." Disgust filled his harsh tone as fear reverberated through Eva. "Then he will have hisssss raven, hisssss dark queen."

Realization swept through her as she began putting his words together. This revolting man planned to finish removing the threads surrounding her; the threads Delta had been gently unraveling that still led to exhaustion and pounding headaches for both of them, even using slow, meticulous methods. He planned not just to remove them, but to rip them out for some unknown master to get to Ravyn.

Rough hands once again forced her mouth open, bruising her lips in their roughness, then inserted a piece of wood between her teeth, forcing her jaws open several inches. Her tongue fought for space, and she could taste the blood from her dry lips that had been torn during the intrusion. Shallow, panicked breaths through her nose were causing her head to swim, leaving her precariously light-headed. She must convince herself to slow her breathing and calm down before she passed out took several long seconds. Inhaling and exhaling slowly through her nose, trying to keep the panic from leaving her breathless, was a losing battle.

Ignoring her struggles, the group circled the table, leaving little room between them. The old man muttered in what Eva now could recognize as Latin even if she didn't understand the words. He began slashing viscously through the air. For several minutes nothing happened, and then Eva felt a pain rip through her entire body. As soon as the pain dissipated another wave racked through her, and another. Louder, the man hissed his garbled words, and his hands slashed the air harder and harder as each wave of pain grew more powerful.

Eva's eyes grew even wider, and her mouth moved to scream around the wooden block, but nothing could come out.

With cold, blank eyes, the three men around her held tight to her legs and chest as she thrashed about, unable to exert even a minuscule amount of control over her body. Her bladder quivered as the water Eva had allowed herself earlier ran down her legs in a warm stream of urine. One of the men grunted but tightened his grip on her leg even as the pungent liquid spread. Silent tears ran down her face, and her teeth bit tightly into the wedge in her mouth. Mentally, Eva begged for it to all end as the evil man cut through the magical bounds with no regard to the pain that shattered her down to her soul.

Hours later, perhaps—time no longer had any meaning—Eva no longer cried or even fought as the pain shook and racked her body. Head rolled to the side as much as it could, staring unseeing at the wall of Latin, she barely noticed when the pain stopped. It was the man's raspy, struggled breathing that cut through the haze.

From a distance, she heard him admit, "Ve are clossssse now, but I mussssst resssssst a bit." It sounded as if two of the guards were walking the old man through the door, their footsteps echoing through her mind. The guard left behind pulled her lips back and worked the wedge free from her mouth. He loosened the strap on her neck, and her head immediately fell to the side, unable to stay upright.

Shivering from the now cold puddle she lay in, she whispered, "Water?" not caring if it ended with another punch to the head. Nothing could hurt as bad as she hurt. Not answering, the man held a water bottle to the side of her mouth, letting it slowly drizzle in, removing and then repeating this a few more times.

In the distance through the haze of pain, Eva could hear thudding on a door, reminding her of when the hellhounds had broken through her own back door. Her heart skipped a beat when she heard a pitiful howl followed by more pounding. These were the first sounds outside of the room of pain that she'd heard since she'd entered. Was Baby Boy all right? Sharp barks punctuated the howling and pounding. Surely he was!

After a respite, the men shuffled back in. At least his steps weren't as lively now, Eva thought bitterly, knowing that no matter the pain or discomfort the witch faced, it wasn't nearly as much as she felt.

"Can't we just kill her to destroy the thread? It would be much simpler and faster than this," a guard grumbled.

*Yeah.* Eva thought bitterly, *this has been really rough on you.* Never in her life had her body felt so much pain. It continued to pulsate through her from her limbs to the ends of her hair.

"We don't know where the undead queen'sssss thread would go. It could disssssapear, yesssss, but it could choossssse another. Dessssstroy. Then death." The old man's tone indicated that her inevitable death was less than nothing, and her stomach rolled, realizing that there was a good chance no one was coming to save her. If they were coming, wouldn't they be here by now?

"Damn, I wish that mutt would shut up," another guard cursed as the hellhound howled from the basement.

"Yeah, why don't you go down and shut him up, or even chain him back up?"

"Hell no. Even those puppy bites burn. We need to get another tranq spell first. I can't believe you idiots didn't have extras."

The arguments floated around Eva's head as Baby Boy kept up the banging and howling. Then the sound changed slightly; it added a crack to the mix, and then a yip of excitement. Another bang was followed by a longer crack. Eva smiled, imagining the door cracking and falling open for Baby Boy to escape. Maybe he could get back to his family. *Run,* her mind fleetingly begged of the pup, knowing he couldn't hear her. *Save yourself, little one.*

"Oh shit, close the door!" The room erupted in panic as the men shouted, boots thumping as they ran toward the door, slamming it closed and causing the room to shake a little. A howl shook the upstairs as the pup celebrated his escape from the confines of the damp dungeon. His heavy paws stomped through the house, ending a moment later outside the door.

*"No, go, Baby Boy!"* Eva wasn't even sure if she spoke the words aloud. *Run, run, run,* her mind screamed to the puppy. Then the room reverberated as he slammed against the closed door. Eva shut her eyes as the old witch began hissing his unknown chants and garbled words again. In Eva's mind, it sounded as if the hellhound's barks had multiplied and that sharp barks surrounded the room. but that wasn't possible. He was just one pup. Her mind was cracking; that was it.

Then all hell broke loose, or at least that was what Eva would tell others later after the explosion and chaos settled. Despite the fact that she could only see bits of the room, the simultaneous crashing on both sides of the room and not the door gave Eva the hope that help had arrived via the three large, drape-covered windows. Her eyes darted back and forth as bits of deep green drapes were flung around the room. Lithe figures in black floated in and out of her vision with a flash of silver . . . swords? She could only imagine the guards' surprise when faced with true adversaries and not an injured, chained up woman or a puppy missing his mama. Their feet crunched on the glass as they floundered around the room, unprepared for this sudden entrance.

Shouts, grunts, and thuds surrounded her and frantically, Eva tried to shift her head to see what was happening around her.

The wizened old man stood above her, looking more angry than scared, raising a thick, prehistoric-looking, black-handled knife above her head. "Die," he hissed.

Eva couldn't even close her eyes. If this was it, she wouldn't die with her eyes closed.

But an unearthly howl filled the air, and a glint of silver so quick Eva barely saw it flashed above her. Then in slow motion, the decrepit creature intent on destroying her dropped the knife as the hand holding it flew in a different direction. His face changed quickly from anger, then shock, then pain before he dropped out of her line of sight and a spray of blood clouded her vision, forcing her to close her eyes.

Blinking rapidly to clear out her sight, she saw Oliver's beautiful, bloody face appear above her. With a clank, he dropped his sword to the ground and gripping the chains with both hands, he tore the links apart, finally releasing Eva from her captivity.

With bloody hands, Oliver gently unraveled Eva

and helped her into a sitting position. Wrapping his arms around her back and torso, he leaned his head gently against hers as both Eva and her limbs moaned in relief. Breathing in Oliver's essence brought her comfort, and for several steady breaths, she took him in, as her body continued to tremble against him from the trials inflicted upon her. Over. It was over. Unless her mind was shattered, he'd come for her. He hadn't forgotten her.

"I've got you now," he whispered against her face, pressing his lips against her forehead, ignoring the filth that covered her. "I'm so sorry," he chanted over and over as his bloodied hands steadily and carefully removed the blocks and restraints from around her face and then the rest of her body.

Eva wanted to tell him that it was okay. Everything was okay now. Barely recognizable, garbled noises formed in her throat torn raw from hours of screaming as she struggled to form words.

Scooping her up like a child, Oliver turned and looked in rage at the shriveled man who clutched his bloodied stump of an arm against his face, mewing in pain. Lifting his chin in defiance, he opened his mouth.

"Don't," Eva managed to breath out, but Oliver already had a leg pulled back. He kicked the witch across the room into the wall, letting loose another flurry of dust as the creature moaned and slid down the wall in slow motion.

Surrounding Eva were the figures in black who had come through the windows to rescue her, while the guards who had taken part in her torture were now silent, bloody and unmoving on the floor. Eva couldn't even allow herself a minuscule amount of pity for them and if she had energy for even more than existing, she happily would have spat on them. Silently, the group looked at her as the pounding on the door grew louder. Howling somewhere outside had the men shifting around the room, bouncing on the balls of their feet, weapons loosely in hand but upright in preparation.

"Sir, the witches are reporting that the hellhounds have woken but are currently staying outside the house perimeter. We'll need to dispose of them on the way out, to make it through."

One of her saviors inspected the old witch, poking him to ascertain if he still lived.

Surprisingly, in a shocking display of strength, the old creature sat up and pointed his bleeding stub at Eva. "Asssss you scream, he will eat the flesh from your bonesssss and take your ssssstrength and power. The Massssster will devour you and share thisssss world with hisssss Undead Queen."

At his dark foretelling, the pounding on the door began again in earnest as the young hellhound grew frantic at the sound of his torturer's voice. Casually, the soldier flipped his sword and in one swift motion, the evil man's head was removed, rolling along the floor and ending with his open light blue eyes staring at the ceiling.

Eva found herself bubbling out hysterical laughter that cut off sharply as the door split open and Baby

Boy jumped into the middle of a room of armed men. With the wiry, black fur on his back raised in anger, puffs of smoke curling from his mouth, and steam sizzling off his body, it was easy to see him as the predator he truly was.

"No," she croaked as they raised their weapons, perhaps to end him where he stood. "Wait!" Frantic to cut them off before they could also decapitate the young pup, she called, "Baby Boy." Struggling against Oliver's hold, her voice scratched out, "Don't hurt him."

Upon hearing her voice, the pup's ears cocked as he took in the room, searching for its source. After laying eyes on her in Oliver's arms, he dropped to his belly, letting out a yip and wiggling his entire body with happiness at finding his fellow captive, ignoring all other threats in the room.

"Help me to him," Eva ordered Oliver, who dropped down to a squat, but kept one arm raised protectively against the beast.

# Chapter Twenty-Three

*You're barking up the wrong tree.*

Breathless with a combination of adrenaline and relief, despite the danger the young beast offered, Oliver couldn't deny Eva, especially after his neglect had caused her capture and torture. Such a gentle soul . . . How could he deny her anything after everything she'd been through over the past days?

Careful to keep some skin-to-skin-contact, hoping his power would strengthen her, he lowered Eva to the ground. She grimaced; rage filled him along with the immediate need to kill all those who had been a part of this torture again. Her perfect skin marred with purple and green bruises was proof of their extended abuse, with matching echoes under her eyes. Oliver might not trust the hellhound, but he did trust Eva. Sitting her part way on the ground, he supported her while keeping an arm stretched around her in case the beast attacked.

It didn't attack; at least not in the way Oliver feared or expected of the hell-born spawn.

"Baby Boy," she cooed, encouragingly balanced in his grasp, "we did it."

The hound crept closer with his belly to the ground before leaping to cover the last of the distance separating them, landing so hard he briefly pushed Oliver back on his heels before he regained his balance. Without hesitation or worry about the surrounding men, the hound landed on Eva's lap. She wrapped both arms around the demon, pulling him close as he frantically licked the blood from her face. "Hey, buddy, you're a good boy. What a hero. Paws-itively amazing." Glancing at Oliver, she added softly, "You too. Thank you."

Oliver could only awkwardly hug her tighter in his arms, pressing his face into her hair, marveling that they'd found her in time. No doubt they'd cut it close. Too close.

The group watched in awed silence as the hound preened under Eva's attention, before pulling himself off her to explore. He sniffed and huffed around the room while the team continued to observe him warily, determined to bravely hold their ground when his exploration found him too close to them. Finding the old witch's head, he cocked a leg over it and let off a long stream of hot piss as the mercenaries continued staring in disbelief. Satisfied with that act, he picked up the severed hand, promptly lay down with his back to the wall, and began chewing on the wrinkled gray appendage.

Hellhounds were rarely seen. Never had Oliver seen one in any state other than when trying to kill all those around it. From the looks and quiet murmurs among his wolves neither had they, despite their assumed relation to the beasts. Hellhounds were usually bearing down to maim and kill while leaving a trail of stinking brimstone in their wake. This young one looked and acted quite regular canine-like when he wasn't glowing, and if you could overlook the fact that the chew toy was actually a human body part, who was he to judge a fellow predator?

"Sir, the barrier around the house dropped when the old bastard died. All three hellhounds are able to enter the grounds and reports say they're coming straight for the house."

"Tell the witches to snare them again. Even if they can't see them, they can track them, can't they?" Oliver snapped.

The mission coming in had to be quick and precise, the entire location overrun with witches' traps, layered protections, and magical alarms. They'd opted to stun the pack quietly in case completely incapacitating them set off an alarm. Of course, knowing little about hellhounds meant that the stun potion had worn off more quickly than anticipated.

"They've moved too fast, out of range already," came the short report.

The men sized up again despite the fact that their guard hadn't been let down. Shifting heavily back and forth, adjusting the few weapons they were armed with, they awaited Oliver's next command.

Scooping Eva back into his arms, determined to whoosh her out of this hell hole, he noted the pup's eyes and ears perk up and follow his movement. Although Oliver trusted Eva, he didn't feel the same about this pup. Warily, he began backing from the room, preparing for an acceleration back to their safe house. The vamps still outside securing the area could easily outmaneuver the hellhounds as well, but Oliver wasn't so certain that his wolves would be left unscathed even if they did share a common ancestor.

Oliver assumed that if it were the decapitated witch who had brought the beasts to this plane and controlled them, his death made it possible for them to immediately return to the afterworld, which was generally what hellhounds seemed to desire. Looking once again at the tiny hell beast, he began to suspect that it might no longer be Eva they were after. Something else was bringing them to this house of horrors.

Eva's Baby Boy stood up, moving fast toward him; Oliver began to recognize that it didn't want Eva out of his sight, and while he commiserated with it, he also feared the beast had somehow imprinted on her.

"Good boy," she murmured to the beast, who happily wagged his entire body beginning at his tail at her praise, while his tongue lopped out the side of his mouth.

Hesitating, Oliver explained the obvious to Eva, fearing to see the disappointment in her face. "We can't take a hellhound with us."

"He's all alone, and he's a baby." Her brown eyes welled with tears, as if they were, in fact, leaving a defenseless baby behind to fend for himself.

Damn! He hated himself all over again.

"It needs to find a way home, and more are

coming; most likely the ones that attacked you earlier. Even if their master is dead, they might still be following his last command, unable to give up the hunt. That's all they want to do: hunt and kill. Even that little one in there."

As Eva grabbed his forearms, Oliver felt her pulling energy from him, most likely still unaware that she did such a thing. Just a hint of it, before she gained enough strength to struggle from his grip and attempt to stand on her own. Letting her reluctantly go from his arms was the hardest thing he'd faced that day.

"Come here, Baby Boy."

The overzealous pup launched himself from across the room, jumping from a seated position into her arms, pushing her back against Oliver, whose solid frame caught her before she could stumble as much as a step back. "He's not like the others, and he's had a rough few days," she tried to explain as the pup proceeded to lick more grime from her face.

Oliver grimaced, wondering if Eva had forgotten that just seconds before the "puppy" had been teething on a human hand.

"Boss, we've got them coming in fast and hot. We need to get the asset out of here." Even if Oliver had begun to muddle the rescue, his men remained focused.

Rubbing his forehead, not wanting to disappoint Eva, Oliver realized that this particular battle needed to wait until they were safe. "Circle up." With a few hand gestures, he commanded the men to protect their backs as he pointed at another to be eyes up front, placing Eva and a hellhound right in the middle of the circle of protection. Apparently, he'd unknowingly become part of a hellhound rescue mission, but for Eva, he would walk through the fires of hell itself.

Moving quickly through the house could be detrimental if there were more traps in place that hadn't disintegrated at the old man's death. Once they were in the open, they could stagger the vampires and wolves and then back track in two groups along the path they'd already cleared. On alert, the group crept through the house, wary of potential dangers as Oliver carried Eva, who in turn held the unpredictable predator in her arms.

Standing tall, Oliver continued to rotate his head between the areas they passed through, as did Eva's newfound friend. He noted that the pup stayed on alert, alternating between happy licks to Eva's face, then twisting his neck to scan the area and men with wide eyes and perked up ears.

"Stay still," he ordered the pup as his movements attempted to unbalance him, hoping he understood him as much as Eva. The hellhound let out a low whine and licked one of the hands that held Eva, quickly, but complied although his eyes continued to rapidly access his surroundings. The pup already appeared to run on pure instinct, and perhaps that would help him survive—assuming they could all get out of there and get the pup someplace safe to nestle up next to some hellfire.

Two men moved forward to scan the exit door for magic and, finding none, opened it, so the group could file out and regroup in formation, before trekking off the wooden porch to fan out in the yard. The guards there joined the group, with Oliver and his cargo safely in the center of them.

A low voice whispered a warning. "Shit, two o'clock, the witches say they were unable to banish them back to hell. They were moving too quickly. They should be coming into sight now."

Slightly to the group's right, the pack of three hellhounds emerged from the tree line at break-neck speed, determined to reach their quarry. Skidding to a stop about fifty yards from the group, they stood firm, their hackles stuck up as gray smoke rose off their backs. Three sets of red eyes assessed the situation, and their pointed ears twitched in the wind, their pitch black fur soaking up every bit of the fading light.

A few of the rescuers slowly began revolving their swords again, while others clicked out fang and claw, as the two groups warily eyed each other at a standoff. Despite the fact that the mixed group included both wolves and vampires with magnified speed and strength, the hellhounds were also enhanced with similar demon-like abilities. As much as Oliver despised the creatures, he also recognized that they shared a lot of the same characteristics. And the wolves might hesitate to battle a creature that possibly shared the mythological Norse wolf Fenrir as an ancestor.

Except the hellhounds weren't at home here on Earth. A witch—he assumed the dead one upstairs—had called them forth from their home in hell, binding them to him, then forcing them to hunt those he chose. Driven by instinct, they would fight the binding, yet a powerful enough witch could usually dominate and control one, maybe two, but three seemed like an impossible feat. Could another witch still be nearby, wrestling control of one of them, while the others followed pack drive?

Oliver's own instinct as well as the intel they'd been gathering as they tracked Eva to this witches' lair told him the witches in the vicinity had been obliterated. Whirring, his mind tried to consider what could be driving the beasts. Then with a groan of realization it struck him; he would have thumped himself in the head if his arms hadn't been wrapped around Eva and the infernal fucking hellhound pup.

They were looking at a family unit. The witch upstairs hadn't been strong enough to call forth three hellhounds and bind them to him. But he'd been smart enough to get his hands on a pup, then most likely bound one of the hounds to him. With threats against the pup, he kept them all in line to follow his bidding until his death. It wasn't remnants of a last command driving them. It was their pup.

"Eva," he whispered, nodding toward the frozen beasts, which had begun to growl low with a warning clear enough that the threat could be heard across the yard. "I think that's its family."

"Whose family?" At first confused, it took seconds for Eva to realize that the sooty, red-eyed creatures might belong to Baby Boy. "Ohh. Ohhh!" Squeezing the pup nestled against Eva's neck, Oliver could feel the disappointment emanate from her.

Standing her up again but keeping his arms around her and the overgrown pup to help support her, he told her sadly, "It couldn't continue to survive in this place. It needs the heat, brimstone, and hellfire to thrive. It needs its family, and they've been waiting for it. Everything they're doing is for their pup."

"I know." Nodding, Eva struggled to keep the tears from her voice. "Hey, Baby Boy, your mama and the others have found you." The poor little guy had been a prisoner just like her, and he deserved to return to his family as much as she did.

The group fanned out, leaving open space directly between the two sets of threesomes, still remaining prepared for the expected as well as the unexpected. One of the three hellhounds let out a sharp bark, along with a steaming puff of brimstone, and jumped a few feet toward the group, its tense muscles preparing for whatever came next. Eva's armed saviors tensed in anticipation but held the line just as they'd been trained to do, prepared to go down if necessary for the mission.

The noise caught the young hound's attention. His excitement grew, and he licked Eva while also wiggling and struggling to get down from her arms, yipping as he pushed away to find the source of the familiar sound.

Once on the ground, he let out a series of sharp, rapid-fire barks and stumbled briefly over his over-sized paws as he ran toward his awaiting family. Hesitating, he looked back at Eva and laid his ears down, giving a questionable yip at her as his eyes flickered a short flash of red before settling back into blackness.

"Go. Go, sweetie, your family is there. Go with them."

With another happy bark, Baby Boy turned and ran at full speed to the three adult hellhounds. Bouncing around, the group frolicked in greeting, nipping at each other while interjecting the play with joyful yips, clearly overjoyed at the reunion. One raised its head, flattening its ears and letting out a loud, long howl that reverberated through the air around them and had Eva covering her ears in pain as they snapped and popped. The howl tapered off as a fog rolled up around the beasts, whose eyes flared blood red before they simply disappeared. Just as quickly, the fog dissipated too. As it floated away, the scent of brimstone followed briefly and then was gone.

The forces stood in silent awe, watching the situation unfold, before Malthazar's deep voice broke the silence behind them. "Eh! I need to stay around here longer if you keep giving me such adventure."

Malth strolled out of the house, swinging the head of the wizard by his lackluster remaining strands of hair. His own wavy hair was pulled back away from his face, showcasing his two tiny horns. His hands and forearms were covered in blood; like Oliver, he hadn't needed any other weapons. Tossing the head to a startled guard who nearly dropped his weapon, but still caught it with one arm despite the look of disgust that crossed his face.

"Hold that for the boss. Interrogate soon." Malth was a man of few words, but he was correct; a necromancer could see what secrets the witch held.

Oliver's focus had only been on getting to Eva and destroying anything and everything that stood between them.

Bloody and damn, was he shirtless as well?

Malth paused before Oliver and Eva, studying her face. He began to reach out with one bloody paw and before Oliver could stop himself, he growled at his friend. With a guttural laugh, Malth continued reaching out to gently touch Eva's face with one finger, leaving a trail of blood in its wake.

"Sister," he said in his deep, raspy voice, "you have been sorely treated." Dropping his hand back to his side, Malth nodded solemnly to Oliver, confirming his relationship to the woman.

Solemnly, Malth continued kindly, "You're rare, sister. It is rare for a female half-demon to be born of a union. Long ago you were hunted by them. The hellhound that killed your parents could have been searching for you or for them. Retribution or attempted kidnapping? Probably never know. Memories are short in demons or anything that lives forever." With a shrug, Malthazar's clipped words confirmed some of what the group had guessed.

Scooping Eva into his arms and without looking back, Oliver demanded, "Burn it to the ground as soon as it's cleared." The home and land were seeped with dark, blood magic. Eva hadn't been the first to be brought here, but she would be the last. Burning the hovel to the ground was a start, and Hecate's coven would ensure the land was purged. Oliver suspected it might take generations to cleanse the land, but the witches were nothing if not thorough.

Home. Battered and damaged, but still alive. Oliver was bringing Eva home.

# CHAPTER TWENTY-FOUR

*Is having a penis fun? It has its ups and downs.*

The days back in Oliver's fortress passed slowly. Holding her in his arms until he could safely deposit her in his home had offered both strength and comfort to her, literally healing her while he gave her energy that food and drink couldn't provide.

Eva wanted to thank all those involved in tracking and rescuing her, but they all melted away before she could gather her thoughts and wits. Arriving back at Oliver's home had felt like coming home again, but it was much quieter than before. Doors shut with a whisper, rooms emptied quietly when she entered them. In fact, outside of Oliver's housekeeper and Delta, who had performed an oddly quiet but thorough exam of Eva before leaving for her own apartments, only one young wolf had approached her at all.

He'd pressed a cup of coffee into her hands, whispering, "I made you this,"

"Sit," she patted the seat next to her whispering the words hopefully.

The youth shook his head negatively. "He says you need quiet and rest," before smiling sadly at her and slipping from the room without another sound.

The coffee was sweet, too sweet, and the espresso tasted burnt, but she drank all of it anyway. It may have been the best cup she'd ever had. Before she'd been taken, the young man had been one who had lined up daily, joking and jostling in line to get his own too sweet beverage made by Eva. When Sebastian and Ravyn had returned to the west coast, the young wolf had pleaded to stay longer. After a day, she no longer saw him at all either, and she couldn't bring herself to ask where he'd gone. Perhaps he too had moved on and was now on the west coast with the others on Ravyn's security team. Eva hadn't asked; there was no one to ask.

Delta had vanished as well, only a quickly sprawled note that had appeared next to Eva's morning coffee letting her know that the witch was taking a few days off to recuperate. Unsigned, it could have been left by Oliver, housekeeping, or Delta herself.

Now the house echoed with the quietness of a tomb. Ironic, considering its owner was a vampire, she supposed. She floated from room to room like a wraith, searching for signs of life, which seemed to avoid her at all costs. Rooms in which the occupants would silently melt away left her feeling unseen and avoided. Nights blended into days, and by keeping the blinds drawn, she often remained uncertain which was which.

So, she worked.

Someone kept her laptop fully charged, and so she typed and typed, blending a story that belonged both to her and another. Blurring the lines between what happened to her and what happened to book Fala Ishto. Her own kidnapper, torturer, and tormentor became a storybook caricature destined to be defeated by Fala's great love interest, finally giving the heroine the happily ever after she deserved. The fairy tale romance that seemed to elude Eva was given freely to Fala. The words poured out, a balm that left Eva feeling raw and exhausted at the end of each writing session. She often fell asleep at a table or on the sofa with laptop in hand, waking up back in her bed or sprawled on the sofa with a blanket tucked around her and her laptop being charged, ready for its next palliative session.

The clothes Oliver had purchased for her that fateful day had been washed and placed in drawers in the room she returned to. More had joined them, soft lounge pants that she paired with tee shirts and changed each time she showered, which happened every few hours. Memories of the dank, dirty basement sent her straight to the shower. Flashes of the spittle dripping onto her face from the rancid breath of the scraggly-haired witch sent her to the shower. Phantom twinges from the magic being torn from her soul sent her into the hottest bath she could stand just to warm up. She scrubbed until her skin became raw and red before donning clean clothes until another whisper sent her into a panicked shower or bath, once again determined to scrub the sins from her skin.

She sat now at yet another meal while Oliver paced around her, sipping from a crystal glass, watching to make certain she took more than a few bites. Eva wanted to tell him she wasn't broken, but her mouth couldn't form the words. She couldn't trust herself to believe the words. Maybe she was broken. Maybe she'd always been broken.

Setting her fork down while Oliver eyed her every movement like the predator he was, Eva chokingly whispered, "I'm sorry." Despite his supposed enhanced hearing, he only blinked slowly at her, so she cleared her throat before forcing the words out more loudly. "I said. I said. I'm sorry."

Oliver stopped his pacing to stare at her. Teeth clenched; his hands tightened around the glass to the point she was afraid he would break it. Instead, he turned and threw the glass against the wall behind him. Eva couldn't help letting out a shriek and jumping as the glass crashed into the wall, shattering and letting the thick, red liquid ooze down the wall. The fury in his face was instantly replaced with regret as he took a step toward her.

Frozen, her heart pounded rapidly against her chest as he stopped well away from her before sorrowfully pushing a hand through his hair. "No, no, no, no, nononono," he muttered. "This is not on you."

Tentatively taking two short steps in her direction, Oliver stopped and held up both hands when Eva felt herself retreat deeper into her chair. "You have nothing to feel sorry for . . . None of this was your fault. I'm the one who is sorry." His face crumbled. "I'm so damn sorry."

Biting her lip, Eva waited. What could he possibly

be sorry for? Oliver had saved her. Saved her and the young hellhound. She liked to imagine Baby Boy snuggled close to his mama and family, warmed by them and the brimstone they slept on, nothing lingering in his memory of the cold and pain that had been inflicted on him. As bad as her torture had been, she liked to imagine that she'd had a part in saving him. Like lightning, the thought struck her. Perhaps that was Oliver's hope for her. Despite it not being his fault, maybe he wanted to also vanquish the unseen injuries and heart-stopping fears but didn't know how?

Shaking his head, he continued, "No, don't make me into some sort of hero. A necromancer questioned that depraved nob. You were a means to an end. You were standing between him and his Queen Ravyn. Not that the damn thing gave many straight answers. He'd spelled himself to only spout death and destruction along with adoration for his queen. The creature was insane, and it's due to my world that you were caught up in his insanity."

This time shaking her head vigorously, Eva argued, "No one is responsible for that. Ravyn literally saved my life. If I have a choice between death and facing life no matter how hard it is, I will always choose life. One could argue that I'm a weakness for Ravyn, that I put her life in danger by existing when all she wanted to do was help some poor, near dead child."

Standing and pushing herself up and away from the table, this time causing Oliver to stumble back, she added, "No one, and I mean no one, is responsible for what happened except for those bastards who are, in fact, responsible. And since no one has bothered to ask me about anything, I can tell you that he wasn't working alone. He may have called Ravyn his queen, but he also answered to a master."

"Oliver," she pleaded, "I wish we could go back to how we were before. I wish we could laugh and watch movies together. I wish you could tell me about your day. I wish you wouldn't look at me like I'm broken or falling apart."

She took a few steps closer to him. "I wish I knew that what I felt for you was real. I wish I knew it wasn't one-sided. I wish we could just have a chance." Looking at him across the room, she begged him to understand. The air slowly escaped her lungs before she admitted, "I would love to have seen where we could've gone. But I refuse to be a supporting character in my own life. I deserve to be the main character, but I can't be if this is how things are. I just can't be."

In a blink of an eye, Oliver had crossed the space that separated them, as Eva's heart pumped wildly.

"It's not too late, is it?" he asked, his voice gentle and vulnerable, his earnest, open expression breaking her heart again. But the hope in his voice reflected the hope she felt in heart. "I couldn't protect you from any of this. I should have been able to, but I couldn't and I didn't. I don't even know how you can look at me with everything you've faced. All I've done for you is let you down."

"You stupid, stupid man," Eva whispered, closing

the distance between them.

*Main character vibes,* she chanted to herself, squashing the fear that rippled through her body. Before she could talk herself out of it, she held his head in both hands as his anguished eyes met her. Pulling downward, she saw the look change to surprise as she smashed her lips against his, the tightness in her chest easing for the first time in days.

It only took a second before his lips turned soft against hers, matching the intensity breath by breath as she held his face gently against hers. His strong hands went to her sides, pulling her hips invitingly against his own, allowing her to melt into him.

*Finally,* floated through her mind as she opened her lips, darting her tongue out, inviting—no, daring him closer.

With a growl, he lifted her up, pulling her even closer. She wrapped her legs around his waist, feeling the heat rise through her core and move into her lower stomach, urging him closer still, her soft, thin pants hardly a barrier between them.

"I don't want to hurt you," he whispered against her even as she sought to draw him closer, feeling his need snapping through the air, flitting upon her face, teasing her with the desire that was so near.

"You can't," she said as her body demanded he come closer still. "I need you to . . ." Overwhelmed by the intoxication of his desire, Eva could barely form a coherent thought, let alone words. "I need this."

"I want to fuck you until you scream," Oliver admitted as his tongue drew along the throbbing artery of her neck. "And when you get off, I want to bite you right here." He kissed the precise spot as Eva moaned, basking in the energy of his desire swirling about her, just waiting to be fed upon.

Eva leaned back, pushing her heat against him as he groaned, readjusting his grip on her hips to keep her core as close to him as possible. Frantically, she tugged his shirt up over his head, pulling down one arm and then the other until he stood bare-chested against her.

"I need you now." The floodgates, now open, had Eva begging him for what she needed.

"Not here . . . a bedroom," he gasped out between peppering kisses along her neck and face.

In the blink of an eye, Eva found herself lying on his bed while Oliver stood between her legs, gazing down on her with drunken, lust-filled eyes. She was doing that to him.

A pleased, powerful feeling passed through Eva at knowing that his desire matched hers. His body was a work of art, lithe and lean, marred only by a small pucker of scarred skin just to the right of his heart.

"Take off your shirt," he ordered lowly.

Eva scrambled to comply, tossing the offending article to the side as soon as she pulled it over her head. As his eyes darkened throughout, she slowly and lazily reached down to unhook the front clasp of her bra. Removing it slowly as she covered her full, heavy breasts with one arm, wiggling the bit of satin and lace off her shoulders, she watched him watching her like she was prey.

She released her full breasts from the safety of her arms and they bounced slowly down, tightened heavily under the heat of his gaze. Eyes completely black now, he looked down at her as she cupped her breasts with each hand, offering them up to him. "Like this?"

Whose husky voice dripping of sex was that?

Nodding, his chest tightened as he reached once again for her hips, this time sliding the soft leggings off and down her legs to her feet, leaving her exposed to him. Slowly, she lifted one foot out and then the other, making certain not to cover her sex, her desire for him, as it grew wet and fragrant under his dark gaze.

Her eyes dropped to his sweatpants, which grew tighter as he feasted his eyes upon her, taking in all of her without touching her. "I want to remember this moment forever," he admitted, flashing a hint of growing fangs at her as well.

Releasing her breasts, Eva ran her hands slowly down her body, watching his reaction as she imagined it was him touching her. Running her hands down her hips, barely brushing her mound, she pushed her own thighs apart.

"Promises were made, vampire." Her voice sounded strange and heavy to her, and she drew her hands back up her thighs, stopping before they would have touched the spot crying out for his attention.

Pushing his own pants lower on his hips, he slowly dropped them, his cock jutting out toward her at attention. Stepping out of the pants in a slow, fluid moment, he dropped his hands to her wrists, leaning deep between her legs hanging helplessly off the bed. Pinning her body with his own hard body, he pushed her hands above her head.

"Don't move them," he warned as the heat of his body sent pulses of desire through her body wherever he touched.

Nipping at her lip, he rewarded her with a kiss as she complied with a soft moan. Oliver moved down her body, dragging his heavy cock slowly down her body, followed by his mouth, showering each puckered nipple with his mouth until they tightened with sensitivity, blowing on each one softly before moving on down to her waist. She arched her back, trying to force more contact. With a low laugh, he pressed her stomach gently back onto the bed with a soft touch. "In good time, love."

Moving down, he pulled her legs up and with her knees over his shoulders, he dipped in gently between her legs, as she continued to arch up toward him, frantic with need.

"Bunny, if you knew how good you smell to me," he whispered, his breath just catching the edge of her dripping sensitivity as she cried out, wanting to beg him for more. "Vanilla and lavender are my two favorite plants now."

Grasping her hands together over her head, Eva forced herself to not grab him and pull him closer even as her hips bucked closer to his awaiting mouth.

"So beautiful, my impatient one." He gazed at what she felt was her own dampness down her leg. "You will scream so beautifully, and no one will hear you."

"Please . . ." she begged. "Please . . ." as his hot breath continued to caress and promise her things to come.

"Of course, since you asked so sweetly. How can I refuse? When you beg for my cock—and you will beg me for it—I will fill you so full you'll forget all those cockless fuckers from the past. You'll beg for my cum to fill you over and over, until it drips out of you," he promised her as he lowered his mouth on her wet, aching need.

# CHAPTER TWENTY-FIVE

*It's pasture bedtime.*

Satiated, Eva snuggled deeper into Oliver's embrace, slowly circling her index finger over the contours of his chest and down his abs as she floated down from the burst of power that had washed over her.

Despite her relaxed state, power hummed through her. Oliver could feel the vibrations under her skin and wondered if his body felt the same to her. She looked well fucked; well fucked and well fed, flushed and marked by the hours-long session. Pride settled through him; as promised, he'd made her scream, over and over again. But his little bunny hadn't begged him to stop; she'd matched him, taking everything he had to give her. Begged him to fill her with his cock over and over again.

He was content. Content for perhaps the first time in his long life. He slowly let out his breath as her exploration led back up the middle of his chest, and she traced the ridges of the puckered skin while he gently washed away the sticky strings of his cum that ran down her body.

"You're glowing," he stated, touching her pale,

white skin as it shimmered, dancing under the moonlight. Uncomfortably, she rubbed her arm as if to remove the light that emanated from her entire body. Catching her hand, he whispered, "Don't. It's beautiful." He wasn't lying, and truthfully, watching the shimmer was beautiful and mesmerizing. "I could watch you all night long."

With an awkward laugh, Eva admitted, "That will be a first; the fact that you're still awake after sex is a first for me."

Clearly, previous encounters had drained her lovers and while Oliver felt a twinge of jealousy that there had been others, he also felt pride that he was able to share this first with her. He vowed never to love her and then fall asleep. He would always bask in the peace of watching her body process the energy from the encounter. "As if I could fall asleep so easily with you."

Raising her head off his chest and looking more closely at the scarred tissue, so out of place on the rest of his body, she asked, "What happened here?" For a moment, uncertainty stopped her. "I mean, if you want to tell me. It's none of my business. Just because . . ."

Oliver raised his free hand to trace Eva's lips and then moved it down with habit to trace the raised circular flesh. For a moment, the smell of gunpowder and death assaulted him, but it dissipated with a look into Eva's wide brown eyes. Kissing her forehead, he admitted, "That's how I died."

Eva raised her head to look into his eyes, her curls falling into her face. He smiled and kissed the same spot again and pulled her back down to rest against him.

"I was born Oliver Patrick Davis in 1887." Eva raised an eyebrow at this but said nothing, so he continued turning back the years. Sensing her mirth, he laughed. "Yes, I'm well over a hundred years old. Looking good for my age," he teased, knowing there would be no lighthearted moments to his tale.

"My family did well, well enough for me to receive an education. I was fortunate enough to attend the University of Florida's College of Engineering." He absently stroked Eva's hair, winding the silky strands through his fingers; its tantalizing softness overrode the desire—no, the habit—to touch his own scar.

The time rolled back easily for Oliver at Eva's question. The years spent in Florida had been some of the best of his life, his true life. The first time he'd been so far from home, and the freedom it brought. The cheap, shared beers that lingered long on the lips, the lively discussions that often begot table pounding and shouting, but always ended with laughter and a firm pounding on the back of one another even when agreements weren't made.

He hadn't truly experienced the camaraderie of such young men before or since then. The peace. Of course, the young men were long gone now; the bloody war had ensured that. Most likely none had been lucky enough to experience old age. He'd never checked, and his heart softened with the realization that he missed those young men, so hopeful and carefree.

Graduating in 1913 near the middle of his class, which was standard for his life, Oliver found a job in the city of Boston working for an engineering firm whose name now eluded him. Still far from home, he assumed he had plenty of time to settle back down in Illinois, closer to family even if he lived in the city.

Those days were baseless, not like college, one exhausting day running into another. Long days still ended quite often in a bar with a few drinks that were no longer as cheap. Conversations still flowed, but not as freely as in his university days. The office hours converged seamlessly with the evening hours, as the young engineers discussed projects and developed ideas without the constraints of desks, middle management, and time frames. Often the best solutions arose from these evening drinking sessions surrounded by the jazzy music and constant noise of a city always on the go.

And this was his life; of course, there were rumblings of a war in Europe. Newspaper boys shouted out the headlines, and politicians waved their arms about as they spoke of it. But that seemed so far away, places that he'd read about and places that perhaps someday he would visit. But as more and more American ships were sunk around the British Isles, more rumblings began that the president's proposed neutrality wasn't possible.

In April 1917, President Wilson asked Congress to join the war: "A war to end all wars." Today, Oliver's chest tightened in sorrow as he thought of that promise, of that even being a possibility. But during those moments, those days, Oliver fervently believed in what the president was saying. Along with countless other young men, he joined the ranks to protect democracy.

"I wasn't a good soldier," he admitted, staring off into space, looking back over the years. "I was a good engineer, but really that didn't matter. I thought I could make a difference, the same as other young men, I suppose. The war needed bodies, and it was indifferent to strengths and weaknesses."

He was a member of the 11th Engineer Regiment, his unit attached to a British unit. A unit that found themselves in November of 1917 at the village of Fins, digging trenches behind British lines as the war raged on around them. All too soon, Oliver began to realize that the promises of old men were built on the deaths of young men. Even when the church bells rang of British victory, the screams of the injured and dying, as well as the silence of the dead, were deafening.

For ten days, the battle raged, the pounding of artillery and mortars making any amount of sleep impossible. Sometimes, the exhaustion would overtake a man for a few minutes, but true rest was unthinkable.

November 30th, a young, pimply-faced English private arrived at the back lines. Oliver guessed the boy was ten years younger than his own twenty-eight years. His haunted eyes told a different story, a vastly different age; war was imprinted on his soul. Death was a frequent visitor. He spoke in whispers. More men were needed. Any of the injured who could stand

and hold a gun were called back. The Americans were needed at the front. Even a few men might make a difference, might turn the tide.

Just a few whispered words, and Oliver found himself gearing up for battle at the front lines. Digging trenches could wait; this could make a real difference. *He* could make a real difference. Dirty and tired, he clenched his rifle—the rifle he'd kept clean and oiled despite being on the rear lines. Training had taught him that much: clean rifle, dry feet. Most days only one was possible. But all the training in the world couldn't truly prepare anyone for war. Everything was damp, even downright wet at times. Miserable. Supplies were short, but on the bright side, the brutal hunger they felt meant they were still alive.

"The plans of gods and men differ," he quoted quietly.

Eva's hands had quit tracing his body and now clutched him, as if driving the demons away were a possibility.

The battlefield and trenches were soaked in the blood of the fallen. What the rain washed away was immediately replaced. Oliver couldn't begin telling Eva about the horrors. He didn't want those images to mar her beautiful soul. He shook his head to bring himself back to the present. Back from the battlefield.

"It was a bayonet here." He brought up her hand and touched the center of his chest. For a moment, her touch replayed the shooting pain of the lance and then the frightening numbness that followed. "I'm not sure how I wasn't instantly killed. I lay there staring up at

340

the boy. Yes, it was a boy who had speared me. Another boy. A boy whose eyes were filled with sorrow. Both sides were sending boys. There was so much noise and then I could hear nothing. It was as if a vacuum had sucked all the noise and air off the battlefield. Blood appeared on the boy's chest and spread slowly out. Shock and horror replaced the sorrow in his eyes. He let go of the rifle holding the bayonet and fell to the side of me."

Even though he couldn't turn his head to see him, for years Oliver had often imagined the boy's lifeless eyes staring at him as the last of his blood pumped feebly from his wound. What had been his last thoughts? His mother? Was he old enough for a lover? Had he seen whoever had fired the fateful shot that ended his life? Paralyzed and unable to move, Oliver waited for his own death to come.

What Oliver couldn't tell Eva was that as he lay there staring up at the clear blue sky, he had thought, *This isn't how death should come. Can death arrive on such a beautiful day? Who should die on such a fine day?* The battle seemed to have moved on, and a strange, unearthly silence surrounded him—or his hearing had already left him, a merciful prelude to death.

Then a shadow blocked out the sun. A woman. A *woman* on the battlefield bent down over his head, upside down, her eyes even with his eyes. A hood covered her head and most of her face, but even in that moment he had no doubt that it was a woman who peered down at him. A strand of thick, straight black hair fell onto his face, although he couldn't feel it. He willed his mouth to say something, anything, but he couldn't manage even the tiniest of twitches. Oliver wanted to ask if death was a woman, if death was a Valkyrie sent to take him to the heavens? But the words formed only in his mind.

The dark eyes looked down at him and for a moment, he saw a flash of red. Red, which he was sure was his own life blood reflecting in her eyes. This stranger, this beautiful angel of death stared at him for a long moment, turning her head as if to examine his soul through his eyes.

Bending down closer, so close that he would surely feel her breath upon him, she whispered in an unrecognizable accent, "Do you want to live?" Then, pulling her head back, she began her slow perusal of his eyes again, waiting for his response, studying his face and his injury.

Oliver willed his lips to move, willed them to twitch. Willed his eyes to blink rapidly, screaming inside as he realized nothing was occurring. Prayed to whatever gods might listen that she understood that yes, *yes*, he wanted nothing more than to live. Nothing more than to see his mother again, nothing more than to go back to his boring, hopeless, but safe office job, nothing more than to find young women to love and grow plump together with age. He wanted to live. Did this dark stranger know that? Oliver didn't know then but was told later that tears were running down his face. That despite not moving or speaking to her, she did know he wanted to live.

"I'm Ravyn." She bent down and first kissed one cheek, then the other, seemingly un-bothered by the dirt and muck covering him. "This is going to hurt." Then all the pain and more returned.

Laying her hand flat on Oliver's chest where the skin still puckered from the injury, Eva again rose part way up. "Didn't this heal when you, um . . . changed?"

He pulled her hand up to his mouth and again kissed it gently. "So many things healed, aches and pains disappeared, and scars faded. All but this one. It's a reminder of my life and my death, I suppose. Sometimes I forget about it for months, maybe even years, but other times, I can still feel the bayonet sliding into my skin.

"Ravyn carried me from the battlefield under the cover of darkness. I disappeared, assumed dead like so many others at the Battle of Cambrai." Oliver found himself continuing, aching to tell Eva his story, needing her to know who he was and where he came from. "She wasn't a vampire looking to kill. God knows she could find enough blood and death on the battlefield. Humanity fears the unknown and the things that the dark might bring, but really they bring their own evil upon themselves. We don't need to search far for what we need; they serve it to us."

It only took a day and a night for Oliver to heal, to change, and to find himself desiring the blood that flowed plentiful across Europe for another year. Ravyn had been alone for many years at this point, and together they found companionship; friendship and freedom. Ravyn taught Oliver how to live without killing needlessly and without being caught.

"We would go into field hospitals and cure the wounded as best we could, passing through the night like angels of life and death. We used our blood to heal and spare those we could and ease the suffering of those who were not long for this world." Reaching over to the nightstand, Oliver retrieved the bottle of water he'd sat there earlier and took a long pull from it before offering it to Eva.

"After the war ended, we still traveled together for several years as the countries attempted to rebuild themselves. We saw the battlefields replaced with cities. Back alleys replaced the field hospitals, and instead of mesmerizing wounded soldiers in hospital beds, we began enchanting the rich at parties, slowly gathering what we needed to survive. I learned to live in a peace of sorts. Learned how to take care of Ravyn during her hours of sleep, hoping that if I were lucky enough to live so long, someday I might have such a companion."

Oliver allowed himself a sigh as he remembered what had been good years. "Of course, that peace didn't last long. Ravyn told me it never did, but I'd hoped. Before we knew it, another war erupted, just as the nations were starting to heal themselves. This time, the former soldiers who had survived were sending their own sons to die in trenches all over again. Rinse and repeat, it seems."

Oliver took another drink of water, his mouth dry from the memories he found himself eagerly wanting Eva to know about. "After that war, Ravyn and I went separate ways for many years. She didn't really need me. I think she created me in a moment of loneliness, and taking care of her gave me a sense of purpose for a while. We'd spent thirty years together and then we spent nearly that long apart. I came back to the States, and even though Ravyn had spent time in the Americas, she stayed in Europe and even Africa, traveling. There were still places she wanted to visit and people she wanted to see. Hell, she may have taken a long nap just to escape the world for a bit."

Oliver stopped himself. "Eventually, she did come to the States, and we've stayed in touch since then. Clearly, we followed different paths, but between Hollywood and security we've managed to overlap quite a bit. I know without a doubt that she trusts me with her life and I trust her with mine. That's why she knew I would help her when she needed it. I owe my life to her."

"Did you see your mother again?"

He sadly shook his head. "That was the wish of a dying man. I disappeared on that battlefield, and by the time I made my way back here, she was gone. I wondered for years if she welcomed death, thinking we would finally meet again. I disappointed her in life and in death, I suppose. I visited her grave a few times," he admitted. "It called her 'Beloved Mother,' and I suppose that was the epitaph for a missing, forgotten son who couldn't have his own burial."

For the first time since his death, Oliver felt a different kind of hope, one that didn't revolve around living forever alone or even alone with Ravyn. He felt the same hope he'd felt on the battlefield all those years ago, hope for something more than just an eternity of nothingness and boredom.

Eva sat still for a moment, hesitating to ask the question that was on her lips.

Oliver could sense her uncertainty in the rapid beating of her heart. "What is it? You can ask me anything."

A nervous giggle escaped her. "It seems stupid," she admitted. "You've gone through so much and my only question is because I'm jealous or could be." She couldn't bring herself to look at him and buried her face in his chest. A low rumble surrounded her, shaking her head from the vibrations. "Stop," she pleaded.

"No, it's just that it's amusing. Ravyn is a sister to me, and an older sister, at that. I would say mother, but I think she might cut my balls off if I dared make that claim. Never lovers." Oliver gently pulled Eva's face up to look at her and earnestly reiterated. "Never."

A soft smile crossed Eva's face. "Thanks, and thanks for not thinking I'm a jealous harpy. I mean, we did just meet and yes, we did this." A blush crossed her face at the memory of "this."

"Not a jealous harpy at all, but I have a feeling we're seeing some of your succubus coming through. They do tend to be jealous of their lovers and very possessive."

Eva stiffened in his arms, clearly not wanting to think about the newly discovered succubus part of her, and Oliver feared she might pull away from him at the reminder.

"Why did you start security instead of staying with engineering?" she asked in a thinly veiled attempt to change the subject, which Oliver allowed with relief, since that meant she wasn't pulling away from him and his faux pas.

*Don't bring up being a succubus unless she brings it up*, he ordered himself.

"It sort of went hand in hand and as times changed, I needed to evolve with it. Engineering was the foundation and then computers, and then when the Internet came to life, I followed and grew along with it. Cyber security is my main emphasis, but I also have the entire force of physical security to hire out as needed. They're a good balance to each other and in this era are quite lucrative."

"Oliver," Eva began, and he waited. "Thank you for telling me."

He could feel her heart slowing down to a steady pace again as she relaxed into him. His own chest swelled with something he couldn't quite put a name to. Was it relief? Contentment? Happiness? Maybe a mixture of all.

"I dreamed of Ravyn for the first time after I had sex." Eva admitted with quiet words. "Maybe that event solidified our bond or my half demon nature. I never saw her, but it was more like I saw through her eyes. I saw an entire world through her eyes. She has been my connection to the world for so many years. A part of me is unsure how I will see the world now that we are no longer connected."

Oliver wanted to tell her the world was still out there to explore. He wanted to tell her that Ravyn's existence didn't define Eva, but such comments were weak platitudes.

"You didn't feed from me during sex," she questioned hesitantly. "Is that a part of the lore too? I mean, I fed from you. Even though I don't know how I do it, I still did. And if you wanted to . . ." Trailing off, she looked at him, waiting for his answer.

At her suggestion, his cock swelled once again. She did this to him. She made him insatiable, and she gave him permission. Already her heady, sweet scent began to fill the room again; she was insatiable too. Pulling her over on top of him, his bobbing, thick cock searched for her heat. Kissing down her neck as he gently rolled a nipple between his fingers, Oliver determined it was time to bring her heart rate back up again, and leave the past where it belonged.

# CHAPTER TWENTY-SIX

*Make Like a Banana and Split!*

After waking next to Oliver mid-afternoon, Eva lay within his arms, daring only to savor the moment briefly before easing herself free even as his grip tightened in his sleep. Sleep that she knew would be brief for him, during these hours of full sunlight.

Despite her desire to stay longer and drink up the moment, the clock had already begun ticking. Years of escaping one-night stands had perfected her ability to slither, contort, and wiggle free without disturbing the partner next to her. Gathering clothes to wear, she walked barefoot and silent to the bedroom door, allowing herself to look back at Oliver's sleeping form. The vice grip on her heart tightened as she permitted this one last look at him. Perfection. It had been perfection.

Leaving now was for the best. Perhaps the last night and day had been selfish of her. Surely the best night of her life, but how could she be a parasite feeding off the best thing that had ever happened to her, knowing that he might not be choosing her of his own free will? Having him without his freedom wasn't really having him at all.

Instinctively, her hand rose to her neck, still feeling the puncture of his teeth in her skin, the phantom ecstasy that had already closed either due to her own healing ability or some mystical property of vampire saliva. A small part of her wished for the ability to maintain the punctures as a reminder of the night, but no physical reminder remained for a part-demon monster like herself. Just the memories.

Turning, Eva pushed herself to get through the door, where she could silently dress before selfishness overtook her and she stayed. Her backpack, already loaded with what she'd come with, slid easily onto her heavy shoulders. Then, without another backward glance, she did the only thing she was good at. She ran, ran home to her haven.

Leaving the house was uneventful. No one stood between her and the garage, despite the fact that maybe a tiny piece of her wished she'd run into at least one person. The garage door smoothly and silently slid open with her approach, gaping and giving her the view of the drive and sunshine, where once again she hesitated briefly as she fought herself, her intentions, and her own desires. Shifters watched her through the guard house door as she stared straight ahead at the gate, unable and unwilling to meet their gaze. In the end, this gate also smoothly opened for her exit.

The old Suburban, filled with gas and driving better than it had in years rolled smoothly along the highway both toward and away from her greatest desires. As the tires spun along the road, they rhythmically reminded her: coward, coward, coward. She angrily wiped away tears that flowed freely from puffy eyes. Why was she crying? She'd chosen this. This was her decision. Her demon heritage didn't control it, and her grandmother's magic tethers and protections no longer made decisions for her.

At a gas station halfway through her trip, she took down the hanging talisman from the rear-view mirror that her grandmother had given her when she got her license and threw it across the parking lot. After filling the huge tank, she skulked across the parking lot, kicking up dust and gravel as her eyes scanned rapidly for the little yarn-and-jade figure. She snatched it up angrily after she found it in the gravel and tossed it in the passenger seat, where the hanging figure could no longer mock her.

Someone had parked in her carport. A tiny Smart car, one of those that got great gas mileage but took up little to no room and would certainly be no good in a crash. Good God, once the wards had fallen, had that left her home open to any bit of riffraff who wanted to take what was hers? All she'd felt the entire trip was anger and now Eva had somewhere to focus it. She parked in the drive, blocking the small car in. She gritted her teeth while stomping to the doorway, seething, prepared to contact a towing company and having the slip of a car towed away or beat it to pieces with a sledgehammer. She hadn't made up her mind yet, but both seemed viable options.

Stopping at the door, she took in the newly framed

and painted door staring back at her. Oliver had insisted that he would have the home worked on, and she'd half expected things to still be the same. Eying it suspiciously, Eva knelt down in the dirt next to the front porch, searching for the rock that held her old key under a bush that, despite the early summer sunshine, held more dead leaves than living. A shiny new key had replaced her old one.

Hesitantly, she slid it into the lock where it smoothly clicked, suddenly uncertain what would face her when she opened the door. The hellhounds had done a number on her home. Was it even her home anymore? They'd slammed through the back door, ripping through the house before pounding once again straight through this doorway. Not that she blamed them. They were being controlled by the mage's black magic, driven by the unexplainable magic and fear for their little one. However, that didn't change the fact that her house had been in shambles and hadn't stood up well to the onslaught.

Taking a deep breath, Eva pushed her door open, half fearing that the home would still be filled with rubble and the smell of brimstone. Instead the fragrance of lavender and vanilla greeted her—along with a barefoot Delta lying on a new sofa, propping herself up with decorative pillows, a book open on her lap.

*Not one of my works*, flashed through Eva's mind.

"Hey there, girl!" Delta spoke as if her being there was the most natural thing in the world. "Get in here and close the door. Don't let in the flies or whatever flying, crawling things like to come in the house. Although I have my doubts this ole girl would let that happen."

"You drive a Smart car?" Shocked, Eva complied with Delta's request, sliding off her shoes as she examined the room. If a house could be sentient, she would have sworn it welcomed her home. A soft, pleasant buzz reverberated through the room, brushing gently across her face in greeting. New furniture filled the front room, but the afghan folded on a chair was the same as before. The carpet was new and plush, but the pictures hanging on the walls were the same as before. The energy buzzing around the room oddly felt both familiar and new.

Setting her book aside, Delta stood invitingly, smiling, as if it were, in fact, her own home she sat in. "Come check out what's been done here. We tried to fix what we could fix, and only replace what we had to. I know that you'll want to add your own touches to things. I think you'll be pleased with what was done. I know she is."

Eva followed silently, dropping her keys in the bowl by the door out of habit, not daring to leave the vehicle keys in the Suburban now that she knew it was her grandmother's wards that had kept the old SUV safe for years, not the disinterest of locals.

The front room wasn't the only room that had been changed. In fact, its changes were downright subtle compared to what was to come. The kitchen had been gutted; new mint-green cabinets framed in bright white retro appliances, even a dishwasher, fit the now customized space. The old, yellow floral flooring had been replaced with black-and-white checkered tiles. And the wobbly table had been replaced by a bright red table with matching vinyl-covered chairs. The backsplash now boasted mint-green and red tiles, with a fancy coffee machine and syrups taking up counter space and an array of tea choices she knew had to be all Delta.

"Ta da!" Delta waved her arms around. "If anything isn't exactly how you love it, we can get it changed out for you."

Eva examined the kitchen with wide eyes. It was perfect for the house: warm and welcoming, while functional. In fact, she couldn't have designed it better herself given all the time in the world. Her home swelled with pride around her, filling the air with more of the lavender and vanilla scent that seemed to mark its happiness.

Speechless, Eva could only examine the room with bright eyes that she knew glistened with tears. She ran her hand along the smooth counter before opening and gently closing the dishwasher. It was like someone had plucked all the thoughts from her head and created the perfect kitchen for the cottage; a beautiful mix of old and new, bold and simple. A perfect contradiction.

Delta pulled Eva back through the doorway into the living area, before guiding her down the unrecognizable hallway. Suddenly, it seemed twice as long as it had in the past. Showing the first signs of uncertainty, Delta admitted quietly, "We switched things around a bit, but if you hate it we can change it, cross my heart."

Eva went into her bedroom, gasping at how much bigger it looked, finally finding her voice. "No, wow, it's perfect." And it was. The bedspread and pillows she immediately recognized from Oliver's guest room, the same ones she'd determined she must buy. Admittedly, she was a bit sad to see her oversized bed frame gone, but perhaps that was what made the room look so much bigger.

Relief crossed Delta's normally confident face. "I'm so relieved, but this is one of the changes I was talking about. We did extend the wall out a bit. A smidge anyway." She held apart her thumb and forefinger as if the extra square footage were nothing. "But I've been staying here. We moved you to the other room."

Disappointment briefly flickered through Eva; no matter, she could move herself back. She needed her office and even with extra square footage, the layout of the other room no longer worked for her.

Giggling, Delta pulled Eva along the hallway. "We'll check out the main bathroom later. It's been updated, but it's still just a bathroom."

Main bathroom? Her little place only had one bathroom, but Delta had been raised in a world far more affluent than hers; perhaps it was a habit to call it that. Next she would be referring to this as the main level of her single-level home.

Rushing along, Eva barely noted there was an extra door along the way and was more focused on the fact that the old office door had been relocated to the end of the hallway. It was for sure longer, not an illusion. They must have needed to rework the floor plans a bit after expanding her room.

"Close your eyes," demanded Delta and, with the first smile she'd felt in hours, Eva complied while the young witch pulled her into the room. "And *open*!"

"Holy, holy . . . wow!" Eva's mind and tongue stopped working altogether when she opened her eyes. The bedroom—her bedroom—was an entirely new addition, way beyond a small expansion of a few feet.

Her bed was placed in the middle of the room with two windows framing it on either side and even more floor space before the walls. No more scooting between a wall and the bed just to get into bed. Two dressers matched the over-sized bed. Her old, tall dresser had been replaced by the set that went with her oversized bed frame. This time, the comforter matched the one that she'd only recently discovered in Oliver's own bedroom. And if she were to guess, at least fifteen pillows of various shapes and sizes littered the bed.

Delta grabbed Eva's shoulders from behind, pivoting toward the right. "Walk-in closet," she announced. The light was already on, showing that at least part of the closet had clothes and shoes in it. Once again, pivoting her to the left where two doorways stood, she said, "Your bathroom, which I've been told under no circumstances could I use. But you'll die when you see the tub! Seriously, die, but don't die." A giddy Delta gently pushed Eva toward the other door. "But this . . . this is a masterpiece."

It was an office. Not just any office, but The Office. Bookshelves held her books, notebooks, and what appeared to be her research along the walls. A skylight let the sun fill the room with natural lighting, while the over-sized desk had been polished so well, it glowed. Pens and notebooks neatly lined up along the side of the desk. Eva's eyes darted around the room, stopping at a gas fireplace flickering along a wall opposite the desk.

"We kept it simple here," Delta explained. "There is room for a sofa or chairs by the fireplace, and we waited to pick out a chair for you. But you can put up new pictures or whatever all over there. You can enter through your bedroom or just come in through the hallway." She waved in the general direction of the doorway. "Surround sound, so you can connect your music and not always wear headphones. Do you love it? Please tell me you love it! Because if you don't, I'll happily take it off your hands."

Nodding, Eva continued gaping at the room. "What's not to love?" she questioned, shoving down the empty feeling that filled her as she looked at the amazing room. "Seriously, it's amazing. I don't even know what to say. But thank you. Thank you so much."

"I've only been here the last few days," Delta admitted. "It wasn't me who did all this. I mean, I've been resetting wards and pampering that gorgeous garden out there, but you know it wasn't me." Hesitating, not like the normal, outspoken Delta Eva had come to know, she added, "When walls were tore out, we found something your gram left for you. A letter for you."

She handed Eva a folded paper that had been waiting for her on the desk.

*"My dearest Eva,*

*If you're reading this, then I'm gone. This letter is my backup plan. If all went well, in an ideal world, I would have been given the time to explain and if this letter is in your hands, then you're still waiting for that explanation.*

*I've told you I'm a witch, and I know you never believed me. You would smile at me with that cute little smile of yours, big brown eyes, and nod solemn agreement, but you didn't truly believe. But I am a witch, truly I am. I've used every ounce of my power to protect you and keep you safe. And I would give it all again for any measure of protection I could give you, because aside from being a witch I am more importantly your grandmother. I was born to be your Gram. Don't ever doubt that.*

*In the simplest terms, you are half demon. As soon as I saw you, I knew it. I don't think your mother had any idea. I dropped hints or suggestions, but she always remained insistent that you were the product of a one-night stand, a man whose last name she never got. Someone whom I've since learned was an incubus. A demon of lust, which makes sense, I guess.*

*It has been pure luck that your mother's wanderlust inadvertently kept you safe. Demons collect their half-blood progeny, for whatever reason I*

358

*don't know, but if I gandered a guess it would not be for good purpose. And after my son brought you home, I knew I would give, do anything to keep my brown-eyed little girl safe. You stole my heart with that solemn little smile, and I knew instantly I would give my life for you.*

*And so I laid protections on you. Layers and layers to keep you safe, keep you hidden and, sadly, to make you forgettable. It broke my heart to see you left behind, forgotten, but know that I did it to keep you safe and hidden. I won't apologize for that, but I know it brought you grief. I wish I could leave you with more, more knowledge of who and what you are, but my discreet inquiries kept hitting dead ends. No one I found would admit to knowing anything of demon hybrids, so other than passing on the knowledge of what you are, I have nothing else to offer.*

*My home, our home, your home will always offer you sanctuary as long as my magic and the magic of my family holds. Know that you are loved and unforgettable. It took powerful magic to hide you away, but I know that it won't hold you forever. When it breaks, find your people, the people who see you and love you. They will be your protection. And if you're still mourning me, well, buckle up, buttercup, because this is surely not the end of me.*

*Gram*

*PS Remember there are no bad puns. Only unpunny ones.*

*PPS If you remember nothing else I've taught you always remember: Regret is worse than failure. Regret is wondering what might have been."*

*You miss all the shots that you don't take,* Eva finished in her mind.

An unfamiliar half cry, half laugh hiccup erupted from her. Tears welled up in her eyes at the letter, her emotions from everything over the last few days, weeks, and even years overflowing.

Once again, Delta gently led her back into the master bedroom, pulling her onto the bed. "Tell Auntie Delta all about it." The witch lay on her side, pulling a pillow close to get comfortable.

Shaking her head, Eva admitted, "I don't want to talk about the letter right now, but she knew, the entire time she knew. She loved and protected me anyway."

How much easier life would have been if Gram had told her what she'd known. So much hurt could have been avoided. So much loneliness. Realization and anger hit Eva hard in the chest, nearly knocking the breath from her. Gram may have loved her, but her choices had been selfish and wrong. Gram hadn't protected her. She had cursed her existence in a world that couldn't see or remember Eva. Always a new kid, forever unseen and unnoticed. Forgotten. No connections, frozen in a space with no choice for anything different. Surely this had never been Gram's plan?

"Which is better: a long life, not lived to the fullest or a short life full of life, full of adventure?" Eva pondered. "I have lived in the shadow of a life. I want more than that."

The moment lay heavy on them, as the news settled over both of them, their slow breathing in and out the only sound in the quiet room. Delta had done well, Eva considered. The house still felt like home, just more. She could happily live and die here. *Alone, alone,* echoed glumly through her head.

"You're here sooner than I expected," Delta admitted. "I didn't think Oliver would let you leave."

Anger flashed through Eva, briefly replacing the sadness and loss. "No one *lets* me do anything anymore," she said sharply, her words cutting through her own heart before admitting, "How can I be with him if I don't even know if it's his choice or this weird magical tether forcing him to be with me, to like me?" Rigidly, she lay on her back, jaw clicking, staring at the ceiling, refusing to meet Delta's eyes, knowing that she would only find pity there.

"Oh, sweetie, that tether went snip snip the first day I worked on unraveling you. As the newest thread, it was the simplest to completely and quickly remove, since it had barely connected and hadn't begun enmeshing with all the older ones. If you feel anything, if either of you do, that's on you." Delta held Eva's hands in her own. "And even if the thread wasn't cut, the connection can't force feelings. It can help you connect to the other end of the connection, but anything you felt or still feel was and is completely real."

Eva let go of the breath she was holding, and it exploded out as she gasped and nearly cried as the tightness in her chest finally eased for the first time all day. All this time, she'd held out thinking that when the thread connecting them extinguished, so would her feelings for Oliver, as well as any feelings he had for her.

Delta continued sadly, "Oliver was out of his mind when you were taken. He did everything in his power to find you and every minute, every hour you remained gone expounded that grief tenfold. He blamed himself for you being taken, so if he's now denying any feelings for you, he's a liar as well as a coward."

Her eyes downcast, Eva whispered, pleading for understanding, "He didn't deny anything. I just thought . . . I thought, well, going away was the right thing to do. The only thing to do. I couldn't make him a prisoner of my demon side. The only person here who is a coward is me. It's always been me."

"Girl, I don't think you can make that vampire feel anything he doesn't want to feel," Delta admonished her. "He's crazy about you. Not cray-cray like chop you into little pieces and wear your skin so you can't leave him," she amended, causing a sharp bark of laughter to erupt from Eva.

"So how did you get so wise?" Eva hiccupped as she examined the young woman through narrowed eyes.

"Ha-ha! Is this a subtle way of asking my age? Mama Hecate always says to keep them guessing." She mimed zipping her lips innocently. "But I'll give you a hint: I'm older than you. Way older."

Gesturing toward the back yard, Delta informed

Eva, "I think you have company back here. Well, I know you do, and I suspect more company than I can see."

Eva's forehead furrowed in confusion. Visitors had been left in the backyard? As soon as they walked through the new screen door that led from the kitchen to the back porch, a familiar fuzzy face peeked out from around an overgrown lavender bush that blocked a good portion of the view. Tongue lolling out with ears perked up, Apollo let out a yappy bark of happiness when he saw her.

Squatting down with a smile, she opened her arms encouragingly. "Apollo, you naughty boy! Your mom and dad are going to wonder where you've gotten off to." He eagerly rushed toward her and in his exuberance wasn't able to stop before knocking her off balance. He licked her face all over while his tail knocked repeatedly against Delta's legs, whipping her into stepping back and away from the two.

Glancing up, Eva noticed that Delta still scanned the yard, and she followed her gaze, not seeing anything or anyone out of the ordinary. Then hesitantly, another familiar furry face appeared around the bush, acting as if it were a perfectly normal thing for him to do.

"Baby Boy!" Shocked, Eva looked back up at Delta, who still scanned the yard. "You can't see him?"

"Nope, still can't see him, but he managed to get himself and this big fellow into the back yard the last couple of mornings. It literally looks like the big guy is running around playing with an invisible friend. Seeing him bowled over was sort of unnerving, so I suspected he wasn't alone."

Apollo sat on his hunches while the hellhound pup replaced him in Eva's arms, peppering her with rotten egg kisses and nuzzling her neck affectionately. Clearly, the two had become friends while the hellhound waited for her. Had he at one point had other pups to play with? Regardless, he seemed thrilled to escape from her hugs after a few minutes to once again pound across the lawn with Apollo in tow as they wrestled their way along.

# CHAPTER TWENTY-SEVEN

*I love you a latte.*

"*D*amn you, woman!" Oliver's deep voice cut through the room. Standing in the doorway, he continued, "Do you think so little of me that I can't know my own feelings or that you couldn't have talked to me about this before you drove across three states to get away from me?"

"That's my clue to leave." Delta slipped smoothly from the bed and lay a soft hand on Oliver's arm before sliding out of the room. Over the last few days, the two had fallen into a quiet existence together, enjoying coffee and tea respectively in the mornings—after sleeping in, of course—and working on individual projects. Eva would write while Delta puttered around gram's garden cutting, pruning, and tutting at plants that seemed to once again thrive from her ministrations.

They read, listened to music, watched Baby Boy and Apollo play together most afternoons, or in Delta's case, watched Apollo bounce strangely and comically alone around the yard, before settling into Eva's large bed to watch a movie late into the night and finally falling asleep in their respective beds.

Sitting up, Eva watched Oliver shove his hands uncertainly into his pockets. She'd done that; she'd made him unsure of himself. "Do you like it?" he questioned gruffly, examining the bedroom without looking directly at her for several long seconds.

"It's perfect," Eva admitted, standing up although like the first time they'd met, she wanted to run from the room. Silence filled the space as they each examined the other. "Thank you," she tacked on belatedly, which he ignored.

"You didn't take your phone."

"I'll buy another."

"You even left your laptop and all your work."

Holding up her thumb with a wiggle, she told him, "Thumb drive and cloud." Eva had figured she would buy a new laptop as well. Why not? She hadn't wanted to take too long gathering her things. Hadn't wanted to give herself a chance to weaken and change her mind.

"I applied for a passport."

An eyebrow raised at her as if to say *pray continue.*

"I'm ready to live and not just survive," Eva admitted. No longer could she watch her life from the sidelines.

"Why?" he began at the same time, she said, "I'm sorry."

"Why are you sorry? For leaving me? For making me have feelings for you? For being what I dreamed of even when I couldn't dream?" he asked softly, a touch of vulnerability in his voice. The sound broke her heart all over again. "Why did you leave me? I thought . . . I thought we were more than that?"

A half laugh, half cry escaped Eva. "But everyone I've ever been with thought we were more. How can I know when it's real or when I've made it happen? How can you trust me or trust these feelings knowing what sort of creature I am? Being with me literally steals life from you. I'm a parasite. A fucking jailer."

"I'm dead, Eva. How can the life force be taken from the undead? And I would give it to you freely. Not as a way to own or control you, but because I can. How can you steal something that is given freely?" His eyes pleaded with her to hear his words. "If you'd stuck around even a little bit longer, I could have told you this. Whatever I give freely to you doesn't deplete me. It completes me. I've never felt better. I thought after that last night, you could see that. Whatever energy of mine that feeds you, it also replenishes me."

Walking closer, he continued, "Did you think I was a monster or parasite that last night when I took your blood?" Waiting for her answer, his brows furrowed as he considered the possibility that she was, in fact, running from him.

Blushing at the memory, Eva vehemently shook her head. "No, it was beautiful. Perfect." A moment in time that she could hold onto for a lifetime.

"Why would you think it was any different for me?" Oliver questioned. "Am I not deserving of love? Of acceptance? We both are."

Another step closer. Eva stood still, caught between wanting to throw herself upon him and running away.

"I was awake when you left, you know. I kept thinking you wouldn't go. You would make it to the door, then come to your senses and turn around. Then I thought you'd make it to the garage and turn around. Then maybe at the gate you would stop and come back to me. Then I realized you weren't coming back. So I gave you time. Hell, I didn't want to, but Delta convinced me to give you time. And she verbally kicked my ass for letting you go in the first place."

Shaking her head, Eva sadly explained, "You don't know if it's you feeling this or if it's what I've made you feel. I'm just an ex-barista with a knack for hiding away who got lucky with a bit of writing. You deserve so much more than that."

"You are that, but so much more." Oliver's quiet, low voice reached across the room to her. "How can I not be obsessed with you? Not crazy kill anyone who gets between us obsessed"—he paused as he considered his words—"well, maybe. But I own my obsession with you. It's not due to any succubus genetics or blood connections. I felt it the moment I laid eyes on you in the coffee shop. I felt it well before we had sex and well after our bonds were broken. It's due to you and me." He pointed back and forth between the two of them.

"I can only hope you feel even a smidgen of the same obsession with me. And I will regret to the end of my days that I didn't tell you before . . . before we were intimate. I regret that you think that's what I feel, because what I feel is real and so much more."

Hope sprang from Eva, hope followed by shame. She hadn't even given them a chance. At the first opportunity, she'd treated him like all the others who had come before him despite knowing he was different. This time, she closed the space between them. "All you've done is save me. I can't even save myself. Why would you want a damsel when you could have a queen?"

Shaking his head firmly, he argued. "You don't see what I see. You are *my* queen. I don't save you. You save *me*."

"I've been so wrong."

"You have," he agreed, then waited. "If you're a monster, so am I. Maybe you make me less of a monster."

Pointing between herself and him, she clarified, "This is real."

"It is."

"You haven't given up on me."

"Never."

The tightening in her chest began to ease at his earnest tone. "You're not going to become crazy obsessed with me?" For the first time in days, the tension between her shoulders began to relax.

Tilting his head as if considering, he shook his head. "I already am, but I think you know that. I know we're new to this sort of thing." Pushing his hands deeper in his pockets, he continued, "But I want to give it a try, if you want to. I know your entire world has changed almost overnight, and I know that it takes some time to figure it out, but I would really like a chance to be a part of that, if you're willing to have me."

And there it was. The difference. Her past attempts at relationships usually ended with demands and begging or pleading. Being unseen and forgettable was sometimes a better alternative than being hunted and stalked after mediocre sex. Oliver asked her what she wanted; he could wait for her rather than force her to accept his attention. For the first time, a choice was being given to her, and with a flush she admitted to herself the sex *was* phenomenal.

Holding his jaw in both hands, Eva drew him closer, close enough to kiss, while keeping her eyes locked on his, searching for anything that might suggest he meant differently before admitting, "I am sort of a mess. And I'm going to make a lot—and I mean a lot—of mistakes."

Oliver slowly pulled his hands out of his pockets, not breaking their eye contact. "As will I, but this—us—it isn't a mistake."

Eva let out the breath she was holding as he reached out to her hips and pulled her closer, maintaining eye contact, but not pushing for more. She could meet him halfway; she could chase him to the ends of the earth. Instead, she held his face between her hands, bouncing up onto her tiptoes to reach his lips as he turned his head down to meet her, leaving her momentarily breathless before he ended the kiss.

"And I'm sure you've noticed by now that Delta has moved into your house, at least temporarily."

"I thought she was just doing some work on the

wards and helping with this amazing remodel." Now that Eva thought about it, Delta had seemed pretty at home here, and clearly this was why she hadn't been seeing her around since the rescue.

"She is. She was. Or at least she said she was checking things out. Then she took a leave of absence or a vacation. I'm not sure which, but apparently I'm still paying her, and she'll be back when she's back. I quote." The young witch often left Oliver confused, but clearly Delta had no plans of heading back to Chicago any time soon now that Eva considered how comfortable she'd made herself in Eva's guest room, as well as her living room and kitchen. "She's got the right idea," he admitted as he kissed the top of Eva's head, holding her close as if afraid to let her go.

Pulling back, Eva looked up questionably, raising a questioning eyebrow herself.

"I think it's time to step back from some of the day-to-day running of the business. Maybe my partners can step out of the shadows a bit. They all know what they're doing and don't need me looking over their shoulders all the time. Maybe it's time to relax, explore, travel. Maybe bring coffee to my favorite author while she works."

# CHAPTER TWENTY-EIGHT

*Can you put the dog out? I didn't know he was on fire.*

**O**liver slowly shifted his legs, hoping Eva wouldn't notice, but of course she did.

"Are you uncomfortable?"

He sat sprawled in front of the flickering fireplace with his back to the settee and her fitting perfectly between his legs, leaning back against his chest—absolute perfection. Her hair occasionally flitted up to tickle his nose while the fireplace flickered in the mostly dark room, and a slight smell of brimstone mixed with lavender floated through the air.

"I'm perfect, my love," he lied as he kissed the top of her head. But despite the discomfort, the moment was perfect as he squeezed her gently with his arms wrapped around her waist, attempting to settle her in closer.

His heart thumped slowly, strongly, against her. It's a myth that vampire hearts didn't beat. Even though it's no longer necessary, a vampire's heart continued to flicker from memory. Perhaps after many more centuries the impulse for it to pretend to pump blood through a body would fade, the synapsis urges would dissipate, but for now it beat for her.

A low growl escaped Baby Boy, who had easily doubled in size since his rescue. Despite the growth spurt, he still believed he could easily fit across Eva's lap. And technically he did fit, sort of, as long as Oliver's legs braced either side of Eva, supporting both her and the beast while Baby Boy's back side remained on the floor. The young hellhound put up with Oliver's support as long as he didn't move. Oliver refused to fight a dog for Eva's affection, so they'd reached a happy middle ground of sorts during visits.

"Hush now, sweetie." Eva continued caressing the hellhound's ears and neck as he let out a huff and settled down deeper against her. The hound was maturing, losing more of his soft puppy fuzz. With each visit, more wiry, coarse hair replaced the soft fur, but he had yet to lose the puppy glee at seeing her. Several puppy teeth had been replaced by adult incisors, and unfortunately his breath only continued to reek of stronger brimstone the older he got. Eva didn't appear to notice as she snuggled with him, and Oliver wasn't going to be the one to complain; not if she was happy.

Never in a million years would Oliver have imagined that he would be sharing the love of his immortal life with a spoiled hellhound. A hellhound who apparently was growing faster than most thanks to all the nurturing Eva gave him whenever he snuck away from his family for a visit. A bit of his health, Oliver suspected, was also due to Eva's succubus energy that fed the pup every visit. Just as she didn't understand or control how she fed, the same worked in reverse. The demon part of her fed, but the human part of her? Her humanity is what gave energy to others without thought or care.

The fire snapped and crackled, lulling them into a peaceful bliss until Baby Boy's head shot up. His ears snapped forward, and the previously relaxed puppy switched into predator mode as he listened for something they couldn't hear. With a huff he stood, stretching across both their bodies, while Oliver suppressed a groan of relief. Eva had no such pride and let out a discernible moan as she wiggled her legs when the hound's weight lifted off her.

Wide awake with ears twitching, he turned to give a full lick goodbye across Eva's cheek, then met Oliver's eyes for a long moment. With a huff that Oliver dared not translate, the beast turned and jumped into the fireplace, disappearing in the blink of an eye with an audible snap.

"Mama has called," Eva observed dryly as she continued shaking the pins and needles out of her legs. "Nice to know he still listens, sometimes." Neither of them knew how he got back and forth from the demon plane to their home, and Malth, the only person Oliver knew who might know the answer to that, had disappeared as quickly and quietly as he'd appeared to assist in Eva's rescue.

According to Delta, who was still vacationing in Eva's Ohio home, the pup also continued to show up periodically in Eva's back yard with Apollo mysteriously alongside. Not that she could see him, but there were signs, Delta had grumbled, big steaming piles of signs. As much as Delta grumbled, Oliver also knew she kept large dog treats on hand to stay on the beast's good side.

Just a few days after Eva had returned to Oliver's home, the pup had shown up in the living room by passing yet again all sorts of security, all wiggles and shakes, excited to see Eva. He continued to show up randomly and unannounced, sometimes staying for a few minutes and other times a few hours, before being called back home.

"I worry each time might be the last time he visits," Eva admitted once she settled back into Oliver's embrace. Her ability to love so deeply was one of the things he loved about her. Despite losing so much, she never stopped loving.

"Understandable." Hesitating, Oliver added, "But you don't see what I see. When I first saw that a hellhound had attached itself to you, it scared me. All we know about these creatures is what little we've been told and even less what we've observed. But now I know that they have a great love and loyalty to family. He considers you a part of his family and, well, we've seen firsthand what these creatures will do for family." He suppressed a shudder as the memory of what they would do for their family flickered through him. "They will fight daylight itself to be there for those they love."

With her back to him, Oliver sensed the smile that crossed Eva's face at his words. Since she'd come

376

back to him, their bond had only grown stronger, and sometimes he could barely distinguish her emotions from his own, especially when they reflected and amplified.

"How do you always know the right things to say?"

"It's the truth. The truth is always right." Settling down, they continued watching the fireplace flicker as they each radiated comfort and contentedness. The shadows moved along the walls, dancing to the soft music flowing through the room. Leaning down into her shoulder, Oliver whispered into Eva's ear, "Would you be ready to try something new?"

After a long breath, Eva responded with a cautious, "What? I mean, is there anything left to try?"

Oliver's chest shook with silent laughter as Eva leaned forward to turn and look at him. "Well, seriously? And don't laugh at me. Not all of us have lived over a hundred years." Her words were punctuated with her own laughter.

"So much more, my love. But taking your mind out of the bedroom, I actually meant would you like to travel? I know that England was a dream, but I think I can do one better and add a few more countries and continents over . . . let's say the next year or so?"

Her passport had arrived without fanfare a week ago. With a smile, she had opened it, holding it close before sliding it away in a drawer for some day.

"Shut the door! Can you really take that much time off work? I mean, would you?"

"I am Boss Man, after all, and what's the use in

hiring the best people in the industry if you can't trust them to do their jobs?"

Oliver could feel Eva's excitement rise and then sputter before she responded, "What about Ravyn? We've only solved half the mystery. Whoever is out there for her is still out there."

Sighing, Oliver admitted, "I've done all I can for now. It's just a waiting game until the so-called 'master' makes another mistake. Whoever it is has been quiet the last few weeks." He didn't add that they were certainly regrouping from their recent losses and could very well be planning something for tomorrow or two years from now. But as Ravyn reminded him, they couldn't put their lives on hold or the creature won. Necromancy had brought back the old mage briefly, but a failsafe had been put into place and once one question had been asked, the creature's head had shrieked with laughter even as it melted into a pile of putrid sludge.

Another dead end.

"I want to show you the world. You've been stagnant long enough, and it's selfish of me to just want to wrap you up and keep you to myself," Oliver admitted.

"I love being here with you. I love Baby Boy's visits."

"Yes, but you'll love being out there with me as well. Your book is finished, and your fans aren't expecting another one for a bit, so we have the time now."

"My fans wouldn't be satisfied even if I released a

book every week," Eva admitted.

Oliver sensed she was warming to the idea. His Eva wasn't open to immediate change, but he knew her well enough that once she mulled an idea over, even if it were only for a few minutes, she would jump in feet first.

He nodded solemnly, agreeing. "Nothing satisfies those unruly masses, never happy. Besides, maybe you'll find some inspiration out there in the world."

"That sounds . . . That . . . it actually sounds pretty freaking great." Nodding more to herself than Oliver, she added, "But I really need to see a huge windmill." Fanning her arms, she gestured wildly in explanation.

"Anything you want, but a windmill? Why a windmill?"

"Because I'm a huge fan?" While she laughed at her joke, Oliver groaned. "What? Not my best work? Don't worry, I've been collecting travel puns for years. I'm sure I'll find one more to your liking.

"Do you have an itinerary planned or will we just *wing* it? If we fly, it will be air-mazing. It's a-boat time . . ."

"Definitely time for a distraction!" Oliver roared with his own laughter as he wrapped his arms around a gasping Eva before standing, lifting her off the ground.

"Wait, wait, ohhhh, the pilot thickens," she gasped out before he covered her mouth with his own, drowning in the feeling of her against him. Gripping her hips, he pulled her closer, and she responded by wrapping her legs around him, happily allowing the distraction he offered as he edged closer to her heated core.

With a growl, he pulled back his mouth before promising, "Tomorrow. We leave tomorrow." He nipped at her full lower lip, savoring the drop of her intoxicating blood on the tip of his tongue, as she arched fully against him, feeding as well once again on his desire. "Don't pack. We can shop for what we need or just have someone else pick it out and deliver it. I don't want to waste another day."